A Season Past

Christopher Bartley

PEACH PUBLISHING

ISBN 978-1-78036-393-6

Published by

Peach Publishing

For Karen, who took me up into the Wasatch Mountains for the first time.

A SEASON PAST

"Blaze away! You're a daisy if you do."
Doc Holliday to Frank McLaury during a gunfight
behind the O.K. Corral, Tombstone, Arizona, October
26, 1881.

In the year of 1900 Wyatt Earp, Frank James, Cole Younger, Bat Masterson, Emmett Dalton, Tom Horn, Calamity Jane, Bill Tilghman, Harvey Logan, Pat Garrett, Harry Longabaugh, and Butch Cassidy were all still alive and struggling to find their way in a modern world that was steadily replacing the western frontier. The Twentieth Century was not, generally speaking, kind to them.

Chapter One

Autumn 1898

By the early autumn of 1898, before the first freeze, Coltrane knew he'd had enough of the Klondike. With $9,000 stashed in a Salt Lake City bank he decided to give up the prospector's life and return to Utah. It was a state now, had been for over three years since the Mormons agreed to abandon polygamy. There was a valley where he'd passed a summer some fifteen years before, on the run from an angry Arizona posse.

Images of the sky at dusk still haunted him: shimmering orange tints that faded over the jagged outline of the Wasatch peaks, then sudden brightness as the stars fell over like rain. The air in the morning had been cool and fresh with the scent of aspen glades, wild berries, and fields of wheat. In all his fifty-four years he'd never known the quiet that found him there. So he decided to return and live out the years that were left to him in quiet obscurity.

Once he made the decision it was easy enough to sell off his claim. A pair of speculators from Chicago bought it the day he put up notice. They made no secret of the fact they didn't think there would be much gold left in the vein. They would mine it, of course, but that wasn't their reason for the purchase. They wanted it because Coltrane had claimed it, had lived and worked on it. It was his name that excited them, a name they figured to exploit. Coltrane had seen this before and never gotten used to it. People wanted his autograph, wanted to buy him a drink, wanted to brag they had met the famous gunfighter, wanted a piece of his soul.

All Coltrane wanted was to be left alone.

That was why he had gone to Alaska in the first place. He figured no one would know him there. He had arrived in the early days of the rush, had staked a claim that was small enough for him to work by himself. There had been some initial success. But the crowds were not far behind.

Soon the Klondike was filled with the kind of people he was trying to avoid: gamblers, outlaws, speculators, and other assorted riff-raff living on the edge of the law. They had hounded him, had sought him out to hear his stories, had trespassed onto his claim, and worse. Twice he'd had to draw down on young men trying to make reputations. One of them was now buried beneath the Klondike with a simple inscription that read: "Harry Rosen—wasn't fast enough."

Now Coltrane was tired of it and he wanted to get out. He wanted to be left alone. He didn't care why the speculators were willing to pay so much for his near worthless claim. The money bought a first class ticket on a freighter to San Francisco. There he stayed at the Palace Hotel, which had been built back in '75 and now featured electric lights in every room and a private bath, with running water, in every other room. He thought it was the finest hotel he had ever seen, except for perhaps the Hotel Del Coronado in San Diego.

His first night in town he dined at John Tadich's "Cold Day" Restaurant on Leidesdorff Street, between Commercial and Clay. He sat alone at a table covered with a white cloth and was served by waiters in white jackets and black pants. The place was quiet with the hum of hushed conversations. For his meal he had a wide shallow bowl of steamed manila clams, the seafood cioppino with garlic bread, and a bottle of French Champagne.

After dinner he lingered over two cups of black coffee and had a slice of blueberry pie. The pie was too sweet for his taste and he didn't finish it. Later, he sat up late into the night smoking in his room at the Palace Hotel, staring out over the lights of the city, thinking about how it was going to feel to lay his head down on the pristine white linen sheets of the wide bed.

For three days he marveled over how San Francisco had changed since his last visit. It had been nearly ten years. Most of the streets were paved now. You could catch a cable car that would take you down to the bay where freighters came in from ports all over the world.

He spotted several horseless carriages. They were ugly machines steered by smug, wealthy men wrapped in furs. He took long walks through the city, up and down the steep hills, enjoying the exertion after the stifling confinement of the ocean voyage.

Out of curiosity he climbed up Nob Hill, past the mansion of Charles Crocker, the railroad magnate, dead now for ten years. Crocker had once tried to hire Coltrane to work security on one of the Central Pacific lines, but it had been obvious he would be expected to keep the Chinese workers in line. Coltrane had no desire to shoot unarmed Chinese immigrants for a living.

*

On the fourth day Coltrane climbed Nob Hill again and found a bench that faced out toward the harbor gate and the vast Pacific beyond. He rolled a cigarette and smoked it, then rolled another. For forty minutes he watched a freighter head out of the bay and pass the point. He lighted the next cigarette and inhaled.

Seagulls flew above, calling to each other. He thought of his wife, Anne, and decided to send her a telegram. He had not seen her in over six years, though he still cared for her, cherished his memories of their time together. They had been married eighteen years ago, in Atlanta. She had come west with him. For almost twelve years she endured the hardships of life on the shrinking frontier, had stayed by his side as he earned a living, mostly as a lawman. He never earned enough to provide her with the lifestyle she was accustomed to and he could never show her the love that he felt inside of himself.

Anne was tough, independent, loyal, and he never doubted

4

her devotion. Yet living as the wife of a frontier gunman hadn't been easy for her. She suffered long spells of sadness. There were weeks filled with dark moods and inconsolable grief. Sometimes she went days without speaking to anyone, long stretches where there was no pleasure, no gleam in her eye.

When Anne left, to return to her family in Savannah, she had begged him to join her. They both knew there would be no life for him in that town, in the society she came from. It was simple, really – there was no doubt about what they meant to each other, but they could not be happy together. Their desired worlds were too different.

They had parted one rainy morning at a train station in the Sierras. Anne had cried, and they had made promises to each other about the future. Afterwards Coltrane rode up into the mountains alone and hunted for six weeks, but he didn't take much game because he couldn't find the interest.

He wrote Anne every other month, and she wrote him at least that often. Over the years, as he had moved around, the letters often missed him; sometimes catching up to him in bunches. They had never divorced. The bond was still there, unbreakable, and he had been true to her always. He had resisted the temptations that followed him: the prostitutes, the lonely widows who were seemingly everywhere in the west, the younger ladies who wanted to make love to a legend, but cared little for the man. He avoided them all.

When he returned to the Palace Hotel that afternoon he sent Anne a telegram, telling her of his planned return to Utah.

*

In the cool of the evening he stepped out onto the street for a late stroll after dinner. The smell of salt was in the air and a dimming fog was beginning to drift in over the city. At the corner he purchased a newspaper and walked with it folded under his arm. Two blocks from the Palace Hotel he heard the footsteps coming up fast behind him.

"Mr. Coltrane!" a voice called.

His reaction was pure instinct. In one motion he turned and had the large Colt revolver drawn from beneath his overcoat. The hammer was cocked and the muzzle was pushed into the face of a terrified man who stood trembling with his hat pushed back on his forehead, waving a pen in the air. The newspaper had fallen into the street, open and wet now. The man stammered, unable to form words. His eyes were wide and his mouth gaped.

"What?" Coltrane demanded.

"I thought..."

"You thought what?"

"I thought you might sign..."

"I don't sign." Coltrane shook his head in disgust and holstered the revolver. With an angry grunt he turned and stalked off into the night, letting the fog settle in behind him.

*

Early the next morning Coltrane boarded a train headed east, renting a sleeping compartment for the eight-hour trip to Salt Lake City so that he would be alone. He passed the time in the compartment by himself, not even leaving for meals as they were called. He smoked absently and stared out at the broad landscape and then the sharp mountains flashing by.

Chapter Two

Coltrane didn't push the horses. One was a golden claybank he called Bobby-Lee, and the other was a buckskin Appaloosa already named Rosalita. They pulled the buckboard slowly. He didn't mind. He was in no particular hurry and he knew when he purchased them in Salt Lake City that they were riding horses, not meant to pull a carriage. Now he was headed out on his own, figuring to be in no rush to reach Crystal. During the day he stopped often, sometimes to water the mares, sometimes just to let them rest while he smoked beside them.

After all those years in the saddle and the camps his features were rough and sun blown. An old scar creased his cheek down to his neck. He was medium-height and wiry, with short brown hair and stubble of salt and pepper beard. Only moderately handsome in a conventional sense, there was something – a presence, a quality of confidence that would have been difficult to put into words. His eyes were deep blue and he didn't blink often. His expression could be sensitive or cruel, honest or dangerous.

Now he was dressed in clothing that was comfortable to him, not the finer linens he wore in San Francisco, but a pair of denim trousers, a plaid wool work shirt, a lambs-wool vest, and a heavy overcoat. The overcoat was worn and had been patched over many times. His mother had made it for him over thirty years ago when he left the hospital. She had sewn his old unit insignia on the shoulders, the First Virginia Brigade, even though it didn't exist anymore, had been shattered at an obscure crossroads called Spotsylvania Courthouse where he took a ball in the shoulder.

He thought about the Brigade now, as he had nearly every day of his life since the war. He saw the faces, most of them young, sitting around the campfires. He thought of the rowdy games of baseball in the summer heat, the long marches that were usually followed by the smell of powder and death, the sounds of the cannon and musket fire, the screams of the wounded and dying. He thought about Stonewall, sitting so straight and formal in the saddle, then Ewell, who didn't know what the corps was capable of, would never commit it like Jackson would have if he had lived.

Coltrane had volunteered when he was seventeen; a month after his older brother fell at First Manassas. He didn't care particularly about The Cause, barely understood what it was. His family didn't own slaves and didn't understand the argument about states rights. He just knew he had to avenge his brother, had to escape his mother's tears. So he enlisted to fight with the Stonewall Brigade and fought hard for two years in his own backyard, the Shenandoah.

The names of the engagements passed through his thoughts: Cedar Mountain, Second Manassas, Gettysburg. By the battle of the Wilderness he was a Major and had a bayonet scar on his belly. After Spotsylvania, and the bloody crescent, or "mule shoe" as they had referred to it, where the brigade was wiped out, he convalesced at a hospital in North Carolina. The doctors had wanted to take his arm, had said he could die when he refused to let them.

He did not die.

Instead, he recovered and was transferred to Texas, away from the fight, not even to Kirby Smith's command, but to Galveston. Even then he understood what that meant. Not many of the Stonewall Brigade had survived and nobody wanted to see another one fall, as if he and the remaining few others were national treasures.

So they sent him as far away from the cannon fire and musket balls as they could, across the Mississippi blockade. A week after he arrived in Galveston, Lee surrendered the Army of North Virginia to Grant's Federals.

The war was lost.

Coltrane never officially surrendered. He simply slipped away from his new command one night, leaving his uniform, officer's patch, and saber behind. He understood the fight was over, had known it was over when he heard about Lee's trench works around Petersburg. Still, somehow, he couldn't bear the thought of giving himself up to the men he had fought for so long.

He slipped away and headed south to Mexico. He'd been on the move ever since. Sometimes he wondered how his life would have been different if he had never been sent to Texas, had returned to the Corps for the very end. He thought about how it would have been at Appomattox, to march with General Gordon, to stack arms for the Union Army with the last 200 survivors of his unit.

He'd heard the Federal Commander had given the order to his own troops to carry arms – the salute of honor. Goosebumps formed along his neck and arms, as they always did, when he thought of this, pictured the scene, heard the Federal band playing Dixie. He wondered if he'd been there would the war have haunted him as it did, or would he have put it behind him like so many others had.

As he rode slowly through the Utah countryside, he thought about the medals he had earned fighting for the Confederacy. Always there had been words used such as "heroism," and phrases like "bravery in the face of the enemy." But he knew he had never been a hero. He had tried to kill the men who were trying to kill him. That was all. He had killed. It had never been any more complicated then that. Because he had survived when so many others hadn't, they called him brave and they promoted him. He grunted to himself as he thought about that.

He had survived.

And he had been surviving ever since, doing whatever it took, and yet had never been willing to back away from a confrontation or to let another man wrong him. There had been times when he told himself that was all he had, his willingness to stand up for himself, to fight if another man pushed him to.

9

Only now he wasn't so sure what that had meant. There had been too much blood spilled over the years. He'd seen too many men die over little or nothing.

Now he just wanted to experience a few quiet years. It was all he wanted, all he thought about now for himself.

He thought about where he was going, the valley where he had purchased a small cabin and almost a hundred acres of land, where he intended to plant a garden and some trees. He would spend his time with the land, feeling it under his feet, watching it change with the seasons, not moving on just because there was another adventure to be had or men chasing him.

This time he would stay put in one spot and find out what that was like. He would plant some seeds and wait. There were books he wanted to read: novels like *Tom Sawyer* and *The Deerslayer*; memoirs of commanders he had known, served under, or fought against, men like Grant and Gordon; essays by Chamberlain, Longstreet, Pickett; speeches by Lincoln, Davis, Hancock; and monographs printed in Scribner's magazine.

He would read, reflect, watch his seeds grow, and maybe, if he were still enough, peace would come to him. That is, if his past could allow it.

Chapter Three

In the bright sunlight of late afternoon Coltrane stood on the steps of Ryan's Dry Goods. He paused to finish a cigarette and listened to the excited voices of the men gathered inside. Through the window he was unable to see the men, only a girl, standing near the window behind several large rolls of checkered fabric. She appeared to be listening surreptitiously to the men talk.

Coltrane studied her profile through the window for a moment, realizing she was not actually a girl, but a young woman. He took one last pull off the cigarette and tossed the butt into the street, holding the smoke in for a long moment while he listened to the words from inside.

*

"Are you sure? Absolutely sure?" asked one voice.

"I'm positive about it, Sheriff," another voice replied. "He's over there, sitting by himself, eating his supper like it's just another day."

"Probably is just another day to him."

"If it's *him*."

"You really saw him with your own eyes?"

"Absolutely, he's just sitting in there."

"How can you be sure it's him?"

"'Cause I've seen his picture on posters lot of years back."

"That was a long time ago. You'd think he'd changed a bit since then."

"Hogwash!"

"Sheriff, he's not wanted for anything now is he?"

"Not that I know of."

"Could be we just haven't heard about it yet."

"Aw, to hell with it. He's an old man now. Who cares,

11

anyway?"

"Well, I care!"

"I heard he killed six men last year up in Alaska, men trying to jump his claim."

"It's hogwash!"

"Well, what's he doing here?"

"Passing through, more than likely and nothing more."

"Yeah?"

"Yeah! There have been a lot of bodies left behind the places he 'passed through' over the years."

"You figure it out then. We ain't got nothing he'd want here."

"We're not even sure who he is yet…."

"I'm telling you its just hogwash!"

"Hush your mouth!"

*

Coltrane's jaw tightened as he listened to the voices, hearing the fear in them. He let out a breath. It was time to go inside and face them. He had purchases to make and the day was getting on.

For just a moment he considered coming back another day, but he knew the moment was going to come sooner or later. Better to get it over with right now. Besides, he wouldn't allow himself to be pushed back by others. He let out another breath and unfastened the strap on the Colt, just in case.

A movement caught his eye. It was the young woman. She had stepped out from behind the large rolls of fabric to stand with her back to the door, facing the men.

"If you're unsure, why doesn't somebody go ask this man his name?" she suggested. Her tone was haughty, and Coltrane smiled as he pictured the expression on the faces of the men.

"Aw… honey, you shouldn't be here right now," one of the men said.

"I don't see why not. You all standing around worrying about some poor old man, you don't even know who he is. Probably doesn't mean you any harm anyway."

"Sweetheart, you wouldn't understand. He could be dangerous."

"Who is he?"

There was a chorus of voices, and then one came out above the rest. "The man may be a gunfighter, an outlaw."

"He's not an outlaw anymore, I tell you," another voice said.

"We don't even know if it's *him*."

"It is I tell you."

"Aw, hogwash!"

"We better find out for sure," someone suggested.

"Who is going to do that?"

"Leave him alone," was another suggestion. "He's just passing through."

"Would you leave a snake alone?"

"I probably would if I thought he was poisonous."

Coltrane pushed open the swinging doors and stepped into the store. He moved quietly, with an efficiency of motion, no effort wasted.

In an instant he took in the scene. There were eight men standing together, clustered around the register. One of them was a Sheriff and one was a deputy. The sheriff stood watching the other men, absently fingering the strap over his revolver.

All heads in the room turned to stare at Coltrane. He stood inside, to the right of the door, his expression casual. In a shoulder holster hung a large Colt revolver, resting naturally at his left side. When he looked about the room his gaze was aloof, cool.

For a long moment nobody said a word and you could hear the ticking of a clock at the back of the room.

Chapter Four

Highly vigilant, Coltrane approached the counter, watching the group of men, noting the sheriff and the deputy. He looked at the woman again. She had turned in front of him, facing him with a startled but defiant expression.

Young, maybe mid-twenties – she was a bit too thin, but beautiful, with skin that had a mysterious coffee tone. She wore a long beige skirt, with a black blouse that fit her hourglass form snuggly. Her dark brown hair was curly and uncontrolled. Dark circles under her eyes accentuated high cheekbones. There was a slight smirk in the angle of her lips. Her eyes burned with intelligence.

For a moment Coltrane paused, stared back at her, blinking. Then she smiled. Her wide, full lips pulled back slowly as dimples formed and her soft eyes twinkled as they held his gaze.

A moment passed. With effort he shifted his awareness back to the others in the room. He tipped his hat to the young woman without changing expression, and stepped around her, moving toward the counter. Self conscious of her eyes behind him, watching him as he moved, he directed his attention to the small group of men.

Instinctively he focused on the sheriff; saw the man watching him with dark, narrow eyes. Coltrane placed his hands flat on the counter, waiting calmly. His eyes were focused on the man he assumed to be the storekeeper, but the soft part of his vision, the part he concentrated on while appearing not to, covered the group of men, especially the sheriff. He did not speak for a long time.

The men continued to stare at him.

"I'd like a few things," he said finally, quietly addressing the storekeeper.

Ryan, the storekeeper, was nervous now, realizing he had to say something. He stepped around the counter, nodding his head, summoning his voice, which cracked at the first syllable. "How can I help you?"

"I need a few things," Coltrane repeated, holding his eyes softly on the group of men. "Five pounds salt pork, five pounds dried beef, soap, lye, ten pounds of salt, five pounds of flour and five of cornmeal. Some dried beans, two boxes of .45 caliber cartridges and two boxes of .44 caliber rimfire. Do you have potatoes and carrots?"

Ryan nodded quickly as he continued to scribble down the list of items.

"Winter seed for cabbage, potatoes, and whatever else you got. Also, whiskey, kerosene, sugar. Do you have a boy to load all that up for me?"

"Yes, sir."

"That's my buckboard across the street."

"How will you pay?"

Coltrane shrugged. He pulled a wallet from a pocket inside his vest and placed several bills on the counter in front of Ryan, who nodded, doing business now, forgetting to be nervous.

"Passing through?"

"I'll be here a spell."

"Here?"

Coltrane nodded, noting the quiet stir of the men now standing behind the sheriff.

"Would you like to open an account?"

"I'll pay cash money."

"Yes, sir. Give me a few minutes to get these items together."

Coltrane nodded and turned to look directly at the group of men, his eyes cold, waiting for them to make the first move, knowing they had not yet made up their minds. The ticking of the clock echoed loudly in the stillness of the room.

After a moment, the sheriff stepped forward and tipped his hat back on his head. He was a thickset man, short, with a

15

heavy beard and a wide crooked scar under the left eye. His clothing was expensive, unusually so for a small town sheriff. He wore a black silk coat over a white shirt and gabardine vest with a black bowtie and a long gold watch chain hanging from a vest pocket. At his waist hung a pearl-handled revolver with a six-inch barrel that was polished to a bright shine. With his hands on his hips, he nodded and addressed Coltrane for the first time.

"I'm Bryant, been sheriff here in Crystal for six years."

Coltrane nodded, polite, but his expression was indifferent.

"We have a nice little town here, peaceful, if you know what I mean. It's real quiet."

"I reckon so."

"We'd like to keep it that way."

"Don't blame you."

"Like to ask your name, find out what your business is."

Coltrane nodded, as if considering this request. He was aware of the eyes that were on him, especially those of the young woman behind him. "I think you know my name, and my business is only mine, none of yours."

Chapter Five

For two weeks he worked hard on the place, every day, without rest, except in the evenings. It was a small cabin, sitting on ninety-seven acres of land that was at the base of a canyon. It was full of fir trees and elk, and had a stream running through it. He patched the roof, built a sleeping loft to create a small reading room next to the kitchen, repaired the barn stalls, dug a pit for a smokehouse, purchased livestock, hunted and planted a few winter crops. Some days he rode up into the mountains to look down at the large silent shadows cast by floating clouds over the low-rolling hills of the valley.

The work felt good and in the evenings, after it was dark, he would stop to cook his dinner. Usually he ate simple fare such as beans and cornmeal with stewed cabbage and dried beef, maybe a slug of whiskey, although he made an effort to go light on the whiskey. Then he would read for an hour by the light of the kerosene lamp and reflect on the day, feeling good about the work that he was accomplishing, knowing it was good work and that nobody could take it away from him.

He tried not to think too much, tried not to think about the past, tried not to think about the girl – a young lady, really – he'd seen in town, about her eyes, her smile, the ancient, familiar tug of emotion she evoked deep within him, tried to focus only on the work and feeling good about the work, enjoying the open air, the solitude, the hard feel of tools in his hands, the rough sensation of sawing, pounding, digging into the cold earth.

It was honest work, and no one bothered him. He wondered if they were going to leave him alone this time, started to think that maybe they were, but the little voice inside him, the one that had saved his life on so many occasions over the years, kept telling him differently.

On a blustery afternoon in early-October a sudden downpour interrupted his labor. Jagged shards of lightning lit across the sky and rain drenched the land. He stored the tools in the barn and soothed the mares. When it had slowed to a steady, soaking rain he ran across to the cabin and changed into dry clothing.

He thought about fixing a supper, but it was too early to be hungry. Instead, he sat out on the porch, sheltered from the rain, with a wool blanket around his shoulders, a pot of coffee and the whiskey jug at his feet. He rolled a cigarette and while he smoked he surveyed the land that was slowly becoming his, watching the display overhead, and suddenly he couldn't keep the memories at bay any longer.

*

Lieutenant Coltrane led the patrol through the wet Virginia countryside with the rain coming down in sheets now. The distant flash of cannon mingled with the thunder above them. A brigade of Federal soldiers had been spotted two miles northwest of their position, trying to flank the retreating Confederate army. General Ewell had posted extra pickets and now had ordered his brigade commanders to send out platoons to scout the areas past the pickets, expecting an onslaught of fresh Federals.

So far they had seen nothing. The entire army had fought only a few small rear-guard actions, minor skirmishes, fending off the probing enemy. They were surprised the Federal commanders weren't taking better advantage of their retreat, weren't pressing more to hit them before they crossed the river.

To a man they understood that once they crossed the Potomac they were home, would rally, would once again pull together to defend their land as they always had. They felt a confidence on Virginian soil that did not follow them when they moved north.

Coltrane led his men over the rough ground, the muddy

trails torn up by the armies moving over them, the creeks swollen with the heavy rains. The men were exhausted and hungry. No one had slept much for the past week, with almost no sleep at all for the last three days, just hard marching through the rain and mud.

They had not received rations for two days and had survived on moldy hardtack and, on those rare occasions when they were able to pause long enough to build fires, bitter chicory coffee. Since the failure to take Cemetery Hill they had grumbled about the leadership, speculated on what Jackson would have done if he had lived, still commanded the corps.

Ahead of them, beyond a short hill, they heard the sudden sound of small arms fire. The tired unit climbed a crest, moving quickly through a thin copse of trees, not needed any urging from Coltrane or the company sergeant, and then suddenly found themselves looking down a gradual slope toward the source of the gunshots.

Dismounted Federal cavalry, crouched behind a low stonewall, were exchanging fire with a company of Confederate infantry deployed in a line along a shallow depression in the ground at the base of the slope. Although the cavalry unit was smaller than the Confederate company, the higher ground, the better cover, and the repeating Spencer carbines tilted the balance heavily in their favor. Already the ground between them and at the foot of the hill was scattered with the bodies of dead or wounded Confederate infantry. They had nowhere to run, no avenue of retreat. The open ground behind them would allow the cavalry to shoot them before they ran very far, or to chase them down on horseback.

Without pausing to consider the situation, Coltrane gave the signal to fix bayonets. They would take the Federals from behind. Moving quietly through the steady rain, Coltrane led the company down the slope. Using only knives they took out a pair of dismounted Federal troopers holding the horses back from the main Federal line and continued their approach *unnoticed.*

When they were ten yards away they fired their single shot muskets into the backs of the Federals, then closed the remaining distance quickly, charging with a shriek in their throats, slashing with bayonets and musket stocks as they smashed into the Federal line, men slipping in the mud as they grappled.

Coltrane came in with them, ducking low as several shots were fired over his head. He shot one trooper in the chest with his pistol at close range, the muzzle blast opening a large hole in the man's chest and setting the front of his uniform on fire. Then Coltrane turned, shrugged off a saber thrust, and shot another man, his opposite number in rank, in the side of the neck.

Within moments it was over.

The surviving members of the other Confederate unit had come up the slope with bayonets and knives and joined the hand-to-hand fray, ending it quickly. When it was over, Coltrane had lost four of his command, and two more lay dying where they fell.

The ground around them was covered with dead and wounded Federal troopers, some of them almost buried in the mud where they had been driven as others had stepped on them during the fight. They had eight surviving prisoners, two with severe wounds, and twelve horses captured. Many of the horses had bolted when the handlers were killed.

A tall, sweaty man with a reddish beard and a dirty bandage wrapped around his right hand approached Coltrane and saluted. "Sir, the Fourth Alabama is grateful for your appearance on the field!"

Coltrane noted the chevron patch on the soldier's cap, and nodded. "Sergeant," he said in acknowledgement.

"Looks like we've got prisoners, sir. Eight to be exact," said a man whom Coltrane knew only as Wentworth.

"Where's Sergeant Lewis?" Coltrane asked.

"Dead, Sir. Took one of them rifled carbine rounds between the eyes as we were closing on them, Sir. I saw him fall."

"Take his stripes, then."

Wentworth hurried off to attend to this chore. There was no time for sentiment.

"What about the prisoners?" asked the sergeant of the Fourth Alabama.

"They'll have to be transported up to the main body, join the other prisoners."

"Beg your pardon, sir," the sergeant said, nervously, pulling at the bandage, trying to wrap it tighter around his wrist. "We got enough prisoners up there slowing us down already. A few more ain't gonna be appreciated. They only use up the rations our boys need. Besides that, two of these can't even ride, let alone walk."

"Then take the six. Leave the two. If they can survive the night, their own forces will catch up and take care of them."

"Sir, that's not what I was getting at."

Coltrane turned to look carefully at the man; aware of his own men gathered around close enough to hear every word. The prisoners had been herded just out of earshot. "Just what were you getting at, sergeant?"

"I think the lieutenant understands."

"No. I don't. Spell it out for me."

"I'm saying we give these Yankees what they gave to most of my company, what they were about to give the rest of us: death. Begging your pardon, sir, but we ain't got time to be nice about things anymore. We got to report back to the regiment. Those men would slow us. Nobody is going to be happy to see us return with more mouths to feed."

Coltrane took a deep breath, exhaled once. He was tired, so damn tired, didn't understand how it could have come to this, killing men who had surrendered. That was not how he had been taught. You had to have some decency about something, had to draw the line somewhere. Otherwise where did it end?

21

He shook his head, slowly, staring at the ground.

"No," he said aloud then. "These men won't be killed. They're our prisoners. They surrendered to us. We will not dishonor ourselves. You and the rest of your company will personally escort them to General Ewell's Second Corps headquarters. I believe we have captured a colonel among them. Make sure he is treated with the respect accorded his rank. Take the horses too. Ride them if you know how, but leave them for Ewell's staff."

Coltrane turned and walked away from the sergeant. He did not look at the Federal prisoners, most of them now sitting on the stone wall, waiting for his word, wouldn't meet their eyes, didn't want to see the blank resignation of defeat that he had seen in the eyes of other prisoners. Instead he walked away from them, headed part way up the hill and motioned for Sergeant Wentworth to join him.

They still had a patrol to complete, a lot of miles yet to cover. That was the thing. They had their orders to carry out, and the skirmish that had just cost him six men did not count for anything. Coltrane issued several commands to the sergeant and waited for his exhausted men to pick themselves up and climb the hill towards him.

The rain had slowed to a drizzle. The men assembled slowly, fanned out into formation and headed back up the slope. When they reached the top they passed over the peak quickly and back into the relative cover of the trees, then started down the other side, moving at an angle so they were headed to intercept their original course.

They were about a half mile down the long slope, slowed by the growth of underbrush around the trees, when they heard the shots. There were eight of them, Coltrane knew, although they were bunched so close together as to sound more like only three or four. There was a pause and then two more distinct, but muffled shots.

The patrol froze, the men looking at Coltrane, waiting for his reaction. But there was nothing they could do now and time was short, so they moved on.

No one said a word.

There was nothing to say. They walked forward into the darkness of the forest that was before them. Mosquitoes whined about their ears. The distant rumble of thunder receded and the air became heavy.

*

"I never should have left them," Coltrane muttered aloud to himself. "Should have gone back for that."

He found himself shaking, heart racing, a cold sweat broke throughout his body. From past experience he knew that he would not sleep well that night. He did not understand the reaction, the stain of guilt, whenever he thought of those men, the eight enemy prisoners he had left behind with the company from the Fourth Alabama.

Some time later he realized it had stopped raining. He picked up the whiskey jug, tossed the remnants of the coffeepot over the porch railing and went inside for the night.

Chapter Six

During the next few months Coltrane went to town frequently. He did this because he needed start-up supplies and because he hoped people would get used to seeing him. By mere exposure, he thought they might learn they had nothing to fear from him.

On two of these trips he had seen the girl, once at the tavern having supper with the young deputy, once making a purchase at the dry goods store. He was courteous to her and tipped his hat each time. On the first occasion she appeared startled; the next time she smiled and waved at him first. There was no mistaking that she remembered him, knew who he was.

Coltrane never made any effort to converse with her, or with anyone else. He bought his supplies, had lunch in the Red Sky saloon, and went home. Always he was remote, distant from the people of Crystal.

His eyes were alert and cold, revealing nothing.

*

On the first day of December, a day that was clear with sunshine and white clouds spread across the broad sky, Coltrane sat in the Red Sky Saloon sipping from a cup of coffee while his buckboard was loaded with supplies from Ryan's. He had already paid for his coffee and was about to leave when the young lady came into the saloon, glanced about, and walked over to him.

"Sir," she said, meeting his eye. "My name is Elisabeth."

Coltrane nodded politely.

"I've found myself in a particular situation. My horse has come up lame and must be left at the stables. I have more than half a day to pass before I can take a ride home with my fiancé this evening. He's a deputy and must keep guard at the jail until ten o'clock this evening. I was wondering if I might take a ride home with you. It is not out of your way, very much anyway. You pass near my house on your return."

"Do you know where I live?"

Elisabeth smiled. "You purchased the old Barrow cabin, which is about six miles out of town, on the same road where I live, about six miles past my home."

With a smile that was nearly imperceptible Coltrane nodded. "Then you shall have a ride."

"Thank you." She smiled warmly.

*

They rode together, sitting side by side at the front of the buckboard. Neither of them spoke for a long while. Elisabeth watched how he handled the horses, directing them easily, almost telepathically, with short and efficient movements of the reins, at times moving nothing but his fingers to guide them.

"You are rather comfortable with silence," she said at least.

"Yes."

"Most people aren't. I've heard interesting things about you."

"Such as?"

"My fiancé won't tell me anything and he bristles if I mention your name, but others do talk."

"For example?"

"They say your name is Coltrane. For a while you were sheriff of towns in Kansas, New Mexico territory, Arizona. Then, you robbed banks in California and Nevada. You have a wife somewhere. You are still wanted in at least two states."

"Is that all?"

"They say you have shot dead at least twenty men, not counting those you killed in the war."

"You've heard all that?"

25

"Is it true?"

"Some of it."

"Which parts."

"I was a sheriff in Kansas and Arizona. I have a wife."

"Where is your wife?"

"Savannah, probably."

"Do you love her?"

"Yes."

"Did you ever rob banks?"

Coltrane smiled grimly. "Depends who you ask."

*

"You know much about me and I know nothing about you."

"I can tell you," she replied.

"Go ahead."

"I thought about you a lot that first night after you arrived."

"Why?"

"You made an impression."

"Hmmm...."

"You made quite an impression on everyone," she said in a rush.

Coltrane shook his head.

Elisabeth nodded. "A dangerous man with deep blue eyes – you move through the world as if you have no interest in others. All my life I've known men who revealed themselves, their needs, their desires, but not you. You show no vulnerability. You stared straight at me, as if you saw everything, and then moved past me like I didn't exist. The way you handled the sheriff, that bully.... You face down a roomful of men without the slightest sign of concern."

Coltrane nodded. "That's the only way to do it."

*

"Your fiancé," Coltrane said, changing the subject, trying to be polite about it.

"Thomas Hyde. He's the deputy. He was with the Sheriff the day you arrived."

"He's a good man?"

Elisabeth nodded. "Yes, I think so. I've known him since I was twelve. We grew up together. He cares for me."

"Is he good to you?"

"Yes."

"That's most of what counts."

"But there has to be more to it."

"Perhaps."

"Sometimes I wonder…"

Elisabeth talked on. Coltrane learned she had come to Crystal two years ago from Denver, arriving with Thomas Hyde, her fiancé. Her parents still lived in Denver. She worked three half-days each week for a doctor, helping keep his records, assisting with patients. Thomas found a job with the sheriff's office and had recently been made a deputy.

Elisabeth was twenty-four years old, of German ancestry, but she had been born in New England. Her father had immigrated to South America in 1873, coming over from the Caucasus after Czar Alexander II withdrew the special privileges that had been accorded the German communities in Russia since '62. Elisabeth was not close to her father, though she loved him. Relations with her mother were more complicated.

The mother was critical of Elisabeth and her decisions. She did not approve of Thomas. The disapproval was expressed frequently, in many ways, regarding her choice of clothing, her manners, eating habits, living quarters, but it always came down to the same thing: Thomas was not good enough for her.

Stubborn and determined to be her own woman, Elisabeth defied her mother and not only planned to marry Thomas, but she was already living with him before the wedding, still

27

almost a year away.

Coltrane was a good listener. He said little and made just enough eye contact to indicate he was following her words. When they reached her house, Elisabeth invited him inside for a cup of tea.

Coltrane stepped down from the buckboard first, and offered his hand to help her off. She smiled at him, looking down into his eyes, as she took hold of his hand with hers.

"Thank you very much," she said to him.

He removed his hat and wiped his feet off carefully before entering her house.

Chapter Seven

"Of course, everybody wonders about you," Elisabeth said as she poured the tea. "You must know that."

Coltrane nodded and accepted the hot mug. He would have preferred coffee, but he didn't think it would be polite to say so.

"You're so quiet, so serious."

"I reckon I am."

"Why is that?"

"Guess I don't have much to say."

"Why does everyone talk about you the way they do?" Elisabeth asked as she stirred honey into her tea.

"I don't know. How do they talk about me?"

"They say you're dangerous. They fear you. They wonder why you're here and it's in their minds that maybe they need to do something about you."

"Maybe they do."

"I don't think so."

"No? Why?"

"Because you're not the way they say you are."

"Really?"

"You're different than I thought you would be."

Coltrane couldn't help but smile. He licked his lower lip thoughtfully. "How did you think I would be?"

"Mean, rough. I thought you might say 'no' when I asked you for a ride home. I certainly didn't think you would listen to me babbling on like I have been for the last half hour."

"No?"

"No. You're nice, even gentle, the way you handled those horses, the way you helped me down from the wagon."

"I don't know all they're saying about me, but some of it is probably true."

"They say you've killed men."

Coltrane nodded. "When it was necessary."

"They say you're a criminal, that you should have been hanged dead a long time ago."

Coltrane shrugged. "Some men feel that way."

"Some say you should be run out of town before you kill somebody here, that you'll bring nothing but trouble to our town."

"I didn't come here to bring trouble to anyone. I just want to be left alone. I came to find peace."

Elisabeth looked at him and nodded, her eyes heavy. "I believe you. I hope you'll find it here."

Coltrane shrugged, looking into her eyes, holding her gaze for a long moment, then looking away, uncomfortable, aware that he had stared for too long, aware too that she had not looked away, had held his eyes comfortably through the long silence. He sipped from his tea for the first time, then sipped again, suddenly nervous that she was no longer saying anything.

*

On the ride back to his cabin Coltrane thought about the lady, her soft, knowing eyes and coffee-toned skin. He thought about how she had the most beautiful smile he had ever seen.

He found himself thinking about touching her hair, kissing her, and he knew that if he ever got the chance, he would. Even as he thought about Anne and the betrayal that would constitute, and even as he began to feel sick to his stomach at the mere thought, he knew he would kiss Elisabeth anyway.

Yes, if given the chance he would kiss her and do everything else that came naturally after that.

That's how immediate the spell was. He tried to put her out of his mind, but couldn't.

When he got back to his cabin, he put up the horses, unsheathed the lever-action Winchester M1873 that he carried beneath the seat of the buckboard, and walked out into the forest to hunt.

He didn't shoot anything, and didn't even notice the small game and elk that filled the woods. It was almost pitch black before he realized the day had closed and it was time to return to his cabin.

Chapter Eight

Coltrane saw Elisabeth several more times without intending to make a habit of it. On a cold, sunny afternoon she fixed lunch for him when he passed her house with the buckboard filled with supplies. She made hot beef sandwiches, frying the meat first, and then thick slices of bread in the drippings.

When she went riding out his way he gave her a tour of his property, showing off the work he had done on the cabin and barn, the smokehouse he had built. He led her out to inspect the winter garden and introduced her to the hogs and the cows that he had acquired. They walked out into the forest, down a trail that opened up into a meadow where he often grazed the cows.

They began to forge a closeness that others did not see, and would not have understood.

*

"Does Thomas know how much time we've spent together?" Coltrane asked one afternoon.

Elisabeth did not answer right away. She sipped her tea and thought about the question for a moment. It was quiet in her kitchen except for the ticking of a large clock in the hallway. "I told him about the first time I invited you in for tea."

"And he wasn't happy about that...."

"No, I wouldn't say that.... He was indifferent."

"Truly?"

"It bothered him, I could tell."

"So he doesn't know about the other times?"

Elisabeth shook her head. "I don't see the need to worry him." Her eyes flitted away from his.

"No."

"We haven't done anything wrong."

"No. We haven't."

"That's right, we haven't done anything wrong. Yet."

They fell silent, listening to the steady pattern of the hallway clock marking the time.

*

The weeks passed and the winter deepened over the valley. Snow fell and piled thick over the countryside, blanketing the roads, pastures, and fields. Coltrane stopped working on the house and barn. Instead he turned his efforts to chopping wood and hunting. He slaughtered four hogs and, together with the butchered carcasses of two elk, he cured them in the smokehouse.

Always Coltrane remained vigilant to the small noises, to the sounds of the countryside and the forest around him. Past experience had taught him to be on guard, even when there was no apparent reason to be. Every day he scouted his land, wanting to know if anyone was watching him or trespassing. Each day he awoke with the thought that it might be the day someone would try again to kill him.

Mostly he stayed inside the cabin, propped up by the cast iron stove, reading the books he had brought with him. He first read through a pile of old magazines and newspapers purchased in San Francisco, caught up with the events that had occurred earlier that year in Cuba.

He read with curiosity about the war, about the Rough Riders at Kettle Hill, led by a fellow named Theodore Roosevelt and their division commander Brigadier General Joseph Wheeler. Coltrane remembered Wheeler from his own war, knew his reputation as a fighter.

When he finished the periodicals he started on the books. He went through a Shakespeare phase, finishing a play each day for a week, mostly tragedies. Then he started on the memoirs, reading Grant's first because he admired him as one

33

of the strong leaders of the war even though they fought on opposite sides.

The memoir had been published shortly after Grant's death and Coltrane had planned to read it for many years now. He had simply never found time before. Now, he read it ravenously, both volumes, hardly even leaving the cabin for several days.

In some ways he was quite ignorant with regard to the larger picture of the war. He had never read much about the war and had always avoided talking with other veterans since it ended. It was with some surprise that he discovered a strong interest in learning more. After he finished with Grant, he read the memoirs of Colonel Walter Taylor, a staff officer to Robert E. Lee.

He continued to read and read and being alone never bothered him.

Chapter Nine

In mid January a thaw struck. Early on a Friday afternoon, Coltrane saddled one of the mares, the one he called Bobby-Lee, and rode toward Elisabeth's house. The light in her eyes told him she was happy to see him. She was baking bread but didn't care to finish and instead saddled a speckled grey and together they rode out along the Wasatch Front.

As they rode she spoke of her fiancé, and how she thought, but was not completely sure, that he was the right man for her to spend the rest of her life with. She described a new recipe for pecan pie she had tried the night before, a new hat her mother had sent to her from San Francisco, and other mundane things.

Coltrane listened silently as they rode, his eyes scanning the tree line ahead of them.

*

"Can I ask you a question," Elisabeth said. She spoke with an abrupt change of tone and her eyes were distant.

Coltrane nodded, but did not take his eyes off the ground ahead of them. It was colder now, the sky had darkened, and the wind was blowing intermittent gusts. He knew Elisabeth was cold, had offered her his overcoat, but, too proud, she had declined to take it.

"Do you think a man and a woman can be friends?"

"Aren't we friends?"

"It's more complicated than that, isn't it?"

"Because there is the possibility of more than friendship?"

"You must admit – there aren't many men and women who are merely friends. Not in this county. I don't know of any who are. Other people wouldn't understand the friendship that we have."

"Because they would think I'm taking you to bed?"

Elisabeth paused again. Coltrane didn't look at her, concentrated hard on Bobby-Lee, on the trail, on the trees. The ground was rocky and the horses stepped carefully. "I suppose that would be one thought they might have. There is something more complicated about it, something that isn't there in my other friendships. I would never lie to Thomas about having lunch with a girlfriend."

"Do you lie to him about me?" Coltrane looked at her.

Elisabeth bit her lip, nodding. "He wouldn't understand. I guess that is what I'm trying to say."

"Would he forbid it?"

"He might not, but he wouldn't understand."

They rode in silence now, Coltrane trying to understand what she was attempting to express. For what seemed an eternity neither of them spoke. Then Coltrane cleared his throat, uneasy now, but not willing to let go of it. "It is complicated. We have an unusual – perhaps, special relationship."

Elisabeth stared at him, then nodded. "Should we talk about this?"

Coltrane did not respond. They were near the point where they would have to climb more steeply now. He knew it didn't make sense to continue on, and instead reined in the mare, turning her. Elisabeth's horse followed instinctively.

They did not speak for a while, concentrated on the trail, understanding that it was trickier going back down than it had been coming up. Then, without looking at her, Coltrane spoke again, and Elisabeth noticed that his lips were tight, his eyes cold as he spoke. "Under other circumstances.... I would want to be with you if things were different."

He said it matter-of-factly, surprising her. Elisabeth did not respond at first. As the grade leveled out she spurred her mount to a gentle trot, passing Coltrane momentarily, then dropping back to ride beside him. "Did you have to go and say that, what you said back there?" she asked him then.

36

Slowly he turned towards her. "I thought that was what we were talking about." His voice was quiet.

"Maybe so, but did you have to just come out and say it out loud? That just puts it right out there."

"That's the way I am."

"I know. I'm learning that about you."

Elisabeth slowed her horse. She was nervous, but her eyes didn't waver as she looked at Coltrane. They were large and hazel, with a softness that stirred Coltrane in a way that he could never have explained, as if she could see him like no one else could. In that instant, he felt it, tugging at him from someplace deep inside, some place that had not been touched in a long time, as if he had stepped into the light, the heat, the respite from a frozen soulless place, was touched by something blessed, yet achingly familiar, as if he had known her for a thousand years, a hundred previous lifetimes.

Suddenly, Coltrane knew everything was different now. In her face he saw the longing, the desire, and something even more powerful, and he wondered if she could see all that in his eyes too. As they rode on he decided that she must have, because as she spurred the grey to a trot Elisabeth looked over her shoulder and the smile she gave him was joyous.

*

They rode back in silence, both aware they were headed toward his home and not hers.

"Will you teach me how to shoot?" Elisabeth asked as they approached his cabin.

"I thought you already knew how to handle a gun."

"I do, sort of, though I'm not a very good shot."

"I'm not either."

"You must be. You've got to be the best shooter I know."

Coltrane shook his head. "I'm no marksman."

"I don't believe that. That's your reputation."

"It may be my reputation, but it's not the truth. I'm only an average marksman."

"How have you survived if you can't shoot well?"

"I didn't say I couldn't shoot well. I said I'm an average marksman."

"I don't understand."

Coltrane took a deep breath before he started. "There are plenty of men who can, in a quiet moment when no one is threatening them, stand very still, sight their rifle, hold their breath, and squeeze off a highly accurate shot at an unmoving target. They can hit that stationary target or a slow moving animal that is a long way away from them, and they can do that better than I can. That is marksmanship."

"Is that what you are only average at?"

"Yes. It's different if the target is another man, especially if he's shooting back at you and moving."

"I see."

"Physical fear and hesitation make the difference."

"You don't experience fear?"

"I handle it differently than most. Perhaps I'm accustomed to it and so able to disregard it."

"And hesitation?"

"I won't do that. I won't hesitate, not ever. Most men aren't willing to kill another man. The prohibition to take another human life runs deep. Men may think they want to, or need to, or have to kill, but in that heated instant, just before they pull the trigger, everything they learned in Sunday school comes back to them by instinct and they hesitate, or flinch, or shift their aim. During the war I knew of men who fired their muskets over the heads of the Federals, even when they were charging our position with bayonets. They couldn't kill another human. They simply couldn't do it – even to save their own life or the life of the man next to them."

"You never hesitated?"

"Only once, only that very first time. Never once since.

38

You understand; I'm not proud of this? It's a good thing that most men cannot kill."

"I understand."

Coltrane looked at her, stared hard, his lips tight. The dead look in his eyes frightened her. "Yes," he said. "Maybe you finally do." His eyes softened even as he spoke the words.

*

The horses pulled up in front of the cabin. It was colder now than it had been, the sun hidden again. Breath from the horses' nostrils was visible as short eruptions of white smoke as they stood, waiting patiently.

Coltrane climbed off Bobby-Lee and tethered her to the porch railing. He looked up at Elisabeth, sitting tall in her saddle, looking down at him with that look in her eyes again. With a hand on the grey's neck, he started to open his mouth, was going to invite Elisabeth inside, but the words didn't quite form. She shook her head, as if she knew what he was trying to say, and pulled back on her reins.

Her horse took a step backward.

"I should go," Elisabeth said softly. "I've been gone too long. Thomas is probably home by now, wondering where I am."

Coltrane nodded, not wanting her to leave, knowing that she had to.

"Thank you for the ride," she said. "It was wonderful."

Coltrane nodded and watched her ride away, feeling it again in the pit of his stomach and knowing there was nothing he could do about it. He put Bobby-Lee up in the barn and then poured himself a measure of whiskey and sat on the porch sipping it. He did not mind the cold air. He drank slowly and thought about the day.

After awhile he rolled a cigarette and sat smoking it with his eyes half open, thinking about all the words she had said and what they might mean. He wondered if she was thinking of him too and where her thoughts took her. The feeling in his stomach did not subside and he sat there long into the night, smoking several more cigarettes, but not bothering to pour another whiskey for himself.

The sky remained gray until twilight when small cracks of orange and purple shined over the Wasatch for just a moment. Soon darkness settled over the land. There was no moon or stars out and the wind blew fiercely starting around midnight. It howled until dawn, and then began to abate gradually with the first light.

Chapter Ten

Sheriff Bryant and five men approached the cabin slowly.

It was a gray morning, but the thaw was still on, most of the snow had melted into the soggy ground, and birds had reappeared. A thin mist had covered the ground at dawn, but now gave way to an intermittent spitting rain. There was no wind. The riders made no attempt to conceal their approach as they rode fanned out beside each other in a skirmish line formation.

Coltrane heard them when they were a quarter mile away, and watched them for several minutes from inside his cabin. He knew it had been only a matter of time. He pulled on the shoulder rig and checked the cartridges in the Colt before holstering it. Next he quickly checked the Winchester and the Remington shotgun in the rack between the door and the window. Then he opened the door and stood there, arms crossed, watching the riders approach, knowing they could see him standing there waiting for them.

They stopped twenty yards from the porch, forming a shallow crescent of muddy horses in front of him. The riders remained mounted, their eyes on Bryant, taking their cue from him, waiting for him to make the first move, no one quite sure what he would do.

Coltrane remained still while he waited. He had always been good at the waiting. It had been one of the things that set him apart from other men. He had learned never to rush a situation, but instead to let it unfold, always seeming to know when it was the right moment to act.

"Morning, sir" barked the sheriff finally. His voice was gruff.

"Morning, Sheriff," Coltrane replied, arms still crossed. It was a good position from which to draw the Colt from the shoulder rig, a fact that other men had underestimated more than once. "What can I do for you?"

41

Bryant, leaning with gloved hands on the pommel of his saddle, paused and looked around him, glancing up at the sky. "Beautiful day, today, here in the fine state of Utah."

Coltrane made no response. Several of the horses shuffled restlessly.

"Actually," the sheriff growled again, his voice a little louder this time. "It's a little warmer than I like it this time of year, a little gray for my taste. All that melting snow leaves the ground too soft. You've done a lot of work on this place. Old man Barrow never put much into it – too busy drinking the product of his still."

Coltrane nodded. His eyes were on Bryant, but he was aware of the other men too, would have registered any movement in the line, his eyes focused softly. He was particularly aware of young Thomas Hyde, sitting apprehensively on a gray stallion to Bryant's left.

"Any chance you might have a pot of hot coffee on?"

"Nope."

"Don't suppose you're going to invite me in?"

"What for?"

"So we can talk where it's warm."

"Doubt we have that much to say to each other."

Bryant shook his head, feigning a look of disappointment. "I was hoping you'd be a little more hospitable."

"Never been known for my hospitality," Coltrane replied flatly.

"I've got some things to discuss."

"I'm listening."

"Just like that? Right here? Would you mind if I dismounted and came up on the porch?"

"Don't see much need for that. I can hear you fine from here."

"Yeah, but I'd feel better about it."

Coltrane thought it over for a moment. "Alright," he said then. "Just you. I reckon your men can stay mounted. We don't have that much to say. This won't take long."

Bryant nodded, glanced sideways at Hyde and nodded once more, then climbed off his horse, handing the reins over to Hyde. He came up the porch and stood in front of Coltrane, off to the side a bit so that he wouldn't block Coltrane's view of the other men, understanding this was necessary. He kept his hands, still gloved, open in front of him, palms against his thighs. They stood close together now, and Coltrane could smell the strong cologne mixed with the scent of sweat and fear.

Coltrane looked into Bryant's face as the two men studied each other up close. Coltrane observed the neatly trimmed beard and hair, the expensive clothing, the silk shirt, the gold watch chain, the kid gloves. The gloves were not the rugged sort usually worn by men who spent much time in the saddle. On the other hand, Coltrane knew they would be good in a gunfight, their light feel allowing for fine trigger control.

"I've wanted to talk with you," Bryant said at length. His voice was quiet so that only the two of them would be able to hear what he said. "I have to wonder why you're here, in my town. I'm prone to worry about such things. You know, uncertainty can put a man like me off his step."

"Sorry to hear it," Coltrane said.

"Figured I'd come out, in a friendly way, like this, and see about putting my mind at rest."

"Sure."

"Yeah, sure. So what is it?"

"What's that?"

"The reason you're here. Why Utah? Why Crystal?"

"A man's got to be somewhere."

"That's all?"

"This seemed as good a place as any."

"Just that?"

"Just that."

Bryant sighed and brought one gloved hand slowly up to

43

his face and rubbed gently at the corners of his mouth. "That doesn't put my mind at rest. What are your plans?"

"Sheriff, I'm not looking for trouble. Just looking for quiet."

"I'm not particularly enthusiastic about the fact that you've chosen my town to look for quiet in."

"Well," Coltrane started slowly. "I don't reckon I can be concerned with your lack of enthusiasm."

"That's not friendly."

"Neither is showing up with five guns. If you wanted to talk to me man-to-man you could have come by yourself. I might even have invited you in, put on a fresh pot of coffee. This isn't the way to do it. From now on if you want to talk to me, you come alone. I see you out here again with all those men I don't know, I'm likely to feel threatened. I won't accept that."

The scar beneath Bryant's left eye twitched as his lips drew tight. His eyes didn't waver from Coltrane's. "You don't remember me, do you?"

Coltrane studied him carefully. "Should I?"

"I was there the night you shot Jesse Caufield down in Pima County."

"That was a long time ago."

"Eleven years."

"You were there?"

Bryant nodded slowly, his features hardening. "He was my uncle, my mother's youngest brother."

"I see."

"You shot him in the back."

"I hit him in the side as he was turning back to me. He had his gun drawn already, thought he would catch me off-guard."

"That's your story. You should have swung for that killing."

"It was self-defense. If you were there, then you would know that."

"He caught you cheating at poker."

44

"I never cheated – not then or ever."

"You killed him in cold blood."

Coltrane nodded, knowing that further discussion was pointless. "I reckon you can leave now," he said, nodding towards the road.

Bryant nodded too and turned to step down off the porch, splashing through the mud. He took the reins of his horse, put a foot into the stirrup, and swung up onto the saddle in one fluid motion. Once mounted, he sat for a moment, staring at Coltrane, his complexion slightly red now.

"Stay out of trouble in my town," he warned loudly, an angry tone in his voice now for the first time. "Better yet, get out of my county."

"Were you really there that night in Pima County?" Coltrane asked, his voice calm, still standing in the doorway with his arms crossed.

Bryant nodded savagely. "This was a little souvenir from that evening," he said, placing a gloved finger next to the scar under his eye. "I was behind the bar that night. One of the shots hit the mirror. I was picking out glass for a week." With a guttural cry he pulled back on the reins, turning his horse away.

The other riders fell out one at a time, following him single file in a path down to the road. Coltrane couldn't be sure, but it seemed as though Thomas Hyde had lingered for just a moment, looking at him, studying him carefully with a strange expression that seemed more curious than nervous, before joining the others.

Coltrane moved to the end of the porch to watch them until they disappeared into the woods a half mile from his cabin. He stood there watching and listening for another ten minutes. Then he took his rifle and went out into the woods behind his cabin.

Chapter Eleven

"I heard the sheriff came to visit you last week."

They were sitting on Elisabeth's back porch, watching the chickens chase each other around the yard, sipping from cups of hot coffee. She wore a light green wool knit sweater that her grandmother had made. Her hair was pulled back and tied up under a lavender scarf.

Coltrane shrugged with indifference. "He did."

"Thomas was with him."

It wasn't a question so Coltrane said nothing.

"What did he want?"

"Didn't Thomas tell you?"

"He wasn't sure. The sheriff says you're a bad man and it would be better if you left the county. But Thomas couldn't hear what you talked about. He said Bryant was real mad afterwards, said he stayed upset for the rest of the day, was hard to be around, yelled at some of the other deputies for no good reason."

"Can't say that I'm surprised."

"What did he want?"

"Pretty much what Thomas said. He told me to leave, said he doesn't want me to bring trouble."

"What did you tell him?"

"I told him to get off my property."

Elisabeth winced. "The sheriff is not somebody you want to fool around with. He's a bully, and don't expect him to play fair."

Coltrane nodded. "I don't expect that of anybody."

"Not even me?"

"Maybe you, though I'm not sure why."

Elisabeth nodded happily, her smile fading quickly. "I'm serious. Don't take the sheriff lightly. He's mean."

"So am I."

"He killed a man last year, a gambler who had too much

to drink and was shouting vulgarities at the ladies over at the Red Sky saloon. When Bryant approached him, the gambler cursed him and called him out into the street. Bryant never gave him a chance. He shot him right there in the saloon. Thomas was there, said he's never seen such a fast draw. The gambler wasn't even ready. Bryant didn't say a word. He just drew his gun in the blink of an eye and shot the man twice in the chest, killed him instantly. He never had a chance."

"Anything's fair in a gunfight," Coltrane said. "That's the first rule."

"This wasn't a gunfight – at least it didn't have to be."

Coltrane nodded. "I understand your point," he said. "A man who doesn't mind killing is a dangerous man."

Neither of them spoke for a while. They sipped their coffee, which was lukewarm by now. The chickens cackled with excitement as one of the larger roosters attacked another rooster, swiping with sharp talons, driving it away from one of the hens.

"Thomas said there was something else," Elisabeth said. "Something that surprised him, watching you and the sheriff talk. He said it appeared you knew each other. When he asked Bryant about it afterwards, Bryant got mad, cursed him, told him to mind his own business…. Did you know Bryant before you came out here?"

Coltrane allowed one of his rare smiles. "No," he said.

"Is there more to it?"

"Maybe."

"You're not going to tell me?"

"Nope."

"We have to talk about something."

"No. We don't. We don't have to talk about anything at all."

*

Coltrane moved over toward her, slowly across the space between them until his face was next to hers. He looked into her eyes, her beautiful soft hazel eyes, and quite literally felt sick with longing for her. He had thought about this moment for months, laying awake at night, feeling nervous whenever he thought about it. When his mouth was inches from hers, looking into her eyes that were moist with anticipation, he paused.

"Are you sure you want to do this?" she asked, even as she was moving towards him also.

"Yes," he said simply, not knowing what else to say. "Let's do this and get it over with." Then he kissed her.

He felt the heat of her breath, the softness of her lips, their tongues probing gently at first, then harder, more urgently. She placed a hand on his cheek, as if to keep him from drawing away.

Their whole world seemed to melt.

Chapter Twelve

Coltrane saw the ghost in the deepest hour of the night, the hour before dawn arrived.

He awoke in a cold sweat and felt the presence. Unsure if he had been dreaming, he opened his eyes and stared at the apparition. The room was cold and still, and the figure moved slowly past the foot of his bed, reflecting the light of the moon through the window.

Coltrane was unable to move. He watched the figure and saw the soft outlines of a man dressed in frontier clothing: a wide brimmed hat, dungarees, buckskin jacket with fringe, an old Navy revolver. The man's hair curled and flowed down over his shoulders and his mustache hung down past the corners of his mouth.

His eyes were sad.

They faced each other for a long, frozen moment, then the apparition turned, and without a word or gesture moved toward the hearth. He paused there before turning and brought both hands up to his chest, pressing them together, one on top of the other, over his left breast. He continued to stare, motionless now, at Coltrane.

Coltrane stared back, not frightened, but mesmerized. He thought he should know who the figure was, but he couldn't think clearly, couldn't place the face or the movements that were so familiar.

Then, without a sound, the apparition was gone.

Coltrane remained motionless in bed, aware that he was awake. He was sweating heavily and unable to move. He lay there for what seemed like hours, his mind blank, listening to the slow sound of his own labored breathing. Eventually he came out of it. Pushing the blankets away he swung his legs out onto the floor. It was firm and solid to his touch. The fire had burned down to embers.

It was very cold in the cabin, but Coltrane felt warm,

feverish, and he was still sweating. In nothing other than his stockings and the long underwear in which he slept, he sat on the edge of the bed and set a match to the lamp. The interior of the cabin danced with shadows from the small flame.

With difficulty he rolled a cigarette. His fingers trembled. He smoked slowly, holding the smoke in as long as he could and was grateful for the burn of the harsh tobacco in his lungs.

At dawn he poked the fire back to life, added some wood, and made a pot of strong coffee.

Chapter Thirteen

Later that morning Coltrane saddled Rosalita, the buckskin Appaloosa, and rode down one of the trails he knew would lead to Elisabeth. It was cold again. The ground was frozen and the promise of snow was in the air. A lone hawk soared high in the sky, swooping low then soaring up again. Coltrane felt unsettled. He decided it would not be a good day to sit around the cabin with nothing more than his own thoughts for company.

"If I keep moving, I'll be okay," he told himself aloud.

He rode slowly, keeping his eyes on the tree line, vigilant out of habit. He tried not to think of the apparition. Instead, he thought of Elisabeth, of the kiss, of the look in her eyes when he pulled back after kissing her. She had leaned in towards him, encouraging him, and he had kissed her again, longer and harder, certain then that she wanted him to. Afterwards, they said very little to each other. She had smiled and he had felt happy.

Now, as he rode the mare along the frozen trail he felt it all over again. A tingle ran through his body and he felt the warmth of her mouth, her breath, as if she were right there with him. There was sadness too.

Elisabeth belonged to another man.

With confusion, he thought about Anne and the promise he had broken. It was true that he had not seen her for years, but he felt a personal sense of betrayal. He had made a promise to Anne and now he had broken it. The reason did not matter. Now he knew he would live with it.

Coltrane thought about it as he rode.

Guilt was something he was familiar with. You couldn't kill another man without questioning yourself. He had decided long ago that guilt was a luxury he could not afford, a choice he would not make for himself. If you chose to act, then guilt was a hollow feeling for sure and it served no purpose.

With this in mind, he acknowledged to himself that it was wrong to pursue Elisabeth, that it was a betrayal of Anne, and a wrong towards the young Thomas Hyde. He also knew that none of that would matter enough to change the fact that he wanted the lady.

There was something about her, about the way her eyes looked at him, about the scent and feel of her smooth skin, about the texture of her mouth, about the way he felt when he touched her lightly with his fingertips. He could not have put it into words, but there was some intangible quality of hers that was drawing him inexorably towards her. It was as if she owned him now. The spell was complete and total.

So, he rode towards Elisabeth, forcing all else from his thoughts.

*

She met him on the porch, pulling a sweater around her shoulders as she stared into his eyes. He took off his hat.

"I had to come to you," he said simply.

"I know."

"This isn't right."

"No, it isn't."

"Do you want me to leave?"

"You should probably should."

"Okay."

"Wait…."

Then she was in his arms.

*

As Coltrane stepped out the front door onto the porch he spotted a man sitting on a horse, just off the main road. It was Bryant. He was sitting still, with his gloved hands folded over the pommel, waiting, knowing Coltrane was in the house.

For a long moment the rider did not move. Then he turned his horse and rode off slowly toward town without speaking, but it was clear that he had seen Coltrane – that he knew.

Elisabeth stepped out onto the porch behind Coltrane, reaching for his hand. She let out a short gasp of surprise and anger as she realized whom the rider was, releasing her grip on Coltrane's hand.

Coltrane turned toward her and held her eyes with his. Her lips trembled, but her eyes did not waver. He felt the warmth of her gaze and then he turned away from her.

Neither of them said a word as Coltrane untethered the reins and mounted the Appaloosa to ride away.

Chapter Fourteen

The month of February passed quietly. It became cold again. There were two big snows, a week apart and a long frozen spell. Coltrane was content with his books and his hunting. By early March he needed more supplies. His salt and sugar were running low. He had salt-cured more game in his smokehouse than he had anticipated.

The ground was still hard, but the snow was no longer deep. He decided the buckboard could make the five-mile trip into town, so on a clear day at mid-morning he loaded it with dried venison and headed off to do some trading. The mares were energetic and excited as they pranced through the snow and bright sunlight that was reflected around them, happy at the chance to be out of the barn.

The trip took longer than Coltrane expected. Twice he had to climb down from his seat to help push the buckboard through deep drifts of snow. After the second time this happened he walked beside the mares for two miles until the ground leveled and the drifts were smaller.

It was late afternoon by the time he arrived in town and he made the decision to spend the night there rather than return home in the dark. He stopped first at Ryan's, where he sold the venison and made arrangements to pick up the supplies he needed early the next morning. Then he stabled the horses and took a room on the top floor of the tavern.

*

At five o'clock Coltrane was in the Red Sky saloon, drinking a beer at a table in the back, well away from the windows. He was positioned against a wall so that he could see the entire room. No one could come up behind him. Because it was early, and midweek, there were not many drinkers present, only a boisterous group of men at the bar and two men each sitting by themselves.

Coltrane studied the room carefully out of habit. Some of the faces were familiar to him. He was about to take another swallow of beer when Bryant walked in. Thomas Hyde came in behind him, looking edgy.

Bryant glanced around the room and spotted Coltrane. He and Hyde stopped first at the bar, spoke briefly to the barkeeper, and then walked over to the table where Coltrane sat.

"Mind if we join you?" Bryant asked, already pulling a chair back from the table.

Coltrane shrugged. "I'd prefer to drink alone."

Bryant sat down, and nodded at Thomas Hyde who also sat. "A man should never drink alone," the sheriff said.

"On account of what?"

"Loneliness."

"I never minded my own company."

"We'll stay only a minute. Can I buy you beer?"

"I never met a sheriff who ever paid for a beer in any saloon."

Bryant chuckled, nodding his head. "That's true. Come to think of it, I haven't either."

The barkeeper arrived at that moment with three beers, setting one in front of each man. Coltrane continued to sip from the one he already had, leaving the new one untouched in front of him. Bryant and Hyde each took a long pull from theirs.

Bryant set his down afterward, but Hyde only paused, holding the glass in front of his face before taking another long drink, swallowing several times. The large glass was half empty when he set it on the table. Afterward he wiped his mouth with the back of his hand.

"Heard you were in here signing autographs," Bryant said with a malicious grin. The scar beneath his eye shimmered in

55

the gaslight of the saloon.

"I don't sign autographs. Never have."

"Really? I bet you could. If you advertised right, you could charge a nickel and people would line up from here to the street and halfway around the block."

Coltrane nodded. "I don't need the money."

The sheriff nodded in return. "I guess robbing banks has its benefits."

Coltrane ignored this.

Bryant took a small sip from his beer. "Of course there would also be money to be made off your fame if you were dead. Did you know that after Bob Ford shot him in the back of the head they laid Jesse James out on a table and charged people a quarter to view his corpse? They had a continuous procession passing by for three days and three nights. That's a lot of quarters. The only reason they closed down the line was he started to get a little ripe. Heard they did the same thing with Wes Hardin a few years back. Somebody shoot you, we could probably charge fifty cents for a peak at your corpse."

Coltrane didn't react, but he had stopped drinking and the full beer that had been set in front of him remained untouched. The group at the bar started to argue loudly.

"I'd hate to see that happen," Bryant continued, ignoring the outburst behind him. "Hate to see any violence in my town – even if it was you that got shot. Glad to see you sit so careful like, with your back to the wall. That's how they got Hardin, Hickok too. They got careless, left their back open to a roomful of people in a saloon, kind of like this place, and got shot in the back. Neither one of them ever had a chance. Bet there's a lot of glory hunters out there, men wanting to be able to say they're the one who shot down Coltrane, never mind that they had to sneak up on him from behind. At least the sneaky bastard that shot Hickok swung for it. I've got no use for a coward like that. Of course, if somebody has to get shot in the back around here, might as well be you."

"The only one sitting with his back to the room right now is you," Coltrane said, his voice low.

"True," Bryant replied evenly. "Of course, people in this town are my friends. No one wants to see me dead. Besides, I'm just a small town sheriff. No one can make a rep by gunning me."

"You make it sound like a threat."

Bryant shook his head in an exaggerated fashion. "Nothing like that, just thinking out loud, letting you know I can't always to be around to protect you. I suggest you remain vigilant when you're in my town. You never know what might happen."

"I'll consider it."

"Be good to."

"You finished?"

"Not yet."

The noise from the men at the bar continued. The barkeeper had been glancing nervously at the sheriff for the past few minutes. "Figured you might want to quiet that group down a bit," Coltrane said.

Bryant shrugged. "I still have half a beer to drink. Thought we could reminisce a little together, seeing as how we both go back a ways, both remember the way it used to be. There aren't many gunslingers left these days. Not that I'm at your level, of course, but it's almost the next century. Who's going to need us after the century turns? You'll be an unwanted relic of another era."

"There will always be outlaws and lawmen," Coltrane replied.

Bryant grinned, and paused to sip from his beer and then gestured at his deputy. "A few years from now, young Thomas here is going to be chasing the Hole-In-The-Wall Gang in one of them new horseless carriages. He won't have to chase them very far either. If they leave his county, he'll just get on one of them new wired telephones and call the law down the road,

57

tell them to get ready. Outlaws will ride into the next county and find a posse waiting for them."

Bryant chuckled to himself and drank more of his beer, wiping the foam off his mustache with the back of his hand. "Did you know any of those guys, the other legends?" he asked. "Heard you might have passed through Abilene about '71. I think that was the last season as a cattle town. Wasn't Hickok marshal there that year? If I'm not mistaken, I do believe Wes Hardin came through too. Weren't you there also?"

"Might have been."

"You're not sure?"

"Don't recall."

"Seems to me there was a shooting there that very year."

"There were shootings there every year."

"This one was different..... Can't quite place the name: Franks, Frankenheimer, Franklin, something like that. I believe you shot him at the tables after an evening of five-card draw. You don't remember that?"

Coltrane shrugged. His eyes were not on the sheriff. They were staring straight ahead, focused softly on the loud group at the bar, but acutely aware of the sheriff and his every move. "It was a long time ago," he replied.

"He caught you cheating, called you out. You gunned him down right there at the table, just like you did Jesse Caufield. Only reason you didn't hang was your buddy Hickok was marshal and he let you skip town after a few hours in the local jail. Does that jar your memory any?"

Coltrane nodded. "First," he said. "As I told you the other day, I never cheated at cards in my life. Second, the reason Hickok let me go was that he was there at the table playing with us. He saw what happened, saw that Franklin was drunk, was losing bad, started a fight just for something to do. He also saw that I drew and fired only after Franklin threatened to kill me and drew his weapon first. It was clean self-defense."

"Is that a fact?"

Coltrane nodded. "I reckon you better leave now."

"I guess there are two sides to every story, aren't there? Maybe I'll go see about asking those men to keep it down a little bit."

Bryant stood up and Hyde started to, but the sheriff placed a hand on his deputy's shoulder. "I can handle this. Why don't you sit here for a few minutes, get acquainted with our new friend. Doesn't look like he's going to drink that beer, so you might as well help him out."

Chapter Fifteen

The sheriff had no trouble quieting the men at the bar. He spoke a few words and then sauntered out the saloon without looking back over his shoulder. There was no more noise from the group after that. They quickly finished their drinks and then left too.

"He must have a bit of a reputation himself to shut that crowd up so easily," Coltrane said.

"He gets the job done, I reckon."

Coltrane studied Thomas Hyde. He was handsome in the conventional sense, with sandy hair, brown eyes, high cheekbones, and a clear complexion that left him looking even younger than he was. He was big boned, with broad shoulders and large rough hands, outweighing Coltrane by fifteen to twenty pounds. His clothing was casual and dirty from the long day: faded denim trousers, a flannel shirt that needed mending, a worn leather jacket with a flannel lining. He didn't wear a hat.

The young man was nervous, uncomfortable with the situation, and Coltrane figured he was resentful of Coltrane's relationship with Elisabeth. Any man would have been.

"Reckon I should thank you for the hams," Hyde said after a long silence.

Coltrane waved a hand in dismissal. He had left several smoked hams with Elisabeth one morning about a month back. "I had more than I could use."

"Also, I should thank you for looking out for Elisabeth." Hyde's words were polite, but there was an edge to his voice as he spoke.

Coltrane didn't reply.

Hyde nodded. "Elisabeth speaks well of you."

"I think well of her."

"The sheriff has a different point of view."

"Of her or me?"

"Both."

"Oh."

"He's just doing his job."

"We'll see."

"He tries to act meaner than he really is."

"Maybe so."

"I should catch up to him now. He didn't mean for me to sit here all night."

Coltrane noted that Hyde had ignored the beer Bryant suggested he might drink. "Score a point for the kid," he thought quietly to himself after the deputy sheriff had departed.

*

That night Coltrane awoke suddenly from a deep sleep, but found he could not move. The room was cold and still, and the apparition hovered at the foot of his bed again. He was there for a moment, briefly, reflected once more in the light of the moon. His hands were pressed over his heart and his expression was forlorn. He opened his mouth as if to speak, but no words came out.

Then he was gone and after a long while Coltrane was flooded with the realization: it was Wild Bill Hickok, haunting him.

Silently.

Sadly.

Chapter Sixteen

"I heard you had another run in with the sheriff."

"I wouldn't describe it as a 'run in.'"

"Thomas did."

"He's entitled to his opinion."

They sat at his table, eating fried beef sandwiches with homebrewed ale. It had become something of a habit for them. Elisabeth had baked the bread herself that morning with stone ground wheat and oats. Coltrane had brought the beef and ale.

"Thomas said the sheriff tried to bait you."

Coltrane nodded and bit into his sandwich.

"He said Bryant was talking about charging people money to view your dead body and how you better be careful not to get shot in the back like John Wesley Hardin and Wild Bill Hickok."

Coltrane nodded again, but did not speak.

"You didn't get angry?"

"Yes. I did."

"You didn't react."

"He was careful in what he said. He didn't cross the line."

"I thought you were supposed to be famous for a murderous temper."

"That's what they want you to think."

"I've heard stories...."

"Maybe I've learned to control my temper a bit over the years."

"Seems like nothing upsets you now, nothing even affects you."

Coltrane's smile was tempered. "I've learned it doesn't do much good to react to things. If the sheriff wants to pick a fight, it will happen. I don't have to run to it. He'll bring it to me."

"Thomas said you were very cool. He said Bryant was frustrated that you remained so calm."

"He tried to bait me in front of a roomful of witnesses. That was obvious."

"That's not all of it. Those men at the bar and two of the other men in the saloon were his men. He had you surrounded in case anything happened. You wouldn't have stood a chance in there."

Coltrane nodded and studied Elisabeth's face. "I knew what was going on. Bryant isn't going to get near me by himself. He doesn't have the stones for that. I recognized one of the men before Bryant even came into the saloon. I was waiting for him to show up."

Elisabeth smiled slowly, then ran her tongue along the inside of her cheek. "Hmmm…"

"Anyway," Coltrane added, his eyes serious. "I would have stood a good chance in there, even if it came to a fight. Aside from Bryant, those other men are inexperienced."

"How can you tell?"

"It's right there."

"It's not that simple."

"Yes, it is. You can tell from the eyes, from the position of the hands. There's always a tell that gives it away. Men with no experience in such things can't hide it."

"Thomas was in there too."

"I know."

"He has never fired his gun on duty, never been in a shoot-out."

"I know."

"I could have lost you both."

"I know."

"He was glad there was no shooting. He doesn't want to see you hurt or killed."

"I know that too."

Elisabeth frowned. "Yet, he looks up to the sheriff. He thinks Bryant knows what he is doing and doesn't really see what is happening."

Coltrane looked down at his empty plate, not wanting to meet Elisabeth's eyes.

"Promise me something?" she asked quietly after a moment. "Promise me you won't shoot him."

There was a long pause. Slowly, Coltrane raised his face to look at Elisabeth, to study her eyes. "I can't promise that," he said at length.

"Promise you won't, unless you absolutely have to?"

Coltrane nodded slowly, his eyes sad. "Yes, I promise that," he said quietly, knowing even as he spoke the words that he should have said nothing at all and that now it was too late.

*

"Are you ready for us to become lovers," Coltrane said suddenly, not looking at her while he spoke. After he spoke the words he glanced up and caught her eyes.

For a moment Elisabeth said nothing, taken by surprise. "We're both taken," she said finally.

He nodded. "I know."

"I'm not ready."

"I will wait."

"You're so blunt. You come right out and say it. You're so matter-of-fact about it."

Coltrane nodded, seeing the light in her eyes. "I'm rather falling for you."

Elisabeth exhaled sharply, a nervous sigh. Then she shook her head. "Why now? I'm getting married in a few months."

"I can't help the timing."

Elisabeth thought about it. "I know," she said finally. "I'm falling for you too. I wish you had come along last year, before we were engaged. It would have been so much easier."

"Where do we go from here?"

"I don't know. I'm just not ready yet."

"Yet…."

She allowed herself a half smile. He leaned across the corner of the table and kissed her hard on the mouth.

*

"What about Anne?" she asked after awhile. They were holding hands, sitting next to each other on a bench beside the fireplace, staring into fading embers. It was late afternoon. "Won't you feel guilty?"

Coltrane nodded. "Yes," he said.

"Why isn't she with you?"

"After a while things weren't very good for us. We weren't happy together."

"I don't understand."

"It's complicated and I'd rather not talk about it with you…. I reckon Anne and I learned that just because two people love each other doesn't mean they can be happy together. Can we leave it at that?"

Elisabeth nodded. "I will feel guilty about Thomas. I already do. He's a good man."

Coltrane remained silent.

"It wouldn't be right," she said.

"No. It wouldn't be."

"It would be an awful feeling to have Thomas find out about us. I know he would leave me if he found out and I wouldn't get another chance. He would pack a bag and he would leave and that would be it. I don't want to be alone."

"Then you should stay away from me."

"I don't want to. I can't."

Coltrane nodded. "The heart can make us selfish."

*

65

"You seem so certain."

"I am." He could feel the tightness in his stomach.

"Do you *ever* have trouble making important decisions?"

"No."

"You're always this decisive?"

"I never really thought about it that way."

"Thomas is indecisive. It's one of the problems I have with him. That could be why I'm so attracted to you."

Coltrane didn't say anything in reply.

"If I'm honest with myself, there are other problems too," she said. "I'm not sure I should marry him. I'm not sure he's the one I want to spend the rest of my life with."

"Why?"

"There are problems. I need to figure out if they're fundamental."

Coltrane listened. He didn't comment even though he wanted to scream at her, plead with her, and beg her not to marry another man.

He wanted to so badly he could feel it in his stomach, but he didn't say a word. He sat listening, thinking of all the words he wanted to say, but wouldn't.

*

"How come your eyes are so blue?" she asked looking up into his face. They stood in his open doorway, embraced. The afternoon was fading and they both knew she had to leave, but neither wanted to be the one to let go first.

"They just are," he said, uncomfortable with the compliment.

"You know what the worst thing would be?"

"What?"

"If we were lovers and then we stopped loving each other…. That would be really sad for me, and there would be no one to share it with, not if it was a secret. One of us would have a broken heart and no one could ever know."

66

Chapter Seventeen

He stood at the western face of the salient, angrily dubbed the "mule shoe" by grumbling soldiers digging the trenches, facing the open ground in front of Laurel Hill. Bodies were scattered on that open ground, but you couldn't see them now. Noise and confusion swirled around him, distracting him from the rain that had fallen all night long, dulling the senses of even the strongest willed.

Major Coltrane stood with his line, firing over the log and earth breastworks at the dim silent figures moving towards them through the smoke and fog. There was no thought to the action, simply load and fire as fast as you could. Too often the powder was wet and all you heard was the empty click of the hammer after the trigger had been pulled.

All down the line the men paused sporadically in their firing to fix bayonets, understanding that the large wave of Federals would be upon them. The sounds of musket fire and the sharp bursting of artillery shells mixed with the screams of men as they were hit, going down with horrendous gaping wounds, splashing in the muddy water collected along the trenches. Bullets flew thick over their heads and hit the other side of the breastworks with a steady, rain-like tattoo.

Then the first surge of blue soldiers was at the wall, on the other side, thrusting with bayonets or firing through the logs where they could. The Stonewall brigade stood their ground, rallied by the saber waving regimental, battalion, and company commanders screaming to hold at all costs.

Coltrane fired a shot into the bearded, angry face of a Federal who had one leg up over the breastworks. The man disappeared from view, toppling backwards to the other side. Then Coltrane pushed off, stumbling in the mud, and recovered in time to thrust his bayonet into the ribs of another Federal trying to climb over at the same spot.

He felt the horrible resistance and then the give as the

67

sharp point of his blade slid into the man's body. The blade stuck between the man's ribs and his body fell forward, landing on Coltrane as he pulled back, trying frantically to dislodge the bayonet.

They both went down, the Federal screaming in pain and anger. Coltrane wrestled out from underneath him, jerking the musket clear, not even realizing that the bayonet had broken off. He stood, trampling over the man's back, unaware of his muffled screams as the Federal's face was driven deeper into the muddy water. Already the next man was swinging a leg over the wall, waving a pistol, sighting down on a man in gray.

All along the wall muskets and pistols poked over, firing down at an angle towards the men on the other side. Without even turning to look, Coltrane knew instinctively that the gray line, or what was left of it, was being pushed back as the Federals swarmed over the breastworks. He swung his musket, using it like a club now, hammering the stock into the side of a soldier's head, feeling the crunch of bone and seeing the spray of red.

He took several blows himself, punches from behind, then he was scrambling up over the other side of the trench, and trying to get out. Someone grabbed his ankle, pulling him back down into the mud. He kicked hard, with all his might, and pulled free, turning at the top to survey the scene of carnage.

That's when he was hit, the round slamming into his shoulder, spinning him around so that when he fell he landed almost flat on his face. All was suddenly a daze. He crawled through the mud, back toward the sound of the rebel cannons, believing all the way that he was going to die.

*

After he awoke it took a few minutes for him to realize that he was in a cabin set near the base of the Wasatch Mountains and not in a military field hospital surrounded by surgeons who wanted to amputate his arm.

The battle at Spotsylvania Courthouse had been fought thirty-five years before, but he was sweating and shaking with fear as if the fight still raged. The smell of gunpowder and cordite was strong in his nostrils and his ears rang with the thunderous boom of the cannon and musket fire.

His own screams were hard in his throat.

Chapter Eighteen

On Easter morning Elisabeth came to him, smelling like fresh lilacs. She had been to church already. Her eyes were soft and she didn't say a word as she stood on tiptoes and kissed him gently and then more passionately on the mouth. Her lips were full and sensuous, her breath incredibly warm, and he could feel her heart pounding as he wrapped his arms around her.

"I'm ready," she whispered.

His heart beat furiously. "Are you sure?" he asked.

"Yes," she replied, nodding as she looked up into his eyes.

They kissed again and then he led her to his bed where he undid the top two buttons of her blouse.

"I'm so nervous," she told him. They sat on the edge of the bed, holding hands. She looked into his eyes. "I know this is wrong, but I don't care anymore. I'm ready."

"Are you sure?" he asked.

"No, but what if we never make love?"

He leaned over and kissed her, very slowly, gently pushing his mouth, his tongue against hers. As he kissed her he undid the remaining buttons of her blouse. Slowly he pulled it off her shoulders, and then released the fasteners on her riding dungarees.

She pulled her boots off and lay back on the bed, resting on her elbows. He pulled her trousers down and stared in wonder at her body as she lay there in nothing but a black lace top and matching lace underwear. Her skin was smooth and creamy, her exposed flesh quivering slightly as she trembled in anticipation.

Coltrane stood up and began undoing the buttons on his own clothes. She watched him as he undressed, her expression serious, their eyes locking as he slid off his trousers and knelt on the bed beside her. Then he kissed her on the side, near her elbow, and pulled off her black underwear, pausing to kiss the inside of her thighs as he pulled it clear.

He could sense her arousal; smell the scent of her desire. He fumbled with her top and she sat up to help him, unfastening it in the front and pulling it away to reveal her breasts. They were round and full and her skin was very white. She wore nothing but a necklace with a small silver cross hanging from it.

"Kiss me," she said, pulling his face towards hers.

Coltrane lay on top of her then, kissing her mouth, with one hand cradled beneath her neck and the other stroking her slowly. He was shaking badly still and pulled away. She reached for him, touching him softly, trying to pull him toward her, coaxing. He could not stop shaking. Gently she touched him and kissed him for a long while, but he could not stop shaking.

"It's okay," Elisabeth whispered, rolling away from him onto her side so that she could look into his eyes.

*

They kissed for a long while without touching any other parts of their bodies. When his breathing was heavy again she pulled the sheet back. He was ready by the time she reached for him, and he put a lambskin sheath on in a quick motion and rolled his body on top of hers. Their eyes locked as he entered her.

Her eyes closed momentarily as he began to move inside her, then she opened them again and sighed. He settled down on top of her, moving his hips together with hers, their breath matched in a rhythm. She was very wet and they were both trembling again as they felt the closeness of the other. He placed a hand beneath her head and rubbed her neck, searching for her mouth with his. She kissed him hard, then pulled away, arching her back.

A low moan escaped her lips and she moved slower now, concentrating. For the first time they studied each other carefully in a way they never had before.

She played her fingers over the thick hair that covered his chest, the definition of muscles in his chest, arms, and shoulders, the long red bayonet scar across the lower part of his stomach, the smaller round scar on his shoulder. His breathing became urgent. Then he pulled her over on top of him. He caught his breath and stopped moving altogether, looking deep into her eyes for a long moment. She smiled gently.

They continued to move again, faster now and Coltrane could see it building in Elisabeth's eyes.

"Kiss me," he said. She lowered her head with her mouth open to kiss him hard on the lips. She ran the back of her hand along his side, scratching him with the heavy engagement ring she wore. His body twitched involuntarily and he pressed hard against her shoulder with his palm.

As she moved toward him, the cross of her necklace touched his cheek. He ran his hands along her back and buttocks and felt her body tremble as the climax built. She began to shudder with her eyes closed, her breath coming out now in sudden gasps as her whole body shook for a long moment and then she collapsed over him and pressed her cheek against his. They kept going on, deep into the splendid afternoon.

*

Much later, after they were dressed and Elisabeth had brushed her hair, they sat on the edge of the bed holding hands, smiling at each other, but not speaking.

"People are going to ask me how my Easter was," she said. Her eyes were dancing.

He looked away, and then back, felt himself smiling still. The pupils of her eyes were as large as he'd ever seen them. He wanted to tell her he loved her. The words wouldn't quite form, but the feeling was there. They continued to sit with nothing but silence between them. Their eyes would meet and

72

they would kiss and touch as if they might start all over again, although they knew there wasn't time. It was too late into the afternoon.

Finally, Elisabeth straightened. "I have to go," she said. "I don't want to have to explain where I've been."

Coltrane nodded and squeezed her hand. "I know," he said. "It was wonderful."

He smiled at her and she leaned in towards him.

The scent of her perfume lingered long after she left.

*

As the day wore into evening and the shadows lengthened, Coltrane sat alone on the porch, sipping from a cup of whiskey, thinking about the day and seeing her body moving against his, and he knew his world would never be the same again. There was no way it could be. From some small secret place, he understood that she owned him now and he knew he would agree to most anything she wanted of him.

Chapter Nineteen

Three days after Easter Coltrane received a letter from Anne. Ryan handed it to him when he came in to pick up supplies. It had arrived that morning, the first he had received in almost three months.

"Been here about ten days," Ryan commented. "I didn't know how to get it out to you."

"It's fine."

"All the way from Atlanta, Georgia."

Coltrane nodded.

"A woman with your name. Your sister?"

"My wife."

Ryan's mouth fell slack. "I didn't know there was a missus," he said.

Coltrane shrugged.

"Will she be joining you?"

Coltrane didn't answer. He took the letter out onto the front steps of the store and slit open the letter with his buck knife. There were three pages in Anne's distinctive script. As he read, a sick feeling began to spread in the bottom of his stomach.

Anne had been ill, out with a high fever for nearly two weeks and she had almost died. She had pulled through, but then had taken three weeks to regain enough strength to sit up in bed. She had been lucky while others had not.

The epidemic had taken her brother, a cousin, two of the servants. Coltrane breathed a sigh to himself. He couldn't bear the thought of losing her, of not knowing that she was out there somewhere, still connected to him in some way.

As he rode home slowly that afternoon, not pushing the mares to pull the buckboard any faster than they wanted to, he thought about Anne and about the way things had come to be between them. His memories sank into him like placid dreams of death.

*

"I worry about you," Anne told him simply. The house was dark; she was in bed already by the time he got home. Coltrane came into the bedroom, holding a burning candle out in front of him. He set the candle on a table by the bed and pulled a chair over, sitting down with his face close to hers. In the candlelight he could see her soft features, her sleepy eyes, her locks mussed on top of her head. Her nightgown slipped on one shoulder.

"Did I wake you," he asked, and then kissed her on the cheek.

"No. I was worrying about you."

"I'm sorry I'm home so late."

Anne reached a hand out from under the blanket that covered her and Coltrane grasped it in his hand, squeezing it gently. He loved the feel of her hand in his. They sat in silence for a moment, holding hands. The night was still.

"Did you eat yet?" she asked after a little while.

Coltrane shrugged. "I had a bite."

"I left some stew out for you on the dry-sink."

"I'll have it in a minute."

"I'll get up and sit with you."

"Stay here. I only came home for a few minutes, to see you. I have to go back to the jail tonight."

There was silence. He could feel her hand tighten in his. His hours had often been a sore point between them. She didn't accept the fact that he worked such long and irregular hours. At least he wasn't leaving with a posse.

"I wish I didn't have to," he told her.

Anne nodded. "I know. Are you okay?"

"I wanted to sit here with you for a few minutes."

"I heard there was another shooting."

Coltrane nodded, wishing she hadn't heard about it yet. They were still holding hands.

75

"You weren't going to tell me?"

"It could have waited for tomorrow."

"Somebody tries to kill my husband and it can wait until tomorrow?"

"Please, Anne, don't make more of this than it is."

"So, tell me."

"Are you sure you want to know?"

"I'm sure."

"I had to arrest Frankie Gilmore and the Parker brothers this afternoon. They got drunk and killed a man, some stranger, down at the stables in an argument during a craps game. Frankie and Benjamin came easily, but young William went for his gun."

"So you shot him?"

"He didn't leave me any choice."

Anne let out her breath slowly and Coltrane knew she was on the verge of tears.

"You could have been killed."

"That's the risk I take."

"Did he shoot at you?"

"Yes."

"How many times?"

"What difference does it make?"

"I'd like to know. I heard they almost ambushed you."

"It wasn't like that. I was careless. A couple of shots, but they missed."

"Is William dead?"

"Not yet. I shot him in the stomach. They've got him over at the clinic right now." Coltrane shook his head. "I don't think he'll survive long."

"I know their mother. Sally Parker is a good woman. I see her at church. This will be hard on her."

Coltrane nodded and released his grip on Anne's hand. He caressed her cheek with his fingertips. "She is a good woman, and her boys aren't all bad, but they always had trouble *handling their whiskey. They get rowdy, out of control."*

"And now Sally has to bury one of them."

"Maybe both of them soon. They shot a man. It's a hanging thing."

"I hate it," Anne said. "I absolutely hate it. I hate what you do."

"I'm sorry," Coltrane said. His voice was flat, tired.

"Isn't there another way?"

"I don't know of any."

Quietly Anne began to cry. Coltrane continued to stroke her cheek and neck lightly, slowly. He wanted to comfort her more, but he didn't know what to say.

"I've got to get back to the jail," he said finally. He kissed her on the cheek, just as he had done when he first came in, then he pinched out the candle. Behind him she continued to cry quietly in the dark as he left the house.

*

That evening Coltrane reread the letter from Anne, and thought about composing one back to her. He sat up late thinking about her, remembering more of the times they had shared. He missed her and still loved her; and he felt guilty, thinking about the way things were.

Despite several attempts he was unable to finish a reply letter to her and he went to bed planning to write it the next day instead, and dreading it because he didn't know what he would say. He wondered how he could have been such a fool as to love two women at the same time.

Chapter Twenty

By late April spring had arrived in full. Birds appeared out of nowhere and the sun shined nearly every day. There was just enough rain early in the mornings and late in the afternoons to water the flowers and bushes and turn the world green again.

Coltrane sat in Elisabeth's kitchen, sipping a cup of coffee. The kitchen was modern and new, with large white Mexican tile on the floor. The cupboards were a cream-colored wood with clear stain and black knob handles. There was running water in the sink and a pair of electric lamps hung on the wall over the table. Elisabeth was proud of her kitchen and Coltrane had to marvel that he had never been in any like it before.

"Are you okay?" Elisabeth asked. She wore a long dress made of a single piece of dark fabric with flowers printed on it. It went from her neck to her ankles, with a row of buttons down the front, and it was fitted tight, but in a comfortable way. She looked happy and beautiful. It had been five days since they had made love.

"Yes. I'm well," Coltrane replied. He smiled at her and she smiled back. "And you?"

Elisabeth nodded, still smiling. "I glowed for three days."

Coltrane shrugged. "I'm falling in love with you."

"I wish you wouldn't say things like that.

"It's true."

"It makes it seem so real."

"It is real."

"I know." Elisabeth sighed, looked away, then back again. "I'm falling in love you too."

Coltrane reached his hand across the table and squeezed hers. She looked up at him and he felt what was now becoming a familiar aching in his gut. He held her eyes for a moment. They were soft, hazel, and luminous, highlighted by her thick brown eyebrows. The pupils of her eyes were large and shiny.

After a moment he glanced down and studied her hands, fingering the engagement ring with its large, glistening stone.

*

Elisabeth squeezed his hand and looked into his eyes. "Can I tell you something?" she asked.

Coltrane nodded, waiting.

"I don't know where this is going to lead.... At first I tried to tell myself it was only a kiss. One kiss. What did that mean? I've kissed other men, but this was different. I knew it was. No one has affected me like you. I still shudder when I think about that kiss. It was like no other before it. Maybe I was surprised by the gentleness of your touch, the softness of your mouth, the hesitation in your eyes as you pulled away – all that from a man so famous for being ruthless. Perhaps that was it, a need to solve the mystery. How could a man with your history and reputation for violence be so tender? Maybe I had to touch that deep, mysterious, vulnerable spot within you, had to know it for myself. I don't think that was all it was – it was more than that, much more. That is what I've gradually come to realize. It wasn't mere curiosity. There was something about your quiet warmth. I didn't know it was possible to feel so close to someone. You're so intimate. I never expected that."

Chapter Twenty-One

A week later they were together again, sitting in her kitchen. Birds were twittering eagerly outside the window.

Elisabeth let out a long sigh. "This is crazy. I'm supposed to get married this year. I'm not supposed to be in love with you. I kept telling myself that I was just curious, that this wouldn't go anywhere, that I'd pull back from you before it reached a serious point."

"As far as I'm concerned, it's too late for that," Coltrane replied.

"I kept telling myself that I would end this after one kiss. I was going to let it go that far, but no farther. Then I had to make love to you. Just one time; but I know that once won't be enough. I want you too much. I don't want to let go of you."

"Then don't."

"Can I tell you something really stupid?"

"If you must."

"I was trying to figure out a way to put a limit on us, on our time together. I told myself that no matter what happened I would break things off when I got fitted for my wedding dress. I thought there was no way I could be with another man after I was fitted for that dress. There is something about it. It's a symbol. It's supposed to be an important moment, putting on that white lace gown. Every woman is supposed to remember that moment."

"And?"

"I get fitted next week."

"Well?"

"I don't know…."

"Are you going to stop seeing me after next week?"

"I don't see how I can. I don't want to let go of you."

Elisabeth leaned over and kissed him as his heart skipped wildly at the mere thought of her letting go.

*

"I have to go to town," Elisabeth said after awhile.

"We could go together. I've got the buckboard."

"If we show up together in Crystal, people will talk."

"They will."

"They already know we're friends. Right?"

Coltrane nodded. "We've been seen together."

"That means they're already talking about us."

Coltrane shrugged.

"It's hard to know how to behave sometimes. If we weren't lovers I wouldn't hesitate to take a ride from you."

Coltrane shrugged again. "It won't bother me."

"Let's go," she said, suddenly making up her mind. "If people talk, I don't care, let them. We're friends. If people can't deal with that, to hell with them."

Coltrane smiled. "It might be more complicated than that."

"How so?"

"Well, I'm a bit different from most men."

"Yes. You are."

"You understand what I mean."

"I noticed."

Coltrane ignored this. "First of all, I show up in town for the second time this week with no real reason to be there, it may look kind of obvious that I came just to be with you. Second, I don't generally socialize with anyone and people keep seeing me with you, they're going to get ideas about that."

"I don't mind if you don't."

"I don't mind. They'll probably assume that I'm in love with you and that you are humoring me, being kind, allowing me to be with you."

Elisabeth shook her head. "Oh goodness, if anything, it would be the other way around. They'll take one look at my eyes and they'll know exactly how I feel about you. I'm not very good at concealing my emotions. I'm still glowing."

"You're beautiful when you glow."

She smiled. "You're crazy."

"Maybe so. Let's go to town, then." Coltrane stood up and gestured toward his waiting buckboard.

"I'll get my sweater."

Chapter Twenty-Two

Coltrane knew there would be trouble as soon as he saw the three men coming down the street. He was sitting in the buckboard, in front of the library, waiting for Elisabeth. She had gone inside to collect several books that she had on reserve.

It was only mid-afternoon, but the men were obviously drunk. They had been sitting outside the stables down the street, passing a bottle back and forth, when they spotted Elisabeth going into the library. Coltrane watched them cross the street and head towards him.

One of them paused to tip a bottle of whiskey all the way back. Then he tossed it into a nearby water trough and hurried to catch up with the other two. Shop doors closed as they passed. Coltrane had never seen them before, but he knew the type well.

They weren't local and they had the look of men who weren't unfamiliar with the wrong side of the law. They were armed. Coltrane unfastened the strap on his shoulder holster and thumbed the hammer back on the Colt. He crossed his arms and waited without looking in their direction.

"Purty horses," slurred one of the men, the one who had just finished the bottle.

He was a short fellow with a red beard and short red hair. He wore leather chaps over dungarees, a dark checkered flannel shirt, and a walnut handled .38 revolver slung low at each side. A wide brimmed Stetson hung off his back by the drawstring around his neck. The other two were dressed in similar style except they wore narrow brimmed hats and each carried one revolver. They looked enough alike to be brothers. One of them cradled a Remington double-barrel shotgun in the crook of his arm, swinging it casually as he walked around the buckboard.

"Yep," Coltrane said. He nodded curtly, and then looked

away.

"Talkative cuss," said the man with the shotgun.

"We couldn't help but notice," said the first man, "that you came in with a mighty fine looking woman."

"I did," Coltrane replied, giving only the appearance of casual attention.

"Isn't she a little too young for an old-timer like you?"

Coltrane shrugged, not looking at the men now, his chin tilted up as if looking at some point over their heads.

"Perhaps he doesn't hear so well," said the third man.

The one with the red hair nodded. "Could be, Gerald, could be. Maybe we ought to wait out here to talk to that young miss, warn her about her old friend's.... limitations." He chuckled to himself and then looked at the other two.

They laughed loudly.

The one with the shotgun walked around the back of the buckboard again, slowly, as if inspecting it. When he completed the circle he stood on the sidewalk next to his friends, stroking the ear of Bobby-Lee. "Seems to me, an old-timer ought to have a little more courtesy than to keep such a fetching young thing all to himself. You can't possibly satisfy her needs like one of us younger men can."

"All her needs," Gerald agreed, grinning broadly.

"Yesserreee," whooped the man with the red hair loudly. He was the drunkest of the three. He whooped again two more times just for the hell of it and then laughed loudly while looking around.

Up and down the street heads poked out of windows to see what was going on. Elisabeth came out of the library, her arms full of books, and she moved down the steps quickly, pausing at the bottom to look at the three men standing between her and the buckboard. Then she walked swiftly in a path that would have taken her around them.

Gerald stepped sideways, intercepting her. She stopped and stared up at him, hugging the books against her body with

84

both arms. A look of anger flashed in her eyes.

"Afternoon, ma'am," Gerald said, tipping the hat back on his head. "Can I assist you with them books?"

"No thank you, I can manage." Her words were polite, her tone defiant.

"I insist," Gerald replied.

"So do I," said Red Hair. He had come up behind her and reached over her shoulder, snatching off the top book. Elisabeth, turning to glare at him, stood her ground.

"What's this?" Red Hair asked mockingly.

"Edgar Allan Poe. He's a writer," Elisabeth replied. There was an edge to her voice. Coltrane could see her eyes blazing with anger. He knew how much courage it took for her to stand there facing the men.

"Mighty beautiful and smart too!" Red Hair exclaimed.

"May I please have my book back?"

"You really read all these books little lady?" Red Hair flipped the pages of the book casually, pretending to study them.

Elisabeth nodded. "You ought to try it some time, might improve your mind."

"Who says my mind needs improving?"

"You're drunk."

"What's that got to do with my mind? Just because you read these fancy books, you think you're better than me?"

"I never said that. Anybody can learn to read, doesn't make you special."

"You saying I can't read?"

"I didn't say that."

"Well, I can."

Elisabeth nodded, accepting the challenge. "Fine," she said calmly. "Prove it. Read the first sentence out loud to we all can hear."

The other two men began to laugh. Red Hair did not. Instead, his expression changed quickly to rage and he tossed the book over his shoulder. It landed in the grass on the other side of the sidewalk.

A crowd had gathered silently across the street and two elderly ladies stood looking down from the library steps. Later there was speculation about what the red haired man might have said or done next, but nobody ever found out because suddenly Coltrane was standing in front of him, nudging Elisabeth backward.

"I think you should pick up the book," Coltrane said quietly. His voice was low and calm.

"Well, well, well," Red Hair exclaimed. He turned to glance sideways at the other two before turning back to face Coltrane. "I guess the old-timer is feeling a bit uppity this afternoon. What's the matter, old man? You think it betters your chances of getting some of this young thing, you showing off for her like this. We don't mean no harm to no one."

"I'm glad to hear it. Pick up her book and move on."

"I might have done that, excepting I don't appreciate your tone."

"I'm not asking you to appreciate it. I'm asking you to pick up the book and return it to the lady."

"It's okay…" Elisabeth said. Coltrane shook his head, gesturing for her to stay out of it by raising his left hand. He did not take his eyes off the red haired man.

"I think the little lady is worried for you," Gerald said, stepping up closer. He stopped not less than two feet away and stood leaning forward with his face inches from Coltrane's. There was a whiskey stench on his breath.

Coltrane remained calm, his eyes focused softly now, and ready. He understood they were past the point where talking would do any good. He waited silently, easily, seeing everything slow down before him – just like it did every time.

Red Hair's eyes twitched nervously and he took notice of the revolver under Coltrane's left arm. With a sudden grin, he let out another loud whoop. "Look at the Colt in the

86

shoulder rig, boys! Mister, do you think you are some kind of *pistolero*?"

Coltrane didn't respond. He continued to stare straight into the drunk's eyes.

"I asked if you think you're some kind of *pistolero*?" the man said again. "'Cause if you are, I'd like to see it. In my experience most men just aren't as good as they think they are. Is that you? Walking around with that big gun, but don't know how to use it? What's a matter, now? Shitting in your pants?"

Coltrane continued to stare quietly, his eyes devoid of emotion.

"Maybe you're not so tough after all, old-timer? I think it's time to find out."

"You're heeled," Coltrane said quietly. "Get to fighting."

"Well, well…"

There was a pause, a silence, during which the whole world and all of time seemed to come to a halt. Then everything happened at once.

The red haired man started to draw both .38s and Gerald reached for his revolver. Coltrane stepped into Gerald with his left elbow, feeling the man's jaw crunch beneath his blow. At the same time he drew the Colt with his right hand, snap aimed, and pulled the trigger once. The shot hit Red Hair square in the chest, knocking him backwards, off his feet; the two .38s, only half drawn, clattering to the sidewalk beside him.

The man with the shotgun was caught off guard. He still had the large gun cradled in the crook of his arm and as the shot was fired he jumped backwards, startled by the spray of blood that hit him.

Coltrane paused a half-second to see what he would do and then shot the man in the chest when he tried to bring the double barrel around. In almost the same motion Coltrane turned toward Gerald, who had dropped to one knee, and pistol-whipped him on the side of the head, above the ear.

Gerald dropped down and lay still with the top half of his body off the curb, flat over the brick-paved street. Ten feet away the man with the shotgun rolled on his back, struggling furiously for air, sucking in huge, wheezing gasps. His legs jerked for a moment, then he lay still and didn't move again.

As quickly as it happened, it was over.

The street was suddenly quiet again. Coltrane holstered the Colt and walked over to the grass. He picked up the book that had been tossed there, and glanced once toward Elisabeth. With the book under his arm he started over to comfort the mares that were now making anxious, frightened sounds and pulling sideways at their harnesses.

Rosalita turned her head away from him to present her cheek as he patted her on the neck and whispered her name quietly. That seemed to calm the claybank as well.

Chapter Twenty-Three

"I guess you know it's against the law to shoot a man," Bryant said. "Especially in Crystal."

They were seated in the saloon, at a back table, where Coltrane had positioned himself to wait for the arrival of the sheriff. It was just the two of them.

The sheriff had arrived by himself. His deputies were nowhere in sight. His dress was immaculate as usual, with the black silk coat, white shirt, gabardine vest, bowtie, gold watch chain, and the pearl-handled revolver. His kid gloves rested on the table, one on top of the other. He wore a black bowler hat to complete the outfit.

Coltrane nodded his head and took a sip of coffee.

"Probably a man could still hang in this state for killing one man, let alone two."

Coltrane just sipped at his coffee again.

"I wonder if you would let me arrest you." It wasn't a question, but a statement.

"One way to find out."

"I have two problems. One is there were a lot of witnesses to the shooting, including Miss Elisabeth. They all agree those three drunks started the fuss, that you stepped in to protect Elisabeth, and that you did not draw first. They said you fired your weapon in self-defense."

"True."

"Is that the way you see it?"

"Yes."

"That it was self-defense?"

"Yes."

"They left you no alternative?"

"Correct."

"Okay. That's your statement?"

"It is."

"Maybe it looks like a justified killing, self-defense. Hard to arrest a man for that. Which brings up my second problem. Those boys probably needed to be shot. Turns out the red head was Pliney Calderone. He's a ruffian, mostly. Got himself convicted a few years back for rustling cattle, served a few years in the old Wyoming territorial prison. More recently he seems to be wanted for a couple of robberies in the southern part of the state. They say he shot a man over in Nevada last year. My guess is he's been hiding out in Robbers' Roost for awhile."

Coltrane sipped more coffee. The cup was almost empty. He set it gently on the table.

"The other two were brothers, the Earl brothers. I got Gerald locked up in my jail right now. His jaw is broken and his head is bleeding bad. Doc got him bandaged up right now, but he hasn't woken up all the way. Ever heard of a concussion? I hadn't, but that's what Doc calls it. May be a while before we know if he's going to make it, but I think he will. I've seen worse.... His brother, Adam, well.... I reckon we'll be burying him along with Pliney. They weren't much good, neither of them, the Earl brothers that is. Don't know of any warrants out on them, but they were with Pliney, they were headed for trouble."

"Doesn't sound like you're planning to make any arrests today."

Bryant shook his head, an exaggerated look of discouragement on his face. "Not today. As much as I hate to admit it, not today. I'll be meeting with the magistrate in the morning, see what he thinks, but the way it lays now, I reckon there won't be any arrests."

Coltrane nodded and set his coffee down on the table. "I guess I'll be going home then," he said.

"Sit with me for a minute," Byrant said. "Just because I'm not going to arrest you today doesn't mean I don't want to."

"Uh-huh."

"I don't like the fact that you're shooting people in my

streets. Even if they needed shooting. That's not your job – it's mine. I also don't like the fact that you're spending time around my deputy's fiancée. It makes us both look bad. Believe it or not, no matter what I might happen to think of her, I don't want you bringing your troubles into her life. Or his. None of us need that kind of complication around here."

"You finished?"

Bryant's lips tightened. The scar beneath his eye vibrated as the corner of his mouth twitched. "Not quite," he said. "I want you to understand something. I would prefer that you left my town. I've told you that. You are bad news and trouble follows you. Like today. Though maybe it wasn't exactly your fault. I don't want to see any of my citizens caught in the crossfire. I can't force you to leave. Not legally. Not now anyway. I'll be watching closely, though. Are you hearing me?"

"I am."

"Don't look for Elisabeth today. I gave Thomas the afternoon off to see to his fiancée. He's taken her home. Don't you stop over there on your way back this evening."

Coltrane nodded, his jaw set.

"Two more things," Bryant said in a quieter tone. "Gerald Earl isn't going to stay in my jail forever. If his head heals, which I think it will, I can hold him for a while. Public drunkenness, disturbing the peace, attempted assault maybe. That's not more than a few weeks in my jail. Then he'll be out and he may not be too forgiving about his late brother. I heard they were real close and that he's got one swell temper. Might be another reason for you to move along."

"Might be. What's the other thing?"

"You know those witnesses I talked to? Everyone one of them commented on how fast you were. Made me wonder if you're faster than me. I don't think so, but I don't know for sure. I keep thinking one of these days, you keep pushing it, we're going to find out."

Coltrane nodded, pushing the empty coffee cup away from

him.

Outside the shadows were growing long and the air was cool as it swept down the steep grade of Main Street. From all directions people looked at him with curiosity, but did not speak to him.

Chapter Twenty-Four

A week had passed and they were sitting in her kitchen again. Elisabeth had served fresh baked bread, butter, and blackberry jam. The bread was still warm and very good. Coltrane didn't take much butter, but used lots of the sweet blackberry jam. They were drinking coffee and they did not talk for a long while as he ate. Coltrane finished the first piece of bread and she cut another thick slice for him.

"You never hesitated," Elisabeth said.

"Only dead men hesitate."

"It was awful."

Coltrane nodded. "Yes, it was." He spread butter across the bread and then piled on two spoonfuls of the dark jam. He dropped the spoon back into the jam crock and sat back in his chair without biting into the second piece of bread.

"How can you stand it?" she asked.

"I don't have any choice."

"Those men were just going to kill you, maybe me, over nothing."

"That's how it is sometimes."

"I never thanked you."

"For what?"

"I was very relieved when you stepped between me and that man with the red hair."

"His name was Pliney Calderone."

"Yes, I learned that. I also learned he was not a good man. Thomas told me he was a thief and murderer, that he had been in jail once before, and that he was wanted for shooting a man."

"Sheriff told me the same."

"I heard there was a bounty on him."

"So I heard: five hundred dollars, dead or alive."

"It made the Salt Lake City newspapers. You're in the news again."

Coltrane shrugged wearily. "A reporter rode out to my house a few days ago."

"Did you talk to him?"

"No. He left."

"Just like that?"

"After I fired the Winchester over his head a couple of times."

Elisabeth smiled. "Most people would love the fame, but you avoid it. You're so aloof."

"I never asked to be famous."

"Do you feel bad about it?"

"About what?"

"Killing Calderone and that Earl boy."

"What's the point in that? Those men made a decision to harm us. I couldn't let them do that, so I did what I had to to prevent it."

"Are you certain you were right?"

"I'm certain that I was right enough. I didn't have many choices and I didn't have much time to think about those choices. I reacted. I think what I did was fair and reasonable."

"Do you think about it much?"

"The shooting?"

"Yes."

"No."

"I can't get it out of my head."

Coltrane nodded. "I know. That's how it is at first, especially the first time. With time, it should pass." He picked up the bread and bit into it.

"Are you sure it will?"

"No."

*

"You never talk about your past."

"You never ask."

"I guess I figure you'll tell me when you're ready. With most people it would bother me not to know more, but with you I guess I accept it. I'm not sure why. You'll talk about it when you're ready."

"What do you want to know?"

"You'll tell me?"

"Probably."

"I don't know what I want to know. What do you want to tell me?"

Coltrane shrugged.

"What was it like being a lawman in the frontier towns twenty-five years ago?"

"It was a mean time."

Elisabeth listened quietly.

"I don't know what to tell you. Life was not highly valued. A lot of people came out west looking for their fortunes, and some fortunes were made. It was a dangerous, unforgiving life. Between the hardships of the land, the Indians, and the lawlessness, a man often had to make hard choices."

"So, you made them. You came through."

"It took everything I had. Being a lawman meant being willing to kill whenever necessary, to shoot a man down in a moment. You didn't have the luxury of time to make those kinds of decisions. Sometimes it meant being there to see the horrors and not being able to do anything about them."

"Like what?"

"Like after an Indian raiding party, cleaning up the dead. Or seeing the bodies of settler families who died on the trail of starvation or exposure."

Elisabeth shivered. "How awful. Why did you do it? Why were you a lawman?"

"Because I could. It was something I was good at and there was a need. Also, there was a lot of meanness in me then. For a lot of years after the war I just couldn't stop feeling mean. That life provided an outlet."

"The war changed you?"

Coltrane didn't answer for a long moment. "Growing up I had been taught that life was sacred. The war had a different lesson."

"Were you bitter?"

"It left me feeling…. I don't, know…. mean. I don't have another word for it."

"I don't think you're mean."

"I am. Perhaps, I'm not as mean as I used to be, but I'm still mean as they come. You saw some of it the other day. You wouldn't have liked me very much twenty-five years ago."

"I bet I would have."

Coltrane shook his head sadly. "Don't get confused by the things you hear. It was not a romantic time. I was no hero."

*

"You never talk about Anne."

"Not to you."

"Why?"

"Do you want to hear about her?"

"Probably not, but I still wish you would talk about her more. It bothers me that you don't."

"Because you think I'm concealing something from you?"

Elisabeth nodded.

"Like what?"

Elisabeth shrugged, looking down at her empty plate. She wiped off a bit of blackberry jam and licked it off her finger.

"I'm not hiding anything. I can't talk about her to you. I have to keep her separate from you. It's bad enough the way it is. My relationship with her, my feelings for her, our past together. That has to stay private." Coltrane knew after he spoke that Elisabeth was upset. He squeezed her hand to reassure her. "It's the way it has to be," he said.

She nodded and looked away, angry, squinting into the

96

afternoon sunlight that came in through the open window.

*

"You have to go now," Elisabeth said at length.

Coltrane nodded.

"Thomas is leaving the county a week from today. He has to be in Provo for a trial and will be away over night. I'll come to you."

"Can you stay overnight?"

"I'd like to. But you never know... If someone were to come out to the house to check..."

"I understand."

Elisabeth nodded.

Chapter Twenty-Five

That night Coltrane sat out on his porch late into the evening drinking whiskey, listening to the call of the owls that echoed out from the forest. He wondered if he would see the ghost again that night. He had become accustomed to seeing the apparition a couple of times a week now, usually just before dawn. It no longer frightened him and he didn't worry any more about the condition of his mind. He wasn't going crazy – of that he was fairly certain.

The ghost was a companion whom he accepted, had even taken to talking to him, calling him "Wild Bill." The presence was something he didn't understand, though he figured Hickok had come back to him with those sad, warning eyes for a reason. The reason was not apparent. Coltrane would be patient. The reason would be clear to him soon enough.

He rolled a cigarette and smoked with his head rested back against the exterior wall behind him. The whiskey was warm inside of him and he knew he had drunk too much. The forest grew quiet and the moon was on the rise. When the whiskey bottle was low he put the cork back into it and wandered over to the barn.

The mares made appreciative noises as he rubbed their ears and spoke softly to them, whispering the soothing words that no one had ever had for him.

In the pale light cast by the moon and stars of the open sky above he fell back in the hayloft and closed his eyes, allowing the world to spin around him.

*

Coltrane walked into the saloon knowing that every gunman, outlaw, gambler, and drunk would notice the polished Silver Star he wore over his left breast. He glanced around the room, scanning for familiar faces. Territorial marshals could usually count on having at least one old enemy in any saloon they entered. He didn't see any faces he recognized, but he knew he was not welcome.

Several people looked up at him and stared. Nobody smiled at him. He made his way cautiously to the bar, ordered a beer, and took it down to the end of the counter to stand with his back against the wall. The beer was lukewarm, with a strong head of foam. He sipped at it and looked around the room again. For twenty minutes he waited, sipping at the beer, watching the movements around him, ignoring the invitations from whores and cardsharps.

On the other side of the room a piano tinkled bawdy songs. Sometimes the music was drowned out by loud words and angry shouts. Most of the people were very drunk and Coltrane knew he had to watch himself carefully. He drank his beer slowly.

After a long time the man Coltrane waited for came in. He stalked confidently across to the bar and raised a finger at the barman. Immediately a shot of whiskey was set in front of him, followed by a mug of beer. The barman stood poised with the whiskey bottle and refilled the shot glass as soon as it was set back on the counter.

The man drank down half the beer, downed the second shot, and then finished the beer. Both the shot glass and the mug were quickly refilled. He paused then and looked about the room for a moment and then took another drink of the beer. He wiped his mustache and beard off with the palm of his hand, still looking at the room in the mirror behind the bar.

Coltrane noted the way things quieted down. He studied the man carefully. He wore a buckskin jacket and had long flowing blond hair down to his shoulders, a long mustache, and a prominent goatee. His face was weathered by the sun and deeply lined. He also wore a star on his chest, but it did not shine. It was tarnished and stained.

When his eyes set on Coltrane standing at the end of the bar he dipped his chin in a slight nod. His expression was somber. Coltrane finished his beer and set the mug on the counter. Slowly, he walked around the end of the bar towards the man and stopped next to him with his back to the bar, facing the room.

"Been a while," the man said. He didn't turn or extend his hand.

Coltrane nodded. "How are you, Bill?"

"Kicking hard at heaven's pearly gate."

"You look tired."

He nodded. "Yeah."

"Are you alright?"

He shrugged and took another drink of beer. "It's been a long, long weary life."

"Tell me."

"Oh, you know. It ain't so much to talk about."

"I know... You want another beer?"

The man shrugged. Coltrane turned and nodded toward the barman, then put a coin on the counter. The barman pulled two beers and set them on the counter. Then he refilled the shot glass, but ignored the coin. Coltrane picked up one of the beers and drank from it.

"It's been a bad time." Wild Bill Hickok raised the beer mug and took several large swallows. "Had to shoot a couple of drunk trail hands an hour ago."

"Heard you've had to do a lot of that lately."

Hickok shrugged and then tossed back the shot. He shook his head at the barman who still hovered close by, holding the bottle of whiskey.

"'Fact, I heard you shot a jealous husband some time back. Heard he came at you from behind while you were standing at a bar, like you are now. They say you drew and fired over your shoulder, a perfect shot, right through the heart, sighting in the mirror, without even turning around."

Hickok shrugged, his lips drawn tightly back. The whites of his eyes were red and there were dark circles under his eyes. "People say a lot of silly things."

"They do," Coltrane agreed.

"Doesn't mean it's true."

"No."

"There's been some shootings."

"Yeah?"

"People been pushing me. Not leaving me a choice."

"Maybe you ought to move on."

"Nope... Wouldn't make a difference anyway. There's an ancient hellhound after me and it won't stop 'till I'm dead."

"Bill, you don't sound so good."

The man shook his head. "Nope," he said. "I'm kicking hard at heaven's pearly gate."

Coltrane nodded. "Or maybe hell's."

Hickok lifted the mug and drank half the remaining beer. He set the mug on the bar counter. "Or maybe that. You're here for the prisoner?"

"Yeah."

"By yourself?"

"Yeah."

"Dangerous work transporting a prisoner. Especially a killer figures he's going to hang."

Coltrane shrugged. Across the crowded saloon a cry went up at one of the tables. Hickok turned his head slowly and studied the situation. The flat expression in his eyes didn't change, but he lurched away from the bar.

"Damn," he muttered to himself. "I'll be right back."

Coltrane watched as Hickok made his way through the room and spoke to the men at the table for a couple of minutes. There were six men around the table. Two of them were standing, glaring at each other, then at Hickok, as he talked to them. They looked very angry.

Coltrane couldn't hear what was said, although the piano

had stopped and the room had grown quiet. Every head in the room had turned to watch. Coltrane unfastened the strap on his holster.

Without a warning one of the men seated at the table reared up. Hickok was faster and shot the man in the stomach. There was a swell of shouts throughout the saloon and then all was quiet as Hickok glared around, the revolver still in his hand, smoke rising slowly from the muzzle.

Coltrane had his own pistol drawn and ready. He pointed it around the room, over the heads, waiting to see what would happen.

When nobody moved or said anything for a long moment Hickok holstered his pistol and made his way back across the room towards the bar. Before he even reached Coltrane the noise swelled again and the piano resumed play.

When he was standing next to Coltrane again Hickok drank down the remainder of the beer.

"You had my back," he said.

Coltrane nodded.

"Thanks."

Coltrane shrugged and picked up his beer.

"It's been damn ugly here."

"Yeah."

"About that prisoner," Hickok said then. "He got himself shot trying to escape last night. I guess one of my deputies saved you the trouble of a transport."

*

In the faint light of dawn Coltrane opened his eyes to find himself unable to move. He could think and look about, but had no control over his arms or legs and it was a struggle to breathe. The panic of the dream passed quickly as he lay there waiting.

Then the misty apparition was beside him, kneeling in the

hay, hat in hand as if in consolation. The ghost passed a hand gently over Coltrane's forehead. The touch was cool. His voice, when he spoke, sounded both near and far away and his tone was sorrowful.

"You know who I am. Be still and listen to the only words of advice I have to give. You've lived your life by the gun. Sometimes you haven't had many choices, but you haven't learned the lessons you were meant to. It's not too late. Even now, it's not. There are other ways. Stop living by the gun. Don't follow my path. Find another way. Open your heart."

*

As the apparition faded into the mist of dawn Coltrane slowly found he could move again. He sat up in the loft, drenched in sweat and shivering from the cold morning air. The pile of loose hay shifted beneath him. The mares shuffled about, restless in their stalls. Rosalita snorted and shook her head about slowly.

Chapter Twenty-Six

As soon as Elisabeth came through the door Coltrane knew something was wrong. She handed him a bottle of wine, gave him a quick kiss on the mouth, and walked past him into the cabin. He had a fire going and it was warm.

Coltrane waited.

"I don't want to talk about it yet. Can we sit quietly for minute?"

"Of course."

Elisabeth sat down at the table. Coltrane put the bottle on the table and sat next to her. Her eyes didn't rise to meet his. Without saying a word he leaned over and kissed her gently on the cheek. After a moment she smiled sadly, looking up into his eyes, and held out her hand.

"You've had your wedding dress fitted," Coltrane said. It was not a question.

Elisabeth nodded. "Yes," she said.

"I'm sure you are beautiful in it."

"I don't know…"

"I do. Now you have come to tell me you can't see me anymore?"

Elisabeth shrugged. For a long moment she said nothing. Her eyes were sad. "I don't want to," she said finally. "But…."

"You have to."

She shrugged again. "I don't know if I can let go of you. I have to try…. At least, I need to take a break."

Coltrane sighed and leaned away from her.

"I wish this were easier. I don't know what to say."

"What do you know?"

"I know that I love you."

"You're breaking my heart," he said simply.

"There's something else."

Suddenly he knew what she was about to say, though he waited quietly for her to say it.

"I'm late, very late."

"You're with child?"

She nodded.

"Is it mine?"

She lowered her chin and stared at hands. "How could I know?"

"I think you might."

Elisabeth didn't look up, didn't answer.

"What do you want?"

"I don't know what I want, and I have to figure it out. Thomas has been good to me. I don't want to hurt him, and I don't want to lose him. I know I'll never be able to have you. You can't tear yourself away from Anne – and even if you did, how long will you be around? If Thomas found out about us, he would leave me. I don't want to end up alone."

"So you must go?"

"Not right away."

Coltrane nodded.

"I want to make love with you one last time," Elisabeth told him, squeezing his hand hard.

*

They made love ferociously and in the middle of it he asked her to tell him that she loved him – and she did. She whispered the words three times, a little bit louder each time.

After she left, Elisabeth rode home by herself. She wouldn't let Coltrane escort her.

She never did learn that he followed her home, quietly, from a distance to make sure she was safe. For almost an hour he stood beside his mare in the dark, beneath a small copse of aspens, watching the lights of her house until they flickered off.

Chapter Twenty-Seven

To cope with the pain and loneliness Coltrane went on a long hunt. He had a lot to think about and he had decisions of his own that he needed to face.

It was late May and the ground was soft from four days of rain. The sky was overcast when he left and when he was about two miles out it began to rain steadily, but he did not turn back. He rode on, letting Bobby-Lee pick her way up through the canyons and up along the snow covered ridges of the Wasatch Mountains. Rosalita followed along behind. While he traveled he tried not to think about Elisabeth.

Over the years he had learned to clear his mind, to focus on the moment-to-moment details of survival. As long as he kept moving he was all right. It was something he had learned during the war, during those long marches through the countryside. All day long he rode numbly, his mind blank except for the senses that were attuned to the land around him.

Before dark he moved down to a lower elevation so he would not have to sleep in the snow. On a small plateau he paused and slept on the ground for a few hours, wrapped in his poncho, indifferent to the wind and the rain that howled loudly. At dawn he was up and moving again. The claybank, seeming to sense his quiet despair, bore the burden of the long ride stoically.

On the second day out Coltrane stopped a couple hours before twilight to make a camp.

"This is far enough, girls," he whispered to the mares.

They were up high enough that the air was very cold. He could see his breath. The rain had stopped several hours earlier. The ground he chose for the camp was flat with a view down through a canyon towards the valley. It was surrounded by large orange rocks and aspens and was set about thirty yards from a shallow mountain stream that was flowing, fed by the intermittent spring melt above. Coltrane chopped extra firewood and cut several long aspen branches to make a lean-to.

"Sorry, sweethearts," he whispered to Bobby-Lee and Rosalita. "You won't have a roof over your head for a few nights."

The mares didn't seem to mind. Coltrane brushed them carefully and talked to them all the while, then fed them a dinner of oats and carrots. For himself he made a meal of cornmeal and smoked pork.

Coltrane slept well that night, enjoying the crisp air in his lungs and the feeling of independence and liberty that came with being so far away from people. For once he slept through the night, without dreaming or waking.

In the morning he cooked a breakfast of cornmeal mush and drank a pot of coffee that he made in a low saucepan. It had been awhile since he had tasted field coffee. It was thick and black, and he had no sugar or honey to sweeten it with. He savored the bitter taste of the grounds that got into his mouth as he drank.

Memories of other camps, from the rainy fields of Virginia to the dry sands of Arizona, drifted back to him. After he cleaned up and led Bobby-Lee to the stream with Rosalita trailing behind, he sat on a rock in the sunshine to watch the mares drink.

He thought about Elisabeth for a while, thought about how much it hurt to think about never holding her again. For fifteen minutes he sat still until he decided it was enough and he led the claybank back to the camp.

"I can think about Elisabeth later," he told the mares as they walked together through the aspen forest.

Bobby-Lee snorted and peered over at him, seeming to understand. Coltrane stroked her muzzle and rubbed her ears. At the camp he spread his firearms out on a blanket and began to clean them, starting with the Colt, fearing that the rain and moisture might have gotten to the barrels.

It took him almost an hour to clean and oil the revolver, the Winchester rifle, and the shotgun. He worked slowly, meticulously, knowing he could have finished the chore in a third of the time, but allowing himself to become mesmerized by the familiar motions. Afterward he holstered the Colt in the shoulder rig and secured the long guns in their sheaths. If he had been serious about the hunt he would have started by now, but he didn't care about the hunt itself and so he passed the remainder of the day in the camp.

For three hours he sat propped with his back against his saddle, reading about the battles of Chickamauga and Chattanooga. He had not fought at either battle, but had known men who served in that campaign with the Army of Tennessee. He remembered how they had described the fighting and the ground. It had been dangerous ground, with high bluffs and rocks. He knew the territory. It was beautiful land, but very dangerous if you were fighting on it.

Coltrane read first from a monograph in Scribner's magazine, an account written by a war correspondent who had followed the Confederate forces in the war. The correspondent's lack of respect for the Confederate leadership of General Braxton Bragg was plainly evident. Instead the writer, a Southerner, praised the Union General, George Thomas, who held the line at Snodgrass Hill even while the rest of the Federal forces were routed. Later nicknamed the "Rock of Chickamauga," Thomas' stand had allowed the Union army to form an orderly retreat and regroup near Chattanooga. It had been fierce fighting, with bravery on both sides.

After he finished the monograph Coltrane read a section from the *Memoirs of W.T. Sherman* describing the attack on Bragg's right during Grant's push out of Chattanooga. He didn't read about the battles for Atlanta or Sherman's march to the sea. He wanted to focus on the one campaign.

With amusement he noted how little space Sherman

devoted to his own role in the battle of Chattanooga, how he rationalized his lack of success against the Confederate troops at Tunnel Hill even while the rest of Bragg's forces were crumbling along Missionary Ridge.

Coltrane remembered the stories from veterans of Patrick Cleburne's division, men who had held the far right of the Confederate line against Sherman's assault. They had simply outfought him and held the ground.

When Coltrane was finished reading he set the books aside and prepared a meal. While he cooked he thought about the battles, saw the men moving towards each other through the trees, some pausing to fire their muskets, others falling, as the acrid smoke spread across the fields and forests.

He could hear the thunder of the cannon and the cries of the wounded, and he could smell the gunpowder and the death that covered the ground. As the shadows of the afternoon grew longer, his mind drifted away to other battles, ones in which he had fought and seen friends and comrades die.

*

It was almost dark by the time he came out of his haze. He picked up the frying pan and the coffeepot and led the mares back down to the stream to drink while he washed. When he returned to camp he fed the embers of the fire and brought it back to a blaze again.

The sky was clear now and full of stars, and the air was still. The mares had found a sheltered place to settle and appeared content. Coltrane propped himself up against the saddle and watched the flickering of the campfire.

He thought about Anne, about her quiet presence and gentleness. He missed her and wondered how she was and tried to imagine her in Atlanta. Also, he thought about Elisabeth and felt startled at the intensity of his emotions, and he wondered how he could ever be happy again without her, without the sensations he felt every time she touched him.

"Don't think about her," he said out loud to himself. Rosalita sighed in return.

*

Coltrane remained encamped for three more days without hunting. He took long walks through the woods and slept more than was usual for him. In the afternoons he read other parts of Sherman's memoirs, this time from the beginning, and spent long hours sitting still listening to the minute sounds around him.

He ate nothing more than the cornmeal and dried meat that he carried with him, and some wild berries that he discovered on one of the walks. On the morning of the seventh day out, he woke up early, before the sun was showing and knew it was time to return.

Chapter Twenty-Eight

Coltrane did not hurry back. The trip down from the mountains was physically easier on the mares, but the footing was more perilous. He took two and a half days to make the ride, stopping often to rest. When he was down from the Wasatch heights he took a course that would take him past Elisabeth's home by mid-afternoon.

*

"I was afraid you had left for good," Elisabeth said. She pulled the door open and embraced him.

"I thought about it."

She leaned against him and he put his arms around her again.

"I always want to touch you," she said.

He nodded and pressed his lips against her forehead.

"Where did you go?"

"Into the mountains, on a hunt. Did you look for me?"

Elisabeth nodded. "Tell me about your trip."

"There isn't much to tell. I rode up high, encamped, stayed a few days, and then came back down."

"Did you hunt?"

"I didn't feel up to it, but it was good to be away. I had a lot to think about."

"I'm glad you're back."

Coltrane nodded, not knowing what to say. His mouth was dry.

"I missed you," Elisabeth told him.

"I missed you too."

"Can you come inside?"

"I'm awfully dirty from the trail."

Elisabeth grinned. She had never seen him with seven days of growth on his face. "I like the beard," she said.

"You do?"

"It's very handsome." Her eyes danced and he felt the tightness again in his stomach.

"You've had your hair cut," he said, noticing it now for the first time. It was still tousled, but shorter than he had seen it.

"I did."

"You are beautiful."

"Come inside. I don't mind that you've been on the trail."

"Maybe I shouldn't."

Elisabeth took him by the hand and pulled him inside. Coltrane took off his hat and washed his hands and face at her modern sink with the running water. The towel she handed him was fresh and clean, and smelled faintly of laundry soap. Then he drank a glass of water and looked at Elisabeth again as she leaned against the counter with her arms crossed. His heart raced.

"It's been a hard week," Elisabeth said quietly.

"For me too."

"I don't want to be without you."

"It's not that simple," Coltrane said quietly. "I've only ever taken life – I've never brought it in to this world. I had a lot of time to think about matters over this past week, and I think it might be best if you leave Thomas and marry me once I get a divorce from Anne."

Elisabeth stared into his eyes and a smile broke across her face, and then she was moving across the kitchen towards him and he took her into his arms and kissed her as hard as he could for a long time. "I'll need to think about it," she whispered to him eventually.

"Of course."

With total disregard for anything else they fumbled into the bedroom, stripping their clothing off quickly, and made love on top of the bedspread with the broad light of day streaming in through the windows and the possibility that Thomas could walk through the door at any moment.

Chapter Twenty-Nine

Coltrane heard the riders approaching, two of them coming in fast, and checked the Colt. He knew the big revolver was loaded, but he spun the cylinder out of habit anyway. It was near dusk and the sky was a soft hazy purple as the sun began to dip past the mountains. He watched from a window as the riders came into view. It was Bryant and Thomas Hyde.

Coltrane stepped out onto the porch to wait for them as they rode up. After they had reined in their horses neither one made an attempt to dismount. Bryant was dressed as sharp as usual. He wore the bowler hat and the kid gloves despite the fact that the air was warm. He eyed Coltrane for a moment before speaking. Coltrane waited without comment.

"Been looking for you," the sheriff said.

"So?"

"You're not easy to find."

"I'm right here."

"Yeah, but it seems you've been away."

"Maybe so."

"Thomas heard from Elisabeth that you returned yesterday. She said you stopped by their house on your way home."

"True."

"I guess you don't care to say where you've been?"

"I guess not. I guess you didn't really come all the way out here to ask me where I've been."

Bryant shook his head slowly. "Gerald Earl is out of jail."

Coltrane nodded. "Good for him."

"We couldn't hold him. I checked, but there were no outstanding warrants on him, and the magistrate said I had to let him go. Did my best."

"Okay."

"Thought you might like to know."

"Thanks."

"I don't think you should wait around for him."

"I'm not waiting for anybody."

"He swore to kill you for what you did to his brother. I think you should leave the county."

Coltrane nodded, expressionless.

"Look," Bryant said, his voice tightening. "There's no sense in you waiting around to get shot in the back, because that's how he'll do it. He's got friends that could help him if he needs it. Those friends are worse than he is and some of them liked his brother too. Why don't you just move on? There are plenty of other quiet places you could go. This spread can be sold – we'll see you get a fair price for it."

"I reckon not. This is where I chose to settle. It's where I live. It's where I'll stay."

"You're a stubborn son of a bitch."

"Yes, I am."

"You won't last long out here by yourself, not with Earl's crowd gunning for you."

"Folks have been making predictions like that for a lot of years."

The sheriff considered this and then shrugged. "Yeah, I guess maybe they have. One of these days someone's going to be right." His tone was angry and after he spoke, he stared hard at Coltrane for a long moment. The scar under his eye trembled. Then, without so much as a glance at his deputy, he turned his mount and galloped off the way he had come.

Coltrane nodded and looked at the deputy; conscious that this was the man Elisabeth had chosen to marry. "He's sure in a hurry to run me off."

Thomas shrugged and studied Coltrane's face for a long moment. "Look after yourself," he said. They were the first words he had spoken and they were sincere.

Coltrane gave an informal salute and watched as the young deputy backed his horse around and spurred the mount to catch up with the sheriff.

Chapter Thirty

"I don't want to see you hurt," Elisabeth said. "I couldn't bear it if anything happened to you."

They were sitting on her back steps with cups of tea, watching the chickens feed. It was the first really warm day of the year. Summer was near. Coltrane leaned in close and brushed his lips against her cheek. She turned toward him and looked at him with those eyes. "Don't worry about me," he said quietly.

"I can't help it."

"Is this about Earl?"

Elisabeth nodded and sipped her tea. She paused to add more honey, stirred it, and then sipped again. "Partly. It's also about Bryant. Thomas said the two of them rode out to your place last week."

"They knew I had been away. Apparently, they had been out looking for me."

"I think you should go away again, for your safety. You're in danger here."

"There's danger everywhere."

"Gerald Earl swore to kill you. People in town are talking about it. After he got out of jail, Earl went right out and got drunk and told anybody who would listen that he was going to come after you. He means to kill you."

Coltrane took a sip of his tea and then held the cup out in front of him with both hands. "People say a lot of things when they're drunk."

"A lot of people in town believe he was serious."

"He may have been serious. There's nothing I can do about it. Earl tried to kill me once before and he wasn't good enough."

"Next time he'll have friends with him."

"He had friends with him last time."

"Yes."

"They were measured for pine boxes."

"Do you have to be so damn stubborn about this? We all know how tough you are."

"This isn't about being tough."

"Then what's it about?"

"It's about a code. It's about not letting anyone on this earth tell me where or how to live my life. I do no other man harm or insult and I expect no man to do either to me. I learned a long time ago that you couldn't let another man push you. If you do, he'll never stop."

"What about Bryant?"

Coltrane shrugged. "What about him then?"

"Thomas says he's furious."

"He'd like me to leave too."

"Yes, he would, but he'd settle to see you dead."

"Probably so."

"What is it between you two?"

Coltrane shook his head. He looked down into his teacup.

"Thomas has the idea that you crossed paths somewhere else, a long time ago."

"No, we never did."

"What is it then?"

"He saw me kill his uncle."

"Did you?"

"Yes."

"So you knew him before you arrived here, you knew you killed his uncle."

"No."

"What does that mean? 'You didn't know you killed the man?"

"I knew I killed a man. I didn't know it was his uncle."

"Oh... Is there more to it?"

Coltrane shook his head slowly, and then shrugged. His eyes were far away, looking out past the fenced in enclosure that contained the chickens, squinting into the sunlight.

"You don't want to talk about it…."

"I don't."

They were silent for a long moment. Elisabeth sighed. "I worry about Bryant more than I do Earl," she said at length.

"So do I."

"Thomas thinks Bryant fanned the flames with Earl."

"I wouldn't doubt it."

"He's not sure, but Thomas knows that Bryant spent a good bit of time speaking with Earl. He thinks Bryant talked to him about you, made it seem as though you had gloated after killing his brother. I just know he fed him ideas about you and how to kill you."

"I've known men like Bryant all my life. If they can get someone else to do their dirty work for them…"

"I don't want to have to bury you," Elisabeth said. She was angry.

Coltrane nodded, thinking about the familiar words.

*

"I don't want to have to bury you," Anne said.

"Please don't worry about me."

"I can't help it. I couldn't stand it to have to be the one to cry over you as they lower you into the ground while some stranger with a white collar says fancy words."

"Stop it."

"You don't understand, do you?" She was nearly hysterical. "You don't know how it hurts to be sitting here by myself, worrying about you while you're out there. That's just on ordinary days, those days you put on that damn star promising to come home in the evening. It's even worse when you leave town on those overnights. I never know when or if you're ever coming home."

"Anne, please…."

"You try to reassure me, I know you do. It's not enough."

117

"What do you want from me?"

"Give it up."

There was a long pause, while Coltrane thought about it. "Okay," he said finally, his voice flat. "I will. For you."

Anne shook her head sideways, her anger giving way to slow tears. "I know you would. You'd do it for me. Or at least you'd try it for me. But what would you do? You wouldn't be happy with anything else... It's who you are. Or at least who you've become."

"I can give it up."

"What would you do with yourself?"

"I'll find something."

"No, you wouldn't. I know you better than that. You'd be miserable. You'd resent me. I'm not going to have that hanging over me day in and day out."

"Then what?"

"I know you love me. You don't say it very often, but I know you do."

Coltrane nodded, meeting her eyes.

"... but sometimes love isn't enough."

*

"Are you listening to me?" Elisabeth asked.

Coltrane looked at her suddenly and nodded unconvincingly.

"You just drifted off, didn't hear a word I said."

"I'm sorry." Coltrane sipped the last of his tea and set the cup down on the steps. "I should get going," he said. "I don't want you to worry. People have tried to kill me for a lot of years. No one's ever succeeded."

"I know that, but you're not a young man anymore."

"True," Coltrane said, his lips tight. "I'm an old man, can barely fend for myself."

"That's not what I meant."

"Of course not."

118

"Look: the days of the Wild West, with shootouts and Indians and cowboys riding the trail are over. It was a time that required men like you. Those days are gone. That season is past. Cattle are moved on trains now, not by eager young men on horseback with six-shooters strapped to their sides. The Indians, the ones that are left, are on reservations. Even the shootouts are different. Men don't carry guns anymore, and there aren't many Civil War veterans left to notice. In a few months it's going to be the twentieth century. There won't be a frontier – no more wild towns or territory to tame. We're going to have running water, electric lights, and telephones in every home. We won't even ride horses much some day. We'll have motor carriages to take us where we go."

Coltrane looked down at the backs of his hands and nodded.

"I worry about you so."

"I know," he said quietly. "Have you given thought to my question?"

She looked away without answering.

"I best be going home now," Coltrane said after a while.

He kissed Elisabeth quickly on the cheek and carried his teacup back into the kitchen. Elisabeth did not follow him inside.

Chapter Thirty-One

The summer came and the days passed quickly into the golden heat.

Coltrane saw Elisabeth whenever he could. They went for long afternoon walks, holding hands tightly as they passed through the woods and meadows. She told him she loved him and he said the words too, surprising himself with how easily they came out.

They made love passionately with the windows open and the breeze blowing over their bodies and then lay together on his bed talking quietly. Sometimes he would turn towards her while she spoke and, not hearing her words, study her face, noting the freckles on her cheek and the soft lines around her mouth.

He would touch her skin and marvel at how smooth it was.

He would kiss her softly and draw himself up next to her while she looked up at the ceiling, talking, as if unaware of his presence. Then she would smile at him and he would feel it in his stomach and he would want to cry, but he never did. And all the while she refused to give him an answer or even talk about the proposal he had made. Gradually he began to give up hope that she would choose him.

Sometimes he thought maybe he was going crazy, could not understand the feelings that he had for her. Yet when she touched him or looked at him with those eyes he knew he was not going crazy. To love her so much, as he did, made complete sense in those moments.

At night, when he was alone, sitting on his porch looking at the broad sky, he thought about the child that was growing within her. She wouldn't confirm it, but he knew it was his. Somehow he just knew it, and that drove him in a way that nothing ever had.

One afternoon as she was dressing, Coltrane reminded her he wanted her all for himself. Elisabeth replied, "If it is meant to be, it will happen."

It made him sick to think about those words and the fatalism that meant it might not happen.

*

Coltrane continued to spend most of his time alone, working on his land, hunting, and farming. He read daily. Elisabeth gave him a collection of plays by Ibsen, which he finished in two days.

He didn't care for *Hedda Gabler*, but found that he liked *A Doll's House* very much. It had been Elisabeth's favorite. He acquired a library card and began borrowing books, including *The Adventures of Sherlock Holmes* that had been published first in Strand magazine.

He also paid more attention to the news by reading newspapers and magazines when he visited the library. Technology and scientific advancements fascinated him, especially the work of Marconi who invented radiotelegraphy, and Karl Benz and Henry Ford who were developing the production of motorcars.

He caught up on old news, including the discovery of radium by a female scientist in France the previous year, Queen Victoria's Diamond Jubilee, and the famine in India that killed many thousands in 1897.

Politics also caught his attention. He preferred the nationalizing policies of the Republican President McKinley and avidly read the debates that were shaping around the coming election of 1900.

He followed professional baseball, a game he had enjoyed in his youth and had played with other soldiers during the long, dull periods between battles. He read about the Boston Beaneaters and the Baltimore Orioles. The Orioles were led by John McGraw and Wee Willie Keeler, who had a 44 game hitting streak in 1897.

He also followed the games pitched by Cy Young, guessing for himself that "Cy" was likely short for cyclone, and he read about the labor disputes, the reserve clause, and the newly created American League that would compete with the Nationals.

For a while, the ghost of Wild Bill Hickok appeared less frequently and didn't speak much to him anymore. Coltrane only saw the apparition early in the morning; during those brief moments when it wasn't really night any longer, but it was not quite morning either. He didn't mind the ghost and sometimes smiled to himself when he thought about how he could never tell anyone.

*

Meanwhile, the town of Crystal was changing. In preparation for the turn of the century they paved Main Street, installed electric streetlights, and moved City Hall to a new, more modern building. The Red Sky saloon and tavern had indoor plumbing installed and the town's first Department Store opened across the street from Ryan's.

Several motorcars made occasional appearances. The citizens were proud of their growing city and hung flags in front of their homes and businesses. Other events also took place. Sheriff Bryant left the county for a month to bury his aunt in Pima County Arizona, leaving Thomas Hyde in charge while he was gone.

When Bryant returned he seemed different. He was quieter, more inward, and it was noted that he actually appeared to be grieving for his aunt, which surprised many people who knew him.

One other event occurred that caught the attention of people around town. Gerald Earl got himself arrested in Wyoming for shooting a man in the foot during an argument about a horse.

In late August dark storms came and hovered over the valley for a week. Everywhere the ground turned to mud and the streams overflowed their banks.

Chapter Thirty-Two

They made love in the afternoon and then lay together, sharing a pillow on Coltrane's bed, with their hands clasped.

"I have to marry Thomas," Elisabeth said quietly. "We leave week after next. I'll be gone for almost a month. We're getting married in Denver at my parent's church, then we'll take a train to Chicago for our honeymoon."

Coltrane remained silent.

"This is crazy. I'm going off to get married and I can't bear the thought of being away from you."

"You could marry me instead."

"You know why I can't."

Coltrane didn't respond. He lay still, staring up toward the ceiling. She squeezed his hand hard and he knew she was struggling to hold back tears. When he turned toward her she had her eyes closed and then she rolled away as he kissed her lightly on the cheek.

*

"I have a question," Elisabeth said, rolling onto her side so that she could watch Coltrane's face. "You don't have to answer, but please don't lie to me."

"I won't."

"Thomas thinks he's learned something about Sheriff Bryant that might explain why he has a grudge for you."

"I thought it was because I killed his uncle."

"Thomas said Bryant was distraught over the death of his aunt. I guess she had been married to the uncle you killed."

Coltrane nodded, still looking up at the ceiling. "That would be Ellen. She was a beautiful woman, a good woman."

"You knew her?"

"It was a long time ago."

124

"Were you lovers?"

Coltrane smiled slowly. "No."

"I'm sorry… I just thought…"

"Shhhh, it's okay."

"Did you know Bryant returned to Crystal with another man, a friend of his from Pima County?"

"No."

"He's an older fellow, probably about your age. I guess he's a constable down there."

"Do you know his name?"

"Anderson something."

"Billy Anderson?"

"That sounds right. Do you know him?"

"I remember him. He was one of Caufield's cousins. He was there during the Pima County feud and then afterwards."

"Why is he here?"

"Maybe he and Bryant are friends."

"I think they are, but he's a lawman too."

"That doesn't mean much."

"What happened in Pima County?"

"It was a long time ago."

"Tell me."

Coltrane was silent as he thought about it, staring up at the ceiling. The corners of his eyes tightened. "If you really want to know," he said then, quietly.

"I do. Please tell me."

*

"In '85 I was a Federal marshal in Arizona. I rode with several deputies. They were men I knew and trusted. In '86 one of my deputies, a man named Frank Beamon, ran for sheriff of Pima County. Frank was a good man, a southerner from Alabama, a Democrat, but not really political. He would have made a good sheriff and so I backed him.

125

"I didn't want to lose him as my deputy, but I backed him because I knew he was the right man. The man he ran against was Jesse Caufield, the incumbent sheriff. Caufield was married to Ellen Caufield, and apparently he was Bryant's uncle. Caufield was sneaky and dishonest in my view. He claimed to have fought for the Federal Army at the battle of Antietam, but nobody believed that.

"Mostly he was a small time rustler and gambler and he took money to look the other way when certain people wanted to do things. The only thing he had going for him was that he was an amiable fellow who seemed to make a lot of friends, and he was married to the most beautiful woman in the county.

"The election was close. About half the county was Democrat and the other half Republican, and there was a newspaper for each side. It turned ugly. The Republican newspaper would print a story filled with lies about Beamon, saying how he had probably been involved in a stagecoach robbery. Then the Democrat paper would fire off a story refuting this, saying it was a frame, that Sheriff Caufield had robbed the stage and planted evidence. So the feud grew wildly.

"That went on for several months prior to the election. The bitterness of the newspaper editorials grew meaner and meaner in the weeks leading up to the election. They printed all kinds of stories, both sides did. Didn't matter to those men if they printed the truth or not. The whole county was mesmerized and people bought more newspapers than ever before.

"People bought the newspapers every day, both of them, just to see what would be claimed next. Every crime that was committed in the county became a political issue – as did every rumor. They slandered Beamon and everyone associated with him, including me. Caufield got it too, I reckon.

"Two weeks before the election *The Standard*, the Republican newspaper, ran a story saying that Frank Beamon and Ellen Caufield were having an affair and they questioned

Beamon's character, saying he wasn't fit to be a sheriff. You can imagine. That was pouring kerosene on a fire.

"Caufield lost control at that point. He arrested Frank Beamon and his brother James on some false charges and locked them in his jail for three days. He refused to set a hearing before the magistrate. There were rumors that a mob was gathering to lynch the Beamon brothers. I intervened with two of my deputies, Lewis MacDonald and Will Forsyth, to take them out of jail.

"Nobody was hurt, although we did have to draw down on a couple of Caufield's deputies, including the Bond brothers who wore stars, but had reputations as bushwhackers and robbers. They had come down from the gold rush town of Virginia City, Montana, and were two of the meanest, lowest men I ever knew.

"Two nights before the election Frank Beamon was killed by a shotgun blast as he walked down the middle of the street under the full glow of the streetlamps. The killer waited for him in a dark side street and ambushed him as he walked under a streetlight. He was killed instantly and no one ever found out who killed him, although everyone suspected it was the sheriff himself. Of course Caufield had five of his buddies swear that he was a playing cards with them at the time of the shooting, so nothing ever came of it.

"Caufield easily won reelection with nobody to oppose him on the ballot. It was a mess after that.

"Caufield ran that town like it belonged to him. His greasy fingers were in everything. Saloons and gambling halls paid him bribes to leave them alone. Every small business in town had to contribute to the 'protection' fund. The offices of *The Freedom Page*, the Democratic newspaper, were vandalized so that they dared not print anything critical of Caufield. Beamon's friends were harassed and his brother James was arrested again and held without bond for two months until the judge could be summoned to dismiss the case.

"That continued for almost a year. Things came to a head in '87 when I shot Jesse Caufield during a poker game. We were playing five-card stud at a saloon called the New Yorker. It was a strange time and a strange place. Even though you might have been sworn enemies with someone that didn't stop you from drinking and playing poker with them.

"At the table that night with Caufield and me were Lewis MacDonald, Duval Bond, Earnest Bond, and Sims Gossett, another one of Caufield's deputies. We had been playing and drinking for several hours. Caufield was very drunk and he was losing bad. He wasn't a good loser, and when he went bust, he lost control. He talked about Frank Beamon and how he had deserved what he got. He accused Lewis of cheating after he'd won several hands in a row, then he accused me when I started to win.

"I don't take that from any man. We both stood up. Caufield pretended to turn away, but then went for his gun and I shot him dead. It happened so fast, nobody else had a chance to move. I covered the Bond brothers and Gossett as they yelled threats at us. MacDonald and I got out of there and left town for a few days. We should never have gone back."

*

There was a long silence in the room. "Then what happened?" Elisabeth asked.

*

Coltrane continued to stare at the ceiling, his eyes far away. "It was a bloodbath. A week later Lewis MacDonald was ambushed in the same spot as Frank Beamon. There more killings after that. A couple of Caufield's deputies were gunned down outside of town. Earnest Bond was shot coming out of the barbershop. He didn't die, but he lost his right arm and was never really right in the head after that.

"James Beamon and Will Forsyth were murdered. Their bodies were found rotting at a campsite, still in their bedding. They had been shotgunned in their sleep. They didn't even make it out from under their blankets. A Mexican silver medallion that James Beamon wore was missing. Duval Bond was overheard in the *New Yorker* bragging that he had done it. There was a rumor he was showing that silver medallion around like a trophy."

"That's horrible."

Coltrane nodded. "That was Pima County in the mid eighties."

"Did anybody ever do anything?"

Coltrane shrugged. "There was no way to prove anything."

"So Duval got away with it?"

"In a manner of speaking. He left the county soon after that."

"What did you do?"

"I left too. Anne had had enough. We went to San Francisco."

"That was the end of the feud?"

Coltrane shook his head. "A year later four of Caufield's deputies and other friends who were involved, including the editor of *The Standard*, were killed, one by one. No one ever found out who did it. Two of them were found hanging from trees. One of the dead men was Howard Anderson, Billy Anderson's brother, the man Bryant brought back to Crystal with him recently."

Elisabeth remained quiet.

"I guess Duval Bond was killed a few years later in Texas, along with Floyd Parsons, another one of Caufield's deputies. I heard they found James Beamon's silver medallion hanging around Duval's neck when they went to bury him."

Elisabeth let out a long sigh. "So much killing. Is that why

Bryant hates you so much?"

"I think it must be."

"You didn't know him then?"

"No."

"Do you know who killed Duval Bond?"

"What difference does it make?"

"It seems you were the only one of Frank Beamon's friends who survived."

Coltrane shrugged and sat up on the edge of the bed, allowing the sheet to fall away from him. "Yeah, well," he said slowly. "I wasn't exactly the only one. He had other friends. I think it's time to get moving now."

"Is Billy Anderson here to look for you?"

"I don't know why he would be."

"Yes you do. Somebody hanged his brother."

Coltrane stood up and reached for his shirt, fastening the buttons slowly and with focused attention. His jaw was tight and he did not look at Elisabeth.

"Can I ask one more question?" Elisabeth asked.

Coltrane nodded, still working on the buttons.

"Was it true about Ellen Caufield and Frank Beamon having an affair?"

Coltrane shrugged and looked at Elisabeth. She lay still on the bed with the sheet folded off her now. Her naked body glistened in the dimming light.

"Were they in love? Is that what started it all?"

For a long moment Coltrane didn't answer. "Probably so," he said finally.

He went and stood out on the porch to smoke and stare out towards the tree line while Elisabeth dressed and brushed her hair.

Chapter Thirty-Three

It was nearly dusk by the time Elisabeth left. After she was
gone Coltrane saddled Rosalita and rode out to clear his head,
but he could not elude the past.

*

*"The camp is not far," Coltrane said to the two men who rode
with him.*

*He knelt beside his mount, studying the ground in front of
them, looking out over the beautiful valley on either side of
the narrow river. It was late afternoon. They had ridden hard
all day, stopping only four times to water the horses. Their
own needs had been ignored. Coltrane knew the other two
were tired, but he was determined to settle the matter once
and for all.*

*"Perhaps we should rest the horses overnight, go in early
tomorrow," said one of his companions, a younger man
named Jackson Forsyth.*

*The other, a Mexican named Juan Roderiquez, nodded.
His eyes drooped with fatigue.*

*Coltrane shook his head slowly. His expression was
serious. "I'm not going to chance losing him."*

*"Aw, but we've got him now," Forsyth said. "He's not
going anywhere."*

*"That's what I thought last time. I'm not going to lose him
this time."*

*The other two fell silent. They had learned to read
Coltrane's moods, knew it was useless to argue once he made
up his mind. Coltrane remounted and they rode along the
crest of the ridge, winding parallel to the river. For forty-five
minutes they rode without speaking.*

They spotted the smoke first, then saw the tents pitched

near the trees, near the shade and the cool relief of the flowing water. The smell of cooked food floated up to them and made them hungry. They had not had a hot meal in two days.

Without a word they dismounted and studied the camp and the ground in front of them. From the ridge they could count three tents and seven horses, but saw only two men moving about.

"What's the plan?" asked Roderiquez.

Coltrane shrugged and bit down hard on a toothpick he had been chewing on for the past mile. "We ride down there and shoot Duval and Parsons."

"Just like that?" asked Roderiquez. He had been a ranch hand in Pima County, working for the Beamons. He had bravely fought Indians on at least two occasions, but he was not easily a violent man.

Coltrane shrugged again, his eyes on the camp. For a long moment he didn't respond. Finally he spit the toothpick out of his mouth and nodded. "Just like that."

"They'll hear us coming," warned Forsyth.

"Probably so."

"Give them time to get ready. Be three guns against seven. Not great odds."

"Maybe. You got to consider we'll get in pretty quick, two or three of them won't be ready for us. Of the ones that are, couple of them will decide it ain't worth it. They'll run or they'll freeze up. We'll have the sun at our backs. It will be in their eyes. You also have to consider who we are, how good we are. No. I like our odds well enough. Let's get on with it."

Roderiquez was visibly nervous. "We're not going to arrest them?" he asked.

"Hadn't figured on it," Coltrane replied quietly.

"But you're a lawman. You deputized me and swore me to an oath, to uphold the law."

"Out here I am the law." Coltrane's eyes were hard, unblinking in the fading light.

132

"It ain't fair to simply kill them."

"No, it ain't, but there ain't no fairness out here. Did they show fairness to Frank Beamon? Or Jackson's father?"

"That's not the point."

"Maybe not, but we didn't come out here to worry about shades of gray. Now, saddle up."

"You're a lawman," said Roderiquez. There were tears in his eyes.

Coltrane unpinned the Silver Star from his chest, looked at it for a moment, and then tossed it into the tall grass behind them. "Not anymore," he said.

*

"Please don't do it this way," Roderiquez pleaded. He was the only one not mounted now. He stood in front of the three horses and his hands trembled as he held the reins of his horse down at his side.

Coltrane shrugged and pulled back gently on his reins, forcing his horse sideways, closer to the Mexican so that he could look into his eyes. "You're a brave man, Roderiquez. I know that. You have nothing to prove to me or to Jackson. If you don't believe it is right to ride down there and do this, then you better wait up here. We'll be back in a few minutes."

Roderiquez swallowed hard and nodded. Coltrane realized he was crying too hard to speak.

Coltrane turned away, glanced toward Forsyth. "You ready?"

The younger man nodded.

They spurred their horses down the slope.

*

They rode down the grade, across the field, through the sparse

133

grass as fast as they could and closed in on the camp with their pistols drawn. A hundred yards out a cry went up and they could see the men in front of them scrambling, some reaching for firearms, others heading for cover.

Moving at a full gallop Coltrane fired his Colt at a man who stepped out from a tent with a rifle in his hands. The first shot went wide and the man raised the rifle. The man fired off a shot, levered the cartridge out of the chamber, and fired again, missing both times. Coltrane's second shot hit him squarely in the chest, knocking him backwards onto the tent, collapsing it around and over him.

More shots were fired and Jackson Forsyth, riding slightly behind Coltrane, gave a cry and fell from his saddle. Coltrane heard the cry, but didn't slow up or turn around to look. Forsyth's horse veered off and Coltrane charged into the camp alone. Ahead of him he recognized Floyd Parsons kneeling behind a camp table that had been up-ended.

Parsons was rapidly firing his revolver, sending a spray of bullets over Coltrane's head. Coltrane held his own fire until he was only ten yards away and then he fired three times, snap-aiming directly at the table in front of Parsons.

The shots went through the thin board of the table and hit Parsons in the chest and stomach. Coltrane jumped his horse over the table and in the moment that he looked, he knew with a certainty born of all his experience that Parsons was dead.

Coltrane reared his horse around and saw three men standing together with double-barrels pointed at him. He jumped off his horse and drew his own shotgun from its sheath, then charged the men on foot.

Duval Bond yelled a loud curse and fired from his hip, triggering both barrels in rapid succession. The buckshot skipped around Coltrane's feet and pellets tore at his overcoat. He felt several sharp stings on his thighs and arms. He didn't waver.

Duval Bond cursed again and reached for his pistol.

Coltrane raised his shotgun to his shoulder and pulled the trigger. The blast of double ought buckshot nearly cut Duval Bond in half and he fell backwards, collapsing in a bloody tangle of flesh. The two men who had been standing with him ran away as fast as they could and Coltrane let them. There was no other movement in the camp.

The shots reverberated loudly in the narrow valley and then all was suddenly quiet.

*

Coltrane saw it clearly in his mind as if it were happening again. Rosalita brought him back to the barn all on her own. It was well after dark and the bright stars were spread out in the sky and shining above them.

Chapter Thirty-Four

Sheriff Bryant and Billy Anderson were sitting in the saloon together drinking beer when Coltrane walked in and pulled a chair up to their table.

"'Evening, Billy. Been a long, long time."

There was a moment of silence. Anderson set his beer down and wiped at his lips. "Yes, indeed," he said, and then looked at Bryant. His eyes were nervous and flitted about.

The sheriff's smile was cruel. He drank down part of his beer. "Funny you should show up," Bryant said after a moment. "We were talking about you. Buy you a beer?"

Coltrane shrugged.

Bryant waved his hand at the barman and then pointed at the table and made a circle motion with his finger. "I was just telling Billy how some things haven't changed much over the years, how you're still killing people and getting away with it. Was saying how you gunned down Pliney Calderone and Adam Earl on the street one afternoon some time back."

"In self-defense."

"Sure it was." Bryant's tone was even, unconcerned.

"There were a dozen witnesses."

"Just like the time you shot Jesse Caufield."

Coltrane nodded. "Just like it."

Billy Anderson cleared his throat, but did not speak. Instead he raised the beer to his lips and took a long drink. When he set the glass down his mustache was covered with white foam. He wiped at it with the back of his hand, then smoothed out his mustache with the tips of his fingers.

In his late thirties, he was a large man, with a wide face, weak chin, and thick, gray sideburns that made his face seem even wider. He was dressed in a navy blue suit with a dark wool tie, and he wore wire-rimmed spectacles that had slipped part way down his nose. The constable pin had been carefully polished and was fixed to his vest. Its prominence, when you looked at the man, was intentional.

At that moment the barman arrived with three fresh beers. He set them on the table and backed away quickly without collecting the empty glasses.

"I reckon that bothers me some," Bryant said after the beers had been distributed, his eyes fixed on Coltrane. "You're always in the right. Always justified. I figure you're pretty good at egging people on, nudging the other guy to reach for his gun first, making it look like it's his fault."

Coltrane swallowed a mouthful of beer. "Maybe so."

"That's the reputation you carried with you into Crystal."

"I never heard it that way before."

"What brings you to town this evening?" Bryant asked. Without waiting for an answer he drank down half of his beer and set the glass loudly on the table in front of him.

Coltrane nodded toward Billy Anderson. "Heard he was here, thought I'd stop by to say hello."

"We were never friends," Anderson said quickly. His voice was strained, as if he were holding back emotions that he could barely contain. When he raised his glass his hands trembled slightly.

"True enough. I heard you were in town though, sporting a badge. I figured if you were looking for me, I'd make it easy for you."

Anderson paused a moment before replying.

"Just a minute…." Bryant started.

Coltrane cut him off, holding up a hand. "I think the man should speak for himself."

"Who said I was looking for you?" Anderson asked. His tone was belligerent.

"Nobody said that. I just didn't figure you came all the way from Pima County to rehash old times with Bryant. Heard you were wearing your badge around town. Maybe that meant something."

"So?"

"So here I am."

"Are you daring me to arrest you?"

"No."

"There's no warrant out for you."

"I thought you would have brought something up."

"I don't operate that way."

"Why not? You're friends did in the old days."

"Is that why you killed them?"

"I killed Jesse Caufield in self-defense. You were there. Did you see it some other way?"

"Yeah, I was there. What about the others?"

"What others?"

"My brother. Duval Bond. Floyd Parsons. Others."

"What makes you sure I killed them?"

"I know you did. We all know it."

"Did you see me?"

"No."

"Did anyone else?"

"Probably. They just ain't talking."

"Then what makes you think it was me?"

"Who else could it be?"

"You don't have a warrant?"

"Not this time."

Coltrane swallowed another mouthful of beer. "Then I better not see you out my way. I catch sight of you on my land, I'll figure you're not there for any lawful purpose."

Billy Anderson's lips tightened. "Is that a threat?"

Coltrane shook his head. "No, sir. Just the way it is."

"We could take you right now, if we wanted to," Anderson said.

Coltrane nodded and edged his chair back a few inches. "Maybe so."

"We could," Anderson said again, his voice becoming hoarse. "Two guns to your one."

"Only one way to find out."

Bryant remained still, careful to leave his hands on the table in front of him. "I don't think we need to do it this way, boys."

"Seems your friend is hell-bent on dying early," Coltrane said, watching the sheriff.

"You were never that fast," Anderson said. "Not in the old days, not now."

"True. Then again, fast ain't everything – ask Jesse Caufield. He was always supposed to be faster than me."

Rage filled Anderson's face. "You bastard."

Coltrane nodded and pushed his chair slowly back from the table. His eyes were focused softly on a spot between the two men.

Bryant held up both hands, palms open so that Coltrane could see he meant no threat. "That's enough, Billy. Shut your mouth now."

Billy Anderson turned his head and looked at the sheriff.

Bryant nodded vigorously. "There isn't going to be any shooting in here tonight. Right, Billy?"

Anderson didn't respond.

Bryant spoke again. His voice was louder this time. "I said, there isn't going to be any shooting in here tonight. Right, Billy?"

Anderson nodded his head dumbly and looked away. His lips were trembling visibly.

Coltrane waited silently for a long moment. Then he pushed his chair back further from the table. "If you're not going to arrest me, and you don't figure to shoot me, I guess I'll be moving on."

Anderson didn't look up, and Bryant just nodded. Coltrane stood up.

"Wait a minute," Bryant said. "I'll walk you out to the street. Billy you wait here for me. I'll be back in a few minutes. I need a private word."

Chapter Thirty-Five

Although it was fully dark outside now, the street was well lit by the electric lights that had been recently placed. They created an odd atmosphere of night-to-day, with rings of orange light and areas of discrete shadow.

"Billy Anderson's harmless," Bryant said quietly after they were out the door.

They stood together on the porch of the Red Sky saloon, just left of the entrance in a deep pocket of darkness, shielded from the streetlamps by the roof-overhang. Coltrane had his back to the wall and was well away from the window. He didn't trust Bryant, but he trusted Anderson even less at this moment and half expected him to come out of the saloon shooting. Coltrane had seen it go that way before. Men who had backed down from a confrontation out of fear sometimes acted impulsively moments later, spurred on by shame and anger. Especially when they had been drinking.

"Is that how you see it? To me, it seems he could be one of those back-shooters you've warned me about."

Bryant grinned. The scar below his eye gleamed in the dim light. "That got into your head, didn't it?"

"What do you want, Bryant?"

"Just a quiet word."

"I'm listening. Talk fast."

Bryant nodded. "I want to make sure everything stays calm tonight."

"Meaning what?"

"I don't want any trouble between you and Billy Anderson."

"I'm leaving."

"I know that – and Billy's going to know it. I just want to make sure you know he knows it."

"Talk plainer."

"Look, I know there is bad blood between you two. I just want to make sure you understand that he did not come here

140

looking for you. He's on a holiday."

"With that badge shined up like that?"

"Well, he *is* showing off a bit. I can't help that. Yet he's harmless. My aunt's death was hard on him. He needed to get away. I invited him back here for a few weeks. That's all. He didn't come here for you."

Coltrane shrugged. "That's fine," he said. His voice was whisper quiet.

"I don't want you worrying about him. Tonight I'm going to watch him. I give you my word that I won't let him out of my sight and I won't let him leave town."

"What about the rest of the week?"

"In the morning he'll be sobered up and he'll have cooled down. He's harmless."

Coltrane nodded. "Anything else?"

"No."

Coltrane moved past the sheriff and started toward the far end of the porch.

"Oh, one other thing," Bryant said softly.

Coltrane turned. "Yeah?"

"I guess Elisabeth will be going off to get married soon. You given any thought yet to her wedding present?"

Coltrane felt a sudden knot in his stomach. He said nothing.

Bryant smiled widely at him. "You must be real happy for her, marrying a great guy like young Thomas."

Chapter Thirty-Six

On the day before Elisabeth left for Denver she rode out to see Coltrane.

They took a long walk through a narrow path that Coltrane had cut through the forest. With their hands clasped tightly, they walked slowly and did not speak.

Coltrane looked at her often as they walked. She would turn and look at him with those eyes, but she said little. It was early autumn and the leaves had not yet begun to turn. The air was quite warm and still. The forest was quiet.

They moved through the aspens and stopped several times for Elisabeth to pick wild flowers that grew on small bushes close to the ground. Several times they stopped to hold each other and Coltrane thought she might cry.

The forest opened into a meadow where cows and goats had grazed recently. The grass was short and the ground was soft and covered with deer tracks. Above them the sun shined intermittently between cumulous clouds that were very thick and white. The scent of clover was strong.

"This is a beautiful meadow," Elisabeth said.

Coltrane nodded, looking only at her.

"I used to fantasize that I would be married in a meadow."

"We can sit for a while."

"Yes, let's do."

They chose a place near the center of the meadow. The ground was firm and rose slightly so that they could see the open space around them in all directions. They sat down close together and looked at each other. She leaned toward him and kissed him on the cheek. Afterward, Elisabeth lay back on the grass so that she was looking up at the sky.

"There are marvelous clouds up there," she said.

Coltrane didn't look up. He studied Elisabeth's face, her eyes, her nose, the freckles on her cheek. "I'll take your word for it," he said quietly.

"Why do I feel so sad?" she asked.

"For the same reason I do."

"If other people knew what we were feeling they would think we were crazy."

"For not being together?"

"I wish I could explain to you why I have to go through with my marriage to Thomas."

"You don't have to explain," Coltrane said.

"It is something I have to do. I owe it to him."

"I understand a thing or two about obligations."

"That makes it sound so cold, doesn't it? As if I don't care for him, but I do."

Coltrane nodded.

"I don't know how I would tell someone else about you. We're not just lovers. It's more than that. The word 'lovers' seems inadequate. In my mind I don't even use it."

"What word do you use?"

"I don't have a word. It's like I've known you forever. We're ancient."

Coltrane smiled sadly.

*

Coltrane shifted on the grass, moving his holster carefully. The reposition meant he could draw it quickly if he had to, even from the seated position on the ground.

"That gun is with you everywhere, isn't it?"

"Yes."

"Do you sleep with it?"

"I keep it nearby."

"Under your pillow? What if I slept in your bed?"

"Then I would find another place for it."

"When was the last time you slept without a gun nearby?"

"Before the war."

"Since you were seventeen?"

"Sixteen."

Elisabeth let out a breath and shook her head. "That's a long time."

*

"Would you like to hear my fantasy?"

"Yes."

"Someday I would like to sleep in a bed with you."

Coltrane smiled.

"What I mean is that I would like to sleep with you, next to you, all night, and in the morning wake up with you and see your eyes in the light."

"It would be nice."

"I think it would be wonderful," Elisabeth said.

Coltrane nodded, smiling at her. There was no point in telling her how restless his sleep was. He didn't want her to know about the nightmares, the terrors, or the apparitions he saw at night. Elisabeth made a sound deep in her throat and leaned in close to him. The sun shined down hard upon them and squirrels twittered about at the tree line.

*

"I feel so sad about this," Elisabeth said.

"Don't," Coltrane told her.

"Here I am going off without you to have this ceremony, the honeymoon, leaving you out. I should be having this with you. I should be marrying you, but I just can't. It just doesn't make sense."

"I know you care for him and he's a better match for you than I could ever hope to be."

"It's not the same as it is with you."

Coltrane didn't reply.

"If I was married to you, I wouldn't let you out of my sight," she said eventually.

Coltrane rolled towards her and placed his arm across her breasts and pulled her towards him. He kissed her cheek and then put his mouth close to her ear and whispered.

Chapter Thirty-Seven

The next morning Elisabeth and Thomas left for Denver to be married in a large church that her parents belonged to. Elisabeth was away for five weeks. While she was gone Coltrane tried not to think about her, but without much success. It was easiest when he worked, so he worked hard on his land almost every day, even in the rain.

He put up almost a mile of split rail fence to enlarge the grazing area for his cows, knowing as he worked that it was not necessary. He chopped large piles of wood for the winter and hunted and then smoked large quantities of venison and other game.

On the morning of the day Elisabeth was to marry Thomas Hyde, Coltrane started drinking. He sat on the porch with a fresh bottle of whiskey, a small glass, his tobacco pouch and papers, and a history of Caesar's wars. He poured the whiskey carefully into the glass until it was half full. Then he held it up to the sunlight for a moment, studying the dark hues swirling in the glass as he tipped it gently back and forth.

He took the first sip and held it in his mouth for a moment before swallowing. It burned slightly on the way down and he licked his lips before taking another swallow. He set the glass on the bench and picked up the tobacco pouch. With little fanfare, he rolled a cigarette and smoked it while staring out over the land, willing his mind to stay blank.

When he was finished smoking he took another swallow from the glass and then another, and afterwards he reached for the whiskey bottle. This time he filled the glass all the way and set the bottle down beneath the bench. He rolled another cigarette and opened the history before lighting the cigarette.

The whiskey felt good inside him.

He tried to read, but he was too preoccupied. Caesar was leading troops into Gaul, but all he could think about was Elisabeth walking down the church aisle in her white dress to marry another man. He drank more whiskey and tried to focus on the book.

It took him half an hour to read the first page and when he finished with that and went to turn the page he had no idea of what he had been reading. He took another swallow of whiskey and refilled the glass. He rolled another cigarette and tried to concentrate on Caesar. After awhile he set the book down and stared off toward the horizon.

It was another four days before all his bottles were empty and he stopped drinking. Once he sobered up, he vowed not to drink again until she returned.

*

Near the end of the fourth week he went into Crystal for supplies. As he came into town he spotted Bryant and Billy Anderson on the street, smirking at him as he went past them in the buckboard. Even after they were out of sight, Coltrane could feel the anger surging within him, the desire to kill suddenly stronger than it had been in long while.

On the way home the past came back to him again.

*

The posse had been close behind them for two days.

They had spotted the riders cresting a ridge behind them while they stopped to water their horses. Of course they knew the posse was after them. They had seen it pass them by shortly before they crossed the Arizona border. Now they were surprised to realize just how close it was.

Coltrane had figured the posse would give up once they got away from Arizona. He had not counted on their persistence and he wondered how they kept so well supplied with fresh horses. Their own horses were tiring. They could not keep going much longer without rest.

Coltrane looked back at his companion who had fallen behind again. Juan Roderiquez, the Mexican, appeared to be dozing in the saddle.

Coltrane reined in his horse and waited. "Hey," he said softly.

Roderiquez opened his eyes wide, momentarily startled.

"You were sleeping."

"I am very tired."

"We'll rest now."

"Good. I am very tired."

"There's a small stream over there, but we can't afford long."

"How much time between us and them?"

"Not more than two hours. Maybe less."

Roderiquez nodded. He dismounted and led his horse behind Coltrane's down a narrow path to a stream. While the horses drank, the two men filled their canteens. Roderiquez splashed water on his face and Coltrane surveyed the woods on either side of the stream. The sun was warm and the air was very still.

*

"How fast are they gaining on us?" Roderiquez asked.

Coltrane nodded. "Very fast. They've been able to get fresh horses. We haven't."

"Then they will catch us soon."

"Yes. Unless we outsmart them."

Roderquez shrugged. "We could go up the stream."

Coltrane shielded his eyes from the sun and looked in that direction for a long moment. "Yes," he said finally. "That's what we'll have to do."

"It will slow us down."

"It will slow them down too."

Roderiquez shrugged again. "Not if they simply ride up the banks as fast as they can. They will catch us in the middle of the water."

"They wouldn't know which direction to take."

"It's a big posse. They could split up."

"Yeah, but that doubles our chances in a fight."

"You figure Billy Anderson is leading the posse?"

"Probably."

The Mexican let out a long, tired sigh. "I am really very tired," he said slowly.

"I know."

"Let's go."

*

They rode the horses upstream, wading carefully in the shallows for an hour before it happened. Roderiquez was twisting in the saddle, staring back the way they had come, straining to spot signs of movement behind them, when his horse caught a hoof between two rocks and stumbled forward. Coltrane, who had taken the lead, heard the shout and the splash and turned just in time to see both the rider and horse going headfirst into the water.

*

The horse had broken both front legs and she couldn't even drag herself out of the stream. Coltrane slit her throat with his buck knife to keep her from drowning. Juan Roderiquez had a broken arm and no horse to ride. The two men huddled quietly beneath the trees on the bank of the stream.

"You will have to leave me," Roderiquez said.

Coltrane shook his head, although they both knew Roderiquez was right.

149

"Listen to me," the younger man said. He was in a lot of pain and his voice was strained. There was blood on his face from a cut to his forehead. "It is you they want. They will not bother with me."

"They'll know one of us is down, but they won't know which one. They'll have to look for you."

Roderiquez nodded. "Maybe I can elude them on foot. I will pretend I am a bear and climb a tree." He grinned through clenched teeth.

Coltrane shook his head. His eyes were serious. "Not with one arm."

"Yes."

"I don't know."

"They do not care about me. I did not shoot anyone in Texas."

"They may not see it that way," Coltrane replied.

"There were witnesses. They will take me back for trial, and those witnesses will be called. They will testify that I did not shoot anyone."

"Though you rode with me."

"Is that a crime?"

"It will be in their eyes."

Roderiquez shrugged. "There is no choice. You must go on. Ride."

"Will you fight them?"

"No. I will head off into the woods a mile or two. If they follow me, that will take them off your trail. If they do not follow me I will find a town and then I will be okay."

"If they catch up to you?"

"I will surrender and go back to Arizona for trial. I am no outlaw. The people in Pima know that."

Coltrane lowered his eyes and nodded.

*

Coltrane eluded the posse and spent the summer hiding out in Utah at the base of the Wasatch Mountain range. Three months after he had left Juan Roderiquez by the bank of the stream he learned that Billy Anderson's posse had caught up with the Mexican not more than an hour later.

The former ranch hand had surrendered peacefully and had been hanged immediately from the nearest tree. Nobody in the posse had even bothered to ask his name before they fastened the noose around his neck.

*

That night Coltrane thought about heading back into Crystal to kill Billy Anderson.

As he lay in bed, unable to sleep, he was visited again by the apparition of Wild Bill Hickok.

"Everyone you ever rode with is dead," he heard a voice say.

Chapter Thirty-Eight

Four days after she returned from her honeymoon Elisabeth showed up at Coltrane's door.

"Hello," she said tentatively as she climbed the steps to his porch. She wore denim riding trousers, knee-high boots and a brand-new leather overcoat. Her hair had grown out and she wore it pulled back in a clip. Her mouth was dry with anticipation.

"You're back," Coltrane said, meeting her at the door, overwhelmed by how beautiful she looked.

She nodded, unsure of herself.

"You look so beautiful."

"Thank you. I gained too much weight."

"I like voluptuous women."

"Sure you do."

Coltrane smiled sadly. "It seemed like forever."

"You haven't put your arms around me."

"You're a married woman."

"You don't want me?"

"I thought you wouldn't want me."

"I do want you."

Then she was in his arms and he was kissing her as hard as he could.

*

"Are you okay?" Elisabeth asked later.

They sat on the porch. He had been working on the bench. It was sanded smooth and comfortable, but it still needed a coat of varnish. She sipped from a cup of warm cider. Coltrane shrugged the question off without answering it. His eyes were far away, staring off over the trees.

"I need to know," she said after awhile.

"I am okay."

"Have you been sleeping?"

Coltrane shrugged again, not wanting to answer the question.

"You have that look in your eyes. You haven't been sleeping much, have you?"

"No," Coltrane finally replied.

"I know there are other things that keep you awake."

"I'm okay," he said, his voice forceful this time.

"You don't have to talk about it if you don't want to."

"I don't."

"What did you do while I was away?"

"I built a fence."

"I saw it. What else."

"A little hunting. Not much else."

"I've been worried about you."

Coltrane didn't turn to meet her gaze.

*

"I know I made a mistake," Coltrane said after a while.

"It wasn't your decision," she replied.

Coltrane nodded and continued to stare off into the distance. "I could have stopped you if I tried."

"We'll never know."

Elisabeth drank the rest of her cider.

*

"Do you feel different about Thomas now?"

"What do you mean?"

"Has marriage changed things?"

Elisabeth nodded slowly. "Yes, I think it has. Standing up there in front of all those people, saying those things to each other. The words are powerful. You can't say them without their having an effect on you. Especially with the whole world watching."

"Affect you how?"

"My commitment to Thomas is real. It feels stronger. You can't say all those words without…"

"I don't understand. How can feelings become stronger just because you say some words in a church."

"Don't be angry."

"I'm trying not to be. Explain it to me."

"I feel sad about this in a way, sad for you. I'm confused."

Coltrane smiled sadly and shook his head slowly. He did not tell her that he had prayed for her every night as he lay in bed.

*

"Things didn't go well with my mother," she said after awhile.

"Really?"

"She got sick the morning of the wedding and almost missed it."

"Why?"

"Maybe because I married Thomas."

"Why?"

Elisabeth sighed. "She doesn't much care for him. I've told you about that."

"She shouldn't be that way."

"I guess there's more to it. I spent most of the week before the wedding with her, shopping, making preparations. We talked a lot…" Elisabeth paused and looked at Coltrane. His eyes studied her carefully. There was no expression on his face.

"I guess I spent most of the week before the wedding talking about you," Elisabeth continued. "My mother asked why I wasn't marrying you."

"You told your mother about us?"

"No, but I'm rather sure she figured it out. I get kind of happy whenever I mention your name."

"What did she say?"

"That I must be in love with you. She said I was marrying the wrong man."

*

"Will you make love with me?" Elisabeth asked softly, her face hidden in the shadows.

"Perhaps, only one more time," Coltrane responded.

And much later: "I want to take you this way."

"Nobody has done that for a long, long time."

"I want to."

Slowly, Elisabeth began to kiss her way down Coltrane's body.

*

"You make me feel so special," he whispered.

"You are special," she whispered back.

Chapter Thirty-Nine

They dressed slowly. Coltrane loved the way she looked, sitting on the edge of the bed with her legs bare, and he loved the fact that she was not shy about letting him see her body.

The day had advanced and the shadows across the room, over the loft, were long now. Purple streaks of light filtered through the haze of clouds that ran over the mountains to the west. The air had grown cool and the moon was on the rise in the late afternoon sky.

"It wasn't different, was it?" he said. He fastened the buttons on his shirt and walked across the floor, still looking at her, studying her carefully.

"No," she replied, and then she smiled at him. "Did you think it would be?"

"I feared it might."

"Me too." She pulled her stockings on, one at a time, slowly, while he watched with his arms folded across his chest.

"I guess you have to leave now?"

Elisabeth nodded. "I've been meaning to ask you if everything was quiet while I was away."

"Everything was quiet."

"No problems with Sheriff Bryant?"

"None at all. I only saw him once."

"You heard Billy Anderson left town? He went home to Arizona."

Coltrane shrugged. He hadn't heard.

"That's good news isn't it?"

Coltrane shrugged again. "He'll be back. He won't be able to stay away."

"He might stay away."

"No," said Coltrane with certainty. "He won't."

"How can you possibly know that?"

"I just know."

Elisabeth shook her head. "You're determined not to allow yourself any peace. Why must you be that way?"

"You're wrong about that. It's not me. It's my past, and I can't escape it."

"Do you really think your past has doomed you, has determined that you're not to have any peace in this life ever?"

Coltrane smiled sadly and turned away. He opened the door as Elisabeth came towards him, and then he leaned against the doorframe, with one foot on his porch and the other inside the small cabin.

"We can't escape our past, can we?" he said then.

Elisabeth didn't know what to say so she didn't say anything at all. He watched her go as though it might be for the last time.

Chapter Forty

Coltrane spun the cylinder on the Colt and replaced it in his holster. He checked the action on the Winchester, dropped a handful of cartridges into his saddlebag, and then led Bobby-Lee out of the barn.

Almost in one motion he grabbed the pommel, placed his left foot in the stirrup, and swung the right leg over the saddle. The movement was smooth and graceful. He'd done it thousands of times in his life and didn't even think about it. Beneath him the mare moved instinctively, bucking forward, excited to be going out without the buckboard in tow.

He had not slept well. He thought about Elisabeth and what she had said about Billy Anderson. The more he thought about it, the more certain he became: Billy Anderson wasn't going to let go. He'd be back, and the fact that he'd even left in the first place made Coltrane wonder about what that was for.

It was still early when he started into town. After a quarter mile he headed off the dirt road, into the sparse trees on the east side of the road, moving slowly, wary of the road. His eyes scanned forward, alert for any movements, and he studied the ground carefully, memorizing it. He rode parallel to the old dirt road, keeping it within his sight off to the right.

Much of the ground was open and flat. It was mostly farmers' fields and meadows. This part of the country didn't concern Coltrane, but there were other parts that did. Several areas that flanked the road with aspens or ravines would make good spots for an ambush.

"Here's where I'd set up," he said aloud to himself and the claybank at one point. He nodded his head grimly. The road, flanked by trees on either side, snaked over a rise and then dipped suddenly down to a narrow bridge over a ravine.

"Or maybe here," he said aloud two other times. He didn't notice how the years of experience had taken over, automatically guiding his eyes and his thoughts as he moved

158

through the countryside with a tactical eye toward the land.

By the time he arrived in town he was confident that he knew the trail now. He would never ride blindly through the three spots that he had identified. As much as possible he would avoid taking the buckboard to town. When that was inevitable, he would stop short, unhitch one of the mares, and scout forward before riding through.

He would be especially careful on the way back from town.

*

Coltrane found Bryant sitting by himself in the Sheriff's office. There were thin piles of yellowed, heavily fingered, cards spread out in front of him across his desk. His jacket was off, but he still wore the gabardine vest and gold watch chain. The smell of fresh cigar smoke hung thickly in the air.

"Never figured to see you walking into my jail without a shotgun pointed at your back," Bryant said after a moment. His face wore a false, cruel grin. Turning his eyes downward, he studied the cards laid out before him. "You play solitaire?"

Coltrane grunted and pulled a chair towards the wall opposite Bryant's desk and sat down with his back to it. He rested his open hands, palms down, on his lap and relaxed. He did not remove his hat.

Bryant, still not looking up from his game, turned a card over and swore softly. "Guess I lost again," he said.

"Came to ask you about Billy Anderson."

Bryant glanced up, squinting slightly into the sunlight that came through the window. "What about him?"

"Heard he left."

"He did."

"When's he coming back?"

"Didn't say."

"Will it be soon?"

"Couldn't tell you. I got the impression he was gone for

good."

Coltrane shrugged indifferently. His expression did not reveal what he was thinking. "We both know he'll be back. Even if he said he wouldn't be, he will. That's his nature. He won't be able to help himself and you know it."

The sheriff nodded quietly at this and appeared to think it over. From the breast pocket of his vest, he produced a dark slender cigar. He clipped both ends with a silver cutter and rolled it around on his lower lip. He wet it with his tongue, and then struck a match to it. The smoke drifted up slowly towards the ceiling. "You've made a lot of enemies in your lifetime," he said finally. "I guess that could make a man paranoid."

"Billy Anderson has sworn to kill me."

"So have a lot of other men."

"Most of them are dead now. I don't have to worry about them."

Bryant nodded slowly and studied the ash slowly collecting at the end of his cigar. "Well, I imagine they are dead. Do you hear their souls crying to you at night? I've heard that happens to some killers as they grow old. Maybe you should repent and confess your sins."

Coltrane shook his head. "I'm only looking to be left alone."

"Might be too late for that."

"Might be."

Bryant took a long pull off the cigar. "Look," he said after he had exhaled. "There's bad blood between you and Billy. There isn't exactly a pleasantry between you and me either, for that matter. I've known Billy a long time. He thinks you killed his brother. Matter of fact, I believe it myself. Couldn't say whether you were justified in doing so. I wasn't there. It might have been self-defense, though at that, I rather doubt it was. Still… That doesn't mean he's planning to come gunning for you. If I heard that he was, I'd have to warn him off. That would be my duty as sheriff. If I failed at that, I'd be duty bound to warn you. This is my town. I don't want bloodshed."

Coltrane said nothing. He remained still.

"Don't you think this vendetta has cost the lives of enough men?"

"Yes. I do."

"Aren't you tired of it?"

"Very tired."

"Then why not let it go now."

"I would if I could; I will if others let me."

"We've all lost people in this feud."

"I didn't start it."

"Some people think you did."

"Frank Beamon was the first to die. He was my friend."

"Nobody knows who killed him."

"Somebody knows."

Bryant shrugged. "You understand my point."

"You're saying I started the Pima County war when I shot your uncle, Jesse Caufield. I'm saying that, first, it was self-defense, and, second, Frank Beamon had already been gunned down by then. The bloodshed started with Frank's death. I had good reason to defend myself."

"I'm not going to argue with you. All I'm saying is that we've all lost somebody. I think it's time to let it go."

"Maybe so. Be easier to do that if I don't see Billy Anderson around here again."

"You blame him for the Mexican?"

Coltrane nodded slowly and his eyes, cold and blue, narrowed.

Bryant met his stare for a moment then looked away, gazing toward the window. "What was he to you?"

"We rode together."

"He was just an old Mexican cattle hand."

"We rode together, and he was a man."

"Okay," Bryant said, nodding. "We all have our principles. If I were you, I'd forget about Billy Anderson. He's not the one you should be worried about."

"I suppose that would be you?"

Bryant allowed himself a thin smile. "Well, under certain circumstances perhaps, but I was thinking of the Earl boy."

"What about him?"

"He's been raising a little hell over in Wyoming. Perhaps you heard about it."

Coltrane shook his head.

"He's been keeping with some bad company since his brother got killed."

"Is that a fact?" It wasn't a question.

"Part of the Wild Bunch we think. Somebody spotted him with Harvey Logan and Will Carver last month."

"I hadn't heard."

"Last week Earl and some others knocked over a bank in Lawton. Shot a clerk. People say it was Earl that did the shooting."

"The clerk die?"

"Not yet, but he still might. He was shot in the mouth and people are saying that Earl's talking about you and the revenge he's planning for his brother. Seems like he might be the sort to back-shoot a man – or to stand behind a tree and shoot him with a rifle as he rides by."

"It's interesting that you put that idea in my head. I might have thought the same about Billy Anderson."

"Not Billy. He wouldn't do that. It's not his style, but you better watch out for Earl."

"I'll keep my eyes open."

"Or you could leave. Head off to California. Earl would forget all about you and Billy Anderson wouldn't know where to find you. You wouldn't have to worry about either of them. Why don't you go? You've been moving around all your life. What's another trail to you?"

Coltrane stared hard at Bryant. His eyes were expressionless. "You know that's not going to happen."

"I guess you can't leave because of the woman?"

Coltrane didn't move.

"You think people don't see her riding out your way? Do you think they can't count the hours she spends with you?"

Coltrane stared coldly at the sheriff, but he made no response.

Bryant took another puff off the cigar. "It's none of my business, is it? Go on, tell me that."

"Why should I? You already know it's none of your business."

"More men get themselves killed over a woman than any other reason. It happened in Pima County. Remember? Men don't think too clearly when they have a woman on their mind. They take chances they otherwise wouldn't. They get sloppy, foolish. I've seen it happen too many times. Are you any different from those other men?"

Coltrane didn't respond.

"I don't think you are. You're tough, but you're still a man."

Coltrane stood up. He brushed his hands against his thighs and stepped sideways toward the door.

"Tell me something before you go," Bryant said. "Is she worth it? Is she really worth it when you consider it all?"

Coltrane stared quietly for a long moment. "Tell Billy I see him around here again, I'll be talking to him with my Colt."

With that Coltrane stepped back out into the sunlight and rode out of Crystal at an easy trot.

Chapter Forty-One

The days went by and nothing much changed in the valley.

"Do you think people know about us?" Elisabeth asked one afternoon. They were sitting at her kitchen table with steaming cups of coffee set in front of them. Coltrane added milk to his and stirred it idly. Outside it was warmer than usual for the time of year, but the sky was overcast and a light rain had been falling all day.

Coltrane paused, staring at the cup in front of him. "Probably," he said.

"I wonder what they think."

"What would you think?"

"I would think we were lovers."

"That's why we can't continue like this."

"Let's not talk about that today."

*

"Have you seen Sheriff Bryant recently?"

"Not for several weeks."

"I'm glad."

"Why?"

"I think you're wrong about him and Billy Anderson."

"How so?"

"I think they're going to leave you alone."

Coltrane shook his head slowly. His eyes were distantly focused. "They won't."

*

"You heard there's a bounty on Gerald Earl now?"

"No."

"The Union Pacific wants him. They've hired the

Pinkertons to bring him in."

"They're tough enough."

"I know."

"What's the reward?"

"Five thousand dollars."

"Not bad."

"Dead or alive."

"Either way, that's a lot of money."

"The bank clerk died."

Coltrane sipped his coffee, finishing it. "I guess so."

"Five thousand dollars."

"There was a time when that kind of money might have got me on the trail."

"Not now?"

He shook his head.

"You're not worried about him?"

"What for?"

"He might come back."

"I think that's a story Bryant cooked up to distract me."

"You really think so?"

Coltrane nodded. "Yes."

"I'm worried."

"Don't be."

Elizabeth looked down at her coffee. She had hardly touched it and now it was cold.

*

"Can you believe the new century is almost upon us? Nineteen hundred – it has quite a ring to it."

"It makes me feel old," Coltrane replied.

"You are old."

Coltrane grinned and swatted at her.

"I'm teasing you."

"No you're not."

"Well, sometimes you do seem old fashioned. It's not the 1860s anymore. You don't even have a telephone out there."

"There's nobody I need to talk to."

"Or running water."

"The well pump works fine."

"I bet you've never even seen a moving picture."

"I've seen real life. What do I need moving pictures for?"

She shook her head in mock frustration. "Do you think you'll ever get one of those motor carriages?"

"Hard to see why I would ever need one."

Elisabeth reached across the table and covered his hand with both of hers. "Sweetheart, soon we'll be living in the modern world. You will have to adapt to it sooner or later."

Coltrane smiled. His eyes were sad and poignant as he gazed at Elisabeth.

"Somehow," he said finally. "I doubt I will."

Chapter Forty-Two

In the evening he sat out on the porch by himself. He wrapped a blanket around his shoulders and sat in the dark smoking. He thought about Anne.

*

"How many more will you have to kill?" Anne asked. Her voice was quiet. Her expression was blank, but the anger behind her words was evident.

"You know I can't answer that question."

"I know."

"That's your point, isn't it?"

"Yes."

"I can't take it anymore."

Coltrane nodded. He pulled a chair back from the table and sat down next to her. It was mid-morning and the sunlight came in brightly through the lace curtains. *"Can we talk about it?"*

"I've tried to talk about it. For years I've tried to talk about it. It never did any good."

Coltrane nodded again, aware of the sudden tightness in his gut. He waited quietly, knowing what was coming. He didn't look at her.

"You hardly sleep at night and when you do you toss and turn about. You grind your teeth so hard I think you must be about to shatter them. Sometimes you speak or cry out and I know you're dreaming again about the horrible things you have seen. There's a terrible haunting in your soul. I don't know how to soothe you."

"I'm sorry."

"Don't be sorry. I pity you."

"No…."

167

"It breaks my heart to see you that way, to know you're suffering so. If it was just that, I could stand it, I could stand by you."

"I know I'm difficult to live with."

"Yes, you are. The long silences, the moodiness, the rage. Even the coldness in your touch... I could stand all that because I love you. I do, but I can't take the killing anymore. I can't take those long periods when you're away from home and I have no idea where you are, when you're coming back to me, or even if you're still alive. Do you understand that? I can't take that anymore. That's what I can't take."

Coltrane nodded, staring down at his own hands on the table in front of him. He still did not look at her.

Anne sighed slowly and then shuddered. "I'm sorry about Juan. He was a good man. They had no right to hang him. There's nothing you can do about it now. It serves no good to blame yourself. I know you do, but you're not the one who put the rope around his neck and tightened it."

Coltrane lifted his head up and saw that tears were rolling slowly down Anne's cheeks. "I should never have left him there," he said quietly.

"You have to let go of this."

"Not yet, I don't."

"You can't kill everyone in Pima County."

"I don't have to. Just one more."

Anne shook her head. "You don't even remember why this all started."

"Yes, I do. I remember everything."

"I guess maybe you do."

"I do."

"Well... and that's too bad."

*

"I remember how happy I was the day we were married,"

Anne said after awhile.

"I was happy too," Coltrane replied.

"It was a beautiful ceremony."

"You were beautiful that day."

"I'm glad your mother was there."

"Me too."

"It was special."

"I always wondered if maybe you had wished for something different, something larger."

Anne shook her head. "I just wanted you."

Coltrane smiled at the memory and they held hands for a long moment, and after awhile he became aware that she was crying softly.

*

"When I think of you," he said, "Which I do often, I always think of you as you were when we first met. During all these years together, you haven't changed one bit in my eyes."

She smiled sadly through her tears. "You don't see the lines?"

He shrugged. "No. I only see us as we were so many years ago."

"It's hard to let go of that memory, isn't it?"

"Yes."

"And the attachment to what we were then."

"Yes."

*

"Where will you go?" he asked after awhile.

"Home. To Atlanta."

Coltrane nodded. "Will you divorce me?"

Anne shook her head. "I don't think so. I still love you. I

just can't live with you any more out here. You could come to Atlanta. I would welcome you there."

"I can't go there."

"Will you divorce me then?"

"No."

"You might change your mind later."

"I doubt it. I believe I will always love you, no matter."

"I guess I know that. I wish you could have told me more often."

Coltrane nodded.

"I wish you could have shown me more often too."

He nodded again, feeling ashamed.

"Why does it feel so bad then?"

"I guess that's its nature."

"Must it be?"

Coltrane didn't reply. After a moment he shrugged. "Where does that leave us?" he asked.

At first she just shook her head, unable to speak as she struggled to hold back her sobs. "Simply broken hearted," she managed after several moments had passed.

*

The temperature dropped sharply about midnight. Inside the blanket he began to feel the cold. He stood up, pulling the blanket tighter around himself and walked to the edge of the porch. For a long moment he stood there, staring up at the wide clear Utah sky, so bright with starlight, thinking of all the words he should have said to Anne so long ago.

A little later he thought about the fact that he also loved another woman – and with a passion he had never known before, and he felt deeply ashamed. He turned to go inside the cabin, knowing sleep was still a long way off.

Chapter Forty-Three

It had rained during the early part of the morning. Now the sky was a soft gray and there were brief moments when the sun came through. They walked down the path together, holding hands, not speaking. The ground was soft and wet.

When they reached the meadow there were puddles of mud and water to step over. In his pocket Coltrane carried a piece of paper with a few words he wanted to say. His throat felt dry and he had that tight feeling in his stomach.

Elisabeth kept looking at him with those eyes, which made him feel very weak. He squeezed her hand and she squeezed back, looking at him. His throat really did feel quite dry.

"Right here," Elisabeth announced finally. She stopped at the top of a slight rise in the ground where the earth was firmer.

Coltrane stepped up close to her, facing her. He still held her hand tightly. "I have something to say," he told her.

Elisabeth shook her head, as if she didn't trust her voice to speak. She looked up at him and waited. He fumbled with the paper, unfolding it slowly. Above them the clouds shifted and then they were standing in a bright beam of sunlight that played down around them.

Time seemed to slow and there was only the two of them, standing there together and Coltrane suddenly became aware of how nervous he felt. He cleared his voice and read silently from the paper to himself, and then he folded it and put it back inside his pocket.

His throat was dry.

When he spoke, his voice choked back several times with the emotion that swelled within him. After a few minutes, he stopped talking and looked at Elisabeth. Her eyes were large and moist. She squeezed his hand.

After Coltrane said the words he looked at Elisabeth, thinking how incredibly beautiful she looked with those big eyes. He waited for her to speak.

"I'm overwhelmed," Elisabeth began.

"You don't have to say anything."

"Yes, I do." Her voice was shaking with emotion and in the end she said nothing. Instead, she squeezed his hand again and then kissed him quickly on the side of the mouth. Before she could step away, he pulled her body tight against his and held her for a long moment without moving, feeling her warm breath against his ear.

"Now what?" he asked afterwards. The sun had disappeared again and black clouds hung thickly overhead.

Elisabeth smiled. "I think we should head back before it starts raining again."

*

Later they sat on his porch watching the downpour.

"It was incredible," Elisabeth said. She shook her head slowly.

They looked out across the fields, silently watching the rain come down in sheets from the dark, dark sky.

Chapter Forty-Four

"Everything feels different now," Elisabeth said carefully.

Coltrane didn't say anything. He just waited with the tightness gripping his stomach.

"Thomas was looking for me that day."

Coltrane nodded, waiting.

"He came home mid-afternoon. He was upset I wasn't there. He was very worried about me. Remember how hard it stormed that day?"

"What did you tell him?"

"I told him I went out riding and got caught in the storm. I told him I took shelter in a barn until it passed over. I don't think he believed me entirely. I was so nervous, I'm sure he sensed something was wrong. I felt very bad about it."

"Did he say anything?"

She pursed her lips and her eyes moved away from his. "Thomas is starting to know about us, our past... I felt sick to my stomach, literally sick to my stomach when he asked me where I was. You should have seen the painful look in his eyes."

Coltrane felt the distance between them and pushed himself back from the table. He stood up.

"I guess I should be riding on," he said. He put his hat on and walked out the door without looking back.

Elisabeth didn't move from her seat at the table.

Chapter Forty-Five

A few weeks later Elisabeth told Coltrane that she had to stop seeing him entirely. Coltrane was not surprised. It had been coming since that moment on the porch with the rain pouring down around them.

"Are you okay?" she asked afterwards. Her tone was more irritated than concerned.

"I will be." His tone was cold.

"I wish you'd say something."

"If you really want to hear..." he said quietly.

"You don't owe me anything; there isn't anything I can expect from you. You don't have a commitment to me, and I don't have one to you. I'm married to Thomas now. There isn't anything you have to give me. You've never sacrificed anything for me." The edge to her voice remained steady. She was angry.

Coltrane nodded, not knowing what to say.

"I'm married now to Thomas – he's the one who made the commitment to me. At least with him I have a husband."

Coltrane bit down hard, tightening his jaw. Her words dismissed everything between them.

"None of this has made any sense. You know that. I'm married to Thomas and here I am making love with you, feeling totally overwhelmed by the thoughts and feelings I'm having only with you. The most incredible emotional experience of my life is with you, and we don't even belong to each other and there's nobody I can talk to about it. It's not right. I can't continue doing this. I have to think about my child."

"I've never suggested it was right – and remember, we stopped making love for that very reason. You're a married woman now, and I respect that."

"How do you live with it?"

"I just do, because I have to and I've accepted the balance all this means."

"I don't know how I can continue. I felt so ashamed and so guilty when Thomas asked me where I was that day."

Coltrane nodded. The reality of the change between them was clear.

Elisabeth caught her breath. "If Thomas finds out about our closeness, he would leave me. I have no doubt of that and I would lose you too eventually, to one cause or another. I don't want to be alone. I don't want to raise my child alone."

"Why are you so sure you would lose me too?"

"We both know."

"I don't know…"

Elisabeth shook her head. "That day in the meadow – you didn't even leave your gun at home."

Chapter Forty-Six

Coltrane had time on his hands. With an effort that was almost tireless, he turned back toward working the land again. He worked sixteen, eighteen hours a day, sleeping very little. The work felt good, even when it exhausted him.

It was an effective distraction and it accomplished things that no one could take away from him. Once an acre of crops was planted, a ham smoked, a calf birthed, a moose shot, it could not be undone, and in the evening, with the setting of the sun and the first drink of whiskey, Coltrane would stand out on his porch gazing out at the land knowing that he had finished good, hard work. The drink brought a measure of relief.

It was the work again. In the work he began to find hope of redemption, knowing that he was walking his own path, taking care of himself, and that was entirely in a decent and honest way. In that way the work felt like a blessing, every blister and bruise on his hands a benediction.

As with days from his past, when he had been riding the trail hard, he was not thinking about the desperation that filled his soul, focusing only on the moment to moment, surviving each hour, each day as it came, not looking ahead or behind.

In the evening, after rinsing the dirt of the field off his hands, he poured a strong drink of whiskey and always drank the first one quickly, then the second and subsequent ones slowly. The immediate burning sensation as he swallowed the first ounces of the harsh whiskey reassured him that the numbness was not far behind.

When he felt the glassiness in his eyes he began to relax into it, knowing that another night was almost there, and would then soon be over and another day, another chance to work the land, would start. He smoked his cigarettes slowly, deliberately, relishing the feel of the warm tobacco smoke in his throat.

When he ate, he ate simply: corn mush and bacon, canned fruit preserves, boiled cabbage, smoked meats. He would sit with the plate on his lap, bench tipped back on the porch, feet on the railing, chewing absently as he stared out over the wide land that was greening before him in the pale dusk.

Often, after setting the plate aside he stood leaning against the rail for long periods, letting the sky grow dark around him, watching as the silhouettes of the trees faded gradually into the night and the glow of the stars above intensified and spread out silently, ceaselessly.

In the loneliest of moments, shortly after the darkness had settled, after the last faint streaks of purple had disappeared beyond the mountains, he promised himself he would not give in to it, was not lonely in the way that another man would have been.

There was only the noise of the crickets and the occasional sigh or braying of the mares to remind him of the other creatures in the universe. He drank the whiskey with carefully paced sips, making promises to himself that seemed reasonable in the darkness, only to have them slip away long before the emergence of the merciful dawn.

*

The letter from Anne arrived mid-way through the fifth week. It was waiting for him at Ryan's. He had not heard from her in over two months and he had not written to her in over five. He did not read the letter right away. Instead he put it in his pocket, ignoring Ryan's questions.

He bought his flour, sugar, and shotgun shells without comment. The sun was shining hard when he came out onto the street to load up the buckboard. He rode all the way home before tearing the envelope open and even then he did not read it right away.

As the sky settled over slowly, he set the letter on the table

177

and poured himself a drink of whiskey, knowing that it was too early to start drinking, but not caring enough to wait. It was still only late afternoon and the mares needed tending.

He drank the whiskey, emptying the glass in one drought. Then he poured himself another and put the cork back in the jug. Outside he heard the sounds of the mares shuffling about. Bobby-Lee was uncomfortable in the harness rig still attached to the buckboard.

Coltrane stood there on his porch with the whiskey sensation burning down inside him. He ignored the discomfort of the mares and picked up the letter. He stepped over to the light of the window and read it carefully.

My Dearest,

I have not heard from you in a long time, the longest since our separation. That means you are either dead or have found someone new in your life. I fear it is the former, but hope for the latter. If you are still alive, please write to me. I must know. If you have found someone else, I would understand.

My love, Anne

It was only one thin piece of paper, most of it unused, and it was the shortest letter she had ever written him. Coltrane folded the letter carefully and then set it into the fireplace. For a long time he watched as it burned.

When it was no more than a frail black sheet of ash he stabbed at it with an iron poker and it crumbled to nothingness. He turned away from the fireplace, away from the heat, and poured another drink of whiskey into his glass. He would write to her. It could no longer be avoided. He knew that and he felt deeply ashamed as he thought about it.

With the glass of whiskey in his hand he stepped out onto the porch and watched the mares while he drank. They stood still now, waiting patiently for him. When he was finished drinking, Coltrane set the glass on the first step and went down to them. They lowered their heads to his face, sighing hot breath into his ears. He rubbed their muzzles and ears.

"My sweethearts," he said softly.

Bobby-Lee rubbed her forehead against his chin; Rosalita nuzzled the back of his neck.

"Let's go on into the barn, girls," he said quietly after some time had passed.

They followed him. He took their harnesses off and began to brush them, still thinking of Anne.

*

Her body was poised above his. She was muscular from the hard work and yet soft to his touch. They moved together, carefully at first, then more urgently, the rhythm familiar after so many years. She understood his needs and he understood hers. Her eyes were closed, and then half open, staring without seeing towards the ceiling.

Coltrane looked at her body. He studied her pale skin in the firelight of the room. His hands touched her lightly along the curve of her spine and his fingertips brushed over the gentle contours of her hips. They each breathed heavier as they sensed the pace of the other.

With a half cry Coltrane wrapped his arms around her, pushed her back, sideways, rolling her over so that he was on top now, slowing the pace. His mouth hovered lightly above hers. He kissed her on the mouth, then the cheek. Their eyes locked for one long moment and then Anne closed hers. She arched her back suddenly, then stiffened and held still.

Afterward, they lay in bed holding hands tightly, not speaking for the longest time. The fire burned itself out and the room became dark. The only light was the glow of the moon and the stars that spilled in through the window, reflected off the lake.

Anne rolled towards him, hugging him tightly. Her face

was snug against his cheek. She sighed and Coltrane felt the moisture between them, unsure if the tears were hers or his.

"You're leaving tomorrow, aren't you," he whispered.

"Yes," she said in the dark. "You know I have to."

"This was the last time."

"Yes."

A loon called from somewhere on the other side of the lake. Its cry was lonely and serene and then the night was entirely silent.

*

After he put the mares away, Coltrane went inside and wrote the letter to Anne that he knew he had to write. It took him two hours to compose, though it filled up only two pieces of paper. He sealed the envelope and set it next to his hat.

*

Early the next morning the apparition reappeared.

It was sitting on the foot of Coltrane's bed when he awoke at dawn. Coltrane rolled over onto his side, blinking, rubbing his eyes, waiting. The first streaks of gray light hovered over the horizon, punching faint shadows into the cabin.

Out past the barn, a rooster was crowing and the cows were making restless noises. Sometime in the night the fire had gone out. The morning air was cool and Coltrane realized he was shivering. He lay still and waited. The ghost moved toward him, hovering.

"Am I going crazy?" Coltrane asked out loud.

The apparition did not respond.

"I thought you had left," Coltrane said.

The ghost of Wild Bill Hickok shook his head slowly.

His eyes were sad and sympathetic. For a moment he

lingered without attempting to speak or gesture.

Then he slowly faded into the gathering sunlight as the force of day arrived and Coltrane was alone again.

Chapter Forty-Seven

In the pink light of dawn Coltrane saddled Bobby-Lee and headed into Crystal to mail the letter.

*

On his way home Coltrane found Elisabeth waiting for him just off the road, a mile past her house. She sat in the saddle of her mount, speckled grey, shaded by an aspen grove. She wore black leather riding boots, a pair of black gloves, a black skirt with subtle gray pin stripes, and a black calico blouse that was open at the throat. On her head she wore a black Stetson with the chinstrap drawn up tightly. Coltrane felt his stomach tighten.

"You weren't going to stop by," she said. It wasn't a question. She urged her horse towards the road as Coltrane waited quietly for her to climb up the embankment. Bobby-Lee stood motionless, her ears back.

"No. I wasn't."

"Are you angry?"

"I didn't think you wanted to see me, didn't think it was right."

"It's been over five weeks."

"How are you?"

"Well, enough, I'm starting to show a little."

"Just a little perhaps."

"Can I ride a little ways with you?"

Coltrane shrugged. "I don't see that I can stop you."

They rode a short way without speaking. The horses moved slowly, sensing the mood of the riders. It was late morning and the sky had become overcast. Light fog floated along the road, holding especially to the low areas off to their right.

*

"It's been difficult," Elisabeth said.

"Yes," Coltrane replied. "It has been for me too."

"Do you mind terribly seeing me right now?"

"You look as beautiful as ever."

"That's not what I meant."

"Usually people say 'thank you' when they receive a compliment."

"Thank you."

"I wish you didn't. Maybe it would be easier."

*

A quarter mile from his cabin Coltrane pulled up and waited for Elisabeth to turn her mount.

"Are you coming all the way home with me?" he asked.

"Do you want me to?"

He shrugged. "I don't think it's a good idea."

Elisabeth stared down at the ground. Her eyes were serious. "No," she said, tilting her chin back and up. "I'd like to talk to you, though."

"Then let's ride up there." Coltrane pointed toward the Wasatch Range.

Elisabeth shook her head. "I'm not feeling up to that today. Can we sit on your porch?"

Coltrane sat quietly for a moment. "I'm not sure I'd trust myself."

Elisabeth smiled sadly. "I won't take advantage."

"Sure you won't." Coltrane smiled thinly for the first time since seeing her.

*

Elisabeth perched on a stall railing in the barn, while Coltrane brushed Bobby-Lee and fed her a pile of oats. Her own mount, the speckled grey, was tethered near a trough and was drinking rapidly.

"I'm torn," she said. "I've wanted to talk with you, wanted to explain."

"You don't need to explain. As you said that day, we don't owe each other anything."

Elisabeth sighed. "That didn't come out right. I didn't mean it that way."

"You said it that way."

"I'm sorry if I hurt you."

"You did what you had to do. Somebody had to get hurt. We both knew that."

"Do you regret being with me?"

Coltrane stopped brushing for a moment, his eyes held still on the mare. "How could I regret loving you?"

Elisabeth smiled. "I wish we could have two paths in life."

"So do I."

She nodded.

Coltrane started brushing again, moving in long, slow arcs across the mare's side. "But we can't, so we have to make our best choices for the one path we have."

"I'd like to tell you something about Thomas, to help you understand."

"There's no need."

"I'd like to."

"I don't want to hear it. Thomas is a good man. There's no need to explain. I'm sure you've made the right decision. He loves you too and he's likely to be around much longer for you."

Coltrane resumed brushing and neither one of them had anything more to say.

Chapter Forty-Eight

Thomas Hyde rode up to Coltrane's cabin in the late afternoon. The sky was wide and the sunlight bright. A quiet breeze filtered through.

Coltrane was seated on the porch. The bench was tipped back and he had his feet up on the rail. He smoked slowly. He had watched Thomas approach for several minutes now and had checked the Colt under his arm. He was already on the third whiskey of the day.

Without saying a word Thomas dismounted and tethered his horse to the bottom railing that ran along the side of the porch. He climbed the steps and Coltrane held out the whiskey bottle without saying a word.

"Thanks," Thomas said and tipped the bottle back. He drank a long swallow, grimaced, and then took a second, smaller drink before handing the bottle back. He eyes were tired and beads of sweat formed along his hairline. He sat down on the bench.

"Congratulations," Coltrane said.

Thomas stared blankly at him. He wiped at his mouth with the tips of his fingers.

Coltrane studied his eyes. "Elisabeth told me you are going to be a father."

"Am I?"

"That's what she told me. Didn't you know?"

Thomas shrugged noncommittally. "Does she love you?"

"What are you talking about?"

"I know she was out here today. I know you two are close. People talk. I've heard things."

Coltrane shrugged and then shook his head. "She loves you."

"Maybe so, but I'm asking if she loves you as well."

"I'm telling you that she loves you and that's all you should be concerned about."

"Is it?"

"Don't you think you should leave it at that?"

"And the child?"

"What about it?"

"I'll always wonder."

"That's foolishness."

"Is it?"

Coltrane looked at him, studying his face carefully. He looked down at his hands as he rolled another cigarette and nodded his head solemnly.

"You seem more certain than I am," Thomas said.

Coltrane lighted the cigarette and exhaled with deliberation. "Let me tell you something, son. There's enough heartache in life as it is. Don't go letting your imagination make any extra portion of it for you."

"I'm asking you as a man, is there a chance that you're the father?"

"No," Coltrane said without pause. "None at all."

Thomas thought about this for a long moment. His eyes looked out over the land, absently focused on some point off in the far distance. "Can you spare another sip?" he asked after awhile.

Coltrane handed the bottle over. "Help yourself," he said.

Thomas took two gulps from the bottle and then wiped his mouth with the back of his hand. When he was finished drinking, he replaced the cork and leaned over to set the bottle at Coltrane's feet.

"There's another reason I came out here this afternoon," Thomas said presently.

Coltrane grunted. He continued to smoke slowly.

"Billy Anderson arrived back in town last night. I asked Bryant about it, but he wouldn't tell me anything. I don't like the way they're acting."

Coltrane nodded without speaking.

"I just thought you ought to know. I don't think they're

planning to do any riding tonight."

Coltrane nodded again. "I appreciate it. I really do."

Thomas stood up and started down the steps. When he reached his horse he looked back up at Coltrane and paused. "I'm hoping Elisabeth won't ever have to know that we had this talk."

"She'll never hear it from me."

Thomas' eyes didn't waver for a long moment. Then he nodded and mounted the horse. "Thanks for the drink," he said before turning the horse and spurring it to a gallop.

Coltrane raised his glass at the receding figure. "Good luck, kid," he said much too quietly for the rider to hear.

Chapter Forty-Nine

That evening Coltrane thought about what was coming. For a while he sat on the porch smoking and thinking about what he needed to do. When the second cigarette was gone he went inside the cabin and lit all the lamps that he had.

It was time to clean his weapons. He started with the shotgun. After he broke it open he oiled the parts carefully and cleaned the barrels even though they were not dirty. When he was satisfied, he loaded both barrels and put the gun back in its rack before starting with the Remington. He worked quietly and efficiently.

He spent the most time on the revolver, carefully oiling the cylinder and pushing small patches of cloth through the barrel. It was a ritual for him. He understood this as much as he understood the necessity for the gun.

He didn't have to think about anything while he worked. His awareness was not focused on the task or even on Billy Anderson. No decisions were contemplated. The passing of time was not noticed. He simply cleaned the guns, allowing his mind to rest easily while he worked.

Once he was satisfied with the barrel and the action on the Colt he loaded it, putting a cartridge into each one of the six chambers. Then, from a shelf in the back of the cabin he brought down several boxes of ammunition and a leather pouch that held shotgun shells.

Working slowly still he rechecked the loads in the rifle and the shotgun. With his thumb he flicked open the smallest ammunition box and began refilling his gun belt, placing a .45 caliber cartridge in each of the empty loops, inspecting each one carefully before he placed it. The stocks of the rifle and shotgun each had ammunition bands as well. He filled these next, putting eight cartridges on the Winchester and five shells on the shotgun.

Finally, he replaced the Colt in its holster, pulled it on

over his shoulder, secured the long guns in their wall racks, and looked around the small cabin. He stood there for a long moment.

In the dim light of the fire and the kerosene lamp he studied the books on the shelf. There was the literature of Cooper, Shakespeare, Longfellow, Twain; memoirs of Grant, Longstreet, Gordon, Chamberlain; biographies of Napoleon, Washington, Jefferson; speeches of Lincoln, Davis, Hancock; the Holy Bible. Most of these he had read. A few he had not, and now knew he never would.

He paced the length of the room, holding the lamp before him at eye-level, stopping at the small chest of drawers in the corner. The lamp balanced easily on the chest and he pulled out the top drawer.

From between two folded shirts he carefully removed his only photograph of Anne. It was held in a heavy silver frame. He studied the image of the woman carefully, smiling as he felt her beauty and her presence, and he was glad that he had already written and mailed the letter to her. He stared at the photograph for a long time and his eyes filled slowly with tears.

Without thinking consciously about it he stepped out onto the porch, carrying the photograph with him. He stood there; looking out into the darkness with the stars gleaming brightly overhead and he knew without any doubt in his soul what the next day would bring.

*

For six straight blessed hours that night Coltrane got the best sleep he'd had in months. Anne's photograph and the Colt were clutched on the bed next to him. He awoke before dawn, in that very still moment just before the roosters began to call, and looked about the room. The vague reflection of the apparition moved across and settled at the foot of his bed.

"Bill Hickok," Coltrane said softly. "Why do you come to me?"

The figure didn't appear to speak, but Coltrane heard the words anyway. "I think you know."

"There is nothing left for me to do."

"You can leave here."

"I can't do that."

"You can leave and go to her."

"I won't leave. This is my land."

"Don't use the gun."

"I don't know any other way."

"There can be tenderness."

"It's too late."

"No. It is not."

"I don't know that way."

"You have learned."

"I cannot escape my past, anymore than you could."

"You can learn from me."

Coltrane shook his head. "I cannot escape this – it will find me no matter where I go."

The apparition nodded sadly and fell silent.

For a long time they sat there together until the light of day began to sift over the horizon and the ghost of Wild Bill Hickok faded slowly into the pink glow of the morning.

Coltrane sat up in bed and he knew it was time.

Chapter Fifty

It was still early in the morning when Elisabeth arrived. She rode in at a gallop and came up very close to the porch. She did not dismount. Coltrane was standing on the porch, sipping a cup of coffee. Both the rifle and the shotgun were near his reach, leaning against the rail, unsheathed.

He was freshly shaved and washed. His gray hair was combed back neatly and he did not wear a hat. He wore his best white shirt and the heavy leather gun belt was looped over his shoulder blades, carefully tied in place.

"You have to leave immediately!" Elisabeth shouted. "They're coming for you."

Coltrane set his coffee cup down on the porch railing and picked up both long guns, one in each hand. "Ride away, Elisabeth," he said calmly. He started down the steps towards her.

Instead of turning the horse, she dismounted quickly and stepped towards Coltrane, allowing the reins of the speckled grey to fall unattended to the ground. "You don't understand," she said. Her voice was agitated, louder now than it needed to be.

"It's okay."

"There are eight of them. They're not more than fifteen or twenty minutes behind me."

"Hold on."

"Sheriff Bryant and Billy Anderson came by our house this morning to get Thomas. They had five other riders with them, including Gerald Earl and one of his partners. They've been deputized to arrest you!"

Coltrane smiled thinly. "He deputized wanted men?"

"Please go! You have time. You can get away."

His eyes narrowed and a muscle in his jaw twitched. "Elisabeth, you must know that I'm not leaving."

"Please!" Elisabeth looked at him. Her eyes pleaded

silently as they filled with tears.

Coltrane shook his head slowly, and then he turned to rest the long guns against the steps. When he turned back to face Elisabeth his eyes had softened. "Come here. I don't want you to worry. Hold me for a minute."

"I don't understand."

"Just for a minute," he said. His voice was reassuring, his expression relaxed.

Elisabeth put her arms around him, holding him tightly. He squeezed her back for a moment, letting his cheek fall down against hers. "I don't want you to be upset," he whispered in her ear.

"You still have time to get away," she replied softly.

"I'm not leaving. This is my land, my home. Nobody will force me off it."

"I love you."

"I know you do."

"I don't want to lose you."

"Hush." He brushed his lips against her cheek and for another moment they stood silently, swaying together with the Wasatch Mountain range looming silently over them in the distance.

*

Coltrane heard the riders first and pulled back from Elisabeth to look over her shoulder. She let her arms drop to her sides and turned to look back the way he was facing. There were eight of them, still almost a half-mile away.

"Please, go away from here," Coltrane said.

"Only if you go too."

"I can't do that."

"Then I'm staying as well."

Coltrane looked around for a moment. "Let's go to the barn. You can stay with the mares."

192

He picked up the long guns, grabbed the reins of the grey, and walked unhurriedly over to the barn. Elisabeth followed him. Inside the barn Coltrane opened a stall and led the horse in, pointing toward a stool at the back of the stall for Elisabeth.

"Sit here," he said.

Elisabeth sat down and started to shiver. Coltrane knelt beside her and cupped one of her hands in his, studying her face, noting every detail. It was the most beautiful face he had ever seen. "I don't want you to worry," he said. "It is time. There's nothing anyone can do now. This must follow its course."

"I can't bear the thought of being without you."

"We knew this wasn't going to last forever. I believe you know I'll always be with you."

"And I with you." Elisabeth tried to smile.

"There's one last thing," Coltrane said.

"What is it?" she asked between halting breaths.

"I left something for you on my table," he told her quietly. "It's a letter granting you my estate. There are instructions that direct you to a lawyer in Provo. He will handle everything and no one needs to know. The proceeds may be useful to you one day – or to your child."

"Our child."

"No. Your child with Thomas. That's the way it has to be – don't ever let anyone else ever think otherwise."

"Oh no," she sighed.

"Yes, sweetheart."

Coltrane kissed the back of her delicate hand and then held it against his cheek for a moment. He stood up, moving away from her to the front of the stall.

Elisabeth was weeping softly now. "Thomas is with them," she said quietly. Her wet eyes were down.

"I know," Coltrane replied.

"He didn't want to ride with them, but it's his job."

"I know that too."

"I couldn't bear it if he was killed either."

"Shhhh," Coltrane hushed. "I know that." His tone was not unkind. "I don't want you to worry."

Elisabeth nodded. "What are you going to do?"

"The only thing I can do." He said the words gently as he stroked her cheek. "Please take care of the mares for me."

*

Coltrane turned away and walked to the far end of the barn. He could hear the riders clearly. They were very close now and were moving slowly, cautiously. Coltrane stepped out of the barn and stood behind a low split rail fence with his shoulder next to the corner of the barn.

He held the double-barrel shotgun in his hands, the muzzle pointed toward the ground, and watched the men approach. They were fanned out about ten feet apart from each other, with Bryant and Billy Anderson in the middle. Thomas Hyde was in the line, near the end on Coltrane's right, and Gerald Earl rode at his far left. Most of the men carried Henry rifles or Remington's as they approached.

Coltrane stood still and waited in plain sight. When they were thirty yards away from him they stopped. Everyone except Earl dismounted and stood in front of their horse with the muzzle of their rifle pointed downward.

Earl rode several steps past the line and stared fiercely at Coltrane as he leaned over the pommel. He did not speak and after Coltrane returned his gaze without flinching for a long moment Earl looked away and began to cough.

Chapter Fifty-One

"Gentlemen," Coltrane said in an even voice. "It's a beautiful day in the fine state of Utah."

"It is indeed," Bryant said loudly across the distance between them. "You look splendid this morning, sir."

"What brings you out my way?"

Bryant nodded once and tipped the bowler hat back on his head. He was wearing the expensive kid gloves. The gold watch chain glinted in the sunlight. "We have a warrant for your arrest for the murder of Duval Bond in Texas. Will you come quietly with us, sir?"

"Duval was killed a long time ago."

"According to this warrant, he was murdered by you," Anderson said. "In cold blood. There are two witnesses who will testify to that."

Coltrane smiled grimly and shook his head, dismissing this comment. "Bryant, are you deputizing wanted men now?"

"I was afraid we might need every available gun to bring you in. I figured they're the lesser of two evils."

"Do you really intend to arrest me?"

"Yes."

"For trial in Texas?"

"Arizona."

"Are you sure? Because I see Billy Anderson with you and I figure you might aim to hang me from a tree right off, rather than take me all the way back to Arizona. Isn't that how it went with Roderiquez?"

Anderson's face reddened and he couldn't restrain himself. "That damn Mexican got what he had coming to him!"

"We mean to take you in for trial," Bryant said, interrupting, without glancing at Billy Anderson. "You have my word on that."

Coltrane nodded.

"Will you put your gun down and come with us now, sir?"

Coltrane appeared to think about it for a moment, and then shook his head. "Reckon I can't do that."

Bryant rubbed his chin thoughtfully. "You can't possibly mean to shoot with all of us standing against you."

"I won't have to if you leave."

"You know we're not going to do that."

"I reckon so."

"What does that leave?"

"It's up to you now."

"You're good, but you're not that good. You must know that."

"We'll know soon enough."

Bryant frowned and looked down the line at the men on his left. Gerald Earl's horse snorted, and moved back a step. Above them a hawk soared across the sky. Billy Anderson moved first. He brought the muzzle of his Henry rifle up and fired off his hip.

The shot went wide and Coltrane let loose with the shotgun. The blast caught Anderson in the chest, slamming him backwards with a force. Some of the shot scattered and hit the next man over in the neck. He went down too, with his hands clutching at his throat.

With the first shot most of the horses broke and the men scattered. Earl's horse reared back, and then lunged forward. The only man who did not flinch was Coltrane. He swiveled quickly, aimed the shotgun at Gerald Earl, and let go with the second barrel. Both rider and horse went down in a spray of red.

Coltrane dropped the shotgun and grabbed the Winchester. Still standing beside the barn he levered off three fast shots. They hit Earl's partner in the chest and stomach and he dropped backwards. Then Coltrane was moving. He dove sideways, away from the barn. Rolling past the fence, he drew the Colt in one motion.

Still lying on his side he squeezed off two shots, hitting

the deputy on the far right twice in the chest, and then he was moving again.

A series of shots hit the fence and the frame of the barn, near where he had been standing moments before. Coltrane ran a short ways along the fence, fired once, and then ducked down.

"Coltrane!" Bryant screamed.

Gun smoke gathered over the small field in front of the barn. Horses dashed from the confusion. Coltrane took a deep breath, counted to three, exhaled, and then took another deep breath, listening for a lull. When it came he reared up and leaped over the fence.

He was almost hit by a horse that came towards him, galloping hard, then veered off at the last second with loose reins flapping behind. A figure behind a puff of smoke shouted and turned towards Coltrane, bringing around the muzzle of a rifle. Coltrane brought the Colt up first and his finger tightened on the trigger.

There was another shout and the man's face appeared through the smoke. For just the thinnest of seconds Coltrane froze. It was young Thomas Hyde. Their eyes met and everything slowed in that moment.

Bryant came out through the smoke beside Hyde, firing twice as he dodged forward. Both shots hit Coltrane in the lower part of the chest, knocking him back a step. For a moment he stood there breathing heavily, staring at the two men through the smoke. With a flick of his wrist he tossed the Colt away from where he stood and then he fell over onto the ground and rolled onto his side.

Echoes of shots continued to ring through the valley. Somewhere a horse whimpered in pain and a man's voice cried out in anguish.

"Jesus," Coltrane heard one of the deputy's say. "He killed five of us." Then his world began to narrow and all sounds became slowly muted.

He felt like he was floating.

Chapter Fifty-Two

Coltrane laid staring up at the warm sun, blinking, and struggling to breathe. He thought about Anne, thought about Elisabeth, knowing he should never have loved like he did, never have given up so much of himself, never have allowed the emotion and the pain to have brought him to this point; and yet despite all that he still loved, would do it all over again if he could, still loved so deeply that it was the only pain he could feel, the pain of love spreading through him so that nothing else mattered, not even the wounds that were bleeding his life away.

The ghosts of Wild Bill Hickok, Roderiquez, and so many of the others, some in gray, some in blue, seemed to pass over him as dark shadows in a spreading twilight. Then Elisabeth was beside him, kneeling, cradling his head against her, shielding his eyes from the sunlight, rocking silently. Heavy tears filled her eyes and ran down her cheeks.

She ignored the calls of her husband who was moaning her name, pleading with her to come away, and in that moment Coltrane felt the warmth, the quiet that is possible for all souls. Their eyes locked and their hands gripped tightly, understanding what the moment meant and all they were losing. They had been together before and would meet again and again until maybe in some distant tender world they got it right.

No words passed between them.

Above them the hawk soared across the wide, wide Utah sky.

Clouds floated over, obscuring the sun. The cool valley breeze became still and then he started to fade, smiling faintly as he looked up into her moist eyes, realizing now that his season was at hand.

THE COLD ARDENNES

Hitler's Ardennes Offensive in December 1944 caught the Allies by total surprise and pushed their lines back dramatically, such that American newspapers dubbed it the "Battle of the Bulge." German Panzer divisions and 450,000 troops attacked a weakly defended sector of the Allied line, taking advantage of heavy snowfall and overcast weather conditions that grounded the Allies' air forces. However, determined resistance around Eisenborn Ridge and the small town of Bastogne, prevented German access to critical roads and disrupted their offensive schedule, providing time for the Allies to regroup and the weather conditions to improve. The offensive was a last desperate gambit for Nazi Germany, though with 89,000 American causalities it was the largest and bloodiest battle fought by the U.S. during World War II.

Chapter One

Late summer 1945

The roads between the small towns in Texas seem to go on forever, especially if you are on a Greyhound. I sat in the front right row, staring ahead over the headlamp beams that cut into the night ahead of us.

I'd been riding for hours and had run out of things I wanted to think about, so I focused on the driver. He was a tiny man with stringy hair, a burn scar on his cheek, and a low jaw that seemed to grower slacker by the hour. He didn't smoke or chew gum and I had to question his character for that. I wondered why he wasn't as miserable as most of his passengers. He seemed oblivious to the hour, while they were a tired group, country folk mostly, hanging over their seats into the aisle, not talking to each other or managing to sleep.

If I took the most charitable view, it was possible to believe that maybe the driver was damaged goods. I had to let him have that because that was how plenty of people had come to see me. I considered that for a while as I sat by myself in the darkness. He had never asked my name, where I was from, or what I'd just come home from. He didn't care and he wasn't interested in knowing.

A lot of guys were coming home now and they all had their stories. Stories were a dime a dozen. Everyone knew that. By now, we'd heard them all and we were all tired of them. My story wasn't special either and I wasn't going to bother anyone with it.

Listening to the rattling drone of the bus as the miles rolled away, I drew a slow breath, paused, and then exhaled forcefully. I didn't want to talk to anybody about my past, and I sure as hell didn't want to know about theirs. That's probably how the driver felt by now. I couldn't blame him. He'd probably heard it all and then some. I pushed that thought away to stare out the window at the flat lands, waiting for the glow of the lights that had to be there, somehow, up ahead. I couldn't see them yet.

Eventually, the creaking bus slowed near a desolate spot just outside of Monahans, shortly past the sign that said population 3,944. It's a town no one outside of the Odessa area has ever heard of, the seat of Ward County, Texas, though part of the town is actually in Winkler County. It was heat-crackled territory where the Comanche and Mescalero once roamed some seventy years ago.

I glanced at the old field watch I wore strapped to my wrist. It was a few minutes after three o'clock in the morning, but that didn't bother me because I wasn't sleepy anyway. My body felt disoriented and I hadn't slept much since getting off the ship. The driver called the stop just as we reached it, though I was standing on the first step down toward the door with the duffel over my shoulder by the time we came to a full halt.

When the door screeched open I was out onto the gravel shoulder of the road, kicking at the dust. The bus was already rolling again by the time I turned around, before the door even fully closed. For a moment I saw the driver's disinterested face in the glow of the cab lights. His eyes stared down the lonely road ahead of him.

Suddenly I was alone.

There was nobody there to greet me. Nobody knew I was coming home. I wasn't even sure myself who was left. Sally had long since broken things off; Johnny was probably still in jail; and my brother had fallen with a lot of other Marines on some Pacific island I didn't even know how to pronounce. My old mother was probably still in the same run down house I'd grown up in, though it had been four months since her last postcard and only the Lord knew how long since her last day of sobriety.

There was no reason to hurry.

I dropped my bag onto the gravel and lighted a cigarette. Now I only had four left, but I didn't worry about that. The air was hot and muggy – real, real hot – but I didn't mind that either. Anything was better than the bitter cold. My frostbiten toes still hurt and they reminded where I'd been. For a while I stood there with old thoughts. They weren't pleasant and I shook my head against them, trying to shake them from me. That didn't help.

I leaned into the night and reminded myself where I was. Europe was a long way behind me. The memories rolled on anyway like a lousy B-movie. For a good while, I stood there with them, tolerating them, waiting. Then I decided maybe that wasn't such a good idea and that I should let them wash away on their own. I tried to smile at that thought as I let it play out.

In the distance I could see lights, probably a gas station at the edge of the city. I didn't mind walking. I'd done enough of that over the past year that a two mile walk into town didn't bother me at all – even if I didn't really know where I was going or what I would do when I got there.

When I finished my cigarette, I decided not to think about the past I'd left behind. After all, it was just that, right? It was the past – it was over, finished, kaput. I reminded myself for the thousandth time: there was nothing to be gained by dwelling on it.

I picked up my duffel and started walking toward the lights.

Chapter Two

The morning was gray and tired.

"What are you gonna do?" she asked.

"I don't know, Ma, whatever there is to do."

"Don'tcha have a plan?"

"Didn't expect to ever need one."

"What's that supposed to mean?"

"They have newspapers here? Maybe you heard about the war."

"Don't sass me, son of mine. I'm still mourning your brother, may he rest in peace. They never even recovered his body. It's out there somewhere in the mud and sand, ten thousand miles away from here, in the jungle of some tiny, meaningless island. Who ever heard of Peleliu?"

To avoid the sour expression on her face, I looked down at my plate and didn't say anything. The egg she had fried for me had tasted fine, but the toast had mold on it and there was no butter. We were sitting at the old table in the kitchen. It was really just a board propped up on cinder blocks with a stained gray cloth spread over it.

She'd let me in when I'd knocked just after six o'clock in the morning, but she didn't say much and she didn't make any fuss about seeing me. I assumed she was fighting a hangover. Age had caught up to her and turned her hair gray and creased her face and lips deeply with lines that had only been starting to show the last time I'd seen her.

It had been almost two years since I'd left home and now every part of being back only reminded me of decay and decline. Something about being away and then coming back made it seem stark, more apparent than before.

After a long moment of silence, she got up slowly and pulled her bathrobe up behind her so she could retie it tightly around her awkward body as she moved. She poured something from a jar into her coffee mug and returned to sit at the table again.

"Money's a little tight. You're gonna have to help out if you wanna stay."

"I've got a little saved up," I replied.

"You'll need to get a job."

"Do *you* have one?" I asked resentfully.

She didn't answer. Instead she took a long pull at the coffee mug, drinking it down fast in a way you couldn't do with coffee that was very hot. Afterward she pulled a face and fussed around with her bathrobe some more.

"Well, you know where your old room is. Might as well settle in there for now."

I ambled down the narrow hallway with my duffel and opened the door. The room was about as I had left it, only with a fine layer of dust over everything and the mattress had been stripped bare a long time ago. Sunlight came in through the window and cast a long, angled panel on the naked wood floor. I stepped onto it and kicked my shoes off and unbuttoned my shirt.

That's when it hit me in a wave: I was so damn tired.

With my head on the pillow and my feet dangling off the end I stared up at the ceiling. The old house was quiet. I had to give it that at least. Lying there alone, I thought about some of the other things that had happened in that bed.

Sally had been my first, snuck into the house one night after my mother had passed out. I must have been sixteen at the time. She'd been a little older than me and seemed to know so much. At least she had taught me a lot – how to touch a woman, how to whisper to her in the dark, how to delay the moment until she'd had hers.

I thought about Sally. She had broken my heart with the letter she had sent me six months after I'd left. I couldn't blame her, though. How could I? Even I didn't expect to come home. Why should she wait around for some guy who was likely to be dead soon?

Chapter Three

I'd been seventeen in 1942 when I'd left home to join up. Not sure why I did it. It just seemed the right thing to do. Everyone else was doing it. Up to that point in my life I'd never been more than sixty miles from home. When you're young, you don't know any better – you don't even know how poor you are – until you get away and see other parts of the world. Now I'd seen plenty of it and I knew more than was good for me, though I wasn't going to be one to complain.

Nothing had changed in Monahans except me. I was different now.

After a few hours of sleep I left the house and walked six blocks down to Handrow's diner. It looked the same as I remembered, though it had a new banner hanging inside the window and the menu prices were higher than they had been. A hamburger was fifteen cents now. I ordered one and asked for a Coca-Cola with it. The counterman wasn't anyone I knew from before and he just grunted and turned away after hearing what I wanted.

"Hot day again, eh?" I said after him, mostly just to be saying something.

"Yep" he replied without turning around.

"Guess you get used to it, though," I continued. I didn't like looking at the back of the man's shoulders. That annoyed me, even though he was fixing my lunch.

"Yep," he said again, still without bothering to turn around.

Irritated, I swiveled on my stool to look around the room. It was empty except for an older couple in the corner and a woman sitting with a small child in one of the booths by the front window. I didn't recognize any of them and they didn't look at me.

When my hamburger arrived there were two of them and they were each placed on the lower half of a toasted bun and topped with a pat of butter. The upper halves of the buns were turned up and piled with lettuce and sweet pickles. There was also a small plate of French fried potatoes and the iced Coca-Cola I'd ordered.

"You want catsup?" the counterman asked.

"I only ordered one hamburger," I told him. "And I didn't order any fries."

The old guy nodded without looking at me. There was no particular expression on his face. I studied him for a moment. He was probably in his fifties and I judged he'd seen his share of hard living. The skin on his nose was bubbled from too much sun exposure and there were heavy concentric half-circles of skin hanging below his eyes. His knuckles and his ears were scarred up awfully bad. He'd probably been a boxer at one time. That didn't explain the jagged line descending down from his jaw to his neck.

"Forget it," he rasped. "Just eat what you like. There's no extra charge."

"What for?"

"Son, does there have to be a reason for someone to treat you decently?"

"I ain't used to it, is all."

He nodded, but his eyes remained vacant of any particular expression. "I know," he said roughly. "I remember, myself. When I came home from France in 1918 no one knew me anymore. If my name was familiar they struck up just enough conversation so they wouldn't have to feel guilty afterward for not talking to me at all anymore. That's what a lot of them proceeded to do."

I set my fork down and looked at him. "You were in the Great War?"

"Yep," he said, meeting my eyes for the first time. "France and Belgium mostly. I was U.S. Army for ten years before the war started. My division was one of the first to go over there."

"How was it?"

He pursed his lips, but his eyes didn't change. "Kid, you

208

should know better than to ask me about my war. I won't ask you about yours."

"How did you know I was in the war?"

Now he smiled for the first time and lighted a cigarette off a match that he shook out and dropped on the floor. "Instinct, I guess. You've got the eyes and the shoulders – the posture of a man who's been in the Army, carried a pack. If I barked loud enough, I'd lay bets that you'd salute. I never saw you around here before, so assumed maybe you just came home from somewhere. What theater were you in? Which unit were you with?"

"Thought we weren't supposed to ask each other about our wars?"

He shrugged and his lips almost formed a smile, but they didn't. "Might be okay to swap a little info on our units," he said, softening his tone as he worked the cigarette. "Just the basics."

"European theater. I was 101st Airborne."

He took another drag off his cigarette as he thought about what I'd told him. It meant something to him. "Normandy?"

I shrugged and then nodded. "We dropped the night before."

"Bastogne?"

I nodded again.

He sighed. "Nuts," he said then with a half grin.

"How'd you know?"

"I read the newspapers. You saw a bit, huh?"

"Sure, I was there for some of it, part of the great Allied race across France and Germany, starting somewhere near Saint-Mihiel. What about you?"

He leaned forward with this elbows on the counter and his sagging face close to mine. When he spoke, it was in a coal-burnt whisper: "I was infantry, humping with the First Army under Black Jack Pershing. We passed through Saint-Mihiel too. You had Patton, we had Blackjack – two mean sons of bitches who knew how to kill Germans dead."

I nodded. "They sure as hell did."

"Neither wanted to quit at it either. They both wanted to go on to Berlin – had the men and arms to do it too."

"That's for sure."

"What's your name?" he asked.

I told him. "What's yours?"

"Can barely remember, but for some reason everyone calls me 'Bill.'"

Without any further palaver, Bill turned back toward his grill and began to clean it as though it were the only thing in the whole world that mattered to him.

Chapter Four

As I was finishing the second hamburger two fellows came in and sat at the counter near me, leaving just one empty stool between us. Gruff and unfriendly, they ordered their lunch in low angry tones. Bill ignored them, treating them the same way he had treated me when I first came in. They didn't seem to notice and I decided maybe they were regulars and not folks I needed to tangle with on Bill's behalf.

After I finished eating, I placed a dollar bill on the counter and waited until I could catch Bill's eye. When he could, he drifted around and picked up the bill and sniffed at it. A moment later he came back with a few coins and spilled them onto the counter in front of me. I sorted out two dimes and then pushed the rest together in a tight pattern, sliding them across the counter with the palm of my hand over them.

Bill had moved on already. He stood at the other end of the counter with his arms crossed, frowning at the newcomers. I lighted my last cigarette and sat there with it, smoking and listening.

I didn't want to leave if there was going to be trouble. I watched the men while I smoked and after awhile one of them, the one that was three seats over, noticed me and said something. His friend turned to look at me over his shoulder. He was within my reach. I thought about how easily I could smash my soda glass over his head before he could even get off his stool.

"Come again?" I asked loudly.

"Said: what do you want?"

"Nothing," I replied. "Just finished my lunch, relaxing for a moment before I move along."

"Why are you staring? I don't like the way you're looking at us."

I shrugged. Out of the corner of my eye I could see Bill backing up to the cutting board behind him. I guessed he was reaching for a knife. "Wasn't looking at you," I said. "I was thinking, didn't mean any harm." Maybe if I had managed a smile that would have ended it, but then maybe I didn't want to end it.

"You should go think somewhere else, Mister."

I restrained my urge to assault them by asking a question instead. "Hey, you fella's know where a guy could find a job in this town?"

From the corner of my eye I saw Bill relax a little.

The one closest to me joined the conversation. His voice was low and calm. He had a very different tone from his friend, and his body language was sort of easy going now that we were talking. "What kind of job are you looking for?"

"Any kind," I replied.

"What are you good at?" He didn't seem the least bit hostile and his friend had become quiet.

I shrugged because I didn't really know. "I'm strong, hard working. Don't have much education, but I'm not stupid."

"You just need a chance, right? Is that it?"

I nodded and took the last drag off my cigarette.

The other man, the loud one, spoke up again. "Maybe you should try knocking on a few doors. It's a good afternoon for that. If I were you, I'd head two blocks over that way and turn right – it's the edge of where businesses, businesses that hire people, can be found. You ought to give it a try."

I stubbed the cigarette butt out in an ashtray and climbed off the stool. "Guess I'll do just that," I said with a glance toward Bill. He stood relaxed now, with his hands on his hips, watching me with a slight smirk on one half of his face. It broadened in response to my informal salute.

"Hey kid," the quieter man at the counter called after me. "Depending on your luck this afternoon, you might try drifting into Hacket's Saloon tonight about eight o'clock. The beer is cheap and usually cold and there'll be honky-tonk music. A lot of folks gather there and it's a chance to meet some of the people who might be interested in hiring a guy like you. Strong, hard working, and not stupid still counts for something around here."

Not being sure what that meant, I went out through the door into the bright heat of the afternoon. Blinking a few times I turned my squinting eyes in the direction of where the businesses were said to be.

"What are you doing, mister?" asked a small child, twelve, if she was a day, sitting on the curb in front of Handrow's, sucking on a straw.

"What have you got there?" I asked her.

"Malted milk."

"Bet it's good. I just had lunch myself," I said.

"Its not what I asked you," she chided. "I asked what you are doing, Mister."

I looked up toward the hot sun, as I drew a heavy breath. Sweat had gathered already and was starting to roll down the small of my back. "Right now, I'm standing in the afternoon heat, talking to a smart-aleck child, trying to decide what to do next."

"I'm not a 'smart-aleck' and I'm certainly not a 'child,'" she cried abruptly. "I'm fourteen years old."

"You're not."

"Am too."

"What's your name?"

"Sylvia."

I considered that for a moment as I noticed something about her eyes. "Sylvia, do you have a sister named Sally?"

"Sure I do, and I don't like her very much."

I smiled politely as it dawned on me. "Why not?"

"She's mean to me. She's mean to everyone."

"I used to know your sister a long time ago. How's she doing anyway?"

"Just fine, mister. She's got herself a fella, and she's doing swell. He treats her right fine too. Who are you, anyway?"

213

"Don't you know better than to talk to strangers?" I challenged her.

She didn't back down an inch. "Mister, you better know that strangers in this town don't stand a chance."

I wasn't going to argue with her. Instead, I walked the two blocks down and then turned right, as had been suggested. Small businesses and shops lined the street on both sides for at least four blocks. I paused for a moment to survey them. There were a couple of bakeries, several clothing stores, a furniture outlet, a mortgage house, an insurance office, a butcher's shop, a pharmacy, two grocers, a diner, and an establishment that might have been a real restaurant.

I also noticed two banks sitting there, baking under the hot sun. Pedestrians on the street walked by them without paying them any attention. That observation planted a few thoughts in my mind.

For the next two hours, I walked the street up and down, looking for opportunities. "Help wanted" signs were posted in a handful of windows. I poked into those places first to make inquiries and then I walked the street again, being less particular the second pass through.

I went into every joint that was open, just to inquire. Unfriendly eyes met me more often than not. At the soda fountain in the back of the pharmacy, I was served a root beer with a scoop of vanilla ice cream in it. The proprietor wouldn't take my dime. I guess he felt some pity for me. That didn't help. I left the dime for him anyway when he wasn't looking.

Frustration began to wear me down.

The words were different, but the message was the same over and over again: "Love to help you son, but we got no work. Business has been slow. Nothing personal."

Chapter Five

Early in the evening I shook my mother awake. She'd passed out on the sofa, still wearing the bathrobe she'd worn at breakfast that morning. Lines on her face and neck from the cheap fabric on the sofa showed up in the light when she sat up to glare at me.

"For dinner I picked up pork chops, potatoes, and a few other items." It was all I said to her, though a lot of other words that I could have said crossed my mind.

She rolled off the couch slowly, clutching her bathrobe at her throat, and looked about the room with a glaze of disorientation. I went into the kitchen with my package to unwrap it. Behind me, I heard her coughing. The sound was ugly and for the first time ever I realized her health was probably quite bad.

I got the potatoes and two carrots peeled and boiling in a pot of water, and then I found a cast iron skillet and heated it over one of the stove burners. I chopped up an onion. When the skillet was hot, I scrapped in a little lard, waited a moment, and then tossed in the onions and laid the pork chops in over it all. After that I ground pepper and salt over everything, reduced the heat, and placed lids over both pots to let them cook.

Five minutes later, I turned the chops and ground more salt and pepper over them. I opened a bottle of beer and tore open a package of Chesterfields and lighted one.

Mother came into the kitchen at that point, dressed and ready for the first time that day. She wore a light gray blouse and a black skirt that dropped well below her knees. I looked at her and she studied me. It occurred to me that she was almost pretty, like I had thought she was when I was little.

"A woman could almost feel human with cooking odors like that around," she said, smiling for the first time since I'd been back.

I handed her a bottle of beer and offered her one of my cigarettes. She was still in her late thirties, and with a little effort she was capable of looking nice enough. The thought occurred to me that if she would cut out the booze, she could look real nice. When I wasn't angry with her, I felt sorry for her. She'd been dealt a tough hand all her life and she'd never found a way to play it well.

For several minutes we sat smoking and drinking our beers quietly without talking to each other at all. When I stood up to check on the pork chops, she stood up with me to watch over my shoulder. I removed the skillet from the stove, and tilted the lid off it to let the steam rise out. I turned off the burner beneath it and set it down again. On impulse, I poured in some of my beer and then slid the pan around by its handle to circulate the liquid inside it. I replaced the lid and turned the heat down. The potatoes still needed more time to cook. I let them be.

"Where'd you learn to cook like that?" my mother asked once she had another cigarette going. Standing with her legs crossed and with one arm folded over on top of the other, she held it away from her face so that smoke rose up toward the ceiling without bothering her eyes.

"Field camps in England."

She made a sour face. "How did it go today?"

She didn't want to hear about my war experiences and I wasn't going to bother her with them. "I didn't find a job, if that's what you're wondering."

Standing close to me now, she stared up into my eyes and smiled through her fatigue. She'd always had pretty eyes and I guess she'd always known how to use them. They were light brown and large, and had small dots, like freckles, around the irises. "You can't expect to find a job on the first day of searching for one."

I nodded and then shrugged. "Well I didn't."

"Where did you look?"

"Everywhere I could. There weren't many open doors."

"Meaning what?"

I set a large serving fork down on the counter and turned toward her now, with my full attention. "Do you think I didn't try?" I asked sharply. "Is that it? I walked the entire length of downtown, all the way from one end to the other and then back again – twice actually. I rang bells, knocked on doors, talked to people. Where did it get me?"

"This town!"

"That's right."

"Surely, there must be something out there for you."

I stared at her and noticed the anxiety in her expression. "It's okay, Ma, I'll be okay. It takes some time. I've got the lay of the town now and I've met a few people. It'll be all right. Tomorrow I'll look again and I won't be a stranger. Eventually I'll find something. You'll see."

"I sure hope so. We're gonna need the money."

"Are you really so desperate?"

She stared at me hard and then turned away. "There's nothing coming in. Since your father left us, I've had nothing."

"My father didn't leave *us*, he left *you*," I said with controlled anger.

"Is that how you see it? When was the last time you heard from him?"

Not having a good answer to that question, I turned away from her to stir the pot with the potatoes in it. I felt the shame rising through me and I knew my neck and face were suddenly bright red. Leaning over the steaming pot, I hoped the rising heat of the cooking masked my reaction to her comment. She'd intended to hurt me, but that didn't mean I wanted her to see it.

"I'm sorry," she said, suddenly quieter now. "I can't hold you responsible for the dissipations of your father. I really am sorry for that. Won't you forgive me?"

I almost believed her, and in fact, I wanted to, but from

long experience I knew better. What I said was: "You can relax and not worry about me. Within a few days I'll find employment somewhere, somehow in this God-forsaken town. It'll be alright."

The potatoes were cooked soft now. I drained the water and mashed the potatoes with the carrots and a couple tablespoons of butter and some salt and pepper. We ate the pork chops and the potato carrot mash without talking much, though my mother acknowledged it was one of the better meals she'd eaten in a good long while.

At least she gave me that much, though I new what it meant.

Chapter Six

After dinner I wandered down the hall to my bedroom and lay on the bed with my feet hanging off the end of the bed again. I was thinking about Sally and our first time together and the things she had taught me during those hot nights. She'd been my first. Her perfume – lavender and vanilla – was real to me, as was the feel of her skin against mine and the scent of her breath, so hot against my mouth.

How many nights in the Army had I thought about her, dreamed about her? There were too many to count, even after her letter arrived. Some sergeant had torn it up in front of my face and yelled at me to get over it. I understood what he meant.

We'd all seen what happened to a guy when he got that kind of letter. No one wanted to see another GI take a bullet on purpose. Still, there were times when Sally was all I had, where she was the only reason I continued to fight and to live and I'd had to do some pretending to make that work.

One of the things she'd whispered to me in the dark the night before I'd left was that every boy like me should have a girl like her, a lover who could teach him things. She was six years older than me and she liked to think she had provided the kind of instruction that a younger guy needed to learn how to please a woman. Maybe she was right about that. The more I thought about it now, the more I thought she probably was.

When I asked her how she had learned the lessons herself and how many men she had been with, she'd replied those were the kinds of questions a gentleman should never ask a lady – and wouldn't want to know anyway. That had left my imagination plenty of room to play, and it sure did play.

Now that I was home again, I didn't know what to do with myself. I lay there in the bed, smoking my cigarettes slowly, staring up at the ceiling through the early evening hours, watching the shadows move across the ceiling and the wall.

Sally was on my mind.

If I was honest with myself, she was always on my mind, had been ever since I'd left. The letter she'd sent me hadn't changed that. For a couple hours I lay there, staring up at that damn ceiling, smoking occasionally, thinking of her, wondering about her, wondering where she was now, thinking about who she was with now, how she might have changed.

Even as tired and messed up as I was, I knew that wasn't good for me somehow, but I didn't know how to change it. I thought about it and smoked and got nowhere with it.

Eventually an old tune went through my mind and, concentrating on it, I played it for all it was worth, hoping it would change my mood. It didn't. After an hour of that, I planted my feet on the floor and drew a breath.

Chapter Seven

The eastern sky at dusk settled into a rainbow of horizontal colors transformed by the current of dry lightning at its periphery. I stopped by Handrow's diner again for a chocolate malt and a package of Chesterfields. Bill wasn't on duty and I didn't linger. The little girl on the sidewalk was long gone and I didn't give her another thought after noting her absence.

At a few minutes past eight thirty, I walked into Hacket's Saloon and I took a seat at the far corner of the bar. From there I could see most of the tables in the room as well as the small stage and the entire bar. The odor of stale beer, burnt tobacco, peanuts, and urine was heavy in the air. It was like every other low-end bar I'd ever been in, from Texas to Germany.

There was some comfort in that. I thought about the guys in my company as we'd moved into Germany late in the war. Some of them were obsessed with finding Kraut treasure – gold, art, and other things nobody ever actually found – or souvenirs, like swords, helmets, insignia. Those things were all over the place, though I'd never cared about any of that stuff. Sure, I didn't mind pick up something that I could sell or enjoy right away, like a bottle of wine, but to me the rest of it was nonsense.

What use was I going to have for a Lugar once I returned to Texas? I was pretty sure I wasn't going to want anything around to remind me of the war. Now that I was home, I was sure of it.

We'd been there for one reason and one reason only: to kill Germans and end the war so we could go home. Souvenirs were a distraction and the guys that looked for them were bringing trouble upon themselves. I couldn't square with the idea of taking a memento off a man I had just killed. For me, the killing was enough. It kept me level.

That said, most of the guys in my unit were usually ready to blow off steam and have a good time. I was right there

221

with them. As the war drew to a close, we gradually became euphoric, careless even. Early on, none of us had expected to survive and then suddenly it seemed like we just might. Hope brought optimism and cheer, but also, an occasional tragedy. We tried not to think about the invasion of Japan. We were all on notice to be sent over there. The officers warned us about it and how many of us might be killed once it started.

That meant time in cheap bars and houses with ladies who didn't have very much. I didn't go for the ladies so much, but I was happy enough to spend my combat pay in the bars where there was wine and beer, frenetic music, and disorganized gambling. I liked that scene well enough. Somehow it appealed to me.

We had all the guns, so we made sure we never lost at the gambling, but somehow the house always got it's money back on the alcohol and the ladies. I guess in the end we all got what we wanted – and most of us got what we deserved. It was a lesson I had vowed to remember.

On the raised platform at one end of Hacket's Saloon, a four-piece honky-tonk country band was plinking out one sad love song after another while a small group of people gathered around the tables in the front row to drink and dance together. An inebriated woman in a tight dress danced all by herself as she glanced wildly about the room, evaluating her potential partners. Her eyes and hips were herky-jerky, though nobody appeared to be paying her much attention.

I crossed my arms on the bar and made myself as small as possible. The music chugged along within it's measure, driven steadily by the rhythm section – the drummer and the bass player were actually pretty good, better than their band mates, better than the material I thought.

Smoke from a Chesterfield filled my lungs. I let it burn and enjoyed it. Looking around the room I guessed it was a slow night. When the bartender, a heavy, graying man in his late fifties, finally came over to me. I asked for a cold beer.

He only nodded and then he turned away from me, as though I didn't matter.

I considered following after him with a comment, but remembered I wasn't in Germany anymore and decided to let it go. I was a civilian now and back in the United States. It was time to get into step with what that meant. Somehow I had to find a way to fit in and pretend like I belonged.

With the cigarette in my mouth, I drew a calming breath through it. Before I exhaled, I pulled the Chesterfield and held it in front of my face to contemplate it. Soon I took another slow drag and grinned to myself as I set it in the ashtray on the counter. There was a mirror behind the bar and I caught a glimpse of myself – or at least of a fellow who looked something like me, though I didn't recognize the glaring eyes that seemed to glow a high yellow.

When the beer arrived I drank it down quickly and asked for another one. The bartender looked at me kind of funny, but he didn't say anything and he drew the second beer and placed it in front of me.

I wanted to tell him I wasn't stupid, but instead I said: "Thanks, Ace."

He seemed to like that. "You wanna run a tab?" he inquired.

I spread a five-dollar bill on the bar with the fingers of both hands and then pushed it over to him. "Let's see how far this will take me," I said.

He picked it up, studied it, and then folded it in half and pushed it down into his apron. With a hard grin he said: "You got few more coming – hope you can hold it, soldier."

I shrugged and tried out one of my various smiles. "I'm not here to drink much. Was hoping to meet up with a guy that encouraged me to come in."

"That a fact? What kind of guy are we talking about?"

"The kind of guy who didn't give his name," I admitted. "He seemed to have some role around here in this town. I thought maybe he was important. He let me believe that, anyway."

The bartender considered this and then shrugged. "Buddy, that could be any number of guys around here. Lot of guys like to think they're important. Can you say a little more about him?"

"Sure," I smiled. "He was easy going, with a quiet voice. Said 'hard working' was a good quality in a man. I just need a chance and he seemed inclined to give me one."

"Yeah?"

"Do you see anything in that?"

He shrugged, indifferent. "No, I don't see anything much in that."

I grinned. "This guy said coming in here could be an opportunity for me to meet some of the people who might be interested in hiring a guy like me."

"That a fact?"

I was growing tired of hearing him say that. "Yes, it is a fact," I assured him. "It's what he said, word for word."

"How would I describe a guy like you to someone who might be interested?"

I nodded patiently, going along with his game. I lighted another one of the Chesterfields and exhaled. "Easy," I told him. "I'm strong, hard working, and on my better days, I'm not too stupid."

"That a fact?"

"You better take it as one," I replied, smiling along with him now like it was all good fun that we were having together. It was in my thoughts to pick up the glass of beer he'd brought me and hit him over the head with it. I could have brained him easily and it wouldn't have bothered me none to have done so. But then I'd had too many thoughts like that since coming back and I knew that kind of behavior wouldn't get me anywhere I wanted to go.

"Well then, soldier," he said slowly, backing away from me as if he could read my mind, "I think I know who you're looking for."

"Why don't you let him know I'm here, waiting to see him?" I showed him my best friendly face.

With his oblong, heavy eyes close in front of mine, the bartender squinted a little as he stared back at me. "You've got me whistling a tune now. I guess I'll do just that." With a strange expression pasted on his face, he moved away from me toward the other end of the bar. I watched as he picked up a telephone receiver and spoke a few words that I couldn't hear.

I drank my beer and waited and tried not to think about killing anyone over something as trivial as a funny look. My eyes continued to roam about the room. They kept finding their way back to the bartender. He was careful not to meet my gaze, which caused me to trust him even less than I had before. I watched him as he went about his duties. Self-consciously he pulled beers and mixed drinks, glancing over at me every now and then furtively.

Chapter Eight

Ten minutes later a man wearing a large western-style Stetson showed up and took the stool next to me. The brim of his hat tilted down over his face and concealed his eyes and his expression.

"Buy you a beer?" he suggested.

"I wouldn't say no to that," I replied, pushing my empty glass away from me.

After a nod toward the bartender, the man turned toward me and leaned an elbow on top of the bar. He set the wrist of his other hand in the crook of that elbow and studied me quietly.

He was a large, burly man, with sun-darkened skin around his chin and neck, and he had the appearance of one who had put on a good bit of weight recently. When he smiled, I noted that his teeth were a bright white color and they were very straight.

That told me he had money and access to good dental care. I guessed that he had never served. On his wrist, he wore a large, shiny watch – a Rolex model that I'd heard of and had never seen before. After a moment he lowered his chin so the hat brim shadow covered his eyes and the upper half of his face again.

"Do you know who I am?" he asked seriously. With the way his lips pursed, I recognized his insecurity and the fact that he didn't want it to show. I still couldn't see his eyes very well except to know they watched me carefully.

I shrugged casually. "Sorry. I don't, but I've been away for a few years, so don't take that too personally. I don't know who anyone is anymore."

He grinned broadly, showing me more of his fine teeth. "Of course, you're allowed that."

"I don't follow."

"You're newly back in town, one of our returned war

heroes, no?"

I shrugged the same shrug I'd gotten a lot of mileage out of lately. Then I gave him the same line of chatter I'd practically memorized by now. "I was in the war," I started. "A lot of guys were. It was a big effort. Most of the real heroes are dead. The guys telling tales are a dime a dozen now that the fighting is over. Any man can tell a story. Me, I didn't do anything more than the next guy in my unit and lot less than many of them did. I fought for those guys; and they fought for me. Other then that, I just wanted to make it home alive and I did, so I got lucky. What's your point?"

"Heard they gave you a medal."

"They gave everybody a medal."

"They didn't give everybody a Silver Star."

I shrugged and picked up the fresh beer the bartender pushed across to me and took a large swig from it. It was almost as cold and as sweet as the first one had been. I could feel it now, the clarifying warmth. It spread through my mind and shoulders, into my ready hands as I drank half of it down, hoping to quiet something inside me.

"Maybe I got it wrong?" the man in the hat suggested.

I stared at him, swishing the glass on the counter between my hands. "The war is over. What difference does it make now?"

"Maybe I'd like to shake your hand."

"No reason for that. The guys that came back are just the lucky ones. That's all they are. The only thing that separates me from the ones who didn't come home is that I was fortunate. Too many of my brothers are still sleeping over there, sleeping forever in places like the Ardennes Forest, Normandy."

"It must be a tough thing."

I shrugged, growing annoyed now. I wasn't going to shake his hand over this. "It is," I said.

"All right then, we'll leave it be," he replied after a moment.

I lifted my beer and finished it in a series of swallows. The

227

man in the hat watched me drink, and then he raised his own glass and followed suit. The bartender smiled at us and then moved along the bar to draw two more beers.

"So why are you here?" the man asked after we had our fresh cold beers.

"It's where the beer is served."

He smiled to acknowledge my quip. "Maybe you're looking for work?"

"Maybe I am."

"Are you the guy that was in Handrow's earlier today?"

I considered this question for a moment and then nodded again. "I think you already know I was."

"One of my buddies might have talked to you."

"Sure," I said, smiling cautiously.

"What did he say?"

"He was a quiet-spoken man who encouraged me to drift in here about eight o'clock tonight. I think I have done that. He said the beer would be cold and a swell honky-tonk band would be playing."

"That sounds like something he would say."

"Well, he did – and he was right."

"Pardon?"

"The beer *is* cold and a swell honky-tonk band *is* playing."

"Did he say anything else?"

"He said 'strong, hard working, and not stupid still counts for something around here.'"

"Yep, he sure got that right," the man replied, grinning now as though he knew it bothered me. He slid his half-empty glass back and forth between his hands, rapidly on the counter top.

I smiled and finished my beer.

"My name is Willard Haynes, but people call me 'Wrench.'"

"Why do they call you that?" I asked.

"I never really knew. It's what they've called me since I was five or six, and it's stuck with me ever since."

228

"Well, Wrench, I have an old, silly nick-name too." I shared it with him and we shook hands and laughed about our goofy nicknames and finished our beers together, warming ourselves up to become swell pals.

"Maybe you ought to come on back to the room over there and talk to the Johnny," Wrench said eventually. "He's boss these days, and he's got a good handle on what he's looking for and we do need some right guys for what lies ahead. You know how it is."

I didn't, but instead I said: "Is he the guy I met in Handrow's?"

Wrench just smiled and climbed off his stool. "Could be," he said, enigmatically. "Could be."

I stood up and followed him toward the back of the joint.

Chapter Nine

We passed through a narrow hallway with off-white paint on the walls and the same paint dripped carelessly on the bluish concrete floor. The passageway had dim yellow light bulbs in the ceiling spaced at four-foot intervals. It led us to a back room well behind the bar. You could still hear the honky-tonk music pumping away, though it was muted now.

Wrench pushed through the door and I followed in behind him with my hands clenched. There were three men sitting around a table. Maybe they had been waiting for us. I looked at Wrench and then I looked around at the other faces. They were hard, somber, and unrevealing. One of the men raised a glass to me silently and then held it to his lips.

The room was poorly lit and heavily shadowed. The only illumination was a single shaded lamp that hung about two feet over the table. Squinting as my eyes adjusted to the low light, I recognized the two men I'd seen earlier at Handrow's Diner. I realized the man who had raised his glass was the man who had been the quieter one at Handrow's, the one who had encouraged me to come by Hacket's Saloon. He was smiling and his eyes were bright enough that I wondered if he'd taken something illegal.

"Glad you came by, kid," he said. His voice was thick and a little raspy from too much smoking and drinking on the night. He chewed his lips and waited for my reply.

"Well, here I am," I said. "What's it all about, anyway? You got some ruckus that needs a play?"

"Come on in, grab a seat, kid. You've already met Wrench out there at the bar, so now meet some of the other guys. I'm Rainey. This is JD. He was at Handrow's with me earlier."

I nodded at JD, and he nodded back without baring any teeth.

"JD's always half-angry, very grumpy," Rainey explained with a wave. "He's easily concerned that things aren't going the way we want them too. Don't mind him. It's just the way he is. Over here, we have the boss, the man everyone in this town answers to. Meet Mr. Hacket."

I nodded. "Mr. Hacket, it's a pleasure."

"Pull up a chair, kid," Hacket said to me in a casual drawl. His voice was loud and buoyant; his face was friendly, smiling even. He had large white teeth that contrasted with the dark, dimpled skin of his suntanned face. A shock of dirt-blonde hair hung to one side down over his forehead.

I found him to be a man-child – one of those guys who had been popular with the girls in his youth and had managed to find everything come easily all the way along – except that middle age took him by surprise when he discovered he was no longer in high school.

Hacket's hands rested in his pockets and his elbows were out wide at his sides, a gesture intended to project self-confidence and an easy welcome. I moved into the room with my own arms down at my side, my hands carefully in sight, and I took the chair that had been kicked out from the table for me.

"Have we met before?" Hacket said, squinting at me even as he broadcast his large, perfect grin.

"I don't think so, sir. I'd remember."

"Heard you just got back from Germany."

"That's right, sir." I nodded and found one of my cigarettes, twirling it between my fingers. Somebody set a bottle of cold beer in front of me. I didn't look over my shoulder to see who it was, but I caught the heady scent of perfume and a woman's sweat. It struck me as familiar and I stiffened.

"When did your hitch start?"

I told him the month and year.

"They say you killed a lot of Krauts?"

I shrugged. I still didn't know how to react to comments like that. They made me uncomfortable. It was one of those awful things that a lot of people wanted to hear about. A man

231

like Hacket should have known better.

"Tell us a story," Hacket encouraged.

"Not sure what you mean."

"You had adventures over there, share one with us."

I shrugged at that. "Sir, there was nothing adventurous about killing. It was hard, slogging, ugly work that never got easier the more you did it. It involved a lot of mud and cold and noise during the artillery barrages. Men don't die easily, they never do."

Hacket nodded, accepting my response graciously as though he knew exactly what I was talking about.

"Ever heard an artillery barrage yourself?" I asked him.

He shook his head and seemed suddenly disinterested. "Listen up, son, it's okay. You earned the right to talk about it or not. Go on, have a drink."

I picked up the bottle in front of me and took a good swallow from it. Wrench had moved around to stand on the other side of the room, just to the side and a little behind Hacket. There was an empty chair there, but he didn't sit in it. I could see his bulging waist directly across the table from me. His upper body and face were blocked from my view by the low-hanging lampshade and the dark shadow that swelled above it.

"Kid was a hero," Wrench said quietly, earnestly. "Remember, we heard that from old Jemma's cousin?"

"I remember," Hacket said, nodding while he continued to stare at me. His meandering smile curled in a way that made me uneasy. "Maybe we should talk a little business now," he suggested with a shrug. The manner in which he held his hands up and toward me made me consider going across the table to cut his throat.

It was an impulse I held in check.

Chapter Ten

"I'm proud of you for killing Krauts in the war," Hacket started. "It shows you got guts, shows you got character."

I could only shrug that off. "I guess we all did, those of us who where there."

"How many?"

For a good long moment I didn't say anything.

"How many did you kill?" he asked again when my pause had grown too long for him to stand.

I shrugged it off again. "Kind of hard to say. How often could you tell for sure, and when did you ever have time to count?"

"What did you shoot?"

"Rifle – the standard M1 they gave us. Sometimes a BAR, sometimes a mortar or bazooka, depending on the day and the situation, often times depending on who had just been hit. It was small unit tactics – movement and fire. We had to be light and mobile and we had to be expert at everything we had."

"Long range killing mostly?"

"Sure, plenty of that. Not all of it was, though. There was close up work too, if that's what you're wondering about. I had a .45 and I have blood on my knife. Some of it got on my hands, face, and inside my mouth. That's just the nature of it. War isn't neat and clean as Hollywood likes to pretend. Men don't die with poetic last words. They curse and scream and cry and beg."

Hacket showed his tilted grin and brought the back of a hand up to his face. "Alright, kid," he demurred. "You headed off the next question I was going to ask. How does it feel to be home?"

I shrugged. What could I say to that?

"I guess they didn't throw you a parade, did they?"

That made me laugh, though I don't know why. "Maybe I missed it?" I countered.

233

Hacket shook his head grimly. "Come to think of it, they did throw a parade a few months back, after the first group came home. You know the first boys they shipped home were the ones still sitting in England when the Nazi's surrendered. Most of them probably never even got into the fight, but they sure had plenty of medals and ribbons and polish to show for it. They're the ones that got the parade – and the girls. After that, everyone moved on with life. How does that feel to you?"

It felt rotten of course, but I wasn't going to give him the satisfaction of admitting it. I lighted a cigarette while I thought about what my response should be. I watched his face as I exhaled.

"A parade wouldn't have done much for me," I said finally.

"Them other boys seemed to enjoy it plenty. They marched quite sharply."

I didn't say anything, just took another drag off my cigarette.

"Well, if a parade wouldn't do much for you," Hacket started. "What would?"

"I need a job."

"What kind of job do you want?"

"Anything that pays the bills."

"What are you good at?"

"Don't know. I've been in the Army my whole life since I left home."

"What did the Army teach you to do?"

"Only one thing," I replied, stretching a little to stub my cigarette butt in the tin ashtray on the table.

Hacket twitched a bit, which told me something, and then he covered it with a chuckle from deep in his throat. "I see your point," he said, his voice raspy now from the effort. "I might have some ideas that could make sense for a guy like you."

"I'd like to hear them," I assured him.

A sound behind me caught my attention and I turned my

head to follow the hips of the woman with the familiar scent of perfume and sweat as she moved around the table and settled down into Hacket's lap with her hair tossed back over his shoulder.

I already knew her by her scent and the lush sway of her hips.

When she lifted her head and her face came into view below the lighted reach of the lamp, I recognized her, as I knew I would. It was Sally Parker sitting there on another man's lap, staring at me with those golden eyes. She was my Sally, the one I'd known from the hot nights all those years ago, the one who'd written me the letter that had changed everything. From across the table she stared at me with a challenging gleam in her eye. I stared back at her for a while.

Confronted with her half-drunk smile, I remembered all the rest of it even though I didn't want to. Her grandmother had come back to Texas from the territories after losing her first two sons to the law and she had raised a second family right there in Monahans. That grandmother had died of a fever six weeks after her granddaughter had reached her tenth birthday.

I'd heard the story, though it had never meant much to me until I'd received the letter while I was in Germany. The letter. *The goddamn letter.* It had changed everything, had almost got me killed – according to the Master Sargent who had pulled me off the line and slapped me around for a day or two.

My memory of the time was poor. Maybe I'd been drinking. Maybe it was the natural effect of stress on the human mind.

I didn't know.

I simply had little memory of the days after the letter had arrived. They said I'd gone a little crazy and maybe I had, but they didn't complain about it either, because I'd been especially good at what they wanted me to do, which was killing Germans after that.

Chapter Eleven

"Oh hey, buddy, do you know Sally – Sally Parker, my little girl, right here on my hip?" Hacket spoke in a rushed, clipped manner that told me he already knew the answer to the question. He knew it too well, in fact. He was flaunting her in front of me and enjoying the discomfort it caused me.

I did my best to hide it, though I knew I stared at her for just a little too long. Sally was still a petite beauty. At most, she was five-foot-three and ninety-five pounds with her clothes on. Her jawline was clear and tight, her sharp eyes and short hair were dark, and she had almost no breast or hip development. Still she was the sexiest woman I'd ever known. She had a fashion of wrapping a man around her little finger, and somewhere along the way I had decided it was a talent that she had been born with.

My gut clutched. I hadn't seen her in over three years. I watched as she squirmed intentionally on Hacket's lap, looking about, wearing nothing more than a skin-tight dress with black and white vertical lines that came up short of her knees, and a pair of canvas sneakers. Her make-up was perfect. Dark eyeliner and heavy rouge accentuated the contours of her face – the high sharpness of her cheekbones, the narrow point of her nose, the shallows of her cheeks that led down to her cherry-red lips.

As I looked at her she didn't avert her eyes from mine, though she pretended not to remember me. "Seems we might have met once, perhaps long ago," she said quietly with a gentle smile.

I opened my mouth to reply, but no words came out.

Then her eyes darted away from my face to stare into Hacket's eyes as if he were the only man that had ever mattered to her. That cut me deeper than anything she could have said. Then she gave him a light kiss on the cheek and ran a hand up through the hair on the back of his head as she whispered something into his ear. He smiled and then laughed as though there was something funny going on, a private joke perhaps. I wasn't in on it and I knew I never would be and I could feel the sour taste of anger starting to burn hot at the back of my tongue.

"I think we were talking about a job," Hacket said, as if picking up on my response.

"We were," I told him. "You said you might have some ideas for a guy like me."

Hacket nodded and then looked at the girl on his lap, tweaking her chin between his thumb and forefinger to raise her face up to his. "What do you think, darling? Should I help a war hero find a job? He served his country and surely, as a society, we owe him something."

She didn't look at me. As far as I could tell she was barely aware that I was still in the room. "Whatever you think best, honey," she cooed, staring into his eyes with that smile I knew too well. "Those boys had it rough over there. I hate to think of what they went through."

"We can stop here," I said, standing up. My chair slid back away from me a little too hard, too fast. "I'm not looking for pity. Don't want it, don't need it, won't take it. I'll find my own damn job."

"Wait," Hacket called. "Don't go. Come on, we're all friends here tonight."

I told him what I thought of that, using a few phrases I'd picked up during boot camp.

I was almost to the door before Hacket started laughing and apologizing at the same time. After a short pause, Wrench and the others were laughing too and calling for me to come back to the table. I stopped at the door and turned around. The faces I saw were all smiling and laughing and gesturing, waving at me to come back, as though I'd successfully passed some unspoken hazing ritual.

The joke was on me – or perhaps there was no joke at

all and they had all been rolling along without a script, just thinking they were funny and we were all laughing along together. But no, I didn't really think that was it.

"Is there a job or not?" I asked of nobody in particular.

"Don't get your nose out of joint," Hacket said. "Come back around here day after tomorrow and talk with Wrench. He'll have something for you to think about, though you have to understand, we already have our operation developed and things are rolling smoothly. Before we bring you on board, there will have to be a test. Do you mind?"

"Why should I? I've already passed more than a few of them."

He smiled broadly. "I don't think you should mind at all. You've already come through the first part rather nicely."

I shook my head and spewed out a few more of the phrases that had set them off laughing. Then I turned back toward the tunnel that led out into the bar. I was trying to appear cool as I moved into the lights and frenzy of the saloon, but inside I was madder than I'd been in a long time.

The honky-tonk band was lurching through an up-tempo version of an Ernest Tubb song: "Walking the Floor Over You." I should have gotten out of the joint and gone home right then, but I wanted another beer.

Good judgment had never been my strongest suit.

Chapter Twelve

She caught up to me before I'd had a chance to swallow the first drop. The bartender was sliding the draft across the bar to me with the foam head melting off the top as she slipped onto the stool beside me.

"Put that on my tab, Gene," she said easily to the bartender. He smiled pleasantly and turned away and busied himself wiping his hands on the towel that was tucked into his apron.

"Thanks, Sally; but I'd rather drink alone tonight," I told her. I brought the cold glass to my lips and licked the cold foam off the rim.

"Oh, darling." Her voice was soft and emotional. It held a texture of empathy I hadn't expected as she rested an open hand on top of my forearm. Her touch was quietly electrifying. Her fingers pulsed against my skin. "Don't be that way about things," she whispered. "There's no point to being so stubborn. Those boys in there didn't mean you any harm. They're just too dumb to understand. Hacket doesn't know anything about us. I've never told him the first thing about you and me."

I wasn't sure I believed her – or that it mattered anyway. "There isn't much to know," I replied coldly.

Sally pouted her lips for a moment and then her face brightened. "You didn't really expect me to wait for you all that time? Did you? I never thought you did. Why would you? For all I knew you were going to be away for years – and we both know you could just as easily have been killed or maimed in some horrible way. What was I supposed to do? A girl in this town has to make her way and she only has so many years to do it." Her voice was almost pleading.

I wasn't looking at her. I was staring down into my half empty beer glass now. "For instance, you could have done what plenty of other girls did for their man overseas. You could have waited awhile, and you could have encouraged me to come home safe and sound and given me something to look forward to. You could have given me something to stay hopeful for."

"You really think a lot of girls did that?"

I shrugged. "Plenty of them seem to have done that for the guys in my platoon."

"Is that what the guys in your company thought? Maybe they were naïve. How many of those girls were spreading their legs for the very next hometown guy who hadn't left yet for overseas? You ever wonder about that? Would you prefer that I had lied to you? Because that's what a lot of girls did to their guys. They kissed their beaus good-bye and wished them well in the war, and then they hopped into bed with one guy after another among those who were still left behind. Some of them even told themselves they were contributing to the war effort that way."

"That don't make it right," I said quietly.

Sally crinkled her nose at that. "I know a girl who was writing to three different beaus in the European theatre and two in the Pacific. You think she really wanted all five of them to come back home in one piece? Where would that have left her? Sure, she cried it out real hard as word came home that one by one they were either killed in action or severely wounded. In the end though, only one came home unscathed and she quickly married him, and then she sent 'Dear John' letters off to the two who were laid up in military hospitals somewhere over in Europe."

"You think that's okay?" I asked her.

"I didn't say that," she replied forcefully, pulling her hand from my forearm. "It's just the way it worked."

"Do you really think that makes me feel any better?"

"Oh honey," she sighed, and looked away, turning her head.

"Stop it," I said. "Just stop it."

Sally sat still for a long moment and then put an arm over my shoulder and leaned her tiny body against me so that her mouth was close to my ear. I could feel the heat from her breath and it caused me to shiver with arousal. For a moment I wanted to pick her up and swing her, though of course I didn't do any such thing.

"As I recall, you served in the Airborne," she whispered.

I shrugged a little and shifted away from her on my stool, leaning my weight back. "The hundred and first."

"The Screaming Eagles, right?"

"That's what some people called us."

Her smile managed to be both cunning and compassionate at the same time. I felt it in my gut like a punch.

"I am proud of you," she said in a softer whisper as she moved even closer to me. For a moment I thought she was going to kiss me, but she didn't. I was aware of her perfume. It still smelled like lavender and vanilla, exactly as I remembered it. "You stopped the Nazi's at Bastogne," she told me. "That must have been really something to have been a part of."

"It was," I agreed, reluctantly.

"The newspapers called it the Battle of the Bulge?"

I held for a moment and then nodded. "I guess they did call it that. It was a pretty good name for what happened. Hitler surprised us with a winter offensive and bulged out our line and nearly got past us. We could have lost the war. That's how close it was."

"What was that like?"

I shrugged, unsure of what to say.

"Please tell me something," she whispered. "I want to know more about it."

Reluctantly I began to tell her. "It was cold and the snow was deep. We didn't have enough food or ammunition and it was a hard fight for several days. We almost didn't survive, but we did. We held on to each other, and we held our positions. Eventually, the Germans backed off and moved out around us after Patton broke through with his armored divisions."

"You didn't quit, did you?" Sally encouraged with her

241

bright, shiny golden eyes.

"Didn't have a choice," I corrected her. "It wasn't valor that kept us going."

"No?" she said in a whisper. "I don't believe that."

I tried to smile for her. "We fought for each other and we weren't heroes. So, don't think that we were. We just did what we had to do to bring each other through each new day."

"I suspect only the men who talk that way are actual heroes."

I didn't say anything in response to that. Instead, I finished my beer and looked around the room.

"I'm sorry about that back in there," she whispered, gesturing with her chin to indicate Hacket's back room.

"No need to be," I told her.

"Yes, there is. He shouldn't have treated you like that, and I shouldn't have either."

"Forget about it," I told her.

"I don't want him to know there is any history between us. He doesn't know. That's why I acted the way I did. I am sorry. You deserve better after all that went between us."

"There isn't anything between us now."

"You are so cold when you talk that way."

"What other way could I possibly talk?"

"Well, you can't talk that way now," she said quietly and firmly, as if she could will it to be true. "You can't be certain there isn't anything between us still."

"Wake up, Sally. This isn't a fairy tale. We were kids back then, and now we're both somebody else. The world is different and so are we."

"I don't believe that we're so different."

"You should know it," I told her.

"Maybe, but maybe it doesn't matter. I'm here right now, staring into your face, searching your eyes with mine. Doesn't that count for something?"

I didn't say anything. I didn't know what to say, didn't

want to dare think about it.

She stared at me with eyes that were wider than the open sky. "Won't you kiss me now?" she breathed hotly into my mouth. "Please? Maybe just for old time's sake? Just kiss me. Kiss me now."

Her last sentence wasn't a request.

It was a command and I followed it.

Chapter Thirteen

When I headed back out into the hot night, I realized I'd sweat clean through my shirt and it stuck to my back and shoulders. I unbuttoned it to peel it off. With just a t-shirt to cover my chest, I tied the shirt around my waste, forming a knot with the long-sleeves. I had to walk home, but I didn't mind.

The street outside Hacket's Saloon was quiet and still. Streetlamps shined modestly at twenty-foot intervals, covering the distance between them with a faint light. Half a block down the street I paused to light a cigarette when I heard the footsteps behind me. I turned and waited with the Chesterfield smoke burning in my lungs.

"Best be careful with that little girl," a voice said. "She's a hot one." It was Wrench. He stepped out of the shadows formed by the corner of the building I'd just passed. His face, when he came up close to me, was taut and frail in the yellow light over our heads.

We were still within the glow of the neon halo that advertised Hacket's Saloon. I turned halfway and took a few sideways steps so that I was just outside the arc of light. Wrench continued to walk slowly toward me without seeming to notice the meaning of my movement.

"That's probably good advice for any guy regarding any girl," I said after I'd exhaled. I held the cigarette cupped low in my left hand so that it wouldn't illuminate my face. My right hand I held beside me, just out of Wrench's line of vision.

He didn't seem to notice that. "Maybe so," he said evenly, "but that little girl in particular is one to be careful with. She's the boss' girl."

I shrugged. "Maybe you know something I don't," I suggested.

Wrench stopped moving when he was about ten feet away from me. "I saw what happened: she kissed you while the two of you were sitting together at the bar. There wasn't anything sisterly about the kiss either and I noticed you didn't exactly push her away. A cynical guy could suspect it wasn't the first time you've kissed."

"Maybe we go back a ways," I conceded. "So what? Sometimes a guy can't always escape his past entirely, but she's with Hacket now. She made that clear enough and I accept it. Why bother to make anything out of it?"

Up close to me now, I could see Wrench's face. It was a pale blonde under Hacket's neon lighting and the lines around his eyes and mouth showed as deep scars that suggested something about his character. Slowly, something about his face spread into an angry smile that didn't conceal much.

"I kissed her once myself," he confessed maliciously. "It was a year ago, after she met up with Hacket and well after she and I both should have known better, but we didn't let that stop us. In fact, we didn't stop there either. One kiss wasn't enough for either of us, and I think you know what I mean. She's that kind of girl. Some of them just are around here."

I held up the palm of my left hand, waving the cigarette that was still between my first two fingers. "You can stop your story right there," I told him. "I don't need to know the rest. If you want to brag to the boys, I'm sure you can do that somewhere else."

In the dim light I could see Wrench's smile fade. Maybe he'd thought we would share a bond over our experience with the same woman. I'd seen other guys do that before in other circumstances. To me, Germany was a long distance away and a long time ago and I wasn't inclined to be friendly to another man over sharing a girl in my own hometown.

"Anything else you want to say to me?" I asked.

"Matter of fact, there is. I want to show you what I got, thought it might connect us in some way – you know, the tie between those who have served."

Wrench rolled up his left sleeve well past the elbow, and then he pulled it up to show me a green tattoo of a hawk coming down, claws first, on an obscured insignia.

It didn't mean anything to me and I said so.

"You got one?" he asked aggressively.

I wasn't going to show him everything, but I rolled up one sleeve to show him the black spade I had on my upper shoulder.

"That's nice," he said, nodding, as the meaning of it hit him. "Airborne."

"Where did you serve?" I asked.

"Regular Army."

"Where did you serve?" I repeated.

"I joined up kind of late, never got out of the states."

"No need to feel bad about that," I said. "I guess we all did our part."

"I was ready to go," he asserted. His eyes glowed an ugly red under the streetlights. "My unit trained and trained, but we never got out of North Carolina. Germany surrendered a week before we were scheduled to ship out. After a couple months, they sent us to California and we thought we were in for the invasion of Nippon, but that never came to be either." Wrench's expression soured as he spoke the words, as if the Japanese surrender had been the most unfortunate moment of his life.

"You were lucky," I assured him. "Nobody wanted to invade those islands."

Wrench moved his shoulders around eagerly, and then rolled his sleeve back down past his elbow. "I wanted to get into the fight," he said. "Now I've missed my chance and it won't come around again."

"Don't feel too sorry for yourself," I warned him. "There are plenty of men who saw the fight and wished they hadn't."

"Does that include you?"

I shrugged off the question.

246

Chapter Fourteen

My mother's house was dark when I got there. I assumed she was asleep or passed out in her bedroom. I took my shoes off at the door and tiptoed in and down the hallway to my bedroom. As I passed her room, I could hear soft murmurings behind the door. For a moment I wondered if she was with someone, but then I realized she was alone, muttering in her sleep. I almost felt bad for her.

In my room, with the door locked, I got undressed without turning on the light and I lay on the framed bed with an unlit cigarette in my mouth. Crosshatched shadows laced the wall and appeared to move slowly while I stared at them. I was tired, but I didn't feel sleepy. It was a feeling I was familiar with.

I couldn't see it, but I could sense the night sky up there. It hovered high and hard, filled with the bright stars that looked down upon us. At times I hated it. It was the same indifferent observer here in Texas that I'd cursed in the forests of Germany and Belgium.

Eventually I lighted the Chesterfield and took my time with it. There was no rush. I knew I wouldn't be falling asleep any time soon. While I smoked slowly in the dark, hot room, I stared up at the ceiling and thought about how relationships change over time and how new ones appear and the order of things you once took for granted gets all jumbled and reshaped. Did anything ever last? I was coming around to the notion that nothing ever did.

I thought about Wrench and Sally and Hacket and the other men Hacket had around him. They weren't my friends, though perhaps they would be my path to a living wage, or perhaps a score that would set me up for something. I didn't trust them and I couldn't see why they would trust me. Maybe they needed me. They probably did, I decided. I was the guy with the experience. That's how it was.

In the dark, I lay on the bed with my hands beneath my neck staring up at the ceiling, ignoring the shadows on the wall, thinking about the cold. It had been cold in the Ardennes, so very cold. When the American lines had first bulged out under the weight of Hitler's Panzer divisions and their surprise attack, it had been too frozen and the weather too harsh for us to jump into the area by parachute. So we'd moved out overnight, through drizzle and sleet, scavenging for jackets, meals, and ammo as we went, collecting a lot of what we got from regular Army troops marching out past us in the opposite direction.

We were going toward the fight and to a man we each knew it, and knew what that was likely to mean. It wasn't the longest march we'd ever done and most of it was accomplished riding in the back of trucks and on the front of the small number of armored tanks going our way. Yet, we were a small unit, going in alone, watching a long parade of defeated men walking out past us. They were leaving the field demoralized. We knew what that meant. It was hard, unforgiving ground and we went into the night knowing the danger we were being sent toward.

The temperatures dropped rapidly, but we kept going, huddling together as best we could to conserve heat and comfort each other. Most of us were still young, but after Normandy and Market Garden, we weren't kids any more. We had seen and done and survived everything. We were tough, battle hardened, and dedicated to each other, though we'd seen plenty of death and destruction and we each had that callous layer, that protective armor, that went up against anyone new coming in to the units. To a man we instinctively mistrusted any officer above the rank of major.

Still, we were proud of what we had already accomplished and we fought for each other – not for some great cause. There was a guy in Dog company that had lost his right eye to a ricochet near Eindhoven. He'd maneuvered an escape from the military hospital to rejoin his unit. It seems he'd told more

248

than one lie about his ability to see and shoot straight. We didn't question him. To him, it meant everything to be there. That's what I'd been surrounded by in the Ardennes: men who wanted to join the fight with their unit and were willing to do anything to reach it.

From the strangeness of my childhood bed I stared at the ceiling for a good while longer, thinking about the company and the men I'd known, the men I'd served with, and the ones who had found the light. Across the continent there were cemeteries with rows of crosses. The Texas night air was hot and it reminded me where I was now, so very far away from the cold ground we had fought over.

Some time just before dawn with the night sounds winking at me, I fell asleep in the bed and tossed around awhile until I heard the clatter of my mother in the kitchen, moving a cast iron pan about on the stove. The scent of fried eggs and toast persuaded me to climb out of the bed and pull on a pair of trousers.

"How do you want your eggs?" she asked when I came yawning into the kitchen, though she had already fried them hard.

"I don't care," I told her honestly.

Chapter Fifteen

The next three days passed slowly. At night I slept fitfully, if at all, tossing myself among the sweat-stained sheets and staring at the clock at regular intervals until the sun came up. The high Texas heat contrasted with the sensation of the frozen Ardennes forests that filled my head through the odd moments. I worked at it to push the memories down, out of consciousness. I didn't know why it proved to be so difficult most of the time, but it was.

It just was.

During the mornings I continued to search the city for employment, finding nothing but guilty, blank stares and doors that closed in my face. By early afternoon it was simply too hot to walk the streets anymore, so I typically reverted to Handrow's for a cold malted and sometimes I stayed around long enough for a couple of cold beers. I didn't return to Hacket's Saloon, and I didn't want to run into Sally again.

At times I might have had a little too much to drink, though at least I never woke up on the floor of a county jail cell – or in another city where I didn't understand the language. I also stayed out of trouble – didn't get into any fights or mix-ups with any other women, married or otherwise. Mostly I stayed to myself and spent a lot of time staring at newspapers during daylight hours and the ceiling of my bedroom during the night.

Maybe that was the only sort of progress I could hope for.

It was almost a week later that Wrench found me at Handrow's and summoned me out onto the sidewalk with a waving gesture of his hand. I knew straight away that it was time for the "test" I'd been promised. I finished my beer before joining him.

"You ready?" he asked, when I came up beside him.

It was two o'clock in the afternoon and the sun was high above us and almost hot as one could imagine possible. It must have been a hundred and ten degrees where we stood on the pavement. My shirt stuck to me as though I'd run through a sprinkler. That's how hard I was sweating within the first minute of standing there. I grinned hard with my teeth flashing to show it didn't bother me none.

Wrench wore the same low, wide brim Stetson. It kept the sun off his face and neck. "We'll wait here for a ride," he explained, looking away from my face to stare down the street in each direction. "You okay with that?"

I told him I was.

After a few minutes of standing there in the sun, I lighted a Chesterfield and squatted down on the curb with it, shielding it between my knees. Wrench moved over to stand next to me, but he didn't sit down. Instead he stood with his hands on his hips and looked up and down the street. He was casual about it, but I could sense his growing irritation as the minutes went by.

Soon a Ford flatbed truck turned the corner off to our right and came down the street toward us. The driver double-clutched as he pulled level to us. I stood up.

"Here we go," Wrench said to me without glancing my way.

I tossed the remainder of my cigarette into the street gutter as the truck driver revved his engine a little bit.

"I ain't riding in the bed," I said, as if talking mostly to myself.

"No need to," Wrench said, glancing at me. "There's plenty of room in the cab."

We crossed the street and Wrench opened the passenger side door and held if for me to hop in first. I did as he gestured, and he came in right behind me, slamming the door hard after him. That put me wedged into the middle seat between Wrench and the other man, who didn't look at me. I'd seen him at Hacket's Saloon the other night. He had dark sunburned cheeks and neck, and isolated tufts of black whiskers around his mouth. I guessed his age as somewhere around thirty, and his heritage as a mixture of Mexican and White.

"Where are we going?" I asked.

Nobody answered me.

We drove slowly across town, passing by many of the shops along the main street that I'd visited that very morning. When we came to the edge of the business district, the driver took a long arcing left turn, slowly.

After we straightened out, he accelerated onto a residential street and then pushed fast toward the outskirts of town. Once we cleared the township, we were on a dusty country road that went in a straight line out toward nowhere. At that point, the Mexican driver pushed it hard and we sped along at sixty miles an hour for a long while.

"Where are we going?" I eventually asked again, looking at Wrench's immobile face.

"We're going out here a ways into the country," he responded cryptically with a gesture of a darkened forefinger.

I stared out toward the direction he pointed, but I couldn't see anything worth driving to. I sat back in the seat and closed my eyes, reminding myself of all the times I'd been loaded out to go somewhere when I'd just had to sit there and let it happen.

I'd done it plenty of times before. I could do it one more time.

Chapter Sixteen

For nearly an hour we drove without talking. The bright sun moved across the sky. Somewhere along the way I must have drifted off to sleep. I woke up when Wrench dug his elbow into my side and grunted something I didn't quite catch.

The truck slowed, made a gentle quarter loop onto a grassy field, and then pulled up to a stop under the shade of a tree. The driver shut the ignition off and we sat still for a minute or two, allowing the dust to settle around us. It was almost three-thirty in the afternoon and sun was still blazing hot.

"What now?" I asked.

"Now we get out and look at guns," Wrench replied matter of fact. "And we find out if you can shoot worth a damn."

He was already half way out of the truck by the time he finished speaking. I followed closely behind him. The Mexican driver waited in the truck with a thin cigar that he lighted and his wide-brimmed hat tipped down over his forehead. He paid no attention to us. I glanced over my shoulder at him once when we were about twenty yards away, but he hadn't moved and I decided I didn't need to pay attention to him.

I followed Wrench a quarter of a mile across a dry field to a weather-beaten shack that was set well back from the road. There was no paint on it now and hadn't been for many years. It still had windows though a couple of them were broken and had been stuffed with newspaper. A low stream meandered behind it through a grove of Bur oak trees. There were a lot of bugs in the air and they didn't seem to be deterred by my swatting at them.

"Curious to see what you think of these here," Wrench said.

He led me toward a shed at the back of the small house. Once inside he flicked his cigarette lighter a couple of times to get a kerosene lantern going. When it was lighted it provided enough illumination so that we could see around the small enclosure. Rakes and shovels were lined up against the wall between the shed and the house.

The opposite wall had an old pegboard that held a variety of old tools. There were saws, drills, chisels, hammers, and a shelf that was stacked with small boxes of nails and screws. On the floor were several cans of paint that had been opened and used long ago. I didn't see any sign of paintbrushes or cleaning solutions.

Swinging the lantern as he moved, Wrench picked up the end of an old tarp that was piled in the middle of the space, pulling it off a wooden crate that had been bolted to the cement floor. The lid to the crate was padlocked in two places. Wrench had a key chain on his belt and from it he found two separate keys that opened each of the padlocks. He worked slowly. I helped him tip the lid open and set it against the wall behind the crate.

"What do you think?" he asked as we stared down inside the crate. Slowly he moved the lantern back and forth over the length of it so that I could study what was inside it.

What I could see were two Thompson submachine guns, a Browning M1919, a Browning Automatic Rifle – known widely as a BAR – M1918, and six M3 submachine guns. The six M3s were still in their original wrapping. They had never been fired since leaving the factory.

"What do you think?" Wrench asked again.

"Where'd you get these?" I asked.

"An armory robbery in Waco three months ago."

"You pull the job?"

Wrench shook his head quickly and adjusted his stance so the weight of the lantern wouldn't strain his back. "Hacket knew the guys," he said. "He helped fund the caper and then got a deal on some of the hardware."

"You don't want to be caught with this stuff," I told him.

Wrench lifted the lantern intentionally so that I could see his face as he grinned at me. "Yeah, but what do you think of 'em? They're nice, huh?"

I looked at him. "You had military training. Surely they taught you to use some of these geegaws. What do *you* think of 'em?"

He grinned harder before he lowered the lantern. "I think six of the right men with those M3s could take down Fort Knox."

I stared at his shadowed face for a moment and then shook my head. "Those grease guns aren't worth much. In the hands of the right guys and in close quarters, they can lay down some nice fire. But they aren't accurate past twenty yards and they have a bad habit of jamming. Use them in a city and it would be easy to have a lot of the wrong people dead. Nobody wants dead civilians. What are you going to do then?"

Wrench's face fell a little and he lowered the lantern further. "You're the war hero. Tell me what you think. I want to know."

I didn't like his tone, but I didn't say anything. Instead, I picked up the BAR to inspect it and I moved the bolt back and forth a couple of times. Inside the crate were several military ammo boxes. I rummaged around in each of them until I understood what we had available.

"Here's what I think," I told him. "I'd need to know more about the job we're planning before I could say too much. That said, I think the BAR here and the two Thompsons ought to be all you need to get any job done – especially since I assume everyone will have a side arm."

"How well do you know how to use that?" Wrench asked, gesturing with his chin at the BAR I had cradled in my arms.

I shrugged. "Well enough."

"Yeah?"

"If we're going to use these we ought to test them out anyway."

"I never thought you'd ask," Wrench said with a lazy smirk, swinging one of the Thompson's up out of the crate onto his shoulder. "Let's grab one of these ammo boxes and see what we got."

We each took one handle of an ammo box and between us we carried it out into the field. As we were laying out the ammo on the ground Wrench stood up and tilted his hat back on his head, wiping around his eyes with a red handkerchief.

"What about the other Browning," he asked. "Should we bring it out here now?"

I shook my head. "The M1919 is a terrific machine gun if you're planning to hold off an infantry battalion."

"Yeah?"

"Well, are we?" I straightened up and looked at him.

Wrench grinned and shook his head. "Naw, nothing quite like that. This is west Texas, Son."

"Maybe a company of Rangers?"

"Not that either," Wrench promised solemnly.

"Good," I replied. "So when are you going to tell me what we *are* planning to do?"

"Later," Wrench said. "Once we get to know you a little better and have a feel for what you can do."

"Alright," I said. "I'll show you right now."

"That's why we're here," Wrench replied with his swankiest grin yet.

Chapter Seventeen

While I set up the BAR and loaded several twenty round magazines for it and the Thompson gun, Wrench stepped off thirty yards and balanced four empty Coke bottles on a sawhorse. The sun was dipping behind it, just over the top of the Bur oak trees.

After Wrench was standing behind me again, I shattered the bottles in one easy sweep of the Thompson gun. Then I popped the magazine loose to show him I'd only used half the rounds to do it.

"Not bad," he observed, nodding.

I shrugged. "Ten rounds, four bottles. You got any more of those? I can put the Tommy on single shot if you like and I'm reasonably confident I can hit four out of four."

"I'd like to see that," he acknowledged.

"Set 'em up then."

"Don't have any more empties."

I stared out at the sawhorse. "See the black lettering in the middle, the capital letter 'O'?" I asked.

"I see it."

I raised the Thompson and fired once. That knocked the sawhorse over.

"Let me check it," Wrench said. He trotted out toward the sawhorse and a moment later he whistled.

"What about the BAR? I'd like to see what you can do without the tripod."

"Set it up then," I told him.

Wrench righted the sawhorse and draped an old newspaper over it. The paper curled in the breeze, but stayed in place.

As Wrench tromped back toward me, I picked up the BAR and checked the bolt. Then I popped in one of the box magazines. With the BAR on my shoulder, I let loose with a long burst. The newspaper and sawhorse disintegrated into the air.

I turned toward Wrench and found him staring at me happily. "That's mighty purrrty," he mouthed, though I had to read his lips to know what he had said because my ears were ringing from the echoes of the shots.

Together we walked back to the shed, carrying the rifles and the ammo canister between us. We made one more trip to clean up and then returned everything to the crate inside the shed.

"That was some nice shooting," Wrench said, after he had closed and padlocked the crate. "Truth is I never saw anything like it before. Nobody could shoot like that in my unit, not even the drill sergeants, though we trained almost entirely with M1 and M2 carbines."

"Those were good rifles," I told him.

"They were single shot, mostly."

"That's usually most of what you need."

"Really?"

"Well, it depends," I admitted. "Single shot is for killing men. Automatic is mostly for suppressing fire. Are we finished here?"

"I think we are. Let's go home."

The sun was still high enough, but the heat seemed to have faded a little since we had arrived.

"I've been thinking," Wrench said as we walked back across the field toward the truck.

"Yeah?"

"That kiss I saw the other night."

"What about it."

"Boss wouldn't like it if he knew."

"So?"

"Long as we're friends, he doesn't need to know."

"What's the price of friendship?" I asked coldly.

Wrench jerked a bit. "Aw, now, don't be that way about it. I didn't mean it in that way."

"In what way did you mean it?"

258

"I'm just saying, friends do things for each other. I do a favor for you, maybe some day you do a favor for me."

"Sure."

When we reached the truck, the Mexican driver pretended to wake up and he tossed his cigar out the window before switching on the ignition. We drove back into town without any further conversation and they dropped me two blocks from my mother's house. I was still stewing with the anger inside me.

Chapter Eighteen

"Where have you been?" my mother asked me when I came into the house.

It wasn't late, but she was already wrapped in her bathrobe. Her eyes appeared to have sunk deeper into her head and the skin around them had bunched up just above her cheekbones. A stub of a cigarette with a long ash hung from her lips. "You stink."

I didn't know if she was referring to the smell of sweat and dirt that clung to me, or if I had the heavier scent of gunpowder in my clothing and hair. Mostly I should have kept my mouth shut, but my patience had worn thin over the long day.

"Maybe I do. I'm surprised you can smell anything through the haze of beer and tobacco that swims around you."

"Don't talk to your mother that way." Her words were scolding, but her tone was hurt.

I ignored her and pushed on by, moving into the kitchen where I found there were only two beers left. There had been a full case the day before. I cracked one open without asking permission.

My mother followed me into the kitchen and studied me with an expressionless stare as I drank down most of the bottle in a series of swallows. She didn't say anything. When I finished the beer, she moved forward, toward me so that she could put her cigarette out in the ashtray that was on the table. Her hand trembled slightly as she performed the action.

"So, sue me," I said to her afterward. "I was thirsty."

"Help yourself to the other one," she replied, lighting another cigarette off a match. "You're a big boy, you need your drink."

I opened the second bottle and took a long swallow myself and then handed it to her. She didn't reject it. When she handed it back to me, there wasn't much of it left. I drank that down and set the empty bottle on the sideboard next to the sink.

"Now what?" I asked.

"Are you hungry?" she replied.

"Does that mean you cooked something?" I countered in turn. I knew she hadn't.

"No," she told me. "It doesn't mean anything like that, but I have a can of tomatoes, a few onions, and a couple of pork chops in the icebox. I can get them going quickly enough if you would run out and find another case of beer."

"Schlitz good enough for you?"

"It always has been. You need money?"

"Do you have any?"

She shrugged and turned one shoulder toward me, dropping her eyes down toward the floor. I accepted that as her answer and left the house on foot. It was still light outside, but the sun had dipped past the horizon and the air would cool off a little soon. Fireflies were starting to appear. I walked slowly, not feeling in any hurry.

There was a small corner store two blocks away. When I got there, the elderly shopkeeper recognized me and we made small talk for a few minutes. I hadn't seen him for about six years, though he looked exactly as I remembered him. He was a short slender man with receding white hair, who combed his eyebrows upward for affect. Though he wasn't fat, he wasn't lean either, and his neck didn't fit well within his collar.

"Good to see you. When did you get home?" he asked, smiling brightly and nodding eagerly. I remembered that when I was a child coming in with my mother he had always given my brother and me each a Choward's violet mint.

"I barely remember," I told him. "Some day last week."

He reached his hand over the counter to shake mine. "We're all proud of you and what you did."

"Everybody did their part. I'm sure you did too."

He shook his head briskly. "That's not true, not at all. Some people did a lot more than others. Believe it or not, a lot of us here in the community, we followed the news of the 101st

261

closely. We know what you did, what your unit accomplished. You went over seas and you risked everything and then you came home. We are grateful."

I shook my head, turning my palms out. "I merely played a part. Everyone did."

The man grimaced, reflecting his private judgment on the society around him. "Back home, we had only to deal with the small inconveniences of the effort."

"What does that mean?"

He smiled graciously. "We had to ration things: gas, sugar, flour, food. We lived with some hardship, but nothing like you endured."

"We were all in it together," I replied. "How much for the beer?"

"Nothing tonight," he answered. "Take it as a small gesture of my gratitude."

I hadn't expected to hear words like that and even as I heard them, I was skeptical. The old guy must have noticed my expression because he continued.

"The whole town knows you were Airborne and served in Europe. We followed your division all the way across the Rhine. We got daily reports by newspaper and radio."

I held up a few bills to pay for the beer I had set on his counter.

"How's your mother?" he asked as he took the bills from me. His hands moved quickly and his eyes roamed over them briefly and then he handed them back to me. "I can't accept this tonight."

"Are you sure?"

"Absolutely."

"Thank you," I said. "I guess my mother is pretty good."

"She must be glad to have you home again."

"My older brother didn't come back from the Pacific," I told him. "That weighs on her."

His eyes moved away from mine, which told me that he

262

hadn't known. "Of course it does. I remember him when he was small and the two of you came in with your mother."

"I remember that too," I promised him.

When the beer was packaged, the storekeeper, whose name I had never before known, came around the counter and shook my hand. His eyes were bright and sincere, and he held out another package for me to take.

"It isn't much, he said, "but it will feed you and your mother for a few days. No charge. It's my way of thanking you."

"What's your name?" I asked. "I'm sorry, but I've never known."

"Freddie McGeevers, and I am proud to know you."

I told him my name and shook his hand again before leaving his store. I didn't have the heart not to accept whatever it was that he had given me.

Chapter Nineteen

When I got home the scent of cooked tomatoes and pork shops was in the air. I moved into the kitchen and set the grocery bag down on the table. My mother's eyes were on the case of Schlitz I had under one arm. I set that down too and tore open the package and popped the caps off two bottles, handing one to her. For a while we drank without speaking.

"What's that?" my mother asked eventually, gesturing at the package Mr. McGeevers had given to me.

"You want another one?" I asked, opening two more before she answered. I handed the bottle to her and we tapped ours together before drinking again.

After that I opened the bag from McGeevers. Piece-by-piece I unloaded it. There were two jars of sour pickles, two loaves of bread, a dozen potatoes, a pound of sweet cream butter, a bag of green beans, a jar of salted peanuts, two large Hershey chocolate bars, and four beefsteaks. I laid them out on the counter beside the sink and looked at my mother.

"Mr. McGeevers sent these home with me."

"He's always been the kindest man."

"This kind?"

My mother shrugged and half-smiled and I assumed she knew something I didn't. I stared at her, but she didn't blink. It wasn't worth speculating about. After a moment she softened and pointed with her fingers, showing me where the various grocery items should go.

When I finished distributing them to the cupboards and the icebox, I returned to the case of Schlitz and handed her another bottle. While I had been doing that, she had been serving the meal. A plate of hot food waited at each end of the table. It smelled good and I realized I was hungry.

I took a new bottle and opened it, and then traded my open bottle for the unopened bottle in her hand. She surrendered it willingly and I opened it and took a swallow from it. By now

I was starting to feel a little drunk and comfortable throwing questions at my mother.

"Shall we eat?" I asked her.

"We should, if you'll sit down."

I pulled out a chair and picked up a fork and knife. "Do you want to say a Grace?" I asked.

"I wouldn't know how, anymore," she replied. "Do you want to say it?"

"How can I take that?" I challenged.

"Take it anyway you like."

"I'm not looking for a row," I told her. I said a short, muttered Grace myself and dug into the meal.

We ate silently for a while. Then she said hotly: "You don't have to be that way about it with me."

"Aren't you happy enough?" I asked her.

She frowned and set her bottle down on the table. Her eyes had a strange air about them. "You remember little Jimmy Roberson? I'm sure you must. You played baseball with him ten years ago."

"I remember him," I said. "We were never friends."

"He was two years older than you, ran track in high school and he was pretty good at it back then. We knew his family over at the church. His mother was the one that made the candy baked hams that you and your brother used to love so much."

"What does my brother have to do with this?"

"I'm trying to talk about the old church days."

I set my bottle down and leaned back in my chair. "You mean before dad ran off and you started drinking?"

Mother ignored my wisecrack and I felt bad about making it. She set her cigarette in the ashtray and pulled her bathrobe up tight around her neck, anxiously twisting the cloth there at the base of her throat. She wasn't even forty years old yet, but in that moment she could easily have been mistaken for a woman twenty years older. Hard luck, heartache, and hard

265

living had worn her down quickly over the past few years.

I uncrossed my arms. "What about Jimmy Roberson?" I asked quietly. Suddenly, I understood what I was about to hear. "Did his family receive bad news?"

My mother nodded, staring down at her plate. She'd barely touched her food and I felt sorry for her in a way I never expected that I could. Abruptly she looked old and small, and quite different from the woman who I'd known all my life.

"What happened?" I asked.

Before responding she pressed her hands together in front of her face, as if she were about to start a prayer. "Two weeks ago he succumbed to injuries received during the invasion of Okinawa. His ship was hit by a Jap kamikaze. His family only found out yesterday. You can imagine their grief."

We finished the meal in silence and my mother moved into the living room where she continued to drink until she passed out. Three hours later, I helped her off the couch and guided her to her bedroom. She initiated a detour herself, pulling me into the bathroom where she vomited into the commode. For twenty minutes I sat with her and then led her into her bedroom.

"Lay down with me for a short while," she pleaded, plumping the bedspread next to her with the palm of her hand. "Show your poor mother just a little lovin'."

She was stinking drunk and I ignored her despondent pleas. I turned her on her side and pulled the blanket up over her shoulder and turned out the light before retiring to my own bedroom.

For a long time I lay awake. The shadows of the night crawled over me and moved up the bed, climbing along my moonlight-exposed skin, weighing down on the sheet over my lower torso. Sleep had not found me – or at least I thought it had not. I couldn't be sure, I told myself. Perhaps I had drifted off or floated in some intermediate level of consciousness for several hours without being aware of it.

266

I twitched with a start, finding myself awake suddenly, but unable to move.

The dream held me motionless: the nightmare of an ugly, primitive aboriginal people huddled together in a dank cave. I wasn't sure how I had arrived there or why, but as I studied the stunted, odd-looking, hairy people, I was struck by how happy and affectionate they were with each other. They didn't know how ugly, primitive, or backward they were. I felt sorry for them, but as I awoke, I realized that perhaps I wasn't fit to judge them. Who was I? What did I know?

Maybe they pitied me?

Maybe they should have.

Chapter Twenty

Two days later, in the stifling heat of the early afternoon, Wrench found me nursing a chocolate milkshake at Handrow's diner. He ordered a hamburger for himself, and we sat together at the counter without speaking much to each other while he ate and I finished my milkshake. I took a deep breath before standing up because I knew it would be well over a hundred degrees outside.

"You ready?" Wrench asked me after he'd paid his tab.

"Its awful hot out there." My shirt was already sticking to me.

"Let's go anyway."

We left the diner together and he waved me down the street with him. He was a few inches shorter than me, but walked briskly with a lot of motion in his arms.

"Where we going?" I asked.

"Let's you and I go talk with Mr. Hacket," he suggested. "I guess it's time. What do you think?"

"I think its swell," I replied.

"Are you carrying?"

"Why, is today the day?"

Wrench shrugged and found a packet of cigarettes. He drew one and then offered the pack to me. I selected one myself and we each lighted up off our own lighters. We slowed our pace, but didn't stop.

"No," he said. "We can't go without a plan. You know that and we need you to help us with it. We believe you'll be a good man to have on the operation when we run it – but also important, we need your expertise in designing the caper. I guess in the Army they called it operational planning."

"Is that what it is? A caper?"

"Call it what you like."

"The Army would start by finding a good code name," I told him.

268

"I like that. What do you suggest?"

"Angry Doll," I said immediately.

"'Operation Angry Doll.' I rather like that. What else do you think?"

"I need to know the objective."

"In time."

"Then I don't have much to work with."

We continued to walk together in the afternoon heat.

"You can speak freely with me," he said after a while.

"Here's how it sits: I understand how an operation works in the Army. You identify an objective, make a plan, work out the logistics, pull together the necessary resources as best you can, and then you execute it. I don't know anything about how you and your boss work things here in this town. In the Army you have command and control, and you have structure and discipline. Does any of that exist out here? Does it even matter?"

"Of course it matters," Wrench replied amiably. "Let's march a few blocks more. We're almost there."

We continued through the heat. As we smoked our cigarettes in silence, I counted the blocks out of habit. We walked exactly seven streets over from Handrow's and then we turned right on Euclid Avenue and walked three more. By that time we were both drenched in sweat and we had loosened our ties and rolled up our shirtsleeves as far as we could make them go.

Wrench fanned himself with his Stetson. I decided that was one concession I would not make.

I knew it was harder on him than it was on me because I'd been through far worse. Airborne training saw to that: they made it so hard and miserable that when you finally landed in a combat zone you were able to tolerate whatever pain, fear, and horror awaited.

"We're almost there," he promised me.

I smiled at him, tapping his shoulder to make sure he saw

me. "Where are we going?"

"Hacket has a place, a house. He wants the crew to meet there."

"He wants us to meet at his house?"

"I didn't say that."

"Maybe you meant something else, then?"

"It's a place we use. A house, but he doesn't live there."

"How large is this crew?"

"I'd guess six men, maybe as many as eight. We'll learn when we get there. You have to understand something – he's the boss and he pulls things together."

"If this isn't Hacket's house, won't it seem strange to the neighbors to see all these obvious crooks going in and out in the middle of the afternoon?"

"He's used the house before, never had a problem."

"What do you think that means?"

"Never thought about it."

"Exactly."

"It works."

"Huh?"

Wrench looked at me with lazy resentment in his eyes. "The man's married. He has to have somewhere to tryst with his girlfriends."

Suddenly, I understood all too well. We were going to the house that Sally lived in. She was the one on the hook for this meeting of outlaws. I hated her, but now I also felt sorry for her.

Chapter Twenty-One

The house was a simple ranch style in a non-descript neighborhood. The lawn was well kept. When we reached the door, Wrench hit the knocker three times as if he were passing along a previously agreed to signal, and then he opened the door without waiting for a response.

Six men sat in the front room of the house. One of them was Hacket. He lounged in a chair positioned in the middle of the room with his legs crossed and his head back on the headrest. A cigarette dangled from his lips. His arms splayed out over the armrests with open palms down toward the floor. He looked for all the world like he was already dead, except he blinked his eyes and bobbed the cigarette with his lips when he saw me.

I nodded and tipped my hat.

He ignored the gesture by closing his eyes and pretending that he hadn't seen it. The other five men in the room also ignored me, which I didn't mind. What I did mind was when Sally came into the room with a stack of glasses and a pitcher of beer. I didn't like the way she served the men, moving around with the stacked glasses, pouring the beer for each man in his turn. She was too nice, too solicitous, and too something else that I didn't want to put a label on. Her eyes needled me as she occasionally glanced my way, checking to see if I was watching her. I tried not to look at her.

When she reached me, I shook my head. That didn't matter much because her pitcher was empty anyway. She went back to the kitchen to refill it. By the time she returned, I had moved to take up a position in the far corner of the room, standing with my back to it, with my arms crossed.

Sally didn't look at me and for a little while I almost thought she had simply missed me.

Eventually, she went around the room again refilling glasses. Wrench stood in the entryway, also not drinking. I suspected that was his response to my decision not to drink. He didn't want to risk giving me an edge. At least that's how I read him. As I thought about that, I rather liked the idea. Maybe I'd gotten under his skin after all.

"We're all here," Hacket said eventually, standing up to face the room. "Honey, would you give us a little privacy," he whispered loudly and waved a hand in the air.

Sally didn't look at him, but she left the room again and this time closed the door behind her. It seemed mostly for show. Hacket had to know she could hear everything through the door.

"Thank you for coming," he said to us, "and I'll keep this brief. Most of you know why you are here. For those of you who don't, I'll spell it out. There are two banks in this town and we're going to take them both Friday afternoon coming."

Two of the men started to clap. Hacket held up both of his hands, open palms outward, and encouraged the men to quiet. "Let's not get ahead of ourselves. This is an ambitious job. We have work to do before we'll be ready to pull this off."

"Who are we?" someone asked. "I like to know who I'm working with and the only face I recognize is yours."

"For one thing," Hacket replied, "we're not going to make introductions. Each of you knows me and that's all you need to know. Most of you are out-of-towners. When the job is finished, you each go your separate ways. I stick around to take the heat if there is any. This way if anyone is pinched, they can't rat out anyone but me."

One man stood up, grim-faced, as he flexed the muscles inside his t-shirt. "In that case, count me out. I need to know who I'm working with."

"You know me," Hacket replied firmly. "You know my word is good."

I noticed the other man's eyes were bloodshot red. He wasn't going to let it go. "That's not enough," he declared. "I'm not going to risk my life with strangers, especially if I don't know their names or where they're from."

"No names," Hacket insisted.

The man didn't budge. "Either we make friendly introductions or I walk."

Hacket looked about. "You want names? I'll give you names."

He counted us off one at a time, pointing his finger at each one of us as he spoke: "Jimmy One, Jimmy Two, Jimmy Three, Jimmy Four, Jimmy Five. I'm not a Jimmy, and neither are these other two," he said, waving at Wrench and me. "You all know who I am, so I won't belabor the point. Call these two Frick and Frack. That's who they are to you now."

The belligerent man was still standing, only now he was shaking his head angrily and muttering under his breath. His face was the color of a boiled beet – red and hot and moist. He didn't say anything as he started to walk toward the front door of the house.

He only took three steps and then he wasn't able to go any further. The man identified as "Frick," who I knew as Wrench, blocked his path. More then blocking it with his body alone, he also blocked it with a gun – a .32 Colt revolver, which barked loudly two times.

The bullets hit the man in the chest. The entire jiffy didn't take more than a few seconds and then it was done. Nobody moved.

Hacket smiled mildly as he looked around the room and then at the dead man on the floor. "Anyone else concerned about names?"

No one else was.

Chapter Twenty-Two

"Alright," Hacket continued, pursing his lips confidently. "Let's get to business. Here it is in broad strokes: First, we'll look at a couple of street maps and then I'll show an enlarged drawing of the area. After that, I've got blueprints of the bank interiors. It took a lot of work to get these. I've done a lot of thinking about this and I've consulted with a few guys who know about these things, but I need your help – your eyes, your ears, and your thoughts. Consider this plan a draft – that is, some of the details need to be worked out yet."

While he was talking, Wrench set up an easel beside him. After he flipped through several large sheets of paper, he finished with a flourish and we were looking at a city map of Monahans with several red arrows drawn brightly on it. Large colored dots of blue and green and yellow were also placed on the map.

Hacket paused to turn and study the easel himself. When he faced us again, he was smiling. "This is Monahans. The red arrows are the primary access points to get in and out of town. The blue dots are police stations, the green one is the fire station, and the two yellow ones are hospitals. Any questions so far?"

"Will we have time to study these later?" somebody asked.

"Yes and you'll each be issued a smaller city map. There will be a primary and secondary getaway route marked on them, but you'll need to memorize these in advance and the drivers will have already driven them many times over. Any other questions?"

There were none.

Hacket flipped the page to show us the next sheet. It was a detailed map of downtown Monahans. "This shows the downtown area, the entry streets, the location of the two banks – marked in orange – and each of the buildings on the street and the two streets parallel to it."

"What are the small green dots?" someone asked.

Hacket smiled. "These are possible roof sites for a sniper to set up on."

"Why would we need a sniper?"

"To provide cover *if* the local police return from the diversion before our crew can get out. I don't expect that will happen – but we have to be ready."

The room was quiet. I studied the location of the small green dots. Although they were presented as an afterthought, I knew about the BAR out at "the farm" and I suspected it was the role planned for me. I was to be the sniper.

"So how does this all begin?" another man asked.

Hacket flipped to the next page on the easel. "There will be a diversion," he said simply. On the map, he bounced his finger along several points around the outskirts of town. "No one in this room needs to concern themselves with what it will be, but it will be significant and effective. It will draw the local police and firefighters away from the center of town out to the warehouses. They will be completely preoccupied there for at least an hour and if you know the roads out there, you know there's a bottleneck through which all vehicles have to pass. There's a causeway with a small bridge over it."

"I'll vouch for that," Wrench said. "I've driven that road many times. Once it flooded out there, and it took me a half day of driving around the long way to get home."

One of the men who had not said a word up to that point cleared his throat and raised his hand. "I'm just a dumb Jasper from Oklahoma, but I don't think we can count on one of your famous Texas floods rising up on Friday after all the police have gone out that way."

Hacket smiled momentarily and then his eyes fell hard. "That's why we're going to dynamite the causeway."

The room filled with chuckles, though I knew it meant men would almost certainly die.

"What about the banks?" one of the other Jimmies asked.

Hacket nodded seriously. "That's the right question. What about them? How do we take them down? Think for a moment. At this point in the scheme, we've drawn all the law away out of town and the banks are isolated, but there's still one more step. Someone has to go into the banks and get the money. The first four Jimmies, numbers one through four," and here he paused to count them out by pointing at each of the four men in turn. "You guys are the keys to this caper. Two of you will walk into each bank and take the money and bring it out."

"What are we going to be armed with?"

"Each of you will carry a side arm of your choice. We have .45 semi-autos and revolvers chambered for .44 and .38. Choose whatever you like. You will also each be issued two pineapple hand grenades and two smoke canisters."

"I'd like something with a little more robust firepower," one of the Jimmy's said.

"You shall have it," Hacket averred. "Each pair will have one Thompson submachine gun. It will be up to you guys to decide who carries it. We also have several M3 submachine guns. So each of you will have either a Thompson or an M3 grease gun, a sidearm, and grenades and smoke canisters. Is that sufficient?"

"What about vests?"

"Yes," Hacket replied. "Every man who wants one will have a bullet proof vest."

The Jimmie who had asked the question, nodded his head, satisfied. He had another question: "What's inside when we get there? Do you anticipate armed guards inside the banks?"

"You'll have a chance to see for yourself tomorrow," Hacket answered. "The answer is yes, but I don't think they represent a serious challenge. They are little more than bright monkeys who strut around and pose with their pistols. They flirt with the ladies and share lollipops with the kids, but I don't think they're well trained and I'm sure they've never been tested. I doubt even one of them has ever had a gun barrel pushed against his forehead."

There was a ripple of soft laughter and I sensed the room loosening now with the confidence of men who had lived their lives with guns. The opportunity was clear and tangible to them, and as they looked about at each other, I recognized something else. They were a band of brothers – outlaws to be sure – but men who knew each other not from the accidents of family trees or educations or military service, but from the commonalities of the risks they had taken and the lives they had lived outside the law. They knew the same sacrifices, the same illegal joys.

"Other questions, comments, or concerns?" Hacket invited. He shook his hands out at his sides, encouraging us to speak.

"You mentioned we might have a sniper on one of the roofs," someone started. "What type of firearm would he be operating?"

Hacket paused while he let the question sink in before answering: "A Browning Automatic Rifle. Standard M1918, .30 caliber."

Someone in the room gave a low whistle.

"That's right," Hacket said.

"He know how to use it?" someone else asked.

Hacket nodded. "Mr. Frack over here. He's an expert with the BAR. Uncle Sam trained him well and gave him extensive practice across Europe over the past couple years."

Several men glanced over at me. I didn't say anything or react in any way.

"Other questions?" Hacket asked. He stood still, as though frozen in time with an unlit cigarette waiting between his lips. After about thirty seconds he moved again and lighted the cigarette, exhaling slowly up toward the ceiling. He was still waiting, still looking around the room.

While he was doing that, I was thinking about the Browning M1919 .30 caliber gun I'd seen out at the farm. No one had mentioned it. Maybe it had been one of the options and my suggestion to put it aside had been accepted.

I thought about that and the more I thought about it, the more I couldn't quite let go of the thought. Somewhere out there was another powerful automatic rifle and I suspected it would make an appearance at some point.

"Any more questions?" Hacket asked.

The room was quiet.

"I have one," I said, raising my hand level to my face.

Hacket nodded at me.

"What's the payday?"

"Something north of two million."

"That's nice change," I said.

"Is it enough for you?"

I had to smile at him. "No," I replied.

"How's that?"

I lighted the cigarette that floated between my lips. After exhaling, I said: "There's no such thing as 'enough.' It can't be had."

Hacket didn't mind that comment, but I wasn't finished.

"There is one other thing," I said. "While I can understand why a small town like Monahans might have two banks, I can't understand why those two banks would be holding two million dollars between them – or how you would know about it if they did."

Chapter Twenty-Three

The silence didn't last long. Hacket filled it with his own soft merriment, course and ugly. Nobody else chuckled with him.

"That's a fair statement," Hacket said eventually.

"The statement has a question mark hanging at the end of it." It wasn't the first mission briefing I'd sat through that didn't make full sense.

Hacket was quiet for a moment while he ran a hand over the top of his head, tousling his own hair. "The answer to the question is both simple and obvious. It's an old Texas story: wildcatters hit some good wells out in the Odessa area and they hit more all around Ward and Winkler counties. For reasons that are too complicated to bore you with, the money – profits and payrolls – now run through the banks of Monahans."

"Doesn't make sense to me," I said. "Maybe you should bore us with the reasons."

Hacket's gaze turned sour. "There are no trustworthy banks in Odessa. Those city guys are crooks and everyone in the counties around here knows it."

"Can't be that simple," someone else kicked in.

"Banks in Monahans charge lower overhead," Hacket said.

"By design?" someone asked.

Hacket shrugged. He allowed his half-smile to blossom as he began to feel like he was back in charge of things. "I might have had something to do with that."

"If I understand this correctly," another man joined in. "You're telling us you've planned this score for a long time. You've worked behind the scenes to bring oil and gas money to Monahans on the premise that it's a better banking environment than Odessa is for the oilmen in the surrounding counties. Have I got that right?"

"Yes," Hacket affirmed. He smiled broadly as he let the realization sink in among us.

"How did you sell that idea, and how can you be sure it

won't come back on you after this score goes down?"

"I had nothing to do with the notion, at least not directly," Hacket said. "I did take a few of the right men out to dinner. You know: the men who run the banks and the men who drill the oil. Some of them like to drink, some of them like to gamble, and some of them like pretty young ladies. Some of them like all three. All I did was facilitate things, circulate a few suggestions, and make a few introductions. Human nature took care of the rest."

There were some mumblings and somebody laughed as if in response to a whispered joke. I finished my cigarette and glanced at my watch.

"Where will you be when the knock over happens," one of the Jimmies asked.

Hacket cleared his throat. "On the day and time you all take down the banks, I'm going to be at a meeting with Governor Coke Stevenson in Austin. I will have an alibi and no one will be able to suspect an inside man. My name isn't on anything – and no one will be able to connect me to the robberies, or me to any of you. Besides, Coke is going to like what I have to tell him and he's going to be so happy, he's going to call me his friend."

I contributed another question. "What do we do now?"

"You've been out to the farm," Hacket replied. "You've seen what we have out there."

I nodded.

"That's where the operation moves now. We've prepared it to receive the whole crew, with a couple of exceptions for the two of you who live here in town." He nodded at Wrench and then at me. "By the time you all get out there in a few hours, we'll have food, water, and bunks prepared."

"What about booze and girls?" someone asked.

"There won't be any of that," Hacket responded. His tone was firm, not joking around. "There will be time enough for that after you are all rich men. Tonight you should eat well

280

and sleep, and get ready for the next few days."

"Aww, boss!" one man lamented.

Hacket held up his hand. "Let's be clear. Over the next few days you are going to prepare for what you came here to do. You are going to focus and practice. Not only will you study the maps – meaning you will know the roads, the buildings, the interior blueprints of the banks – but you will be tested on them.

"You will learn your role perfectly, as well as the role of two other men. If anyone falls or if anyone falters, their role will be picked up by another. We will have range practice out at the farm. Each of you will stay until you demonstrate expertise with your pistol, the Thompson gun, or the M3. You are going to be ready for this mission – so ready it will be second nature to you when the time arrives."

I'd heard that kind of talk before and I smiled to myself. "Once we've taken the banks down and have the cash, where do we go from there?" I asked.

"After the knock over," Hacket said, "everyone retreats back to the farm. I do mean everyone. The plan is to lay low for two to three days, maybe four, depending on the situation in Monahans. Once the heat is off, you will each receive your cut and you can go your separate way."

"What is our cut?" someone asked.

"I promised each of you that you would be rich," Hacket responded. He licked his lips, as though tasting the words he was about to speak. "Every one of you will receive one hundred thousand dollars cash money." When he finished speaking the words, Hacket's eyes were alive with the moment.

One of the Jimmy's whistled.

A second Jimmy whistled.

"What's your cut going to be?" I asked Hacket.

There was a moment of silence.

"The math isn't tricky," Hacket said finally. "My cut is one million and two hundred thousand. Out of that I have to pay off my inside sources, pay for the weapons, and pay for the men who set the dynamite diversions that will make this operation possible. I've already spread around a fair bit of coin among the bankers and oilmen involved, and I'm planning to spread a good bit more around Austin. When all is said and done, I hope to clear five hundred, maybe six hundred thousand for myself."

"Nice work, boss," Wrench avowed cheerfully.

"Does anyone have a problem with that?"

"No, sir, I sure don't," Wrench volunteered. "This is a solid operation."

Hacket surveyed the room with his eyes slowly and he finished with them fixed on me.

I shook my head. "I don't have a problem with it," I said. "Why would I?"

The Jimmies didn't say a word among them.

Chapter Twenty-Four

For supper I stopped at Handrow's on my way home and ate a meal that Bill cooked up for me on his grill: two hamburgers, a bowl of fried potatoes, an egg fried over-easy, and four slices of a grilled tomato doused in salt and black pepper.

Bill served the hamburgers on crispy toasted buns with lots of mustard and thinly sliced dill pickles that he had put up himself. I ate it all and washed it down with a glass of beer and then followed it with a chocolate milkshake. It might have been the best meal I'd ever eaten.

"You okay, buddy?" Bill asked me after I'd finished the milkshake and lighted a cigarette.

I lied and told him I was.

"Want anything else, another milkshake maybe?"

I shook my head. "You fed me too well."

"I like to hear that," he smiled briefly.

"I'll take the check," I said. "No hurry, though."

We didn't talk after that. Bill spent his energy working the grill for the three other people who had come in to sit at the counter and the two couples who were at tables along the window. I finished my cigarette and paid the tab he'd set in front of me in one-dollar bills, not waiting around for the change.

My head ached from the day, but I felt good about the food and the encouragement I'd found at Handrows. It was difficult to put into words, but I liked Bill. Despite the age difference between us, it seemed like we came from the same place. He'd had Pershing, I'd had "Nuts" McAuliffe and Patton. We'd both served under fighting generals and nobody back home understood us.

That meant something.

The sky was still light when I stepped outside. The sun had disappeared behind the horizon, but it reflected off the clouds that hovered above. The air was hot and humid. I lighted

283

another cigarette, though with the heat I felt little enthusiasm to smoke it. Eventually I gave up on it and dropped it under my step as I walked. I glanced at my watch. It was almost nine o'clock in the evening and I walked home slowly, happy to let the food and the ideas and the worries of the day settle within me.

Hacket had given quite a performance. I thought about his approach – the plan, the presentation, and the murder I'd witnessed. There had been a reason they'd killed that Jimmy so quickly. It didn't make sense to me, but I knew it did to them. Hacket and Wrench didn't do anything lightly, especially Hacket. Maybe it was how criminals operated in rural Texas, but the more I thought about it, the less sense it made. That told me it made absolutely sense to them in some way that I was unable to see.

The more I thought about it, the more I wondered what Wrench might have said to Hacket about seeing Sally and me together. I couldn't see an angle to it, so I decided he probably hadn't said anything yet. It was easy to worry, though. Wrench wasn't an altruist. If he'd kept the kiss secret, there was a reason for it. I thought about that all the way home.

"Where you been all day?" my mother asked when I came in through the front door. Her voice called from the kitchen and a moment later she peered in through the living room at me.

"Job interviews," I told her, moving toward the dining room, where I removed my shoes.

"Find anything?" she asked, still wiping her hands on a towel.

I smiled to myself, knowing she couldn't see my face clearly in the darkened room. "Sure, The Court of Saint James offered me a permanent seat at the Privy Council."

"Are you sassing me?"

"Never mind," I told her. I was tired and sorry I'd even made the effort at sarcasm. It was a line one of my platoon

284

buddies had used. He'd had a year or two of college that he liked to treat as a silly joke out in the fields of Europe. "I didn't find a job yet, still looking."

"You were gone long enough. What did you find?"

I ignored the implication of her question. "I tore through a lot of shoe leather this morning and I spent a good bit of the afternoon and evening resting my elbows on the counter at Handrow's."

"They have a good grill man there," my mother replied helpfully.

I nodded. "His name is Bill. He's got special talent."

"Oh come on, I didn't mean it that way."

I shrugged, suddenly feeling very tired, exhausted from the day. It had been a long one. "I'm turning in now. You need anything, Ma?"

With a curdling expression on her face she shook her head and said: "Run along and get some sleep if you can."

As I walked past her, I patted her on the shoulder and then disappeared into the darkness of my bedroom. Absently, I turned on the AM radio, tuning it for a moment and then adjusting the volume downward, so that I could hear it, but that it was quiet.

Slowly I undressed by the window, enjoying a light bathe in the moonlight that filtered down through the trees on the lawn and then in through the lace curtains. After a while, I pushed them to one side and stood there with the moonlight on my skin. Something about it felt purifying. Eventually I lay down on the bed and tried to relax while I felt the silhouettes creeping around the walls and ceiling.

Lying under those shadows at night, unable to sleep in the heat and alone with my thoughts, brought it back. I thought about her body and the way it felt against me, the feel of her warm breath against my neck when we lay still without talking afterwards. I wanted to hate her, but I was unable to – I still had the feelings, even now, even after everything. I wondered if she ever really knew how I felt about her. Maybe I wasn't the expressive type, though it seemed she must have sensed the force of my ache. At times I imagined that it seeped through every pore in my body.

We'd had ideas together about how the future could be and during the days and evenings – down by the river – we'd talked about them and the dreams we had and the ways we would live them together. I thought about those times. We were supposed to be forever somehow, and at the time, I'd believed it.

That seemed so long ago, as if it had happened to somebody else. The boy I had been then was somebody I no longer knew. I didn't want to know him anymore. I was ashamed of how weak he was. The old memories haunted me like an invocation, a hex – mocking me, taunting me, even causing me to wish those times had never happened at all. I could wish them away, but that didn't help any.

I lay on the bed with my feet crossed at the ankles and one elbow propped behind my head. The radio played a slow sad tune that fit with my mood. I lighted a cigarette and forced myself to listen to it there in the darkness.

"*Texas rain coming down against the window pane, old country tunes playing along on the radio, the dial glowing, a couple of beers – just enough to get me through the night.*" I hummed along quietly, allowing the lyrics to swell in my mind as though they were part of a song written by somebody I knew well. I could have written them myself.

As in the song, it was raining now – a gentle, steady rain with occasional soft lightning and the reassuring roll of a distant thunder that followed. It was perfect. Perfect and lonely. One of those nights where even if you can't sleep, it doesn't seem to quite matter so much, but its hard not to think about what you've left behind or simply lost. The steady night rain has a way of focusing one's melancholy on the dreams that have been left behind.

I tried hard not to go there, and while I was trying, I fell asleep – sound asleep, so deeply asleep that the angry, grieving demons came out and played roughshod over my soul.

Chapter Twenty-Five

The next morning the whole world was dripping wet and gleaming bright and the sun quickly burned everything it could reach. I sat up in bed and felt sick from the dreams I'd had through the night, nightmares I'd been unable to escape. The images were obscure, though I was shivering mightily as if I'd been out in the severe cold for a long time.

Hoping it was late morning I discovered that it wasn't even six thirty yet. With the T-shirt I'd worn the day before, I mopped the sweat off my face, neck, and hairline. For good measure, I ran it down the middle of my chest and then brought it back up the lower part of my back.

In the kitchen I got a pot of coffee brewing and a line of bacon cooking in a cast iron skillet. When the bacon was half cooked, I pushed it aside with a spatula and cracked open three eggs into the middle of the pan. They cooked quickly and hard as I shoved them around in the bacon grease, and then I tipped the entire pan over a plate, scrapping the eggs and bacon onto it.

After that I set the pan back over the flame and laid two pieces of thick sliced bread in it. The bread crackled and popped in the bacon grease, and after a moment, I flipped each piece over. When they were crispy I set them on my plate with the rest of the food and poured a cup of coffee.

I ate by myself. My mother never made an appearance. Afterward I set the dishes in the sink, changed my shirt, and headed out into the day. It was going to be another hot one.

I walked downtown and paced by Hacket's banks. I walked the length of six blocks on either side of Main Street, making note of the shops and the alleys that were there. The two banks seemed to be the only two banks in town. Then I walked the same six blocks on the streets that ran parallel on either side of Main Street. Periodically, I checked the folded map that I'd brought along to ensure I knew where I was and what I was looking at.

After about two hours under the sun studying Monahans on foot I had a good sense of the layout. I took a break and ducked into a soda fountain a few doors down from the banks. There I had a hotdog and two glasses of root beer.

I thought about the heist plan and the Jimmies laying low out at the farm. I knew they would be shown maps and given time to study them, but none of them would actually scout the terrain, walk the streets, or peek inside the banks we were planning to rob. It wasn't the way I would have run the operation. The more I thought about that, the more I decided it worked in my favor.

As I sat nursing the second root beer, I decided there was one more thing: I needed to get up on the rooftop I'd been assigned to. Hacket's plan provided a way for me to get up there at the last minute. A maid was going to leave a certain door unlocked for five minutes on the day of the robbery. That suggested roof access wasn't easy. Maybe it was designed to discourage me from trying ahead of time, but I wasn't buying into that.

The more I thought about it, the less sense it made. When I left the soda fountain, I walked around the block one time and from the back side I found it. Down a side alley there was a fire ladder right where I needed it. I scaled the three stories quickly and moved around the roof freely for ten minutes, scouting the angles and the views. From the firing position I would have taken, I could see the street below in front of each bank. I also had a good view of the route law enforcement would have to travel if they were responding to an alarm in that area. Hacket had planned it well.

I also noted there were several rooftops in the area that had higher positions than the one I commanded. If additional snipers were in Hacket's plans, that's where they would be. Hacket's scheme put me in a good spot to have an excellent field of fire over the access route for returning law enforcement and the street outside the bank. At the same time, as I stood there and looked around, I could see it wasn't the best position. It left me at a disadvantage to any other snipers that might be set up in the area.

The map he had shown us suggested where they might be. From where I stood surveying the rooftops, I found a position I liked better. For several minutes I watched it and made mental calculations relative to the street below, the access route, and the other rooftop positions in the area. I studied it for several minutes, noting the location of the building and doors that entered it.

After that, I returned to street level and found entry into the building I'd studied. Within ten minutes of exploration, I was up on the roof, charting the area and the streets, and making several final calculations. The work brought a smile to my face.

I'd found my position.

When I finished, I walked home. My mother wasn't there when I arrived. I undressed and lay on top of my bed with a small rotating desk fan blowing directly over me while I smoked four or five cigarettes and thought things over some more. In my mind I had a clear map of the town – the banks, the stores, the streets. I even knew some of the people by sight. I'd been in there and seen the aging bank guards with their revolvers that had never been fired in the heat of the moment.

Over that I laid Hacket's plan and thought about it from several different angles: What would he do if he were running the operation with a focus on accomplishing the mission exactly as stated? What would he do differently if he were running an operation designed to enrich only himself, while the rest of us were expendable?

Then I thought of two other questions. What would Hacket do if he intended that I would first serve my purpose, but that I would not survive the operation long enough to collect my end? What would he do if he needed to create an impression that the criminals behind the robbery were dead and there was no one left for law enforcement to pursue?

While I stared at the ceiling and smoked, I thought about of all this. In my mind I pictured the operation as it was supposed to unfold and also as it might unfold. I thought through the various angles and scenarios – playing them through, and then I turned my mind toward the question of what I would do and how I would survive if my own worst cynical thoughts were borne out.

Chapter Twenty-Six

That night I couldn't sleep so I went for a late walk through the dark and quiet streets of Monahans. Except for me, nothing moved. It was almost midnight by the time I saw the light inside Handrows. I didn't expect it to be open, but I went over and tried the door anyway and it was unbolted.

I pushed my way in.

Most of the interior lights were off. At the far end Bill was alone with his elbows on the counter, smoking a cigarette. The place was utterly quiet. He didn't say anything, but he opened a cold bottle of beer and set it in front of me as I sat down. He opened a second one for himself. Without a word we tapped the bottlenecks together. I took a pull from mine and then looked at him.

He shrugged vaguely under the dim light and shadows that draped us both. "They're not for the paying customers, but I keep a few of them on ice for myself – just for the end of the day. You know. Sometimes I need to drink a few of them. Glad you came by to have one with me."

"I couldn't sleep," I told him in reply.

"It's okay, kid," he said gently. "I usually can't either."

"What do you do?"

Bill shook his head, pursing his lips. "Sometimes I stay open late, like tonight – just for the hell of it. Try to work through it."

"Even though you don't have customers."

"Tonight I have you."

I grinned. "Paying customers."

He grinned back and shot a forefinger at me. "Sometimes it helps to talk a little. You're just a kid still. You don't know it, but you are. Maybe I have something to offer? I'll listen if you care to gab."

"Not much value in talk," I said.

"You'd be surprised."

292

"Are you a Chaplain?"

"No, but I'm old enough to have learned a thing or two."

"Who do you talk to?"

"Me? I talk to my dog. He's an expert at this stuff by now."

"What kind of dog is he?"

"A mutt – big and bushy with soft brown eyes and the floppiest ears. His name is Rickey. He's a pretty good hunting dog and he's seen his own share of things."

"You tell him everything?"

Bill shrugged. "Why not? He's the best listener I know. He ain't here right now, so all you get is me. I'll listen if you want me to, but I can't promise not to give you advice if I think of some. Rickey will moan and even bark a little on occasion. It's probably better than anything I have to offer."

I smiled. "What happened to 'don't ask me about my war and I won't ask you about yours?'"

Bill's return smile was grim. "I know you now and you know me," he replied. "Not pressuring you, but if you want to talk, I'm happy to listen. We're part of the same tribe now." As if to emphasize the point, he opened two more bottles of beer and set them on the counter between us. I chose one and he took the other.

"You don't have a woman?" I asked.

"Wouldn't have need for one," Bill confessed. "I haven't had much interest in that since I came back. I was married for a few years. The wife said I didn't show affection, wasn't intimate. I guess she was right. That part of me was gone and I feel bad that she had to put up with me."

"What happened to her?"

"She left a long time ago. I can't blame her. What could I offer her on the human side?"

"Is it bad?"

"After all these years, I don't mind being alone. I'm comfortable with it."

"What's the toughest part?" I asked.

"Hearing them call you a hero when you know different."

"Yeah," I replied, with a pit growing in my stomach. I knew what he was talking about. "What do you say to them?"

Bill squinted hard at something in the air over my head. When he spoke again, his voice was lower and his eyes were still clinched: "Nothing. Some things are just between you and the witness tree."

Chapter Twenty-Seven

"Tell me something," Bill encouraged a little while later. "What keeps you awake at nights?"

I took a moment, thinking about where to start. "You want to hear a story?"

"If you care to tell it."

"When we reached Bastogne, we were deployed in a long arc and told to form a defensive line, but there wasn't enough of us to do that – not for a real line. Our command posts were spread too far apart.

"So we dug in as best we could. There were wide gaps and we just had to hope the Germans didn't find them. There were frozen bodies around us everywhere. Some were ours; some were theirs. Mostly we couldn't tell the difference. It was so cold in the Ardennes. Have you ever seen someone who's frozen solid?"

Bill shook his head, but he didn't say anything. He smoked quietly and took a pull at his beer, and he looked at me, listening.

I continued. "We weren't well supplied. We were short of everything: men, ammo, food, warm clothing, medicine. Guys that got hit declined morphine because they believed someone else needed it more. It wasn't every man for himself – it was every man for the team. Nobody wanted to be the one to use up too much of what we had. Even with shrapnel wounds and trench foot, nobody would come off the line if they could help it."

"I remember that part of it," Bill said quietly.

"At night we huddled together in our fox holes. We lay three and four together, sharing blankets and body heat. It's strange. I can't ever remember feeling so safe or happy at night as when I was sleeping in a frozen muddy hole with three buddies, sharing one blanket while shells exploded above.

"For a week we did that, surviving, running patrols when

we had to, ducking artillery barrages, and dying slowly from exposure and starvation. At least we were together. We had each other and that kept us going."

"You almost miss it don't you?" Bill asked.

I thought about it a little. "At least I felt alive. I was doing something that seemed to matter. I was a part of something with a group of men and we were in it together. Maybe I'm kidding myself."

"Keep believing in it, kid," Bill advised.

"Really?"

"You were part of something that *did* matter. Nobody can take that away from you."

"Where do you find that common bond now?"

Bill shook his head. "You don't. That's what makes it so damn hard to come home and be a part of this quiet life here."

I finished my beer and Bill opened two more. We drank quietly, each sinking into our private thoughts.

I decided to tell him something I hadn't told anyone else before: "One night there on the line outside Bastogne there were four of us in one hole, one was a medic we valued because he was the one who might keep us alive if we got hit. He was damn good, too – the type who would take any risk to reach a wounded soldier. It took an active effort sometimes to keep him back and out of harm's way."

"We had guys like that in my war too," Bill soothed. "They ran stretchers and ambulance wagons all over the fields of Belgium, France, and Italy. They disregarded personal danger to get the job done. Few of them got the credit they deserved and a lot of them died in service to the units they were attached to."

I lighted a cigarette and exhaled before continuing. "One night, well after midnight, there were sounds from out in the forest in our sector. It was a Kraut patrol going past us in the forest. Hell, they were probably lost. We climbed out of our hole to track them. We couldn't risk the life of our medic, so we told him to stay behind. We pushed him back down into the foxhole before we left it. Three of us crept out toward the patrol.

"Unless there was shelling, the forest was quiet at night. The heavy bed of snow absorbed most other sounds. There were three of us. We tracked them through the snow and came up on them at a makeshift camp; six Krauts brewing coffee over a small fire, huddled around it to catch some of the heat. We caught them by surprise and it was over quickly.

"We killed four of them outright and took two prisoners. In the fight Healy caught a round through the neck. It was plain bad luck. He bled to death there in the snow and died right away. Rickerson, my squad mate since D-Day, was hit in the side, though it didn't seem too bad. I'd never once seen him smile before, so he was a hard one to read. He kept making those same straight-faced jokes he always made, though he never smiled. He never did. There wasn't a lot of bleeding from what I could tell and I patched him up as best I could. All the while he kept talking about the starlets he was going to screw when he got back to Los Angeles and how he would be famous for it.

"So we had two wounded prisoners, but no way to move them. Rickerson agreed I should go back to command and get help. I thought I'd only be gone for a couple hours. Command was less than two miles away. It was the only way and we both knew it.

"But we didn't count on the night. Snow was falling; the wind was fierce. At some point I tripped and sprained an ankle. All that is to say it took longer than I expected to make my way back to the command post. They didn't have any resources to spare. Six hours later, they sent me back out with a three man squad and a makeshift crutch. I had trouble finding my way back to the spot where I'd left Rickerson. In the dark, with the snowfall, the cold, my ankle, it was difficult."

At that point, I realized I was crying, sobbing actually. I

tried to continue, but I couldn't. Bill patted the back of my hand and made small comforting noises. Then he opened another bottle of beer while I got myself together.

"It's okay, brother," Bill assured.

"We found Rickerson early the next morning," I told him after I had recovered somewhat. "He was almost entirely covered in snow when they brought me up to view him. Around him were six dead Krauts. He'd killed the two prisoners before he passed out. There he was: frozen solid, with a hard smile on his face, as though he was happy for the first time in his life."

Chapter Twenty-Eight

By the time I got home my mother was sound asleep. I could hear her snoring quietly. I went to bed shortly after midnight, though I lay there with my thoughts for a long while. I was thinking about how soothing it was to be sure that our time on earth was finite. Without meaning to I found myself counting the nights I might have left.

Maybe I would have drifted off to a sound sleep, but something was bothering me. At first, it was a feeling, a slight sensation, and then it became a tiny a sound. It wasn't loud at all, just enough to register. Then I heard it again and it was familiar. I knew what it was.

As quietly as I could, I climbed out of bed and opened the window. Sally's face appeared in front of me, leaning inward with a drowsy expression on her face. Without a word, I grabbed her upper arms and pulled her inside. Though it had been over two years, the movement was second nature to me.

"Why are you here?" I whispered.

"Just kiss me," she whispered with her mouth already against mine, pushing hotly, probing.

I kissed her. I couldn't help myself.

We settled back onto my bed with her body on top of mine. "Why are—"

"Shhhh," she hushed. "Shut up."

I did and it was too late to stop even if I wanted to. As I stared into her yellow-brown eyes I became separated from time. I loved her impossibly. We made love slowly at first and then faster, each of us urging the other one to finish. Eventually we stopped to catch our breath and our bodies separated. We lay panting in the heat, savoring the whirring air from the small fan.

"Do you still love me?" she whispered.

I wanted to scream at her. "What can I say to that?" I replied instead.

"Will you free me from him?"

"Who?"

"You know who I'm talking about."

I did know. "I thought Hacket was your man." It was a cruel thing to say, but I couldn't help myself.

"I hate him," she hissed.

"He pays the bills."

She turned onto her side to put her mouth next to mine. The heat of her breath singed my face. "He treats me like his property and I hate him."

"I'm sure there's a reason he treats you like property."

She ran a hand over the hair on my chest, absently, almost tenderly, though her words suggested something else. "Are you taking his side?"

"No."

"My daddy always said: 'The dollar buys the vote.'"

"There's truth in that," I told her quietly.

"Hacket carries it too far."

"How does he mistreat you?"

"He locks me up like a canary – a pretty little bird he brings out to sing for him every now and then."

I looked into her eyes. She didn't look away. In the darkness they seemed to glow like two red-hot fires. "Seems like he keeps you in a pretty nice little cage," I said.

"That's what I thought at first. When I began seeing him he was something else. He was fun, easy-going, even exciting sometimes, and he had so much money. He knew how to treat a gal."

"That's when you wrote the letter," I realized out loud. "You thought you'd found something better."

"I'm sorry, darling," she whispered and kissed me on the mouth. "Believe me, I am. It was heartless of me. If I could take it back I would. I've regretted it a thousand times since and it haunts me that I did that."

"You're not so fragile," I told her.

300

"You think it's easy for me, don't you? I've grown up a lot in the last few months. You must believe me. I can see things now and I know I've been selfish."

I didn't say anything. The fan continued to whir and I found myself counting the seconds between clicks. It registered a slight hitch at the same point in every cycle.

"He's not natural, you know," Sally continued. "It's always about his next big deal, the next take down, the next bargain. He talks about 'scores' like other men talk about baseball games. Shortly after he set me up in that house, he moved on – maybe not physically to another woman, but emotionally. You know what I mean? He's cold like that. How am I supposed to feel? I just want a man who will light a fire in the fireplace, pay a little attention to me, give me flowers, pour a glass of wine, and hold me for a short while at night. Is that so hard?"

"He doesn't love you." I said.

She shook her head beside me. "It's not in him. He wants to possess me and keep me on a shelf like an exotic knick-knack."

"What do you want then?" I asked her.

"A house that's mine to share with a man who loves me."

"What else?"

"Maybe a small garden."

"Kids?"

"I wouldn't mind them. He makes sure I don't get them, though. Last December I was pregnant and he forced me to have an abortion. He arranged everything, but he wasn't there for it when I went in. Lord knows where he was, but I endured it alone, just like most everything else in our relationship."

I loved her and I almost felt sorry for her, but I couldn't quite manage that. She'd made her choices and now she had to confront them.

"What do you know about this caper?"

"Not much, though he likes to brag. He's crowed a little about his clever plan to rob two banks at once. He says he's

301

maneuvered several wealthy oil men to put their money in Monahans' banks, and he claims he's got fall guys set up to take the heat so he won't have to. I'm worried about you."

"You're telling me Hacket isn't beyond putting a little English on the ball."

"Yes, darling," she replied.

"I wouldn't have thought any different."

"Always remember, he does what he does best," she said. "He spins tales."

"Meaning what?"

"Every part of this operation is compartmentalized. He tells you one thing and others something different. That's his approach. He tells everyone what he wants them to believe and he keeps everybody separated from everybody else. Why do you think you're not out at the farm with the other Jimmies?"

"He doesn't need me out there."

"He doesn't *want* you out there," she corrected immediately. "I don't know, but I bet you dollars to donuts that he plays them against you. He'll tell them he doesn't trust you and they shouldn't either."

"Toward what end?"

I could feel her head shake in the darkness. "Maybe he's going to persuade them to fear you, as a way of keeping them in line."

"Or?"

"Or maybe he's going to have them kill you when the job is finished."

"Why would he do that?" I asked the question, though I already knew the answer.

"So he can keep your share."

I shrugged and felt the pillow move a little beneath my head. "That wouldn't get him much. He'd have to divide it with the other men."

"Maybe they won't all survive either. Plus, how many other side deals is he cutting?"

302

"Two million is a lot of money. A group of men like us could split it comfortably. Seems like plenty to go around."

"Two million?"

"Right, two million dollars in cash."

"Is that what he told you?"

"It is."

"It's not two million dollars – it's closer to four. I've heard him boasting about it to Wrench."

"I'm not surprised. I don't trust Wrench either."

"You shouldn't. He's Hacket's boy all the way."

I was silent for a moment. "Why did they kill that guy in the house the other day?" I asked.

Sally was quiet for a moment before answering. "I'm not sure, but you know, I think it might have been Hacket's plan from the beginning. He only needed four men for that role, but he brought in five. Maybe that was to cover his bases, but knowing him as I do, I wouldn't be surprised if he brought in one extra with the idea he could afford to make an example out of someone early on."

"Harsh way to send a message," I observed.

"You don't know him like I do. That's what I'm trying to tell you. Other people don't mean anything to him."

"You think he had that man killed simply to make a point?"

"Yes," she whispered adamantly.

"If I understand what you're saying, Hacket is the type of man who would orchestrate a blood bath among his own gang so that he could walk away with most of the money."

"That is what I'm saying, darling. That's why you need to kill him before he kills you."

There. She'd finally said it. I'd been waiting for her to, wondering if she would. I remained quiet, considering the angles, including hers, wondering if she would say it again.

Eventually she did. "Will you, darling?"

"Will I kill him for you?"

"No – will you kill him for us?" I was silent as I thought

303

about the angles some more – Hacket's, Sally's, mine.

Close to dawn we made love again. It started slowly, but toward the end became frantic as we pushed and clawed against each other. Afterward we were silent. I was aware of Sally's hands on the side of my head, stroking her fingers through my short hair.

"What are you thinking about?" she whispered tenderly.

"It was so cold in the Ardennes," I whispered back to her. "So very cold... so very, very cold."

I guess she didn't know what to say to that because she didn't say anything and after awhile longer her fingers stopped stroking my hair. Shortly after four in the morning she slipped out of bed and quietly left the house. She didn't say anything to me before she left.

Maybe she thought I was asleep.

Chapter Twenty-Nine

According to Hacket's plan, the BAR and an ammo canister would be left waiting for me at the designated rooftop position an hour before the robbery, which was scheduled for shortly after nine o'clock in the morning. I assumed it would be there well before that because he wouldn't want the man who delivered it to be spotted in daylight.

My assumption proved to be correct.

By six o'clock that morning, with the sun just fully showing above the horizon, I was on the rooftop. I wrapped the heavy rifle in a green wool blanket, tucked it under one arm, and picked up the ammo canister with my free hand and carried them down to the street and then up again to the new position I had scouted the day before. It was a three-story building and I stopped once on the stairs going up to rest for a moment and switch the rifle to my other arm.

When I reached the stop of the stairs, I set everything down on the floor just inside the door that led out to the roof. I took off the backpack I wore and set it down as well. From inside the backpack I removed my Ka-Bar knife and attached the sheath to my belt on the right side. I fixed a dark green cap with a visor firmly over my forehead. Then I drew out my Colt .45 semiautomatic pistol from the backpack and went quietly through the door, ready in case someone else was already there.

The rooftop was empty. I scouted it quickly. For a moment I stared over at the spot on the other roof where I was supposed to be. That position was entirely exposed to where I stood now. I glanced around to reorient myself to the other rooftop positions that had potential. There were two of them and they were both clear.

Moving rapidly now, I brought all my gear out into the open air and stowed it around the corner from the door in a spot that was concealed from view from the adjacent rooftops.

According to my watch it was not yet six thirty. I likely had about an hour before any one else might show up, possibly even longer. That gave me time.

I unfurled the blanket and inspected the Browning. Then I opened the ammo canister and began to sort through the box magazines. Five of them were already loaded, but I since I had no reason to trust the man who had loaded them, I thumbed the rounds out rapidly and reloaded them myself – along with twenty-five more magazines. If 600 rounds weren't going to be enough I was in real trouble and a few rounds more wasn't likely to make a difference.

By now it was almost seven o'clock and the sun was creeping up. It was going to be another hot one. Working quietly with one ear tuned to the stairwell door, I field stripped the BAR, ran a few patches through the barrel, oiled a few spots on the receiver, reassembled it, checked the bolt action, popped in the first magazine, racked the bolt once, and set the selector lever to "S." Then I adjusted the bipod and set the rifle down on the blanket with several loaded box magazines stacked beside it ready to go.

Slowly I crouched down onto my ankles with my back against the wall, just around the corner from the stairwell door. I scanned the neighboring rooftops. They remained clear. Next, I checked my .45 once and tucked it back into a holster at the small of my back.

Now I was ready.

I only had to wait for Hacket's shooter to arrive.

Chapter Thirty

I felt the evenly spaced steps coming up the stairs even before I heard them. It was ten minutes before eight o'clock, almost fifteen minutes before I was scheduled to appear at the designated rooftop position two buildings over.

I'd been curious to see how many men Hacket would send. If it had been me, I would have sent two, but I only heard one set of footsteps coming up the stairwell.

Exhaling slowly as I moved, I rose up from my crouch and moved quietly on the balls of my feet to wait behind the door. A man I'd never seen before pushed it open all the way and came through it quickly with his eyes already straining toward the rooftop position I had been assigned to. That was all I needed. I took him from the side as he was closing the door behind himself.

My blade went into the side of his neck easily as I stepped through the jab, cutting across the jugular and severing the man's airway before he even had a chance to register his surprise. He fell over and flopped with his feet kicking for a moment. His eyes stared into mine without expression as one hand tried to grasp hold of his neck. His futile movements became successively smaller. After about fifteen seconds he stopped moving and stared with unseeing eyes up into the brightening sky above.

There was a lot of blood and I stepped carefully around him. The rifle he had dropped was a Winchester Model 70, an effective bolt-action hunting rifle. I would have made an easy target if I'd been lying prone where I was supposed to be. Now I had to wonder if Hacket had planned more than one sniper to cover me. I crouched down quickly against the wall and watched the other rooftops. For ten minutes I hunched there, scanning, breathing.

Nothing.

After awhile, I wiped the dead man's blood off my face

and arm as best I could with an old towel. Then I wiped off the blade carefully and returned it to its sheath. The smell of blood after all those months activated something in me. I almost wanted to drink it.

My heart was beating and I felt alive.

Periodically, I scanned the rooftop positions around me. They remained clear.

That's when I heard activity in the street below and a siren started. I scuttled over to the edge and raised myself up to peer down at the street. Below me I could see two fire trucks and an ambulance hauling fast on their way out of town toward the warehouse district. A police cruiser pulled out after them, fishtailing as it struggled to build up speed. A minute later two more police cruisers and another fire truck headed off in the same direction.

I glanced at my watch and then up at the sky above me. Suddenly I was very hot. I noted the position of the sun and then reoriented my attention to the street below. It was just after eight o'clock and the shops and businesses were starting to open for business.

Men in suits walked the sidewalks. Awnings were rolled out and young men in aprons moved brooms around to sweep away the dust from doorways. One of the diners appeared to be emptying out now as the breakfast crowd moved on.

People had jobs to go to, errands to run. Several men –even a few women and children – stood still below me, staring after the emergency vehicles that had gone tearing out of town. They couldn't know the reason for it, but their excitement was unmistakable.

As I surveyed the scene on the street and then scanned the rooftops around me again, I could hear the sirens receding in the distance. I didn't mind that. The town was almost quiet and then two more sirens started up, one right after the other. This time I didn't bother to look, so I couldn't be certain, but they sounded like police cruisers.

I checked my watch again. There was time. It was that lull, that secret, quiet moment before everything started up for real. I knew it well. During the war a lot of soldiers didn't know what to do with that time and they didn't handle the waiting very well. It was the hardest part for some.

I'd become good at the waiting. I'd learned that how you used those last few moments before an engagement could be the difference between survival and death. I crawled over to the wall where I'd sat earlier and fished around inside my backpack.

From a canteen, I took a long drink of water. Then I unwrapped and ate a sliced beef sandwich I'd prepared. It was simple food – hardy and nutritious. Chewing slowly with my eyes closed I willed myself to relax and I pictured the scene below me.

My ears were alert for any new sounds. For a while I didn't hear any. After finishing the sandwich, I drank a little more water, ate two hard boiled eggs from a jar and two sour pickles from another jar, smoked a cigarette – the last one I expected to smoke for awhile, said a prayer, and then relieved myself against the side of the exterior wall of the stairwell.

Just to be sure, I took five deep breaths, exhaling slowly on each one, and monitored the sensations in my body. It was a process I'd done many times in Europe. I pushed back on the thoughts of the Ardennes that tried to enter my mind.

I was home now in West Texas, and it wasn't the least bit cold. There were no German artillery units shelling my position or killing my buddies. Almost mouthing the words aloud, I reminded myself of that fact several times. Without even being aware of it at first, I rested my hand on the BAR for reassurance.

"*Jesus, draw me close to You,*" I whispered. "*Jesus, give me the strength I need today. Jesus, I give myself to You eternally. Hold me close; do not let me fail.*" I whispered the words out of habit and belief and desperation. They had helped me before – they would help me now.

There was nothing more to be done. I was ready.

In the distance I heard four loud booms. That was Hacket's dynamite on the causeway bridge. I checked my watch again and then began to move over toward the position I had chosen. I spread out the blanket and set up the BAR first, with its bipods extended to stabilize it.

After that I brought over the loaded box magazines, followed by the ammo canister just in case. Because you never knew when a gun might overheat or jam in a bad moment, I also picked up the dead sniper's Winchester hunting rifle and checked it quickly. I laid it down next to the BAR as a back up.

I set my backpack beside the stairwell door and quickly tapped the two weapons – the Ka-Bar knife, the .45 – I had attached to my body.

Everything was in its place. Once I was certain of that I lay down on my stomach next to the BAR with my face cradled in the elbow of an arm and tilted the visor of my cap low over my eyes.

I didn't have too long to wait now, though I still had an uneasy feeling. Maybe it was the same uneasy feeling I'd had before every fight. Or maybe it was something different. I'd never been able to tell the difference.

That Browning M1919 .30 caliber was out there somewhere. Humming a low tune to myself, I wondered where it was and if it would make an appearance and who would be using it. I also wondered if they would be any good with it. That question gave me hope because I didn't expect they would be.

Chapter Thirty-One

With sunlight shielded from my eyes, I was about to doze off when I heard the first vehicle pull up down below. It arrived with an unnecessary screech of tires. I raised my head and checked my watch. It was exactly the appointed time for the bank robberies to commence. A moment later there was another, lighter sound of breaks as the second crew arrived.

I kept my head down while I listened and stared at the second hand on my watch. A moment later I heard the first and then a second bank alarm go off. The ringing in the street was loud and harsh. That was my signal to join the action. In one motion I brought the BAR up and planted the bipods onto the parapet that formed the raised edge of the roof. My thumb hit the selector level to "F" for "fire." I sighted down toward the street and waited a moment, scanning for targets.

When a doorway opened in a store next to the first bank, I sighted on it and pulled the trigger three times, aiming wide so as not to actually hit any one. Glass shattered and the door was pulled inward. I switched my aim and surveyed the street.

Nothing moved down there for a while. I grinned to myself with the relief that action brought. It felt good to be back in it again with a hot rifle in my hands.

Just to let folks down there know they should stay out of it, I started picking out safe targets. I shot out storefront windows and then automobile windows of both parked and moving vehicles along the street. I put a round through a traffic light.

When the magazine was empty I ejected it and popped in a new one, switching the selector lever to "A" for "automatic." This time I emptied the full 20-round magazine quickly down into the street, raking a few storefront windows and a trio of automobiles parked along the curb. When it was empty I popped it out and smacked in the next one. This time I fired a random strafe down the middle of the empty street just to kick up some dust and sow a little confusion.

With a new magazine in, I waited a moment, expecting to see the Jimmies coming out of the banks any minute now. I wanted to cover their escape, but they didn't show yet.

Nothing moved, so I raked the street again on full auto in three bursts, just for good measure. As I was reloading, I heard the sirens in the distance, as well as one in the foreground.

When I came up again to sight down on the street, I saw a police cruiser turning on to it fast. I took aim and let loose with three bursts, the entire magazine, and the cruiser turned sharply and then flipped over onto the curb. It skidded a ways before it came to a stop against a telephone pole. It was upside-down. I reloaded and watched it for movement, but nobody climbed out of it.

The unmistakable sound of a Thompson machine gun roared from inside one of the banks. Windows exploded outward and there were screams. I switched the selector level on the BAR to "F" and waited. A moment later people started to run out of the first bank.

They were civilians and they ran with their hands held up above their heads, screaming. Someone at street level fired at them from the other side of the street. The firing came from below me. Two of the civilians fell backwards into a huddled mess together and lay still. Then one after another two Jimmies came out of the bank. Their Thompson guns blazed as they ran across the street in a crouched manner, weaving and ducking. They each had a large bag slung over their shoulder.

A moment later, a Ford truck roared into the picture and more shots were fired down at street level. It was hard for me to see what was happening, but I assumed it was a few police officers – possibly even citizens – that had taken a stand. They were positioned right below me and there wasn't anything I could do about it without revealing my position to them.

That's when the Browning M1919 heavy machine gun made its appearance. A man popped up from the back of the Ford's flatbed and raked the storefronts directly below me.

312

There was a lot of clatter and then a few shouts. The men who'd come out of the first bank tossed their duffel bags into the back of the truck and one of them scrambled up and over the side, into the flatbed.

The other man had turned to face two more police cruisers that were now roaring onto the scene. Somehow they had gotten across the causeway. I watched as he turned and fired the Thompson gun at them, ripping into them with a fusillade of lead. I sighted down on them myself and began to squeeze off shots, aiming for the center of the windshields.

Both cruisers veered to their left and tipped up on the curb hard. The one in front kept going and went through the window of a jewelry store with a loud crash.

The other cruiser managed to right itself at the last moment so that it barreled down the street with the wheels of one side up on the curb for a good twenty yards before it steered back onto the street and smashed head on into the Jimmy who had emptied his Thompson gun.

The impact of the automobile sent him several feet into the air, up over the hood of the on-coming cruiser. He flipped over it and landed on his back in the street and rolled several times. The police cruiser accelerated down the street, away from the gunfight. Gunfire erupted again from the flatbed of the Ford as the gunner with the Browning M1919 reengaged. He shot up the police cruiser as it sped away from him, shooting out the back windows, tires, and the boot.

I watched all this and lowered my head again. Nobody knew where I was or that I was in position to survive the action. With my head down I said another prayer: *"Jesus, draw me close to You; Jesus, give me the strength I need. Jesus, steady my aim today."*

Chapter Thirty-Two

An explosion in the street and the sound of more sirens brought me out of my haze. I reared up for a look. The Ford truck had backed up to be closer to the second bank and to provide cover for the two Jimmies who had come out of it and were now shooting it out with elements positioned below me. There was a lot of smoke and dust billowing out and I knew someone had chucked a grenade into that area.

Down the street I saw three men ducking from doorway to doorway as they made their way toward the fight. One of them carried a double-barreled shotgun. The other two had pistols. I fired four shots their way. I wasn't aiming to hit them – just to discourage them. Flying shards of glass and bits of brick from the rounds I fired seemed to turn that trick. They melted inside the nearest door and kept their heads down after that.

The sirens were closing fast now. At the end of Main Street two more police cruisers came into view and not too far behind them were two fire trucks. Men were leaning out of windows to fire shotguns and rifles, while other men were standing on running boards and shooting pistols with their free hands.

It was a splendid sight to see.

The two Jimmies were nearly caught in the cross fire as the caravan of sirens descended on them rapidly. One of them appeared to be hit and he fell over. Someone jumped out of the Ford truck, which began to move slowly backwards, and ran to pick up the duffel bag of cash the fallen Jimmy had dropped. Once he had it, he dashed back to the Ford and jumped into the bed.

Nobody made an effort to help the Jimmy who had been shot. The last remaining Jimmy made a beeline for the Ford. He was smart enough not to toss his bag of cash in ahead of himself. Instead, he jumped into the flatbed with his duffel still slung over his shoulder. Hands grabbed him and helped pull him in.

I fired single rounds as fast as I could into the two advancing police cruisers. One of them pulled over and the men spilled out, the other one kept going. I reloaded and flipped the selector to "A" and fired three bursts into the onrushing police vehicle. It swerved into a parked automobile and its siren died abruptly. I fired two shots into its front tire just to make sure it stayed there.

What caught my attention next was that the Ford truck was on the move now. It pulled forward quickly and made a fast "Y" turn so that it could go back down Main Street the way it had come. As it moved, I recognized Wrench at the wheel with another man beside him in the passenger's seat leaning half out the window with a shotgun.

The flatbed held four duffel bags of cash, the Browning M1919, and four men – the two it had arrived with and the two Jimmie's who had survived. For a moment I sighted down on it with the BAR I held in my hands, and though I was tempted to, I didn't pull the trigger.

I shifted my gaze to check on the possibility of pursuit. The two fire trucks had just caught up with the police cruisers. One pulled over to check on the cruiser that I had shot up. Firemen were helping wounded police officers out of it and carrying them as best they could toward cover.

The other fire truck navigated slowly around the injured men and vehicles in the street and tried to mount a pursuit of the Ford. It didn't get far because I shot out its two rear tires as it moved past my position. Immediately it rolled to a stop and seemed to sink into the street as it's tires flattened out.

I drew a breath, and in that moment realized that the world was suddenly quiet. There was carnage below me, but the sun was still shining brightly and there were gentle white clouds floating with grace in the sky above the town. I pulled my face away from the BAR and leaned forward to survey the street. I counted five police cruisers and two fire trucks that had been shot up and put out of action. There were two dead Jimmies and countless others dead, dying, or injured on the main street of Monahans.

Hacket's plan called for me to take refuge in an apartment down at street level. However, I knew his plan also called for me to be shot by the man with the Winchester Model 70. So I couldn't assume the apartment he had assigned me to even existed and if it did, it wouldn't be safe for me to use.

One way or another I had to get out of there fast. It wouldn't be long before investigators and police were flooding up onto the rooftops to look for shooters and the clues they might have left behind. I moved swiftly now with a sense of what I needed to do.

First, I checked the pockets of the man whose throat I had cut. I took his wallet, a pocketknife, and key chain, which included a Dodge insignia on it. I fingered it in my hand for a moment as I thought about it.

Next, I filled my backpack with the remaining box magazines that were still loaded, lifted it over my shoulders, and then wrapped the BAR in the green blanket. Before going down the stairwell, I surveyed the rooftop to ensure I wasn't leaving anything personal behind. I'd smoked the one cigarette, and so I picked up the cold butt and pushed it down inside my pocket.

Then I took the stairs two at a time and moved out carefully into the street that ran parallel to Main. Nothing moved there. Searching in both directions, I spotted a Dodge sedan parked across the street, two blocks away. I glanced about. Nothing moved in either direction. Most likely everybody was keeping their heads down, and if they were curious, they were looking out at Main Street on the other side of the block.

I went toward the Dodge and found it was unlocked. I tossed the blanket-wrapped BAR into the back seat, and climbed into the driver's position. The automobile started right up. I drove it forward at a casual pace and found my way out of Monahans.

Once I was out in the countryside, I sped up a little and hit the highway. There I drove west for well over two hours across the flat, dry land. When I reached Pecos I pulled into a hamburger stand.

Chapter Thirty-Three

The thermometer outside the joint read one hundred and six degrees. It felt even hotter then that. I took my cap off and wiped my face on the sleeve of my elbow.

"You hear what happened over in Monahans this morning?" the roller-skating waitress asked as she brought my order out and stood by the window of the Dodge.

"No," I said, "what's the ruckus?" I held the milkshake against my forehead and rolled it across and held it against my jaw.

"A gang of crooks shot up the whole town, robbed two banks, knocked over a jewelry store, and killed a whole bunch of people."

"They did?"

"They sure did!" the girl responded, smiling at me now and then bashfully glancing down at her ankles. She seemed pleased that she'd found somebody to share the news with for the first time. It was probably the most exciting thing that had ever happened in her world.

"They know who it was," I asked.

"Bandits, Mister, and a lot of them, but don't worry the police will catch them right quick," she promised me.

I smiled into her pretty eyes. "It sounds awful," I agreed with her.

The girl looked about and then leaned in toward me. "As much as I'd like to continue our chat, I have to get back to work. My old man runs the grill back there, and he's watching us right now. I can feel his stare cutting right into the back of my neck."

I smiled and touched the visor of my cap.

It only took a few minutes to eat. I was very hungry.

By the time I got back close to Monahans, it was almost two o'clock in the afternoon. I found a small roadhouse, just outside of town, and pulled into the parking area up close to a tree in order to keep the Dodge out of sight from the road as best I could. I sat there for a while by myself thinking while I smoked several Chesterfields. Then I went inside and ordered a beer.

"I heard there was some trouble around here this morning," I said.

"Jesus, mister," the guy behind the counter said, "they tore up the whole town. There's at least twenty people dead, maybe more." He was a short, wiry man with bristled, white hair on the top of his head and down the sides of his face. He'd spent a lot of time out in the sun. By looks he could have been seventy, but I put him closer to fifty. We were the only two people in the joint.

"That's a lot of dead people," I agreed with him.

"They even found a dead man up on a roof – had his throat cut."

I didn't respond to the last part of what he said. "Heard they knocked over some oil payrolls," I said.

The man shook his head as he played with an unlighted cigarette that he rolled around on his bottom lip. "I don't know about that. I guess they robbed the two banks in town, but who knows what they got to show for it? Wouldn't have expected them banks to be worth so much bother."

"Must have been something worth taking, otherwise why kill so many people?"

"I figure you might be right, but you never know out here."

"They know who it was?"

"There doesn't seem to be any shortage of theories. I've heard Indians, I've heard Mexicans... New York gangsters – even heard it might be John Dillinger coming out of retirement."

"Isn't Dillinger dead?"

"Supposed to be."

"You don't believe it?"

"You believe everything you read in the newspapers?

319

Maybe that wasn't Dillinger they killed in Chicago all those years ago. Maybe he set it up so he could disappear and everyone would think he was dead."

"I don't quite follow that."

The bar man poked his cigarette behind one ear. He was having fun now as he leaned toward me with this elbows on the counter. "See it this way. Just suppose old Dillinger set another man up to look like him and take his fall. By faking his death, he could slip away somewhere with all that loot he had cached up and live like a King somewhere, say somewhere in Mexico or Bolivia or some place like that."

I appreciated the cool darkness of the roadhouse and the beer was cold, so I didn't mind indulging him. I nodded to keep him going even though he had paused.

"You want another one, fella?"

"In a minute," I replied. "Finish your theory on Dillinger."

"Don't get me wrong, I'm not saying Dillinger hit those banks in Monahans today. I'm just saying, at least theoretically, that if he had faked his death and run south with his money, at some point he might run out of money. Right? What would he do then? It's not like he's going to take up an honest job, even if he could find a good one. No sirree, he'd have to go back to work and rob another bank or two."

I shrugged and thought about it while he moved away to draw another beer for me.

"Seems far fetched. I think Dillinger was killed in Chicago all those years ago. The Feds got him and they closed the book."

The bar man smiled at me with frustration. "You're missing my point, son. I'm not saying it was Dillinger. I'm just saying, who knows? This is West Texas and anything goes out here."

"Yeah?" I asked.

"Yeah," he affirmed. "You're young. I've lived here all my life, long enough to know. When I was a kid, over forty years ago, the Texas Rangers rode through and made a pact with some of the local Indians. When those Indians came in to collect some part of the deal they had been promised, they were shot down like rabid dogs in the street. It was cold blooded."

"That's awful," I said.

The man nodded. "I saw it as a child. Worst thing I've ever seen in my life. How can you forget something like that? A few of the Mexicans that rode with the Indians had lagged behind and they survived the shooting and tried to get away. Do you know what those Rangers did to them when they caught up to them?"

I shook my head. I really didn't know because nobody had ever talked about it.

"I'll tell you what they did," the man said to me as he tapped the side of my beer glass with a pencil. "They caught up to them, rounded them up, and then hanged them from a tree branch one at a time while their friends and wives watched. They were gathered around the tree crying and pleading."

"Why?" I asked.

"Why? I don't know why. Nobody ever had to explain it. If you ask me what I think about why they did that, I must tell you that I think they did it because they assumed nobody who mattered to them would care. That's why I think they did it – and you know what?"

"What?" I asked.

"Those men were right. Nobody did care and there were no consequences for those men and what they did. Hell, they were Texas Rangers. It's sad, but it's just the way the world is sometimes."

Chapter Thirty-Four

It wasn't hard for me to find my way out to Hacket's farm. When I was close enough – two miles away – I decided to park and hike in. I pulled onto the side of the country highway, behind a thicket of trees, and ate one of the beef sandwiches I'd prepared early that morning in what now seemed like another lifetime. I followed it with a couple of hard-boiled eggs and one of the dill pickles. Then I washed it down with some water from my canteen.

When I was ready, I strapped the knife and .45 semiautomatic to my body again, looped my arms through the backpack, and picked up the BAR to carry it in both hands. From there I started off across the field toward where I knew Hacket's farm was.

It was late afternoon and the gnats were out and swarming. I hated them, but I ignored them as best I could. The air was still and it was very hot. Although the sun was weaker now, it had been out all day baking the earth mercilessly. You could feel the heat rising up through your boots even as you walked. That's how hot it was.

"*At least it's not cold,*" I told myself as I hiked through it.

From across the field I was able to spot the area where Wrench and I had tested the firearms and ammunition. I couldn't see the small house or shed anymore and I wondered why they would have torn it down. I squatted in a thicket of tall grass and shrub trees and observed the area for about fifteen minutes. Nothing moved out there and I eventually decided it had been evacuated. It made sense. Still, I had to go over there and look around.

What I found when I reached the spot, shook me. The house and shed had been burned to the ground recently. It was nothing more than a pile of embers. They were still hot. Nearby were six dead men laying in rows. They had been lined up and then shot down. They included the two Jimmies who had

322

survived the bank robberies, and four other men who I didn't recognize. I assumed at least two of them were probably in the Ford truck that morning. The other two might have been involved in the warehouse diversion and the dynamiting of the causeway bridge.

Their deaths were the work of the Browning M1919. As I studied the way their bodies lay, I could see it in my mind's eye: they had gathered to inspect their haul, dazzled by the bright green cash they would not live to spend, the machine gun cutting them down like wheat before a scythe. The image caused me to shudder.

Hacket had planned his caper so that it would collapse in upon itself, each member being killed off once he was no longer needed. By setting up different small teams that didn't know each other and had only highly specific duties and roles, he had compartmentalized each element of the operation, isolated each man involved from every other man.

For a while I stood there, looking about. The entire area was quiet. Nothing moved. I was the only living creature bigger than a gnat on the acre of ground. That offered no comfort.

I called out Sally's name and when there was no answer, I called it out again.

Still haunted by our past I stared out into the distance beyond the twin points of heartache and loneliness. I walked the land for almost an hour searching for something I could not even have described before I turned and headed back to the Dodge, wounded and burdened by something I didn't think I would ever understand.

Chapter Thirty-Five

I couldn't drive around Monahans forever in the Dodge. With that in mind I drove it back into town well after dark and parked it in the driveway of the house that Hacket had arranged for Sally – the house where he'd held the meeting that day with Wrench, the five Jimmies, and me.

I broke the lock on the front door, turned on an interior hallway light, and went through the house in a hurry. My expectations were low and they were met. The place was filled with the foul odor of feces and urine. It also was empty and had been for at least a day or two. What I found there was not one piece of personal clothing for a woman or anything else you would expect to find if a woman lived there.

Not only were there no personal clothing, but there also were no photographs, no toiletries, no medicines, no personal items, no books, no records, and no evidence that any normal human had ever taken up residence there. The kitchen was empty and devoid of normal things like dishes, pans, cans, and food.

All I found was a small shy dog – a mutt mix of some sort. He'd been locked inside an empty bedroom and he didn't even bark. He was hungry and wagging his tail hopefully when I opened the door. I carried him into the kitchen and set him on the counter and filled the sink with water for him to drink. He lapped away sloppily at that for along time. When he finished with that, I fed him one of my beef sandwiches. He scarfed it down and wagged his tail some more. Then he turned back to the sink to drink some more. Eventually he stopped and stared at me with big happy eyes.

While I tried to rub his ears and jowls, he made small lunges at my face, licking my check each time until I rocked back on my heels and spoke to him more sternly. That worked. He sat down and cocked his head while he stared into my eyes.

I praised him. "What's your name, buddy?" I asked.

He didn't wear a collar, so I named him myself. "Charlie," I said. "That's what I'll call you, but you have to follow my lead. Can you do that, Charlie?"

He didn't disagree with my terms so I lifted him off the counter and set him on the floor. I couldn't understand how anyone could lock a dog up without food or water. The fact that it was Sally's house bothered me. Either she had left him there or she was dead herself. I wasn't sure which was worse.

The little guy followed me as I went through the other rooms in the house. I didn't know what he knew, but I came to think he knew something. He was trying to help me, but I was lost. I was a fool. I wanted to shout out to Sally, but I couldn't. She'd moved on and I was still there, still hoping for some sign that something between us would come back to where I thought we had been.

I was a fool and I knew it.

Chapter Thirty-Six

I approached Handrow's cautiously. The nearby cross street was poorly lit and I led Charlie down it on foot, sticking in the shadows as far to the right of it as possible. The mutt trotted beside me quietly. When we were close I slowed my pace and came to a stop as soon as I had a line of sight on one corner of the diner.

At half past ten o'clock, the lights inside were dimmed. I moved forward a little so that I could see more of the side window. It took a moment, but eventually I saw the motion of what I took to be an arm lifting a coffee mug. There were no automobiles parked within sight.

I glanced at Charlie to be sure he was watching me. Then I trotted quickly around the corner and across the street to the door, which I held open just long enough for Charlie to follow me in before I let it close.

"After what happened today, I wondered if you might show up tonight," Bill said quietly from the dark end of the counter.

I sat down on a stool across from him.

"I see you brought a friend," he said.

"He's with me. I found him abandoned. I named him Charlie."

"Charlie's a good name. You want a beer?"

"No thanks," I said, lighting a cigarette.

"You okay?"

I could feel his eyes studying me in the faint light, trying to discern my state. "Yeah," I replied. "I'm fine."

"Reckon that's all we can ever hope for." He didn't ask the question that was on his lips, but I guessed he didn't have to. "You want something to eat?"

I shook my head. "I can't stay – just came to ask a favor."

"Name it."

"Watch Charlie for me. There's something I have yet to do tonight."

"Sure, for as long as he needs it."

"Thanks."

I stubbed out my cigarette and stopped still, then extended my hand to Bill. He grasped it and held it for a long moment while his eyes continued their study. "Take care, my friend."

I nodded and turned around.

"Good bye, Charlie," I said and squatted down to pat the mutt on the head. He stared at me and licked my arm at the same time. I spoke to him: "Stay here with Bill. Okay? You'll be safe and well fed. He'll watch over you, but you watch over him too. Take care of each other."

I went to the door and opened it and that's when I heard Charlie bark for the first time.

Chapter Thirty-Seven

Shortly after midnight I took up a position near Hacket's home. It was the nicest part of town. The houses were large and the lawns were smartly kept. From across the street I lay down on my stomach behind a hedge and studied the house for several minutes. It was set far back from the street.

Two men with rifles waited in the shadows at the front. They weren't easy to see at first because they were dressed in black and were crouched behind the bushes on either side of the front door. However, they hadn't blackened their faces – a tactical mistake – so I was able to spot them.

A third man patrolled the right side of the house that faced the cross street and every now and then he felt the need to come around and confer with the man in front who was crouched nearest to him. If I'd had a good rifle I could have taken all three of them out in a matter of moments.

Since I didn't have that, I had to find another way. I also had to find out if there were other sentries posted nearby. As quietly as I could, I crawled backward, out of their line of sight, and made my way around the block so that I could approach the house from another direction.

From a half block away, I walked toward the house with empty hands out by my sides. I kept my eyes focused on the darkest areas of vegetation at the side and back of the property. The shadows were deep so I couldn't be certain, but I didn't see movement or anything else to suggest someone waited there.

When I was in position, I knelt down on the lawn behind a tree and watched some more. Eventually the third man came around the house, turning and scanning the street in a clumsy manner. As he passed by me I leapt and took him from behind.

With one hand clamped over his mouth I drove my Ka-Bar knife into his back, slicing through the kidney area as I pulled him backward and down. I laid his dead body quietly on the grass lawn and wiped the knife on his thigh.

That was one down and it had been silent. I moved swiftly after that, knowing my timeline had just been compressed. As quietly as I could, I came around the corner of the house and found the gunner on the right side of the door. I took him in the same manner as the first, forcing my knife into his back. He died without a sound and I laid him down behind the shrub he'd used for cover.

That left one more. I thought about my options. One was to circle around the house and come upon him from his far right. I didn't like that idea. It was too complicated and would take too long, raising too many other risks. Instead, I threw stealth aside and launched myself across the front entrance and into the position I knew he occupied.

He got off a wild shot before I slashed his throat with the Ka-Bar. Blood spurted and I closed my eyes instinctively to avoid the burn. When I opened them he was down, clutching at his throat as he began to bleed out. I wiped my face and then blade off on the long sleeve of my shirt and sheathed my knife as I watched the man wriggling below me, dying.

I recognized him as one of the men I'd seen in Hacket's saloon and I was pretty sure he recognized me too. His eyes held mine as he struggled for a few short moments to staunch the blood that seeped from his neck. Soon he lost consciousness and closed his eyes.

I knew death was only seconds away.

The sound of his lone shot would have alerted everyone in the house. I picked up the dead man's rifle – it was a Thompson gun with a 20-round magazine in it – and turned toward the front door just as somebody opened it.

I fired a burst from the Thompson at the man in the doorway and he fell backwards into the house amid a red spray. I followed in quickly behind him; firing two short bursts as I went through the door. One cut down another man who had been moving through the foyer with a revolver in his hand. The shots echoed loudly in the enclosed space. From there, I moved carefully into the living room and then into the kitchen, firing single shots ahead of me as I moved into each new room.

When the Thompson was empty I discarded it and drew my .45. Wrench appeared, standing in the hallway. He was grinning in a way that I never expected him to. I wondered if he was tougher than I'd given him credit for.

As he was straightening his grin and turning toward me with a shotgun, I fired at him twice, hitting him both times. My first shot caught his elbow and sent the shotgun flying. The second shot hit him in the chest, just below his neck, triggering a snap to his head and body as he flipped over.

I rushed toward him with my .45 out and ready to fire again, though I realized it wasn't necessary. He was wounded badly. There wasn't any time to feel bad about it.

Behind me there was a noise from the kitchen and I spun around fast, just in time to see her shape disappear as she flitted across the doorway on the other side. I drew a breath and then I heard another noise too, which slowed me just enough to save my life.

A man had come through the kitchen right behind her. His hands struggled with a long, double-barreled shotgun – too long for effective use inside a small, confined area. His first blast took a large round section out of the wall next to me and shook the entire house. He didn't get a chance at a second. I put three rounds into his chest and stomach while he was still trying to maneuver his long gun toward me.

Pressing my advantage, I moved forward quickly to shoot the next man in line behind him if there was one. There wasn't. I kept going, advancing into the kitchen, checking to be sure it was clear and then I moved fast to my right, chasing the shape I'd seen go by.

I found her shrinking in a corner by a closet that she'd opened half way. "I didn't do it," she shrieked. "He made me, he pushed me!"

"Come out of there," I told her.

"Don't shoot me, it wasn't my fault," she cried.

"Hush your mouth," I shouted at her. I was angry, but I didn't understand what she was talking about.

"He made me, he pushed me!" she cried again.

I grabbed her arm and shook her around, turning her in the process so that she had to face me. "Look at me," I demanded. I pulled her around and she came up close to me.

Her mouth bit at my ear, whether playfully or viciously I couldn't tell. I felt the heat of her breath. "Love me," she whispered. "I love you. Don't you see that?"

I shook her once with my hand and then pushed off her. "What's the story?" I demanded.

"Only that I love you."

"Stop it."

"I do."

I shook my head. "You never did. As much as I hate to say it, I don't think you ever did."

"He forced me!"

"Who did?"

"Hacket."

"Where is he now?"

"I don't know."

I pushed her with the barrel of my .45. "Tell me!"

Her hands waved between us. "He might be upstairs."

"Does he care about you?"

"What?"

"Does he care about you?" I shouted as I spun her around and pushed her through the kitchen into the living room.

"It's not my fault," she insisted, cowering with her arms over her face.

"Tell me something," I said coldly, as I released her arm. "You left that little mutt locked in a bedroom without any water or food? How can you live with that?"

331

"You mean, 'Sammie'? My puppy? I love him!"

"Like you say you love me."

"Where is he?" Her voice was frantic.

"I found him locked in a bedroom of your house."

Her face told me the story. She didn't know. "We moved out two days ago," she confessed, seeming to shrink before me.

"You could have mentioned that last night."

Shame covered her face. "Where is he?"

"Safe and dry now," I told her, "though to no thanks to you."

She started to cry and I realized that I couldn't afford to indulge her any longer. There was movement upstairs. I turned and looked up at the ceiling.

Sally grabbed my arm, sobbing. I shook her off and loaded a new magazine into my .45 as I shuffled sideways on my feet out of the kitchen. I looked to the left and then heard something to my right.

I turned as fast as I could, but I was too late.

There was a flash and something bit into my side, just below the ribs, pushing me off balance. Ignoring it, I steadied myself against the table and fired through the door. There was an angry cry – a sharp growl almost – and then another man appeared at the bottom of the stairs, firing as he ran through the living room toward the door.

It was Hacket and he was rushing in a panic.

I snap aimed and fired in one near motion. My shot caught him in the side of the head and he fell forward, crashing through the windowpane in front of him as his momentum carried him. I put another shot through the door and dropped down low, leaning forward on one hand with the .45 clutched up next to my chest, listening.

Sweat covered my face and neck and ran into my eyes. Blinking against it, I wiped one side of my face against the shoulder of my shirtsleeve. The air in the room was still. It was so hot.

It took me a few moments to realize it was over. Wrench lay on the floor, a few feet away from me, groaning softly. His open hand moved, clutching at something that wasn't there anymore. I studied his wide-open eyes as the life drained out of him and he became still.

My ears rang from the shots that had been fired. As I straightened up, I saw Sally curled on the kitchen floor, crying, screaming hysterically. I felt nothing for her in that moment. Combat reflexes guided me out the back door, where I cut through a neighbor's yard, hopped a low fence and began to run down the street, dodging into the shadows of the trees when I could.

From somewhere in the neighborhood, a dog started to bark aggressively and that set off several others who began to howl and bark in sympathetic response. I moved through a quiet alley when I came upon it, sticking to the smaller, less traveled streets. Whenever the lights of an automobile appeared, I ducked behind a hedge or a tree to stay out of sight.

Eventually I had to slow down to catch my breath. That's when I noticed the sirens that filled the night. It seemed the entire town must have been aroused. I walked briskly now and somewhere along the way I tucked the pistol into the holster at the back of my jeans and pulled my shirt out over it.

My hand felt something wet and warm and I knew what that was. I was bleeding from the side, but there wasn't anything I could do about it now. I pressed my elbow against it, alternating that with my other hand to keep the pressure on the wound. I thought about Sally and her yellow-brown eyes that I loved so impossibly, and then I pushed her out of my mind. The old instincts took over and I stopped thinking about anything at all.

I kept walking without knowing where I was headed until my mind slowed and my eyes focused enough to realize where

I was going. I'd already come a long way. The highway was only a quarter of mile ahead of me and the lights of Monahans were well behind.

I noticed how quiet it was. The expansive Texas sky stretched darkly above me, though it offered no comfort. I kept walking, thinking intermittently about the cold Ardennes and the things I had done and seen there. When I reached the highway I picked up my pace again on the shoulder, moving into the familiar and easy six-mile per hour trot, running now into the deep, dark, silent indifference of the night with my boots crunching over the gravel.

THOSE APACHE TEARS

He was shuffling around by a huge, white, late model pick-up truck as we came down from the trailhead. Above us the sky was incredibly expansive and blue, unlike anything I'd ever seen before. It was over a hundred degrees and the air was very dry – as we'd been told it was nearly every day in the late spring at Tent Rocks. The limestone formations around us were soft and pale, their jagged orange and brown horizontal colors barely revealed.

"Back already?" the man asked with a genuine smile and a slow wave. His voice was deep and low and held no urgency. Everything about him was unhurried.

"We made the peak, didn't you see us waving?" I replied, grinning back at him. We really had made the peak and had made a token wave, though we knew he would not have seen or been able to recognize us from so far below even if he had been looking upward. Still, we were excited to have been all the way up and back. The terrain and views had been incredible, unlike anything either one of us had experienced before.

The man gently shook his head, still smiling. Dark burnt skin on his face hung thickly like worn leather, the deep lines grooved with Linseed. His brown eyes, split wide apart, danced happily – active participants in his smile – projecting his thoughts out into the obscured sunlight where they disappeared instantly, tiny soap bubbles blown into the air.

"Did you see the large round stone on the trail?" he inquired.

Lisle and I squinted at each other and looked back at him, shrugging, not wanting to admit we had missed it. She leaned against me in a way that was natural and comfortable.

"Maybe three quarters mile in," he continued easily, in a forgiving manner. "Just past a large square cut formation in the middle of the trail. You had to turn sideways to get around

338

it and duck root branches over it."

We nodded, as though we remembered, but in truth there had been several tight points like that. Lisle allowed her infectious smile to beam out and she asked the man a few questions about his life that only a woman could get away with asking a man. I listened as he took her easy and polite questions and turned them into matters that required only simple responses.

He wore a badge that indicated he was a park ranger and when he waved us over to his truck, we followed him easily enough. The lot was only half full and the arriving vehicles that pulled up were mostly families of tourists who scurried past us eagerly without noticing we were there.

"Come on over here," he exclaimed softly, reaching into the passenger side window of his truck. When he emerged, his hands were full of dark pamphlets: small folded maps and brochures to inform us about the national park we were in. He handed them out one at a time, inspecting each for a moment before passing it over to us.

We accepted them politely and put them inside a backpack we carried between us. I pushed them down to the bottom and then slung the pack over my shoulder again.

"How long have you worked here?" Lisle asked.

The man brought his hands up to his cheeks and shook his head, even as he held his face between his palms. "Not as long as you might think, though I was born and raised nearby until I was seventeen."

He pointed with his entire hand perpendicular to the ground, bouncing it up and down in the air, gesturing in the direction where, I assumed, he was trying to tell us he had been born. The bearing he indicated meant nothing to me. I had no awareness of the general area.

"What did your parents do?" Lisle probed.

He grinned to show his appreciation for the question. "My mother taught a little school. I think she was a substitute when there was work. My father drank and when he was sober he worked a little for the county. He died of fever when I was twelve, or so they told me. He might have run away. My mother had a slow decline after that."

"Oh…." Lisle sighed.

It could have been an awkward moment, but it wasn't. The man smiled and touched her shoulder with tenderness. "That was a long time ago, young lady, and I've learned a lot more recently about how my people have suffered. My parents were just a part of that thread."

"It must have been so difficult to grow up with that," Lisle encouraged.

He shrugged philosophically. "My ancestors claimed this land as their own long before any White people came through – even before the Spaniards or Mexicans came through. My people trace back hundreds of years. It was a tough land to live on, as you can probably understand. To you it is hot and barren. To them, however, it was theirs – it had been given to them by a great spirit and they worked hard to survive and make the best of the life they could live on it and they were grateful."

"Did you understand all this as a child?"

"No," he shook his head seriously. "To me, all I saw was the poverty and the early deaths of the men I looked up to. They became old prematurely and died before their time. They didn't have much to live for and many of them drank themselves into their graves. To me, I needed to get away from it, needed to find something different, something that could be my own destiny. I didn't want to live my life like the older men I knew had lived theirs."

"Where did you go then?" I asked.

"My ancestors were warriors. I wanted to test myself to find out if I was one, so I signed up to go to Vietnam early on – early in the war, before it became a social cause. There were no protestors on the reservations in the early 1960s,

340

My mother encouraged me. She gave me a feather that her grandfather had worn into battle."

"What branch did you serve with?" I asked.

"The Army."

"MOS?"

He smiled. "You know something about it don't you?"

I shrugged. "I worked for the government once myself."

"Sure," he replied. "My military operational specialty was: Infantry Rifleman, though I can't remember the MOS number."

"What years were you in country?" I inquired.

"And you also know something about the history."

I shrugged, not wanting to say too much. "My father was in the Air Force. We lived in Taiwan when I was a child. It was 1969 and he went back and forth, in and out of Saigon."

"Then you do know something about it," he conceded, nodding with his lips pressed hard together. "I did three tours," he continued, "including the first one in the Ia Drang Valley in 1965 before I was finished and came back home to a place that didn't know me."

"Three tours was a lot," I observed. "How was your homecoming?"

The man smiled and his eyes were forgiving. "My people barely remembered me and they didn't understand why I had served. It was a different time. You have to understand that. Some thought I was a fool for fighting for the government after what it had done to our people for generations. To them, I had been used. I was naïve, a pawn in their efforts. A lot of my people view your government as an occupying power. It is true, they do not always treat our people with respect."

"My uncle served in that war too," Lisle added quietly.

"Bless him," the man replied. "How is he doing now?"

"We don't know. He was never the same and then we lost track of him a few years after he came back."

The man shook his head sadly. "A lot of decent men were

341

haunted by what they saw and what they did. They didn't have a government or a society that honored their service. They were not respected as warriors. Many lies were told to the people." He shook his head as his voice trailed off.

"Lies are always told about wars," I said.

He nodded. "I must agree with you."

"We painted over the experiences of those who served in World War II, allowed them only to be heroes."

The man brought a large hand up to his face. He sighed. "I wasn't in World War II or Korea, but I have to agree with that. I've shared a bond with warriors from those wars. Our experiences in Vietnam were not so different from theirs. War is savage, no matter the cause."

"Infantry rifleman are at the soul of every modern war fought during the past two hundred years," I mused.

He nodded as though I'd just said something important. "I was in an infantry company. I was your basic grunt. That's what they called us, what we called ourselves. The term had meaning. My rank was private – and I played the same part some of my ancestors played over a hundred years ago. My job was to go in first to find trails, to track down men, and to kill or be killed. It wasn't a movie. There was nothing glamorous about it. It was very real and it tested every man who served there."

As we listened I realized that I was thirsty. For the first time I opened the bottle of water I had carried all the way up with us and not touched the whole way. I took a small drink and then handed the bottle to Lisle. She drank some and handed it back to me. Her smile affected me. I offered it to the man, but he shook his head and patted his hip. I put the cap back on and screwed it on tight and dropped it into the backpack.

*

When he finished talking dispassionately about his time in

342

Vietnam, the man took off his hat and ran a large hand through his hair from front to back. His account had been modest and succinct, devoid of any real details. I appreciated what that meant, but kept that thought to myself.

"Did you see those Apache tears?" he asked.

"What are they?" Lisle asked.

"You never heard of Apache tears?" he asked, genuinely surprised.

"Never did," I replied. Lisle nodded with me. "What do they look like?"

He rubbed a large finger across his lips. "Mostly they are small, rounded nodules of obsidian – essentially black volcanic glass. By reflected light they look opaque, and when held up to the light they appear translucent."

"Are they black?" Lisle asked. She leaned against me and I put my arm over her shoulder, enjoying the feel of her warm skin against mine.

He nodded. "Most of the time they are, but they can range in color – from black to red to brown…. Fifty years ago you could find them everywhere in the Arizona desert, easily."

"Where do they come from?" I asked.

The man shrugged modestly before answering. He seemed pleased to be asked a question for which he knew the answer to. "The geologists will tell you that Apache tears originate from the ancient lava flows. If water were present during cooling of the obsidian lava, the obsidian would hydrate as water entered the obsidian glass, converting it to perlite; but, if it did not get hydrated, the fresh obsidian core ends up being those Apache tears."

"That's what the geologists say?"

"They do, that's what they say."

"What do the ancients say?" I asked.

The man smiled and rubbed his chin, as though I had asked a rare and special question. "Of course, the Apache legends have their own explanation. I'm sure you can well imagine."

"Can you tell us?" Lisle asked. I knew she was interested because she leaned forward toward the man and turned her head so she could hear him with her best ear.

I put my right hand on her shoulder, leaning against her to feel her presence.

The man rubbed the back of his head before he responded. "In the time of my great grandfather, about seventy-five Apaches and the U.S. Cavalry fought a battle on a mountain overlooking what is now Superior, Arizona. As they faced defeat, the outnumbered Apache warriors rode their horses off a mountain to their deaths rather than be killed or captured by the White Man's cavalry. They refused to submit or be captured. Maybe it's hard for people today to understand that choice, but they've never faced anything like what those warriors saw before them."

I understood pride, though I didn't say anything.

After a pause, he continued: "The legends of my people say that wives and children of the warriors cried tears when they heard of the warriors' sacrifice and their tears turned into obsidian upon hitting the dry, hot ground."

"Oh," I said quietly, involuntarily.

Lisle pursed her lips and leaned back against me with her hip on mine, at the same time reaching out to put her hand against the man's shoulder.

The man grinned and made a circle in the air with his hands. "Johnny Cash wrote a song titled 'Apache Tears.' It was back in 1964 that he recorded it. I remember it, vaguely from the time, but have heard it more clearly since then. Ever hear it?"

I shook my head and dipped my chin, thinking about it and other things all of a sudden.

The man hummed a few bars and then sang a few words in a low, deep voice with his eyes upraised toward the sky:

"The young men, the old men, the guilty and the innocent
Bled red blood and chilled alike with fears
The red men, the white men, no fight ever took this land
So don't raise the dust when you pass here
They're sleeping and in my keeping are these Apache
tears."

"That's beautiful," Lisle said. I touched her shoulder and her neck gently.

"Thank you," the man said graciously, smiling now.

"How long have you worked here?" Lisle asked.

"What do you mean?"

Smiling up into his weather beaten face she pursed her lips and then showed her teeth. "How long have you worked here, at Tent Rocks?"

The man's eyes widened as though it took him a moment to understood her question. "Only just a couple of years, actually. For many years I was on the road. Then I was working in a fish hatchery down south for a while. It was a hard life and eventually I came back home to settle some things, much as I had tried to resist doing that."

"How far south were you?" Lisle inquired. She had a focused look in her eyes that I knew meant something.

The man shrugged awkwardly, perhaps not wanting to tell his story in full. "Mexico," he said after a moment. "I was down there for about fifteen years, trying to find something – never did find it – but I guess it was part of my journey to be down there and to learn how to miss my home land. So I finally came back to Arizona and settled."

"You came home. How was that?" Lisle asked.

"It wasn't easy," he replied. "I'll tell you that. It really wasn't easy. One would think it should have been, but it wasn't."

"The war took you away and it was hard to return?" I suggested.

"I might have left anyway. It wasn't clear to me then what

345

was available to me here if I had stayed. I wanted to see more of the world. I wanted to see things and to be exposed to more than I was able to see and know if I stayed here."

"That war was a long time ago," Lisle said.

He allowed his smile to broaden. "Yes, it was, ma'am," he said. "It surely was. It took me far away and into a whole new direction of my life for a lot of years. Now I'm back with my people, trying to settle in and live the life they expected of me all along. Maybe I'm ready now."

"Are you?" Lisle asked. "How is that going?"

"Well," he started, and then paused, turning his head to one side to look up toward one of the peaks behind us. The expression on his face was taut and serious. "I had to learn the ways. You know? To me, they were new ways. There were the customs and the habits of my people. I didn't know any of them, if you understand what I mean by that. I had to learn them all from the beginning, like a child. It's been hard work, hard learning, though I have a good mentor and a lot of support from my community."

Lisle nodded, and so did I. I rubbed her shoulder to let her know I was there, and to reassure myself in some way that I didn't quite understand.

"When are you coming back out this way?" he asked us, smiling again. "Maybe you can attend a tribal dance? You have to ask politely and let them get a sense of you. That's what I learned, anyway. It takes patience and they have to develop a sense that you are sincere. I was living here for a couple of months before they approached me, and then it took a few more months to convince them of my sincerity. Oddly, it might be a little easier for you – as outsiders – to obtain entry."

"I doubt we'll be back soon," I said. "This is our first time here and it may be awhile before we get back this way."

"That's okay," he replied, nodding, slapping one of his fists into the palm of the other hand. "I have to develop patience to learn the ancient ways myself. It takes time. It really does, and everyone around here accepts that. It's a nice thing about this community – people accept that it takes time. I wasn't around all the early years of my life, so I don't know the old ways. Here, they treat me like I'm a child, an infant almost, but it's okay. I don't know the ways, though I'm trying to learn them. My people here accept that. If I don't ask questions, how can I learn?"

"You can't," I acknowledged.

"That's right," he exclaimed. "I can't. I rely on the help of my people, of my pastor here in the community to educate me and help bring me along. After all these years, I'm still trying to learn the ways of my people. Maybe I should have learned them long ago, but here I am, almost seventy years old and I'm trying now."

"You were away from home a long time," I observed.

He smiled broadly, through the pain he must have felt. "From Vietnam to South America and Mexico and a few others stops, and now finally back to Arizona at last, back to the home I never really knew or understood that I had waiting for me."

*

In my mind I drifted away from the conversation, thinking about what the man must have faced in Vietnam, in the Ia Drang and the type of the combat I knew had occurred there. I'd only read about it, but I'd known other men who had been there and they were changed by it.

From that valley my mind went over to my own experiences – the ones I never talked about and couldn't have even if I wanted to. Lisle was beside me, as she had been for over twenty years, and yet she would never know about the dark world I'd once moved in – the things I had seen and done and could never talk to anyone about.

347

There was an image that came to me: of a man's twisted body, of blood – a man I had killed in service to my government. There were the secrets and the lies I'd lived with for so long, the odors and sounds of profound human suffering, the twin feelings of terror and remorse – and the incredible, addictive excitement that rendered everything since then dull and trivial. I pushed all that away and blinked intentionally into the bright Arizona sunlight to refocus my attention.

*

It was time for us to move on soon. We had to drive back to Albuquerque.

"I'm James," I said. "People call me Jimmy."

"Jimmy," he said in a near whisper, as though he were talking to himself.

I allowed myself the same half-smile I used every time I thought about my father as I said my last name out loud.

"Why 'Jimmy'?" he asked.

"It's my middle name, avoids confusion with my father – since we share the same first name."

"What did you father do?" he asked.

Smiling into his thoughts, I said: "My father was an interesting man and he did a lot of different things over the years. I doubt you would know anything about him, though." It was a rehearsed response that I often used and most of the time it worked just fine to deflect any line of discussion that went that way.

"Sure," he replied, squinting for moment as though he caught my hint. "That's fine."

"What's your name?" I asked.

"Nikki-Boy here."

Lisle introduced herself and we shook hands. Nikki-Boy's paw was large, course, and heavy, but relaxed. It felt even bigger than it looked when I grasped it and noted how far my

348

own hand seemed to disappear.

"What's your actual, full name?" I asked, pushing him a bit.

"Nicolas Garcia, but everybody around here calls me Nikki-Boy. I didn't even know that was my name. I had to come back here after being all over the world to find that out from my own people. It took a bit, but eventually they told me. They had to be sure I was sincere. That took time. Once they were convinced, they welcomed me and they told me my name."

"That's really something," I said.

He nodded. "It is. It really is something."

"All over the world and then back, to learn what your name is."

Nikki-Boy nodded, grinning still, and brought his hand up to his chin. "It goes to show you something," he said gently, looking into my eyes.

"Yeah?" I asked.

"You ever read the Bible?" he asked abruptly.

"Some," I said, truthfully.

He thought about my answer and smiled as though he knew something I didn't. "Go back and read the Gospel of Luke – his account of the Prodigal Son. That's what I was. I was a Prodigal Son and then I came home, finally. I had to return home to learn who I was, to find my way, to connect to my past and to my ancestors. Everyone I knew here had given up on me, but I came home and they found a way to welcome me. I didn't expect that, the welcome."

"That changes you, I expect?" I said, thinking about my own father and what I knew of his parents.

"I guess it does," he replied, his smile broadening. "I'm grateful for it, mostly. I would be lying to you though if I didn't acknowledge there is some pressure that comes with it. I won't get another chance and I have a lot of making up to do."

"What do you mean?" I inquired.

"Got to do *Right* now, don't I?"

I nodded, understanding all of a sudden. "No more second chances, huh?"

"It's do or die now."

I nodded and shook his hand again. "I know about that. It was really nice to meet you, man."

"You too, buddy," he replied, and then to Lisle: "And you as well, ma'am."

She smiled, and it was her good smile, the one that blossomed and encompassed the whole world.

Nikki-Boy turned back to me with serious eyes. "Keep a close hold on this one – she's a good woman. I can tell. She hasn't said much, but I know a few things about her that she hasn't offered and I know something about what you've been struggling with too. I can see it in your eyes and hear it in your voice."

"Thank you," Lisle said to him while looking at me.

"May you treat each other well and take good care of each other," Nikki-Boy said, smiling and bowing slightly. "You have a lot of good years ahead of you together if you want them bad enough and if you are wise. Don't be afraid of a little hard work and effort. Keep each other close, don't stray."

Lisle hugged him and kissed him on the cheek.

I shook his hand again and we parted.

*

Lisle and I walked back to our rental car quietly, holding hands. We knew it had been a special day without having to say so. We drove back to Albuquerque without speaking much at all.

That night after our showers and an expensive dinner in the hotel, we lay in bed under the air-conditioner. We curled together, naked, with our legs intertwined and I put my arms

350

around her and held her with my cheek against her shoulder, thinking about things.

Soon her breathing became deep and regular, and though I wanted to tell her how precious she was to me, I couldn't muster the words and I didn't want to arouse her, so I lay there quietly, with my face pressed against her neck, feeling every breath she took, appreciating the scent of her skin against my nostrils. We had been together almost twenty-two years and I loved her dearly – though I knew I didn't always show it as well as I should have. I knew that and I thought about it laying there in the dark.

As I held her in my arms, and in my mind, it was as though she hadn't changed one bit since the first day I had met her. I pushed my own private thoughts away, the ones that took place in a far country and involved death and violence, and I focused on the happiness she brought me.

The image of an old photograph from our past came to mind. It was well over fifteen years old now. She wore a black dress and held a red rose in her fingers, smiling down at it as though she were looking forward to the evening we had planned together. Every time I saw the photograph, even when just in my mind as I thought about it, I fell in love with her all over again.

Every time.

Somehow, I was one of the few, the blessed. I couldn't explain it – why it had fallen to me and not to so many others. Somewhere in the night I fell asleep, dreaming about that and how she was my happiness....

Acknowledgements

I am grateful to my marvelous agent, Sonia Land.

About the Author

As a behavioral scientist and clinical psychologist, Bartley is a professor of psychology at the University of Hawaii, Hilo, HI; and Interim Executive Director of the Trauma and Resilience Center, Department of Psychiatry, University of Texas Health Sciences Center, Houston, TX. He conducts clinical trials, epidemiology, historical and neuroscience research, primarily with combat veterans and military personnel.

He has co-authored over 300 scientific publications (h-Index = 74; total scientific citations > 15,000), including empirical studies of the British Crimean War and U.S. Civil War and a current graduate textbook on psychopathology. Professionally, he has worked with combat veterans since 1991 – and his earliest interview was with a veteran of the Spanish American War and the Battle of San Juan Hill. More recently he has devoted much of his time to the Quick Reaction Foundation (QRF) in Houston, VETTED Foundation in Austin, and to the military special operations community.

He has consulted to US Congress, Department of Defense, Veterans Affairs, and the National Board of Medical Examiners. He has also published commentaries in the *National Review*, *Huffington Post, New York Times*, and *Time*; and has been quoted in the *Wall Street Journal*, *The Economist*, *Washington Post*, *Scientific American*, *Stars and Stripes*, *USA Today*, *Men's Health*, and *Los Angeles Times*, among others.

Made in the
USA
Monee, IL